The Celibate

'It takes courage to write about faith in this faithless world, particularly from a homosexual viewpoint. But in *The Celibate*, Michael Arditti's first novel, the author's anger, conviction and sharp observation hold the reader's attention throughout. An exciting debut' *The Times*

'This deeply spiritual novel ... a carefully crafted, intensely analytical and deeply honest theological quest where the storyline becomes consumed in a broader faith journey' *Catholic Herald*

'A fine political novel. Michael Arditti's eloquently beautiful style burns with passion and commitment. My mind and emotions were engaged for all of its pages. A brave, unique book, this deserves the widest possible readership' *Rouge*

'This pilgrim's progress for the nineties ... the intimacy of the narrative and the clever juxtaposition of modern morality tale with a Victorian murder mystery make for an unusually absorbing read' *Daily Mail*

'I found Arditti's heartfelt, even desperate, plea for tolerance and acceptance moving and honourable, not to mention timely' *Literary Review*

'Arditti's ingeniously constructed narrative ... A thoughtful, intelligent book. I trust that the publishers are preparing to send a copy to every member of the General Synod of the Church of England' *Sunday Telegraph*

'The novel is written with great flair and stylishly explores a conflict of ideas and identity. Undoubtedly one of the most serious and ingenious novels published in recent years' *The Pink Paper*

'*The Celibate* is quintessentially a novel of our time ... funny, witty, and at times hilarious. The narrative takes on an almost Dickensian sweep, though Dickens would surely have found it hard to embrace the diversity of sexual experience and emotions Arditti describes so vividly' *Capital Gay*

'Startling prose that never puts a foot wrong. An evocative and tightly written book marking a brilliant debut' *Oxford Times*

'The novel effectively tackles today's bitter church conflicts between spirituality and sexuality. And the sordid stench of contemporary London is provokingly mirrored in the insatiable desires of body and soul' *The Big Issue*

'The novel has just about everything: ideas, feeling, moral integrity and an inventive plot. An impressive debut' *Yorkshire Post*

'A fascinating book with real religious insight, and what's more, it's got style' Rabbi Lionel Blu

MICHAEL ARDITTI was born in Cheshire and lives in London. He is the author of five highly acclaimed novels, *The Celibate*, *Pagan and her Parents*, *Easter*, *Unity and A Sea Change*, and a collection of short stories, *Good Clean Fun*.

The Celibate

MICHAEL ARDITTI

ARCADIA BOOKS

Arcadia Books Ltd
15–16 Nassau Street
London W1W 7AB

www.arcadiabooks.co.uk

Originally published in Great Britain by Sinclair-Stevenson 1993
This B format edition published by Arcadia Books 2009

Copyright © Michael Arditti 1993

A catalogue record for this book is available from the British Library.

ISBN 978-1-906413-22-4

Typeset in Garamond by MacGuru Ltd
Printed and bound in Finland by WS Bookwell

Arcadia Books gratefully acknowledges the financial support of Arts Council England.

Arcadia Books supports English PEN, the fellowship of writers who work together to promote
literature and its understanding. English PEN upholds writers' freedoms in Britain and around the
world, challenging political and cultural limits on free expression. To find out more, visit
www.englishpen.org or contact
English PEN, 6-8 Amwell Street, London EC1R 1UQ

Arcadia Books distributors are as follows:

in the UK and elsewhere in Europe:
Turnaround Publishers Services
Unit 3, Olympia Trading Estate
Coburg Road
London N22 6TZ

in the US and Canada:
Independent Publishers Group
814 N. Franklin Street
Chicago, IL 60610

in Australia:
Tower Books
PO Box 213
Brookvale, NSW 2100

in New Zealand:
Addenda
PO Box 78224
Grey Lynn
Auckland

in South Africa:
Quartet Sales and Marketing
PO Box 1218
Northcliffe
Johannesburg 2115

Arcadia Books is the *Sunday Times* Small Publisher of the Year 2002/03

For
Crispin Thomas
20-10-1952–13-8-1989

But we preach Christ crucified,
a scandal to the Jews and a folly to the Greeks.
St Paul: I Corinthians I, 23

Tout comprendre, c'est tout pardoner
To understand all is to forgive all.
Mme de Stael: *Corinne* XVIII, ch 5

PART ONE

1888 AND 1988
PROSTITUTES AND PORNOGRAPHY

One

I'd like to start, ladies and gentlemen, by taking you somewhere sordid... This foul and foul-smelling alleyway hasn't changed much over the past hundred years. In 1888 Whitechapel would have been full of little passageways such as these, the absence of street lighting making them especially convenient for prostitutes who needed somewhere to service their clients. And I regret to say that many of them are still used for much the same purpose even today... Incidentally, I know it's dark but I would advise you to be on your guard where you put your feet, or alternatively to take off your shoes as soon as you return home.

Tonight we shall be following in the footsteps and commemorating the centenary of the most notorious mass murderer in British criminal history. And yet by more recent standards his tally was comparatively small; he killed only five prostitutes. So why does he continue to exert such a strong fascination over us now? Partly of course it's because his crimes remain – at least officially – unsolved, but also because he exerted an equally strong fascination over his contemporaries, many of whom perused each gruesome detail as intently as we shall pursue them today.

So where did that fascination lie? To answer that, we'll need to consider the spirit, or more strictly the psychology, of the age. We must bear in mind that the murders took place against a background of late Victorian prurience and prudery, and that despite blanket references to the Victorian age as if the entire sixty years were essentially homogeneous, such attitudes were comparatively new. In 1860 it was quite acceptable for men and women to bathe together in the nude; twenty-five years later no respectable woman could expose a table leg, let alone her own.

But human desires can't be kept under wraps as easily as furniture; and in response to such repression Victorian society was obsessed by the idea of prostitution. The women themselves, dubbed 'daughters of joy' and judged insatiable nymphomaniacs, represented what our great-grandparents found at once most alluring and most abhorrent: a highly potent combination, which underlay their mixed reaction as these particular five unfortunates received what many considered their hideously just deserts. Moreover, although they could hardly approve the violence of his methods, almost all their favoured Ripper suspects came from the respectable middle class: doctors, solicitors and even clergymen, as though it were their better selves keeping their worse selves in check.

For those of you who may take issue with that hypothesis, it's worth remembering that just as in the late 1880s in this country criminologists were beginning to lay the foundations of a far more scientific approach to criminal investigation, so in Vienna a young doctor was taking the first tentative steps towards establishing what in time would prove an even further-reaching human science.

And it was in this very alleyway, ladies and gentlemen, pitch black then as now, that according to eye-witnesses Jack the Ripper encountered the first of his victims. So who was he? And was he indeed just one man? Nobody knows. That is, nobody except me. And who's to say but, if you stay the course – that is the tour – with me, I may not even share the secret with you... So let's go through here to find out where he took her, and what he did.

I'm here under protest; I should like you to take note. Do you take notes? Or do you have a photographic memory – or whatever might be the aural equivalent? I merely ask. Aren't you going to warn me that anything I say may be taken down and used in evidence, or is all this an empty formality? In which case I may as well save my breath.

You hold my life in your hands. I've been a captive audience, but never before a captive speaker. All I've ever wanted is to be a priest; without that I'm nothing. It's my heart's – no, it's my soul's desire. But they wouldn't even promise to keep my place open, unless I agreed to come here. So you hold my priesthood in your hands; so you hold my life.

Last term at college I wrote a dissertation on free will or predestination, but the arguments now seem as academic as the experience seems remote. For what choice have I? Like Martin Luther: here I stand, I can do no other – would you like me to sit down? Anyone who knows me would appreciate the irony: that so devout a Catholic should be forced to resort to so Protestant a precedent. But the Church of England has broad shoulders; it can find room for just about everyone: except, it would seem, for me.

I don't like this room; I don't mean to be personal, but I don't feel at my ease. Would you like me to sit here? I usually kneel to confession. Surely you don't expect me to lie down? I thought that only happened in films. Not that I'm any sort of expert. I think the only film I've seen all year is *The Last Temptation of Christ* and then I walked out when Our Lord was in the brothel. But I don't believe in censorship; I believe we should censor ourselves.

Did you realise the arm of this chair was frayed? I only ask in case you'd like to have it recovered. Has it been worn away over the years like St Peter's toe in the Vatican by the fingertips of the faithful? Only it would hardly be fingertips here but the torn nails of souls in torment. Well, not mine. I put my trust in Christ; he's both my strength and my salvation. I'm perfectly calm.

But I promised to keep an open mind; although I advise you not to try to press your advantage. I'm told you've helped a number of ordinands in the past, including, however hard it may be to credit, several from St Dunstan's. They seemed to think I'd find that some consolation; they were wrong. But I'd like to make one thing clear right from the start: I am not ill. I simply needed rest, not rustication – do I look ill to you? And yet from the speed with which they made to throw me out, you'd have thought that they'd just been waiting for their first opportunity... My chemistry master once chastened me by explaining how little my body would fetch if boiled down to its basic minerals and salts. I warn you now: I refuse to be reduced to psychological loose change.

So what do I have to do to convince you that I'm as sane as any priest; or is that the very last thing you want? Do you intend to ask me the name of the country or the Prime Minister? Are you English by the way? Or are you going to hold up your hand and tell me to count the fingers, and then rule against me if I fail to include the thumbs? I can't win. Though the one thing I refuse to take seriously is any more ink-blots. Or would you prefer me just to chatter on? And if so, what about? My childhood? My sexuality? My dreams? I'm afraid you'll be in for a big disappointment. I've a very poor memory; I'm a virgin; and I never dream. So that takes care of all that. Now is there anything else? Or do we just sit here and try to outface one another for the rest of the hour?

If you'd like, I'll tell you my joke. I was always led to believe that a sense of humour indicated a sense of proportion; so maybe it's a fair test of sanity too. I'm afraid it's the only one I know, but it always went down a treat at St Dunstan's: When is a parson not a person? All right then, when is a parson not a person...? When he's a priest.

I'm sorry; I put it across badly. But then under the circumstances it's hardly surprising. Was it Glasgow that used to be known as the comedians' graveyard? For a fate worse than death they should try you... Are you never going to tell me what you want from me? What is it about me? Why will no one ever give me a straight answer? I was accused without a charge; I was condemned without a hearing. All I ask is a simple explanation. But the silence rings like tinnitus in my ears.

It's no use feigning ignorance. I'm well aware they'll already have given you their version of what happened, and I'm equally well aware that you'll take their word every time. But just for the record you may as well have mine. There's no mystery; you don't have to be Sigmund Freud to figure it out. I'd been under a lot of strain; I admit I'd been overdoing things: what with my academic work and my placement at Heathrow, not to mention preparations for the college pilgrimage to Walsingham, which I'd taken entirely on myself. I ought to have known better. Even when I was a boy, Nanny always seemed to be reminding me that I had a body as well as a mind. Well, on 25 January it hit back.

Although we said our basic daily offices in the college chapel, on high days and holidays we also worshipped in the parish church. And it should literally have been a red-letter day for me, since not only was it my turn to serve at the altar, but it was to be a full High Mass to celebrate the conversion of St Paul. I don't know how much you know about Anglo-Catholic ritual: I suspect very little, and that you care still less. But the one thing you need to remember is that we would be six in the sanctuary. I was to carry the thurible and Jonathan to administer the chalice.

But first he had to deliver his sermon, which he proceeded to do with an obscene lack of reverence for both the time and the place. In my view there are only three subjects suitable for sermons: Our Lord, Our Lady and the Blessed Sacraments. Needless to say he'd chosen none of them, nor despite the occasion had he touched more than fleetingly on St Paul. But I refuse to dwell on it – and I refused to dwell on it. I was preparing for a Eucharist, not settling old scores. And the moment of incensation was soon upon me. I censed the priest. I censed the congregation. I moved to cense the Host at the Elevation, when I caught a glimpse of Jonathan lying in wait at the altar steps. He was staring at me very strangely. I wish I could say he looked contrite, but in truth he seemed to look challenging. It was a challenge to which I did not intend to respond.

It was then that I began to feel faint. My stomach started to heave and my legs to buckle. I was terrified that I was about to throw up all over the altar steps. I steeled myself – I steadied myself as the altar continued to swell. I tried to shout, but my mouth was too dry. I started to stagger. I felt sure I was on my knees even though I was still on my feet. I made one last desperate attempt to right myself and I threw my hand out in front of me. But it was the same hand that was swinging the thurible and it hit Jonathan square in the chest, sending him tumbling and the chalice sweeping to the floor... No! I can't bear... What devil can have been in me? I'd knocked the blood – Christ's precious blood, Christ's holy blood – all over the sanctuary. I was kneeling in the blood; I was a sacrilege. I was red with the blood. I blacked out.

Is it any wonder I collapsed? It was the consecrated blood of Christ seeping into the stone. I was present at the crucifixion but not as one of the mourners alongside Our Lady and St John; I was one of the soldiers who'd pierced his side and spilt his blood. What did they expect me to do? Calmly fetch a cloth and mop it up? Now that would have been perverse; in that case I admit I'd have needed help – if I hadn't already been way beyond it. And it's quite monstrous for anyone to suggest that I was taking a swing at Jonathan. It was the sanctuary, not the school playground. We were two grown men.

I've no recollection of what happened next. I can only go by what they told me, and I take that with a very large pinch of salt. Do they seriously expect me to believe I would ever have rolled about on the floor moaning and groaning, with my thumb in my mouth like an insecure child? It'd be a joke if it weren't such an insult. They were simply indulging their taste for the sensational. St Dunstan's had never known anything like it, and there were some people determined to milk it for all it was worth: never mind that my entire future was at stake.

But even as I was being carried out of church, that had already been determined. They'd decided to send me away. It seemed I needed some time to find myself... They talked more like hippies than priests... I always thought the whole point of training for the priesthood was to find ourselves in Christ. But I was allowed no right of reply.

And they were at pains to point out that it was no reflection on my vocation; it was simply a question of my extreme youth. I was by far the youngest in college. Although you might have expected them to have thought of that before. And anyway, since when has age been any criterion? What about all the saints who were martyred in their teens? No, it was quite simply a convenient, but utterly unconvincing, excuse.

At Balliol I had a friend who was just half an inch too short for the Guards. At least so they'd told him. But he remained persuaded that it was his background and not his height that had failed to make the grade. Well, I hardly have the conventional background for the priesthood. Do you think that that may be what they hold against me?

I used to wish that I'd had a monastic vocation. It would certainly have been far simpler. And I feel I might have been well suited to the cloistered calm of a contemplative life. But I wouldn't have been true to myself. So I had no choice but to accept their conditions; and here I am: a hostage to new experience. But why must everyone imply that I've had it cushy all my life? Cushioned maybe, but that isn't the same thing at all. In fact the first time I've ever felt fully at peace, and I mean the true inner peace of belonging, was last year when I entered St Dunstan's. So what do they do about it? They send me away...

Critics may talk of the Old Boys' network, but it's nothing compared to the Old Clerics'. Father Leicester appears to have a finger in every religious pie in the country – or less frivolously, a friend in every religious house. So he's arranged for me to stay at St Bede's; whilst Brother Martin, the friend in question, has agreed to act as my spiritual director. Although after all that's happened, it's as much as I can do to say grace. But never mind, for as their final trick, I'm tempted to say their *coup de grâce*, they've arranged for me to bare my soul to you.

Another of Nanny's best-loved maxims was that I thought too much; as you can see she was basically consistent, if rarely profound. At least she'd heartily approve of the timetable Father Leicester's drawn up for me, which seems to leave me little enough time for prayer, let alone thought. One of his oldest friends is Father Nicholas Redfield, rector of St Winifred's, the social-work church, and as it's only a stone's throw away from St Bede's, and they even undertake certain pastoral duties in common, what could have been more natural than that he should conscript me on to their programme as a volunteer?

Have you ever had any dealings with St Winifred's in either your private or professional capacity? It's the large redundant-looking building at the far end of Bethnal Green Road. At first glance I felt sure that it must have been designed by Hawksmoor, but on closer inspection it turned out to have been by no one of any distinction at all: which pretty much sums up what I feel about the whole set-up. Please don't misunderstand; I intend no slur on their dedication, simply its direction. Besides, the social work operation is essentially autonomous, and I'm quite sure the Church authorities can have no inkling of everything that's being done in their name, or at least in their crypt. Most of the care-workers don't even believe in God. To them he's simply the landlord of the building, and the archetypal racketeering absentee.

But then to have any property at all appears a heinous crime in their book: not just theft, but exploitation. And what irks me most of all is their closed minds. They may be anti everything establishment, but they must accept that the Church of England is the established Church. And so apart from anything else, they're displaying the most appallingly bad manners: accepting its hospitality and then insulting the host.

The space itself I find claustrophobic. The ceilings are painfully low, and even now the vaults seem to exude an atmosphere of darkness, death and decay, which is hardly helped by the drab decoration: a complex of sludge-grey, olive-green walls, relieved only by several crudely drawn copies of Old Masters, my pet aversion being a Mona Lisa who grimaces where she should smile. But as they were painted by one of the clients, we're supposed to applaud his good intentions – which is pure pussyfooting to me.

'Client', by the way, is the name they give to the people who use the crypt; I can't think why it's the same word you use for me. And they present a pathetic picture: some are homeless, some alcoholic, some completely inadequate; and many a combination of all three. We're surrounded on all sides by the most acute psychiatric problems; and if you were doing your job properly, it'd be them you'd be listening to, not me. Fiona, another volunteer, said that everything had grown far worse since the move to reintegrate them into the community: it might have helped if there'd been any sort of a community there. I said what about the church; surely we were standing right at the heart of it? She just smiled cryptically... and walked away.

To a man – and a woman: I've already been picked up on that point – the rest of the staff seem to have taken against me. They single me out quite openly for the most routine and disagreeable jobs. But I never object; I intend to shame them by my humility. Patrick, the project leader, complained about my body language... Body language...! He claimed I kept the clients too much at arm's length, and suggested I should try to hug them more often. Well, that's all very easy to say, but I even used to find the kiss of peace in the village church hard to stomach. And the congregation there was considerably more fragrant than the clients in the crypt.

Yesterday evening I was asked to wash and dress an old man who had only one leg. He'd been offered a place in an old people's home, but until he'd been 'freshened up a little', they weren't even prepared to let him past the door. So it was left to us to do the dirty work – in other words it was left to me. I have to admit I panicked. I've never had to undress anyone else before, let alone someone with a disability; I wasn't at all sure what to do about the stump. Besides which, he seemed to sense my discomfort and deliberately played on it. I hate to think how many pairs of trousers I must have pulled off him – each one more revolting than the one before; it was like some grotesque parody of the dance of the seven veils. And I can't begin to describe dismantling, or I suppose I should say dismembering, his artificial leg. I finally had to admit defeat and call on Roy, one of the staff, to help me. I told him I'd done as much as was humanly possible. He replied smugly that Christ had washed the disciples' feet, and even the Queen still did so symbolically. So I said that symbolically was another matter entirely; and besides, as far as we knew, none of the disciples had been incontinent. And then I felt deeply ashamed of my impiety, and the ease with which I'd allowed myself to be provoked.

My particular *bête noire* is Vange: short for Evangeline and, to my mind at least, no improvement. She used to be a nun, but she dropped the rest of her name when she dropped her religious convictions and converted to radical feminism. She spent ten years in an enclosed order, and I'm afraid that it's given her a rather one-sided view of men in general and Christ in particular. She now seems to spend most of her free time outside Whitechapel tube station, picketing walks around the sites of Jack the Ripper. And from her response when in all innocence I asked why she found them so offensive, you'd have thought that I'd committed the crimes myself or at least that I was his spiritual heir.

And her values appear as confused as her thinking is woolly. She complains very loudly about social injustice; but if anybody believes in one law for the rich and another for the poor, it's her. She'd just like to redistribute the laws. The crypt is supposed to be a charitable organisation, but she displays a marked lack of charity towards the financiers and industrialists who fund it. At last week's support group she launched a bitter attack on a proposal for a sponsors' service. It seems that they're good enough to pay for us but not pray with us. And I'd have thought that as even an ex-nun she would have shown a little more reserve. As I reminded her, Christ didn't say blessed are the poor, but rather the poor in spirit. But she said that that was just what she'd have expected from a member of my family. And Roy added that the Bible was nothing but scrawls on scrolls.

They refuse to accept that it's not their politics I object to but their inconsistency. Jonathan was exactly the same: constantly insisting that the Bible had been culturally determined and could only be understood in its historical context, and yet at the same time seizing on statements he particularly admired such as Christ's advice to the rich young man to sell up all he had, as though it were a political manifesto which had been launched at a press conference only last week.

It's not that I don't care about social injustice; I care about it passionately. It's just that it's not my prime concern, nor should it be. Whatever else Christ may have said, he quite unequivocally stated that we'd have the poor always with us; but we don't always have him: except, that is, in the person of his priests. Which is why I believe our essential role has to be sacramental: to stand before him at the altar, to stand for him at the altar, and to celebrate his body and his blood.

But do you think they had the good grace to acknowledge it? Not on your life. Instead they set out as usual to wrong-foot me. Vange wanted to know whether, as the Eucharist was clearly so fundamental to both my faith and my practice, I could ever conceive of a circumstance in which I might feel forced to turn someone back at the rail. I was appalled. It was the Anglican communion we were talking about, not some private members' club. So I didn't hesitate for an instant. Never, I said, not under any circumstances at all.

What? Now Roy thought he had me in a corner. Not even the Prime Minister? I couldn't believe what I was hearing. I might disagree with her politics, although as I just said, politics has never been my strong suit, but to try to exclude her from the communion would be to take my cue from that same doctrinaire authoritarianism which is what they claim she represents. And I tried to point out that if I disliked someone, I was under no obligation to invite him to my house for a meal, but I was obliged to welcome him to church. Whatever our differences, the Eucharist is the one meal we can all share. It was Jonathan who always used to assert, for reasons which now escape me, that eating bacon was a political act. Well, eating the Eucharist is not.

I thought that I'd made out a pretty good case for myself; but Vange said that as usual I was talking through my arse... I'm sure she speaks like that to prove she's no longer a nun... And I know for a fact that she subsequently tried to get Patrick to sack me; because Roy took the first opportunity to tell me, with all the malicious glee of a schoolboy sneak. But Patrick was determined to keep me on; and yet from the way he talked, you'd have imagined he was doing me a favour rather than the other way round. Although he felt it only fair to add that he did intend to monitor me... So long as I had no objections. None at all, I said; I have nothing to hide.

I suppose I ought to revel in all the attention: what with his beady eyes and your flapping ears. But I simply feel confused. And as I'm sure you must have realised, it really isn't my sort of place at all. So won't you suggest to Father Leicester that he let me leave? And then if he still insists on my finding myself or whatever, he could at least find me somewhere more congenial: an old people's home say, but one where the residents are courteous, considerate and clean – and preferably still have both legs. So is it a bargain? You're my last hope. I don't think I'm being unreasonable... do you?

Two

You may be interested to know that you – yes, you, madam – are standing on the very spot where Jack the Ripper disembowelled his first victim... No, don't be alarmed. This tour aims to provide a description, not a re-enactment. And although I've promised you surprises, I hope there won't be any quite like that.

First a little social background: in 1860 there were estimated to be 80,000 prostitutes in London. That's one woman in every sixteen; which on a quick head count would mean at least two of you ladies here tonight. It makes you think... Indeed there were thought to be 1,200 in Whitechapel alone. Though these, as you would expect, were very much the lowest end of the market, many of them being drunkards, and most of them diseased. And what led so many women to become prostitutes? Well, it must be obvious even to the most naive of us – amongst whom until quite recently I would have counted myself – that it was far removed from that conventional picture of the daughters of joy. It's hard to imagine any woman coming out to this joyless street to be fingered and mauled and finally spluttered into because she enjoyed sex. But then it's hard to imagine any man visiting a prostitute because he enjoyed sex. In my opinion it could only be either despair or perversity...

No, these women often became prostitutes very young, as their sole means of escape from their stifling families and unbearable living conditions; not to mention sleeping conditions, as whole families were compelled to share the same bed, together with the constant threat of incest to which this gave rise. But any respite proved short-lived, as they were thrown on to their own resources, which in effect meant on to the streets, where they looked for any likely man who might provide them with the fourpence they needed as the price of a bed for the night. And that was precisely what Polly Nichols, the first of the Ripper's victims, was doing before she was murdered here.

Polly was a woman of forty-two, although she looked a good twenty years older: her way of life had taken such a toll. She'd informed a friend whom she'd met a little earlier that she'd already had three customers that evening, but that she'd spent her pitiful proceeds on drink. Now she needed fourpence – just fourpence, ladies and gentlemen – in order to buy herself a few hours' rest. And so she dragged herself out again: for the fourth and tragically final time.

It may surprise you to learn that this deserted street – this heap of rubbish and rubble, flotsam and jetsam – was in 1888 a rather pleasant road known as Buck's Row, with a schoolyard, coalyard, warehouses, terraced cottages and even the local curate's house. But at about twenty to four in the morning of Friday 31 August, two carters, Charlie Cross and Robert Paul, made a discovery which was soon to make it one of the most notorious in the whole of London – so much so that shortly afterwards, the residents petitioned to have the name changed to Durward Street; by which it's still known today. For it was here in this gateway that Cross came upon the body of a woman lying sprawled in the gutter. His first thought was that she must be dead drunk, although he was quickly disabused. But it wasn't until her body had been removed to the morgue that the full horror was disclosed.

For although murder had long been one of the East End's favourite pastimes, and throat-slitting a particularly popular variant, it wasn't just Polly Nichols' throat that had been cut, her whole stomach had been ripped open. And not just once but twice. Her windpipe, gullet and spinal cord had been hacked through. Her vagina had been pierced in two places. She'd been disembowelled and her intestines had been exposed... Yes, I can see even in this light that you've lost your colour. And I can assure you that I didn't describe all that simply for stomach-churning effect – although I do hope, in view of what's to come, that none of you had kidneys for your dinner – but rather to try to drive home the ferocity of the attack. And this was just the beginning. With each subsequent assault the Ripper's hand became more and more frenzied, and his victims' mutilations more and more extreme... So follow me, ladies and gentlemen, on the next stage of our terror tour.

Tell me, are you a Freudian? It never ceases to amaze me that anyone can still take his ideas seriously. I did an option on him at St Dunstan' – we were taught to know our enemy – and I should like you to understand here and now that my faith is in no sense a neurotic projection. It's the most real – it's the only real thing in my life. Wasn't it Wilde who said that a cynic was a man who knew the price of everything and the value of nothing? Well it seems to me that a Freudian is a man who knows the theory of everything and the meaning of nothing... You say nothing, but then I suppose there's nothing you can say.

So what salutary topic do you propose for today? Sex? Aggression? Faeces? Would you like to hear how old I was when I started using the potty or when I stopped using the breast? It's not that I want to put words into your mouth – although if you never intend to speak, I don't seem to have much option – but I would like to know if I'm on the right lines... You're not a doctor; you're an emotional refuse collector. Well, I warn you; you'll discover nothing in mine.

All right: let's admit for the sake of argument – or rather to avoid it – that I had what you call a breakdown; although I myself much prefer the word stress. According to Father Leicester everyone else could see it coming. But then the wife is always the last to know. He was quite adamant that I mustn't feel in any way ashamed about it, any more than I would if I'd tripped up on a step and broken my leg... Oh, sure. Pull the other one; it's got bells on. Or is it still in plaster? I wouldn't know.

Over dinner at college we'd often try to invent new beatitudes. My next-door neighbour stuck one of my favourites up on his door: Blessed are the cracked, for they let in the light. I always used to smile when I passed it. Not any more.

So do you think I'm mad? You can give it to me straight; it wouldn't be the first time. My aunt tried to send me to a psychiatrist when I was ten. It was after I'd declared I'd discovered my vocation. I can give you the time and place if you like, just as I quoted her chapter and verse. It was during morning prayers at my prep school: not usually the most inspiring of occasions; what with the assembled ranks of sleepy, sloppy schoolboys, with their shirt-tails hanging out, scruffy sleeves and scuffed shoes. I had no reason to expect anything out of the ordinary; when suddenly, in the middle of a hymn, my faith began to surge up inside me and to spill over into every part of me, and in one moment of ecstasy my whole life seemed to spring into place. At first I felt completely disorientated; I had no idea what'd happened. I was half convinced I must have spontaneously combusted; and I was astonished when I looked down to find myself still in one piece. I sat down; I even managed to follow the rest of the service. But I knew as I filed out of chapel I would never be the same again.

Unfortunately for you, I can't claim to have heard voices, so you won't be able to mark me down as a paranoid schizophrenic, less suited to a parish pulpit than to a padded cell. And I'm aware that you'd think far better of me if I were to confess that ever since then I'd been plagued by doubts; but it simply wouldn't be true. Nowadays even at a theological college doubt seems a good deal more fashionable than faith. It suggests an open mind – even though the reality is far more of an empty one; intellectual humility – or at least the show of it; and of course respect for the other person's point of view. But I can only state that from that moment on, my vocation has never wavered; and when I finally came to make my first communion nearly five years later, all my previous convictions – all my earlier convictions were triumphantly confirmed.

It remains to this day the most profoundly perfect moment of my life and one I can't ever begin to put into words, not even for you; language itself is far too inadequate and my own command of it far too imprecise. But I'll do the best I can... We'd been preparing for confirmation for nearly a year; although I at least felt that my whole life had been leading up to it. We'd been told to fast that morning, but I'd eaten nothing all weekend; so as I made my way up to the altar, my head was already strangely light, and I flung myself down so eagerly that I scraped my knee.

At last my moment came; I was offered the sacraments. I took them with trepidation; I waited for the transformation. I waited in vain. I felt betrayed by the underwhelming insignificance. The wafer was insubstantial and the wine tasted sweet. I rose to return to my seat, desperately disheartened, when I was stopped dead in my tracks. In one gulp I felt him inside me: his blood pouring into me, his body pounding through me, his spirit filling every part of me with fire. And I knew then that he'd chosen me; I knew then that he was one with me. And we would never be separate again.

The two things I feel sure that you'll want to know, unless you're quite unique in my experience, are did I convert simply as a way of hitting back at my family, and did training for the priesthood provide the ultimate revenge? Such cynicism used to sadden me, but I suppose to expect anything else would be unrealistic when to a good many people my name is virtually synonymous with my race. But I can assure you that over the years I've examined my motives from every conceivable angle, and I remain completely convinced of my own good faith.

Not that I've ever made any secret of my family's religion; nor do I even regret the bitter struggle it's cost. On the contrary I've felt it's yet another tie that binds me to Jesus, Jesus of Nazareth, the Jew who became the Christ. And although in the past, I admit, it may have caused a number of complications, I wouldn't like you to think it'd caused me any complexes. I can truthfully report that I've no complexes of any kind.

But then you may not be a complex person at all – oh dear, was that a Freudian slip? – I mean a person who believes in complexes. And you may not even be a Freudian; you may be a Jungian. I'd prefer that. At least he allows for a degree of spiritual autonomy; he doesn't reduce the whole of human behaviour to a residue of our earliest experiences, or an amalgam of our parents' private parts... Or you may even be a Kleinian. I understand she was no less of a determinist than Freud. Only with him it all happened on the potty, whereas with her it was at the breast. And I find it very sad to see that universal conflict of good and evil reduced to a choice between two breasts. Besides, how do we know which is which? I find it hard enough to know what's what on my own body. I always have to think long and hard when my tailor asks me on which side I dress.

It's not that I wish to deny my early experiences, but I refuse to accept them as formative. Your founding father seems to allow us even less freedom of action than does Jonathan's. And yet God gave us all free will, no matter whether we're born in a castle or a cowshed, with all the love in the world or with none. And as I'm sure you're well aware already, in my case it was the castle, or at least a late Gothic imitation. But I've nothing to hide; one day I'd be happy to take you on a personally guided tour – or are you an armchair traveller as well as an armchair theorist? And I don't know whether you assign any mystic significance to place names, but it was called – is called – Edensor. So at least they must have had a sense of humour in mid-nineteenth-century Kent.

Edensor was my great-great-great grandfather's folly: a castle in the air he'd had built out of Portland stone. In his determination to prove himself more English than the English, he'd commissioned a country house fit for an embattled Scottish earl. From the outside it appears as a vast, forbidding fortress: a bastion with battlements and buttresses, towers and turrets, and even gargoyles, the ugliest of which I was secretly convinced must have been modelled on my aunt – although not quite so weathered nor so worn. Whilst inside he'd allowed his fancy to roam even more freely, and to draw its inspiration from every period of history and every corner of the globe. So there's a music room modelled on a Roman temple and a ballroom taken straight from the Farnese palace, a Chinese courtyard and an Elizabethan hall. Intricately carved choir-stalls from a Flemish convent panel the library. While in the corridors Baroque cherubim consort with Renaissance putti; and in the galleries Rococo seraphim hold canopies over Gothic saints.

It really has to be seen to be believed, and even then you can never be certain, as rooms with trompe l'oeil ceilings lead into rooms with ceilings over forty foot high. But it's not only the sins of the fathers that return to haunt their children, for at night the fantasies of my great-great – oh, ever so many times great – grandfather came back to torment me, as coffers creaked open their lids and suits of armour rattled their halberds and mirrors threw out hideous distortions, and even his crowning glory, the celebrated malachite staircase, threatened to shake off its marble caryatids and send their swathes of swirling drapery tumbling about my ears.

And yet it wasn't just at night that I had to tread gingerly. For every room was supposed to be admired but not touched in the same way that children were supposed to be seen but not heard. And it may have been the eyes in all the portraits that seemed to follow me spookily, or the spy-holes and secret passages that my great-great... oh, never mind – grandfather had had sneakily built into the walls; but wherever I was, someone would always be sure to be watching me. And history, which was so fascinating in books, was merely frightening in the privacy – or otherwise – of my own home.

Even the nursery seemed to have been designed without the slightest consideration for a child. It was right at the top of a tower and shaped like a hexagon; and so I always felt a pang of envy for other people who could talk of sleeping soundly within their own four walls. And it was so heavily embellished, that when the doors were closed, it felt like nothing so much as being locked inside a semi-precious jewel-box. The ceiling was an enamelled sky of cobalt blue with a burnished sun at the centre, from which issued six ribbed vaults, like golden rays encrusted with shooting stars. While the walls comprised mosaic panels of Hebrew history: the most unsettling of which, the massacre at Masada, was re-enacted nightly in the moonlight above my bed.

It wasn't until a long time later that I realised that my mother must have felt even less at ease there than I did. I remember how she used to sing a song about being only a bird in a gilded cage. It never occurred to me that she could mean it literally; any more than when she thanked Heaven for little girls rather than for me. And her cage – her bedroom was genuinely gilded, and inlaid, or so I'm told, with sixty different kinds of marble. And when on sunny days the painted glass windows sent rays of colour over streams of dust, and the heat of the room brought out the incense-breathing scent of her perfume, it seemed to me more like the lady chapel of a Byzantine basilica than anywhere for a mere mortal to sleep.

But then she fell ill and spent longer and longer in bed, although whether she slept or not, I couldn't say. And now, however far back I think of her, I always see her lying down, whether in bed or on a sofa, propped up on piles of pillows, as though she were trying to establish a buffer between herself and the rest of the world. And please don't think I blame her. I know illness is nobody's fault. But then I wouldn't want to lay all the responsibility at God's door, either. So what would you suggest? Still, the problem of human suffering is one that has exercised a great many cleverer minds than ours, if you'll forgive the presumption. So I think on balance I'll stick to prayer.

She began to take all her meals in bed, rather than just breakfast. I heard her nurse describe her health as delicate, and that was only one of the many words I was rapidly having to redefine. But unlike my baby teeth, I couldn't simply put them under my pillow. And along with my new vocabulary came a new self-consciousness. I was no longer able to run up to my mother and fling my arms around her neck and cover her in kisses; but instead I had to think carefully where I put my clumsy, tell-tale hands.

And if only someone had taken the trouble to explain what was wrong, then I mightn't have felt so helpless. I was still a child and so of course I understood pain – no one better – but not yet illness and still less death. I began to despair; not that anybody paid attention. Children aren't allowed to despair; they're simply stubborn or solitary or strange. And... Do you really need to put me through this? It all seems so unnecessary and so long ago. Very well, I can give you the entire story of my life in a single sentence: someone dropped a match; there was a fire; and my mother burnt to death.

Satisfied...? Oh! Oh no, you don't! You think I did it, don't you?

Everybody always has: even my father; though he'll never admit it. That's why he hates me; though he'll never admit that either. But I was at school. There was an inquest. The findings are there for anyone to see... And as soon as he decently could, he took himself off to the South of France. But he didn't take me. And in due course, with undue haste, he married again; and he now lives on the hillside above Cannes, with his new wife and their two sons and their friends and their staff, and a Spanish gardener called Jesus.

He left me in the hands of his sister, my Aunt Sylvia, even though he himself detested her. So if I needed any further proof of what he felt for me, there it was. And yet he insisted I always be grateful to her for having given up her own life to look after me. But I didn't see why. I'd never asked her to. And besides, as far as I could see, she had no life to speak of – at least not the sort that other women spoke of: she had no husband nor children. She'd had a mother, of course; and she was always droning on about not knowing what to do with herself since she died. Well, now she did; and it seemed to me that I presented a far more attractive solution to her problems than she did to mine.

She returned my loathing with a vengeance; and believe me, no one could be either as vengeful or as venomous as her. And she spoke as ill of the dead as of the living, taking every opportunity to deride my mother. For reasons I've never been able to fathom, she reserved her particular scorn for her former profession. To hear her talk, you'd have thought nursing little better than prostitution. I can only assume it was due to a similar proximity to the private parts of strange men.

Not, I'm quite sure, that she herself would have known one from Adam. I'd be very surprised if she'd ever even kissed a man outside the immediate family circle. She certainly seemed to take little enough pleasure in kissing me. Not that she spared herself, or me for that matter. But from the way she'd lift my cheek to her lips as though it were a piece of overcooked cabbage, she never failed to make her distaste abundantly clear.

And her logic was as warped as her love. She claimed that my mother was mad; and as madness was hereditary it would one day manifest itself again in me. Which is a filthy lie! I'm sorry... But do you wonder I was so reluctant to embark on this? Although if I had a fault, I'd say it lay in quite the other direction; I'm steady to the point of stuffiness. If only my hands were equally steady, I could pilot a plane... Not that it's any thanks to her. She insinuated the idea of insanity whenever she could.

Though if pressed, the one thing she would grudgingly concede was that my mother had been a beauty. It was as if she felt safe to grant her that, since not only was physical beauty skin-deep, but we'd all look the same in the grave. And as proof, not long after the fire, she lured me into the Egyptian room at the British Museum, and led me gleefully to a mummy on a plinth. I took one look at the brown skin flaking off the bony face, like the scrawny claw of a roasted turkey, and I lost sight of any other meaning. All I could see was my own mother, not some ancient Egyptian, lying burnt and charred in her unsettled grave. I began to howl, which was precisely the reaction she intended, and the pretext she needed to haul me back home in disgrace. And if ever there were a curse of the Pharaoh's tomb, I invoked it on her head then.

She could even give the kiss of death to Christmas. One year she almost sank the Sunday School nativity play. She'd long objected to my attendance in principle, but my taking part was something she claimed she couldn't ignore. She insisted that I be replaced, and after endless appeals and consultations, they effected a compromise whereby I swapped roles with one of the three wise men. I felt humiliated, which, believe me, had nothing to do with my demotion. And even then I could see that her argument made no sense. For if anyone were indisputably Jewish it was Joseph; whereas the three wise men had come from much further East.

Of course from where I stand now her position seems even more untenable. I remember how she seized every opportunity to remind my father that to be a true Jew you had to be born of a Jewish mother. Which in itself ruled me out. Unless she'd proposed to apply for a rabbinical dispensation, which would hardly have been in keeping with her blistering contempt for all the fashionable marriages that had been 'made in Heaven and annulled in Rome'. Not that she had any right to talk. No one had ever asked to marry her. I only wish someone had; she might have been a good deal happier. And so might I.

And there was one match I was continually plotting: between her and my Uncle Sinclair. He was my mother's brother and my only uncle, just as she was my father's sister and my only aunt. And to my historically charged imagination, it appeared the most perfect dynastic union since the roses of Lancaster and York. I don't think I was particularly romantic; I simply hated loose ends. You may smile, but I was just a child, and children long for symmetry. And so I turned for consolation to the church.

It was the one place where I felt that my aunt couldn't reach me and that I could reach out to God. It was the one place where no one was forever carping at me, and where they seemed to value me for myself. And as I fell to my knees behind the protective screen of my great oak box pew, I began to recapture that sense of security which I knew I'd lost forever at home. And although I was obviously far too young to take communion, I already felt part of a community; and it was a community I was determined to stay a part of for the rest of my life. And I think I was aware even then, however far away I might have been from expressing it, that I wanted to play a special part – to be a part and yet apart: to be a priest.

Please don't get me wrong. It wasn't because I felt myself to be especially virtuous. On the contrary, I've always been painfully aware of all my faults. And yet, whatever our inadequacies as people, they can become our strengths as priests. I expect that must sound the most appalling self-indulgence, or worse, a licence to sin; nevertheless to me it's a spur to ever greater humility. For since I know that it isn't merely in spite of all my failings, but in full acceptance of them, that God has called me, I must be even more aware of my own limitations, and hold myself back, allowing him the chance to speak through me... And that's the way he works through the whole of creation: making virtues out of inadequacies. And it fills me with joy.

Which is why to become a priest, whatever the sacrifice, would for me be no sacrifice. And I'm quite prepared for all the hardships, even the much-threatened loneliness. Although it does seem a little disingenuous to speak of it as an occupational hazard, as if it were an industrial disease. There's humility and there's mock humility, which are two very different things. Besides for me it's just the opposite; it's the inability to become a priest which is lonely. To have to work amongst people who see no point to my existence. To see none myself. And then to be locked in my own inconsequence. Whereas a priest, although he may be alone, can never be lonely. To be a priest is to be peopled with God.

So what do you say? Here am I struggling to express my vocation: to put the ineffable into words. And I don't even know whether you're a believer. And I'm certain you're going to tell me that belief's a very personal thing; but then so's therapy. And I've given away so many personal things about my life; surely it's not too much to ask for just one in return?

You evidently think it is. You prefer to play God than to let me know if you believe in him yourself. Then I'll just have to fill in the gaps on my own. And one thing which I think is common to both my faith and your philosophy is that there are no such things as accidents. So where does that leave me? I keep returning to that fateful Eucharist. I know I said that it must have been the Devil who was in me; well, I almost wish I could be sure it were. Then at least I'd have the chance to redeem myself. But what if my rejection had been far more absolute? Father Leicester might have sent me to you, but what if God had already made his own feelings quite clear; and at the crucial moment – the very moment when we were about to celebrate the sacrifice of his son – he rejected my sacrifice as conclusively and contemptuously as he once had Cain's?

Three

Hello... Are you looking for the Jack the Ripper tour? Then you've found it. I'm sure if you tag along, you'll soon catch up on what you've missed. I'm afraid we've already done one murder, but don't worry, there are still four more to go...

You may have noticed as we walked down Old Montague Street, and skirted one of Whitechapel's bleakest post-war estates, that a large proportion of the inhabitants are immigrants. This was equally true of the East End of a hundred years ago; only whereas now they're predominantly Bengalis and Bangladeshis, then they were mainly Irish and Jews. The effect of such a rapidly changing population, together with the encroachment of the City, with its ever increasing demands for space, was to make the area at once highly volatile and desperately poor. It's tempting to add that little has changed.

In 1888 there were 30,000 people living homeless on the streets of London, as well as another 130,000 who were homeless in all but name, and whose only shelter was a common lodging house where, as I mentioned earlier, fourpence would buy a bed, known as a doss, for four hours; eightpence would buy it for the whole night; and for those too impecunious even for that, there was a rope rather like a clothes-line strung out across the centre of the room, and for a penny they could prop themselves up against that for a few hours and rest as best they could... I don't know whether any of you have taken any of the other London tours, but I understand that some of them have been re-routed to accommodate Cardboard City: our contemporary centre of destitution, right in our cultural heart... It's tempting to add that little has changed.

Four of the Ripper's five victims relied for shelter on one of these public doss-houses. You heard what happened to Polly Nichols when she went out searching for money for her nightly bed. Well, eight days later Annie Chapman, another prostitute in her mid-forties, and a woman already dying of consumption, took to the streets with a similar objective, only to meet with a similar fate. Her body was discovered at six o'clock the next morning, here, in the back yard of number 29 Hanbury Street. Back yards, like alleyways, were particularly favoured by prostitutes, because they too were left both unlocked and unlit.

As you can see, the lodging house itself was knocked down in 1972 by Trumans brewery. Some people wanted it retained as a memorial to Jack and his victims, but the developers as usual had their way. Though it has always been a magnet for the macabre. The first sensation-seekers flocked here within days of Annie's murder, and some of her more enterprising former neighbours made a killing – I'm sorry – from charging them for a sight of the spot where she met her doom. Which, come to think of it, is not so very different from what we're doing now. Though I'd rather not... think of it, I mean.

Annie, too, had suffered the most horrendous injuries. She was found lying on her back with her legs pulled up. Her throat had been slit and her head almost completely severed. Her lower intestines had been torn out and dragged over her right shoulder, along with two large flaps of skin. But what caused most consternation was the discovery that her womb had been cut out and removed.

The theft of her womb has given rise to two specific, although equally erroneous, theories. The first was that the women were killed in order to satisfy the demand for human organs for medical research, and that Jack was in effect one half of a latter-day Burke and Hare. But whilst he may well have had medical connections, they were in fact quite incidental; and besides, his surgery could hardly be called expert, for as well as her womb, he removed half her bladder in what was scarcely the cleanest of cuts. And the second was that Annie Chapman was pregnant, which in view of her age and general physical condition seems, to say the least, highly unlikely, and that Jack the Ripper was actually Jill the Ripper: some murderous midwife, who also practised as a backstreet abortionist and whose professional duties would account for her blood-stained clothes.

Forgive my irreverence, but, ladies and gentlemen, of all the many far-fetched theories that have been put forward to explain the Ripper's identity, the idea that he was in fact a she is not merely risible but dangerously obscene. As you can hardly fail to be aware, a number of these walks have been picketed by groups claiming that they constitute a crime against women; and I'm only glad that our friend here has agreed to stay with us, after the earlier disruption, to give me a chance to refute the charge. And I hope you won't assume that just because I'm guiding this walk, I hold any kind of a brief for Jack the Ripper. My presence here may simply be, contrary to usual practice, the only way to get me out of the home and on to the streets.

But what really would be a crime would be to suggest, even for a moment, that the perpetrator of such murders could be a woman. For they were first and foremost male crimes. They were male crimes par excellence. You might almost say they were the male sex par excellence. For although they weren't sexual attacks in the conventional sense of involving either sexual contact or consummation, the nature of the wounds leaves no doubt that whoever the murderer was, whether an isolated madman or an Establishment conspiracy, the sexual element was of paramount importance.

In particular his obsession with wombs, which he tore out like a series of grotesque hunting trophies – and we mustn't forget that many of the suspects were well-connected English gentlemen, who would have been well-versed in the rituals of the chase – reveals not so much the desire to take revenge on any specific woman as on the very essence of woman herself, and not on her sexuality, but on her fertility – or more specifically on her maternity: the primal power that had brought him into the world. It was as though from out of his madness had grown the ultimate delusion: that he was completely alone and always had been, and that he had never had any attachments – not even an umbilical cord.

And I trust you'll forgive me, sir, for I can see you find such digressions tedious, and I know you're anxious to hurry along to the scene of the next blood-curdling death; it's just that somehow, without my even realising, the ideas of that Viennese doctor have come to play a not inconsiderable part in my own way of thinking; and I feel I have a unique insight, based not, I admit, on painstaking research, but rather on the most painful experience, into the murderer's character as much as his crimes. It was as if as he ripped out these women's wombs, he was ripping out the very womb from which he'd been born, just as he would have gladly ripped up the whole world which he'd been born into – that world in which he now felt utterly lost and unbearably alone. And the greatest irony is that this man, who has passed into myth as the most notorious of mass murderers, was, in his sadistic savagery, trying to annihilate no one so much as himself.

Thank Heaven for St Bede's: a corner of cloistered serenity and consoling sanity amid the desolation of my own life and the dereliction of the East End. I feel inordinately grateful for its smoke-stained walls and its crested wrought-iron gates, as I hurry home from the crypt, and step back into the solid security of a building that has a history and not just a past.

Brother Martin stops me on the stairs. But I know I reek of the crypt, and I long just to soak for hours in a steaming bath-tub and to scrub myself clean, until my skin glows as pink as a pig's in a children's rag-book. But the cistern's old and the hot water's finished, so I jump quickly in and out, before darting back down the freezing corridor to my spartan cell and slipping, shivering, straight beneath the thread-bare blanket and the well-worn sheet.

Sleep rescues me from exhaustion; until I wake again at six to the mocking peal of the Prime bells and the tetchy tooting of the traffic. And I plunge back under the covers, desperate to recover the anonymity of the night. But my pounding head reminds me that it's once again time to drag myself up: to take my pills and return to face – or fight – another day.

I make my way back to the crypt, through sordid streets of tumbledown warehouses and garages which seem to sell nothing but tyres, past drab pubs with purple billboards advertising indigestible lunchtime stripteases, and abandoned shops bricked up and chained and padlocked, in case someone should steal... what: the empty air? From all sides I'm met by the acrid stench of exhaust fumes and the sullen stare of exhausted people; and my whole world seems to be coloured a dirty brown shade of sooty grey. Whilst overhead the bold blue line of the Docklands railway runs mockingly ever on.

And so to work. I've been promoted cook. At least it was presented as a promotion. And I wasn't about to admit that I'd never cooked a meal in my life. They seem to imagine I've been mollycoddled as it is. But I've always understood that any fool could boil an egg... Well, would you have known you had to prick it before you put it in a microwave? And in any case I'd hardly have thought it was a capital offence. But Patrick called me over for what he laughingly described as a quiet word in my ear, though what with his basso profundo, not to mention the echoing acoustic, I'm quite sure it must have been audible to every ear in the crypt. Then all the clients stood and watched, not one of them lifting so much as a finger, whilst I tried to scrape out the mess. And I really don't know what I've done to deserve it; but do it I did.

Then, as if that weren't enough, after lunch we had to attend a staff support group on oppression. Patrick had divided the blackboard into two halves: on one side he'd written the various categories of the oppressed and on the other of the oppressors. The oppressed, as far as I remember, comprised women, blacks, the Irish, the poor, the disabled, gays... gays! While the oppressors were the army, the police, the royal family, the rich and, inevitably, the Church.

We all had to form groups according to whichever of the categories felt most appropriate to our particular oppression; and there was considerable soul-searching as to where each of our primary allegiances lay. After a few minutes I realised to my embarrassment that I was the only one left unoppressed; while everyone else was staring at me as though I were the last boy left on the touchline once the rest of the teams had been picked.

I stood my ground and refused to be intimidated even by their graceless gibes. I felt rather like an early Christian who'd been thrown to the lions. But I was unafraid; I knew I too would discover my Androcles paw. So I said straight out that I wasn't oppressed, that I didn't feel oppressed and didn't we all have a lot of far better things to do?

That didn't go down too well and was followed by a heated discussion as to how I might start to redeem myself. Someone, I expect it was Vange, suggested with her usual perspicacity and charm that I could always write them out an extremely large cheque and then claim my place amongst the ranks of the poor. But I refused to rise to the bait, or stoop to her level, and simply stood stock-still, praying that I wouldn't blush – do I blush? – until Patrick declared, in a tone of consummate confidence, that the greatest oppression was self-oppression. At which point I left.

To Hell with him... that is, metaphorically. How dare he presume to analyse me? He isn't you. They're all the same. They hear my name and then they're deaf to everything else. And I'm caught in a cleft stick. If I go up to the church to pray, then I'm shirking; if I come down to the crypt to work, then I'm condescending. Selfish or slumming: I can't escape. But I'm not as naive as they all seem to think. And while I admit my experience may appear somewhat limited, I did once spend an entire weekend training with the Church Army. I dipped my toes into some extremely murky water, and came across things you – and even they – would never have believed.

Not that I could ever have seen myself as an evangelist; I've always felt I'd be most at home as a scholar priest. But I was persuaded to tag along by a Balliol friend in the Society of Mary, who was testing his vocation and thought it might interest me. Although in the event interest seemed far too tame a word. And it was no ordinary weekend. Lancelot emerged, somewhat to my surprise, with his resolve unshaken: he's now working as an assistant prison chaplain; whilst my eyes were opened to a very different aspect both of the Church's mission and of London life.

I was truly appalled. I'd never before seen such hopelessness, let alone homelessness, as we tramped through the South Bank shanty town of Cardboard City and up to the fun-fur coated women, offering equally ersatz fun, outside dingy Soho clubs; and then back past the emaciated boys with their etiolated bodies, brazenly clustered around the clutter of Leicester Square. And although it was the women whose wretchedness the Church Army captain chose to dwell on, oddly enough it was the boys who made by far the stronger impression on me.

I'm not looking for plaudits, but I would like you to realise that squalor and degradation aren't completely virgin territory to me. I saw enough in that one weekend to last me the rest of my life. And I'd have thought we'd have had our work cut out trying to relieve the victims of such self-evident oppression, rather than self-indulgently searching out more of our own... Nor did I try to banish it from my mind. For several weeks after my return to Oxford I could scarcely sleep for thinking of them. I longed to take the next train back there and succour them. But then I read about the official campaign to stamp out vice in London, and I knew I could sleep sound in the knowledge they'd soon be in safe hands.

Later, when I described the experience to Jonathan, he openly scoffed; in fact he was downright cynical. I couldn't think why until I realised that I'd used the dreaded word; just to call something – anything – an army is more than enough to damn it in his eyes. He's rabidly anti-military. He was even arrested in Whitehall last Ash Wednesday for painting 'Less Ash' on the Ministry of Defence walls. And he was furious when they decided not to press charges. I sometimes think he'd like nothing better than to be a martyr to that – or indeed to any other – cause.

Though on reflection I'm not so sure that what he objected to most wasn't that I'd gone out with the Church Army, but that I'd gone there with Lancelot. It was almost as if he didn't like to think of my having any other close friends, even before we met. Not that I ever really had; I was an only child and a lonely one. And in time I became a lonely adolescent. As now no doubt in time I shall become a lonely old man: the law of diminishing returns and a self-fulfilling psychology. But for a while he seemed set to break the pattern. We spent so long in each other's company that someone even christened us David and Jonathan; even though my name's not David, and Judas might have better suited him... And no, I was wrong; I must have been very naive.

I've never found it easy to make friends. I learnt quickly that there was no one I could open my heart to at school, neither the boys who were trying to destroy my spirituality, nor the masters who tried to break my spirit. And our loyalties were almost as regimented as we were; even God had to acknowledge the prior claims of the Captain of the First Fifteen. Individuality was discouraged while competition was fostered, giving us the worst of both worlds; which is, I suppose, what team spirit really means. They seemed to be trying to turn out leaders of men from the same mould from which they'd once turned out the administrators of Empire, refusing to acknowledge that both the mould and the Empire had cracked.

I cracked: on one occasion all too violently. I don't know whether you were sent to a public school, but the sole respect in which mine seemed to live up to its name was in its total lack of privacy. I refused to see why my private parts should be subjected to public scrutiny or my modesty to derision. I couldn't even use the lavatories without qualms, for there wasn't a single door amongst them. They were open to the world – and to the most flagrant abuses. And there wasn't one of my school fellows who had more than a rudimentary sense of shame.

Don't think I didn't see your eyes light up. One way or another you were determined I should end up in the lavatory; as, if you must know, were several of the older boys. But I'm afraid you'll have to be satisfied with the same reply I gave them. I kept both my distance and my self-respect... Although I sometimes suspect I must be the only boy ever to have passed through a single-sex school without a single sexual experience. Nor did I allow my resolution to falter at Oxford, where the nature of the temptations may have been very different – so much so that at times we seemed to be enjoying a straight run of Leap Years – but my response remained unchanged.

I'm a virgin and I'm proud of it; and at least you have the grace not to snigger. Most people seem to find the very mention of the word irresistibly comic. And it's a sad reflection on the degradation of the language that its immediate association should be one of loss. But the Church's teaching is quite unequivocal, as is the example of Christ. And if some people find it odd that I should extol the joys of married love without ever having known them, even by proxy, then I can only say that Christians are forever talking about things of which they know nothing – I'll rephrase that... It's like the bliss of the after-life: something we have to take on trust.

As a priest, of course, my commitment will go far deeper. And I hope at least that once I'm ordained, I'll no longer be constantly called on to defend my position, but instead may be accorded a little of the respect due to my cloth. And no, I'm not trying to hide behind it – see, I'm only too well aware of the way your mind works, though I sometimes wish that you seemed to be half so attuned to mine – but it's a part of my special relationship with Christ. I don't mean that I see myself as married to him, or to the Church, or any of those other coy conventionalities; but that I shall stand in his person, alone before his altar, for the whole of eternity, and not just till death us do part.

But even celibacy has become a source of controversy; and nowhere more than when it comes to the sticky subject of masturbation, which I know to be one that's very dear to your heart. And for the record, although I can't for the life of me see why anyone should ever want one: no, I haven't, and no, I don't; and as I've told you before, I never dream, so thankfully I've been able to avoid any other involuntary mishaps, such as sleep-walking or bed-wetting, or... anything else.

At St Dunstan's the general feeling was that a commitment to celibacy might still embrace masturbation; as though self-abuse were in some way different from abuse of any other sort, and now that we know it doesn't actually turn us blind, we can quite simply turn a blind eye. We're back to that disastrous recipe for treating the Bible as if it were a kind of salad: picking out the bits we find palatable whilst leaving to one side those, like the Sin of Onan, we may find hard to swallow.

Jonathan, of course, had to go one better, or at least further, and insisted that celibacy might even accommodate homosexuality. For such an intelligent man he could be maddeningly, dangerously perverse. And how did he attempt to justify such a view? Well, I have to admit he had a kind of logic. It is perfectly true that in the eyes of the Church a clergyman – any clergyman – is by his very nature either married or celibate. And therefore, technically, celibacy simply means not marrying. But he seized on this mere technicality with all the specious sophistry of a man who excused his betrayal of his wife and children by the printing error in the Adulterous Bible; and used it to condone an entirely unscriptural, unsacramental, unsacerdotal way of life.

So why? I know that's what you must be thinking – unless you've not been thinking at all, in which case it'll simply be so what? So why did it take you so long to realise what he felt for you? You claim to have been such intimate friends and yet to have had no idea of his most intimate feelings? And yes, I admit; I have to plead guilty: if innocence be a crime. I broke my own rules; I trusted him. I thought he was the friend I'd been searching for all my life: the friend of my dreams – I don't dream: the friend of my soul.

I'm beginning to appreciate the distinction between innocent and naive. A moment ago I claimed innocence; but that's as phoney as Ben Jonson claiming benefit of clergy and getting away with murder, simply because he could read and write. Do you think I've got away with murder? I know Jonathan did. He claimed I'd betrayed his love; when it was he who betrayed my friendship. And yet if love is as precious as friendship and friendship's more precious than life itself, then perhaps... No! I refuse even to think of it. He's hurt me quite enough already. His parting shot, the very last words that I ever heard from him, and the last that I expect now I ever shall, was that I didn't have the courage of my contradictions. At first I thought I must have misheard, so I corrected him. And now I don't even have the consolation of that.

So what are they? Can you tell me? I've racked my brains, and I can't come up with a single one. No, he was the one with all the contradictions; and he was simply trying to shift the blame. Did you know, for instance, that he was also a card-carrying Communist? Oh he was quite open about it – I only wish he'd been as open about everything else... And on the whole it seemed to have been accepted, or at any rate tolerated, by both the party and the Church. And when I warned him of the proverbial danger of serving two masters, he replied that there were many more contradictions within the New Testament itself than there were between the teachings of Marx and Christ. According to him, Communism without Christianity was a society without a heart and, I'm sorry, Christianity without Communism a religion without balls.

He grew up in Deptford; and whatever else his boyhood might have lacked, and I sometimes suspected that it must have lacked considerably more in the telling, it wasn't warmth. He was one of a very large family. I could never remember exactly how large, but then the ramifications appeared to be endless, as one sister brought home her baby just as an elder brother was preparing to move out.

He left school at sixteen without a single qualification, which I still find scarcely credible considering he's one of the cleverest people I've ever met. But he said it was on account of his class, which I took to mean a disruptive classroom, until I remembered his politics. And I must say it does make them somewhat easier to comprehend. He worked alongside his father shifting furniture... His arms are – were – still very strong... Then, impelled by an increasing dissatisfaction, he began to read socialist philosophy and he soon came to realise that his dissatisfaction had been no mere psychological quirk. And he decided to give up his job and resume his education, or, as he put it: Out of the removal van and into the vanguard of the working class.

There were no shortcuts. He took his 'O' levels and then his 'A' levels and then won a place at Oxford. And so he was at Ruskin at much the same time as I was at Balliol. But when I expressed surprise that we'd never met, he laughed and said that it would have taken a miracle or, failing that, a revolution, since we'd moved in quite different worlds.

But then one Sunday evening the miracle happened. For as he was walking down the High on the way back from a rally for Nicaragua, he heard the strains of evensong emanating from St Mary's. And as he had nothing else to do, he went inside; in much the same spirit that you or I might have gone to a pantomime: to recapture the sights and sounds and smells of our childhood. Only he rediscovered God.

It was then that his real struggle began, for at first he was convinced that his faith and his politics would be pulling him in quite different directions; but he quickly discovered that, on the contrary, they were both leading him down exactly the same road, and if not to Rome, then at the very least to Anglo-Catholicism. And so he was confirmed during his second year at Ruskin, and during his third he decided to become a priest. Initially he resisted his vocation even more violently than his conversion. He fought with God until he realised he had no choice but to submit. He liked to compare himself to Jacob wrestling with the angel... Apparently as a boy he used to box.

His parents were overawed, although not unenthusiastic. It seemed that they now had an honour in the family in place of a son. But explaining it to his friends proved far harder. They were all passionately political and he was afraid they might feel he'd let them down. But in the event they supported him wholeheartedly, several of them even claiming to find his decision no surprise. They trusted him to do what was right, for himself and for them and for everything in which they all believed.

You still haven't told me just what, if anything, you believe. But you'd have had to have been living on Mars or in a particularly remote Siberian monastery to have avoided all reference to last year's debate in Synod and the subsequent furore over homosexual priests. At St Dunstan's it proved the occasion for considerable soul-searching, breast-beating and, in Jonathan's case, even open revolt. His sense of injustice knew no bounds and he was very soon spoiling for a fight. Up until then I'd assumed his sexual stance was simply part and parcel of his radical bravado... How could I have read it all so wrong?

Although I was far from alone in counselling caution, he remained determined to make his indignation felt. He began firing off letters in all directions until Father Leicester forbade him on his obedience;

which gave him a second form of censorship against which to protest. But it isn't easy to deny a clergyman a pulpit; even as ordinands we go on preaching practice in our third year. And by a particularly unfortunate stroke of timing, and with the uproar showing no sign of dying down, the sermon on 25 January had been allotted to him.

As soon as he cleared his throat, I could tell we were in for trouble. He'd been due to speak on the travels of St Paul; but before we knew, we were off on a whistle-stop tour through the perversions of the Patriarchs. In his view the whole of Genesis was one writhing, incestuous tangle: starting with Adam's incest with Eve – did you ever hear anything like it? – through Cain's homosexual incest with Abel – no, I very much doubt that you did... Indeed, that turned out to be the sin which Cain was so anxious to conceal and the true murder for which he had to atone.

He then moved on to Lot. As you can imagine, he had a field day in Sodom. It seemed that the original sin of the City of the Plain wasn't the one to which it afterwards gave its name but rather rape, or even simple inhospitality, and that the shift of emphasis had been deliberately designed to take some of the heat off Lot's own subsequent incest with his daughters. Now, please, don't get me wrong, nobody – but nobody – could have a greater abhorrence of incest than I do; but, in his wilful misinterpretation, Jonathan was being almost as perverse.

For would you believe he then took on Noah? Yes, Noah: everybody's favourite conservationist; every child's favourite Biblical myth. But according to him, the man who almost single-handedly ensured the survival of the species later revealed Nature in a very different light. For he fell prone to the same vices as Lot, namely drunkenness and incest. Only he was seduced not by a daughter, but by his son Ham, who, it was authoritatively stated, 'saw the nakedness of his father'. And you could rely on Jonathan to have followed up every reference in the entire canon to seeing and uncovering nakedness, in order to make his meaning uncanonically clear.

The most crucial and irrefutable, as well as to later Bible writers the most shameful and disturbing, of these incestuous unions was

Abraham's marriage to his half-sister Sarah; for it was precisely the one from which the whole tribe of Israel was believed to descend. And so they devoted all their energies both to playing down the blood relationship and covering up its broader implications. And they deliberately accentuated the taboo on homosexuality in order to divert attention from the far more threatening breach of the incest taboo which underpinned their entire faith.

And so for thousands of years a grave injustice had been done to a group of people who'd been made the scapegoats for the innate guilt of every Jew who traced his faith back to his forefather Abraham and every Christian who based his faith on the faith of the Jews. And the same iniquitous bigotry could still be seen at work today in the Synod of the Anglican Church.

His words provoked considerable mumblings of discontent, and the wonder was that nobody tried to stop him. But then I very much doubt whether anyone would have succeeded; for he was a man who'd discovered the truth and as always he was his own best argument: which was that truth, like desire, could never be wholly repressed. And to be fair, his case wasn't based on wishful, or even fanciful, thinking, but on rigorous linguistic analysis – at least of a sort. Although I'd argue that such analysis is utterly redundant. The Bible is no ordinary historical text, but the revelation of God... And yet I suppose that, too, would have been part of his thesis: that it was precisely God's purpose, or at least the early Bible writers' perception of it, to manifest himself through what so many later writers have perceived as aberrant sexuality. And that even if the details of his interpretation were open to question, the broader implications were not... Besides, as you should know better than anyone, when it comes to myths, implications are all.

And I wouldn't be at all surprised if he'd drawn some of his more extreme ideas not simply from the structuralists and anthropologists, but from you. After all Freud was another great myth-maker; he might even be considered the greatest myth-maker of modern times. But he knew where to draw the line. How do you suppose people would have reacted if, instead of choosing classical models for some of his more contentious theories, he'd called them the Lot complex or the Ham complex or even the Cain? He'd have been laughed out of court, or at least out of practice; and you wouldn't be sitting where you are today. Whereas the very archaism of the Greek myths gave them a spurious intellectual authority, flattering his readers' vanities without endangering their deeper beliefs. Though no doubt Jonathan would have argued that if Freud backed away from Biblical myths in favour of classical ones, it was precisely because at the last he too was unable to confront the guilt in his own heart and at the heart of our entire Judaeo-Christian culture; and our first response should be: Physician, analyse thyself.

For the clergyman the equivalent injunction is usually that we ought to practise what we preach, but in Jonathan's case it wasn't merely that it was something he shouldn't have been practising, it was also a sermon that he'd been specifically forbidden to preach. And yet I shouldn't like you to think that his intention had been simply to sensationalise; rather in his usual unorthodox way he seemed to be arguing that it was only by radically reappraising our most fundamental myths that we could arrive at a fuller understanding both of God's purposes and of our own nature, and begin to build a just society here on earth.

I'd dispute that. As Catholics we can hardly ignore two thousand years of Church tradition... But then I never had the chance to dispute with him again. For you already know what happened next. And later that day I saw him for the very last time when, despite strict instructions, he slipped in to see me in the sick bay. He wanted to apologise; he admitted his methods might have seemed underhand. He said he'd longed to confide in me beforehand, but he'd been sure I'd have tried to talk him out of it. And the one thing – the only thing? – I could always do was talk. He stood there twisting his handkerchief; I'd never seen him look so wretched. I wanted to tell him that I forgave him; I wanted to tell him so much. But my tongue hung in my mouth like an epileptic's. And my lips twitched as though I'd had a stroke.

He moved closer to my bed. He towered over me. I sensed his

presence like a bruise that felt blisteringly tender to the touch. The bulk of his body blotted out the light. His bright copper hair seemed about to burst into flames; the wiry russet hairs on his hands and wrists seemed charged with electricity; and all the freckles on his face seemed on fire. His heavy lower lip was trembling and his sea-green eyes looked pitifully glazed. It was then that he told me what he felt for me; and he claimed, on what authority I still don't know, that I felt the same for him, only I was too great a coward to admit it. He said I was lying to myself as well as to him and laying down so much pain for us both in the years to come.

He leaned over me; I closed my eyes. But he was still there; I could feel his breath on the lids. It was hot – scorchingly hot; but it simply felt radiantly warm, like a gentle mistral. I couldn't move. His arms hemmed me in, one on each side, like the twin towers of the Edensor drawbridge. I wanted to draw it up... And then he pulled back the bed-clothes. I couldn't move. I could see his hands – his boxer's hands, his sculptor's hands, his sculpted hands: the marbled, veiny, marble-veined hands of the Michelangelo David. And he tried to lift me up. He said that there was nothing wrong with me. And I could see the tears welling up in his eyes and his face moving down towards mine. And there was nothing else I could do. Nothing. You have to believe me. So I summoned up all my energy, and I summoned up all my spittle, and...

No, that's not true. I don't know what I'm saying, any more than I knew what I was doing then; it was only a few hours since I'd collapsed. I was clearing my throat; he was so close. I simply sprayed him with a little dribble – I took steady aim and I spat. And for a moment I saw that I was the man who'd first spilt Christ's blood and then spat in his face.

He looked as if he didn't know what had hit him. He looked at me as if he couldn't believe it was me. And then he turned and walked away... And suddenly the college appeared to be overrun with bishops. First Jonathan's bishop came, refusing, or so I'm told, to let one mistake destroy such a promising career. There was some talk of his repeating his final year at Salisbury or Lincoln or one of the other more liberal colleges. But I was in bed, and by the time I was back on my feet, he'd already left, without leaving me so much as a forwarding address.

Then my bishop came, together with my Director of Ordinands, and I was discharged from the Sick Bay, only to be discharged three days later from the college as well, and... Well, you know the rest, or at least all the bits that matter. But it makes no sense; how can they expect me to make a fresh start when they've forced me to sit here hour after hour endlessly reliving my past? And how will I ever be able to forget Jonathan? On the contrary, I seem to be worrying about him more and more. What if he should succumb to the sin of despair, and even take it upon himself to end it? How could I live with myself then? How can I live with myself now...? Sometimes I feel so desolate. Do you think I'm self-oppressed?

Four

We're standing at the corner of Fashion Street, a name that clearly speaks for itself, although sadly more on account of the women who made the clothes than the ladies who made the fashions. Are there any Americans here tonight...? I thought so. You may know this street already by repute as it was the one where Jack London lived when he came to England a decade or so later, for Edward VII's coronation. He'd been so shocked by the living conditions he'd seen in the East End that he felt he had to share them. So he sold his new clothes, bought a second-hand suit and moved here for three months whilst he wrote *The People of the Abyss*.

I don't put that forward simply as a bit of local colour, but you asked me, yes, you, sir, the gentleman with the tattoos, what my qualifications were for leading this walk; and I'm afraid I have to admit they're fairly flimsy. I'm not a historian nor a criminologist nor even a professional guide. In fact you'd be amazed if you knew what I originally set out to be. But I have done my homework, and there's one incident Jack London records which for me highlights the reality which lurks behind the Victorian myth and its despicable double standards. He writes of a boy who was arrested for stealing a mere five shillings from a woman. The judge couldn't understand why he hadn't simply asked her for the money. But, sir, he patiently explained, then I would have been arrested for begging... At least he knew where he stood, which is more than can be said for most of his latter-day counterparts who grew up in the belief that they had a place in this world and a value... But that, as they say, is another story. Back to ours. Or rather Jack's.

Unfortunately history doesn't always follow the same rules as topography, and so to anticipate for a moment: it was also on this corner that George Hutchinson was to stand, as he watched Marie

Kelly, the final, most tragic and most horribly mutilated of the Ripper's victims, in conversation with a man who might well have been Jack himself outside that pub. The pub, which then as now was known as the Ten Bells, has a particular significance for our story, for all five of our victims regularly drank there, as we shall now, although, I hope, with a far less violent outcome.

It is in itself a considerable monument to the Ripper, with pictures and mementos covering every spare inch of the walls. However, for any of you who may be unfamiliar with our English customs, you will be expected to buy something. And, of course, should you wish to purchase any of the many Ripper souvenirs, do please ask one of the bar staff, who, I know, will be more than happy to help. I myself will be available to answer any of your questions... And I should warn you that although the other customers may be typical East Enders and very friendly, it's not advisable to point your cameras at them without asking permission first... So let's make our way inside. Then we'll reconvene here in twenty minutes to consider one of the bloodiest nights in the whole of British criminal history: 30 September 1888: the night of the Double Murder.

I deplore the far too easy analogy between the traditional role of the priest and the current role of the therapist. It can only be made by people who clearly know very little of your profession and less than nothing of mine. You may assuage a troubled mind, but you offer no solace to the soul.

As you were clearly determined to stay sitting on the sidelines – on the fence – I'd finally determined to tender my own resignation at the crypt, when, whether by good faith or providence, Laura, who's about the only volunteer prepared to be even halfway civil to me, invited me to go with her on an exchange visit to the Borough Mission: an old-fashioned soup kitchen across the river, where the minimum of cheerless charity is dispensed in the name of Christ.

We were met by two missioners and led down several draughty corridors into a vast, gloomy, subterranean hall. As we walked in, we passed under a notice which read 'The Gospel is for everyone', although it seemed to me that a far more appropriate one would have been 'Abandon hope all ye who enter here'. I'd never been in a room of such unremitting drabness. Men with faces the colour of porridge, wearing clothes the colour of suet, leaned against walls the colour of weak tea. I found myself thinking back almost fondly to the warm-hearted secularism of the crypt. Surely anything would have been preferable to this parody of a church?

Laura and I were commandeered to help hand round the ragged, battered hymn-books to the even more ragged, battered men. I listened with mounting revulsion as in preparation – or was it penance? – for their suppers they were served up platefuls of platitudes. And although they didn't exactly have to sing for it – in fact the ploddingly played hymn-tunes drew a painfully small response – they were expected to pray.

I felt bitterly ashamed. 'Are you a Christian?' one of the missioners had asked me. 'Yes,' I'd replied. And he'd nodded his head as if no other references were needed. But it seemed more like a badge of respectability than an expression of faith. And he wore it as though it elected him to sit at the right hand not of Christ but of Calvin; and his message was equally harsh. 'You may say that these men are parasites,' he told me, 'but we believe they're people'; when I'd certainly neither said nor even thought anything of the sort. 'Treat them with a little kindness, and you'd be amazed how well they respond.' And his Calvinism had become almost Jesuitical.

The preacher began his sermon. But whilst his tub-thumping vehemence held me in thrall, the rest of his audience had clearly heard it many times before. His text was the parable of the great supper and his theme the reversal of roles they could all look forward to when the poor, the maimed, the halt and the blind – and here he appeared to address them each by name – took precedence at God's heavenly banquet. But in case they found such a prospect remote and his promises hard to digest, he cunningly tossed in a number of equally mouth-watering references to the foretaste of that heavenly banquet which was about to be served up to them there, in that very hall, on that very night.

And what exactly was this feast which for him seemed to contain all the symbolic significance of the Mass? Sausage rolls and baked beans. We're constantly warned of the danger of selling our souls, but it seems we can sell our self-respect far more cheaply: as cheaply, in fact, as two greasy sausage rolls and a ladleful of lukewarm baked beans. I thought to myself that at least in Hell they'd have been hot. And my irreverence was all that cheered me.

Then at the end of the meal a short, sharp-faced, blue-rinsed woman, whose function I'd hitherto been unable to work out, majestically made her way over to the urns where the men were queuing up for their mugs of tea, and dispensed largesse – or at least a small tin of cheap chocolates. One each. That's right: one. For which they had to thank her graciously and shake her warmly by the hand. Had it been me, I know I'd have tried to crush it harder than the cruellest playground bully and then thrown her unpalatable chocolate down at her uncharitable feet.

It was then that I thought – I was sure – I saw my uncle. I was amazed; I was horrified; I was obviously confused. The light was appalling. My mind must have been playing dirty tricks on me. And besides, if I'd last seen him when I was eleven, he must have changed beyond all recognition. The man I'd seen was clearly a complete stranger who simply looked now as he had then. But then when I turned back, the man – the mistake – had vanished, as if his mind had been playing the same dirty tricks on him.

What on earth can have caused me to think of him? I haven't done so for years. We have to protect ourselves from our memories above all else; they're the true enemy within. And he was more than just my mother's brother. If it weren't for him, I wouldn't be here today – that is, I wouldn't be anywhere. He was the one who first introduced my parents. He'd been in the RAF with my father; he used to tell me the most hair-raising stories of how they flew Mosquitoes together on bombing missions over northern France. And I was quite convinced that single – or rather double-handedly, they'd won the war.

But at the end of one successful mission – war gives such different values to death – they were shot down over the Channel. They were alone in the water for sixteen hours before being rescued. My uncle always claimed that my father saved his life; if it weren't for him, he used to say, he'd have been done for. And yet nothing was ever quite the same. He had to be invalided out of the air force; and from then on he was prone to the most profound depressions. But when I pressed him to elaborate, he'd just say: You see... everything... no matter. He was the only person who ever spoke in broken sentences. Everyone else had perfect syntax, even when they made less than perfect sense.

My father, on the other hand, was back in the cockpit three days later. He had a new navigator and he flew for the rest of the war. But he never talked to me about his wartime exploits; he never talked to me about anything. And yet he kept in touch with my uncle, and on one of his leaves went to visit him in Westcliff where my grandparents ran a boarding house... which was another of the targets for which my aunt reserved her especial scorn. And she liked to taunt me with the modesty of my origins as fervently as if she'd been Huxley challenging Wilberforce with the origin of the species. Then, having berated me for some minor social gaffe, she'd generously concede that perhaps I wasn't altogether to blame, considering where I sprang from – a line of reasoning that would, with due respect to Huxley, exonerate us all from the consequences of everything that had happened since Adam and Eve.

Do you believe in love at first sight? I do: at least when it comes to my parents. They fell madly, passionately – sanely, soberly in love. And it wasn't simply my aunt who disapproved; my maternal grandfather was also far from keen. I gather he objected to my father's religion... with all the unthinking intolerance of a man who felt he'd done his bit for humanity simply by supporting the war. But my parents refused to let it sway them. And it must have been so romantic: in the black-out with the heady scent of danger, where the only thing that wasn't rationed was love.

And yet, apart from the first delirious moments, I don't like to think of my parents as lovers. It's too arbitrary; and anything arbitrary is dangerous. And before you think you've touched a nerve – one of yours by the way, not mine – it wasn't their sexuality I was trying to keep at bay, but my insecurity. I was quite prepared to share them with one another, just not with anyone else. So I preferred to think of them as bound together by far stronger bonds: not the transitory ties of lovers, but the sacred, indissoluble – and they should never, ever be dissolved – bonds of parent and child.

Although they never talked to me about their courtship or why they'd waited twenty years to be married, I brooded on it endlessly. It was an even longer delay than Jacob's. If they'd married sooner, my whole life would have been different: I might have had brothers or sisters and they'd still have been young. Instead, when I was born, my father was already fifty and my mother forty-three. Ignorant strangers used to mistake them for my grandparents; which made me want to strangle them – the strangers, not my parents, of course.

I yearned to know the reason; but I felt afraid to ask. And would you believe that I've never seen a picture of their wedding? Not a single record of the most important day of my life. The castle is full of portraits of my ancestors, but none of my parents. I had all the strain of a family with none of the surety... I sometimes feel Our Lord was fortunate, notwithstanding St Matthew's exhaustive genealogy, to have been conceived of a spirit and born of a virgin. It wasn't just the desires of the flesh he was spared, but the burden of heredity.

My uncle was my only source of substantive detail; he seemed to need the reassurance of my parents' coupling almost as much as me. He and my mother were twins, although clearly not identical. How could the same identity ever survive the distinctions of sex? But they remained very close. It must be marvellous to be a twin: to have another being so attuned to you that he can understand your innermost feelings better than you can yourself. To have someone you can trust as much as yourself, to be your other self, so that the whole of your life can be as harmonious as the resolution of a Shakespearian comedy. For years *Twelfth Night* was my favourite play.

This is hurting me. Do you enjoy inflicting pain? Or do you work on the same principle as my old school gym-master: that our exercises were only effective when we were on the verge of collapse?

When my mother died, everything changed. My father went abroad and, although he left my uncle in charge of the estate and my aunt in charge of me, I felt painfully exposed. And my fears were to prove well-founded when one day an old man broke into the garden: a man who was to haunt my dreams for years to come... I speak metaphorically; as I've told you before, I never dream.

I call him a man, but that's only by a process of elimination and not on the evidence of my eyes. I've never seen a face like it, either before or since. It was a face that bulged with bulbous folds; that looked as if it had been burnt half to death and then left for years to fester; where the skin had been replaced long before plastic had become just another cosmetic and seemed to stretch and sag and pucker more painfully than the wound underneath.

I was playing in the alleyway of ancient lime trees, the tips of which intertwined like the lattice-work vault of a Gothic nave, when suddenly he stumbled out and thrust his hands towards me. I was petrified. At first I thought he was a ghost, burnt in the fire, who'd come back to haunt me. And then as I peered more closely at the sagging bags of scarlet skin, I was sure I must be staring into the face of the Devil himself. I broke free and ran back down the alley, stumbling over the uneven path of protruding roots. He was the Devil! I tripped. I was pounding the ground to open up and save me... But I was pounding Nanny. As I plunged my head into her soft bigness and covered my head in her skirts, I choked on my own explanations, and then on my own embarrassment; for, as I turned back towards the walking wound staggering after me, I could see he looked equally afraid.

Of course I realise now that his chief fear was that he'd be charged with a far more intrusive crime than trespass; but the only thing that had touched me was his pain. My aunt quickly took control. Humiliation always brought out the best in her: just so long as it wasn't her own. She discovered that he was a vagrant looking for work, and I think my uncle found him something on the other side of the estate, although I never saw him again. He only stayed a few weeks before moving on. They told me he was lucky to be alive; but I would have disputed their definition. What life could it be with a face that no woman would ever kiss and from which every child would back away: a face that betrayed its own friendliness as well as mine; a gorgon's face that turned even sympathy to stone?

And I think that it must have been then that I first came to realise that there was a pain in the world way beyond my comprehension – a pain that couldn't be soothed in any of the time-honoured ways: a hot bath; a warm bed; an outing; a book: a pain of unbearable physicality that ate into itself like a blood-filled Italian sausage strung up in a grocer's, with hard, red flesh seeping through the holes in the string. Burnt flesh. Dead flesh. War flesh.

It was the war that had done it – and not any war, but that particular one – which seemed to be behind everything I could never know, everything I could never understand. If there were ever a question I couldn't answer – even more if there were ever a question I couldn't ask, then there was always the war: that war that'd been over twenty years before I was born but which somehow seemed to hold the key to my entire life.

And as time went by I needed the answers more and more urgently. But there was no one to ask. Even my uncle disappeared: my uncle who was my one ally in my struggle against the strictures of my aunt; whose wet-wool and tobacco-scented lodge seemed to me as homely as the castle was historic, and served as my constant refuge in my prep-school holidays. He was the only adult ever to treat me as an equal... although you might argue that that's not always a good thing. But then there were also times when he himself could be wonderfully childlike. I still recall how he used to swing me above his head until I could touch the ceiling – the castle ceilings were all way out of reach. The moment you can touch something it becomes so much less threatening. No, what on earth made me say that? It isn't true.

Then one day he just upped and left without a word of explanation.

If he could wipe me from his mind so easily, I see no reason why I should waste a single thought on him. And anyway that was twelve years ago. He might be anywhere in the world: planting tea in Sri Lanka, or managing a game reserve in Kenya, or doing whatever it is Englishmen do abroad now that they no longer go on missions. And the very last place he'd ever be is in a South London hall, queuing up for a condescending chocolate. It was just a face; I've been reading far too much into it. Hasn't it been proved that there are only a handful of fictional plots? Well, I expect there are similarly few facial types. And if I hadn't embarked on this therapy, I'm sure I'd never even have thought of him at all.

But once seen, it was a face not easily forgotten. So I determined to find him, or at any rate his double, if only to remove the doubt. And having drawn a blank on my return to the Mission, I decided to search some of the places I'd visited with the Church Army. The route had stuck in my mind almost as vividly as the degradation. Although once again if that's anyone's fault, it's yours. You made me retrace all the steps in my memory. I'm not trying to evade responsibility; but in a very real sense everything that happened did so because of you.

I walked around Cardboard City, but all I could see were boxes. I didn't feel I could knock on a lid as though it were a front door; somehow the lack of space put privacy at a premium. There was no sign of life apart from a group of young boys skateboarding obliviously, as though the boxes contained nothing but rubbish. Which to them, I suppose, was what they did. I crossed Hungerford Bridge, which now seemed the living embodiment of its etymology. And I gave some easy money to the homeless, hungry teenagers, who held up their misspelt pleas for charity at either end.

I turned down underneath the railway arch. I saw all the men blanketed in the gutter, and wondered which would be kinder: to smile in ineffectual sympathy or to avert my eyes. I became profoundly depressed. I felt I'd have had more of a chance with the proverbial needle in the haystack – at least in the right light a needle would shine. So I determined to go straight back to the priory; and I was striding up to Charing Cross in search of a taxi when I passed a young man shivering on the corner. He looked spiky, both in his stance and in his haircut. And you may think I'm trying to be wise after an event of the utmost folly; but I thought of the Good Samaritan and crossed the road.

I smiled shyly; he stared sharply and asked if I were looking for someone. So I said yes, as a matter of fact; and made up my mind to enlist his support. I speculated as to whether there might be a community of the homeless or even a fraternity, or would it be just the same all-pervasive anonymity? Until I realised that whatever else, Uncle Sinclair was hardly likely to have used his own name. I was about to move away, but the power of his presence gripped me. I examined him more closely. I know I'm thin; but he was skeletal. He seemed barely more than a child, but with an adolescent heaviness around the chin and around...

I asked him if he were as cold as he looked, and his look made me realise the inanity of my question. I wished I'd been wearing a scarf or anything to have wrapped him in. It's all very well for St Martin to have shared his cloak with a beggar, but contemporary coats aren't so easily split. So I asked if he were sleeping on the streets or if he had somewhere to go. He laughed and said that it all depended on me; which somewhat surprised me. But when I queried what he meant, he seemed to become far less sure of himself and began to shake. Then I suddenly realised that he'd probably eaten nothing all evening; nor, for that matter, had I. I gazed at him and began to feel achingly hungry: a hunger of an intensity I'd never experienced even after a Good Friday fast. So I invited him for a meal.

He chose the restaurant. Do you like Indian? he asked. I don't – but I did; so we went. And I can't say I took to it. They showed us to a table that was so far to one side it was almost in the kitchen. Every time the door opened, I was hit by a blast of curried air. They played loud taped music; the sitars were synthetic and the waiters looked bored. Their service was decidedly lacklustre; I was tempted to pull rank, but something about Jason – that was his name – persuaded me to hold back.

Once in the restaurant our relationship had subtly changed; he became steadily more confident and I increasingly uneasy. It was hardly helped when he took off his shirt to reveal a flimsy tee-shirt with a Union Jack and the wording: 'We are all prostitutes'. And I began to feel that the parable might not have told the whole story. There might have been a very valid reason why the priest and the Levite had both passed the wounded man by.

He ate his fill. In the intervals between mouthfuls he told me about his life. No, that's not true, he generally contrived to combine them; with the result that if a particularly large mouthful coincided with a particularly long sentence, gobbets of curry spattered across the table. I tried to disregard them; though the brown stain through the 'o' of prostitute stared me right in the face. He was anxious for me to appreciate that he was no dosser; he'd had a good job in a record shop. But when I asked him why he'd given it up he became extremely cagey, mumbling about unfair dismissal. And I was disappointed; I've worked long enough at the crypt to know when I'm being strung a line.

Besides, I'd at last worked out his eyes. They'd been worrying me all evening; whenever he tried to look at me, he'd seemed to be juggling with his eyeballs. At first I thought he was astigmatic. And then it hit me: drugs. I put it to him straight; and he coolly confessed to a few pills and things: uppers and downers, nothing heavy. And before I could dispute his diagnosis, he was offering to supply me, and with things that sounded very heavy indeed. He must have realised his mistake, for he said he was only kidding; and he rumpled up his prostitutes tee-shirt to blow his nose. The brown stain was joined by a greenish yellow smear.

Despite everything, I felt an inexplicable urge to identify with him and with a fellowship that went beyond the bounds of basic Christian brotherhood to a bond of sympathy that was uniquely our own. So I tried to explain that I understood his predicament. And what was more, although they'd been medically prescribed, I myself took drugs that weren't so very different from his.

He claimed not to believe me, which I suppose I should have taken as a compliment. But it just so happened that I'd collected my prescription earlier that evening, and so I picked up my briefcase and showed him the proof. You must think me such an idiot. Is there a consulting room equivalent of the dunce's corner? But at the time I felt that both my confidence and my confidences had been well repaid.

He lolled in his chair and rolled his eyes, and once again pulled up his shirt and scratched his stomach. I stared at his bare midriff and felt a burning desire to know if his skin were naturally dark, or if it were simply dirty. And I suddenly felt an equally pressing need to visit the lavatory; I should never have drunk so much wine. I looked around rather desperately; he pointed me in the right direction. He said that the first thing he did in any restaurant was to 'suss out the loos'. And I remember thinking that it seemed a somewhat perverse priority, especially before he'd even studied the menu. I went out, never suspecting for a moment... And of course, when I came back, both he and my briefcase had gone.

I tried to stay calm. I casually called a waiter and asked if he'd seen my companion. He replied very coldly that he'd just left, telling them that I'd be settling the bill... which he then proceeded to hand me. I wanted to rush after Jason; but having had to whistle for service all evening, there were suddenly half a dozen waiters standing between me and the door. I began to feel desperately sorry for myself, which is the one thing I was always trained to avoid... Although I sometimes wonder why. Given that I feel sorry for so many other people, would it be very wrong to spare a little every now and again for myself?

That's what you get for bringing a boy like that in here, one of the waiters said to me. And his teeth shone unnaturally white. I was furious. So Jason might have looked a bit of a mess, and his table manners would hardly have endeared him to Nanny; but was that his fault? And yet his words and my folly took on a whole new dimension as he explained that he knew Jason of old. There was a club across the street; he often brought men to the restaurant for a meal or, more accurately, an hors d'oeuvre. And I suppose it must have been obvious to you all along; although the thought had never entered my mind. Or had I simply closed it deliberately? And yet he'd seemed so different from those boys in Leicester Square. Not only had he been all alone, he was so aggressively unalluring. And I desperately tried to exonerate myself; I told them I was training to be a priest. At which they just looked embarrassed. And I realised that to them, far from being any justification, that compounded the crime.

I wanted to demonstrate my good faith to the entire restaurant. But when I looked around, everybody had left except for a party of pot-bellied salesmen, one of whom rested his stomach grossly on the table. And I suddenly remembered yet another of Nanny's nursery admonitions: that all joints on the table should be carved; and I longed to pick up a knife and plunge it straight into his all-too-conspicuous consumption. To cut and thrust and slice and slit. To hide my blushes in the red of his blood and my humiliation in his pain. And... But the violence of my reaction appalled me. And I hurriedly paid the bill.

Everything fell into place: Jason's rapid changes of mood, his smirks, his flirtatiousness, even his tee-shirt. And I felt sick. How could he have even imagined it? I'm twenty-three years old: only four years older than he was himself, or at least than he claimed to be. I thought it was only in old men that money took the place of desire. Tell me honestly, am I really that repulsive? So that his unquestioning assumption had to be that the only love I could get was the love I could buy. Jonathan hadn't seemed to think so... Jonathan... But maybe I've changed; if people's hair can go grey overnight, why not their faces? Maybe my features are etched with an inner ugliness... And the man with the overhanging belly belched and wiped his slobbering lips with the back of his greasy hand. His companions laughed. And I gulped as I saw myself reflected in a mirror or at least in the pupils of Jason's eyes.

Why would he rush off so quickly, with only a monogrammed briefcase containing nothing but some *Readings for the New Christian Year* and three bottles of pills, when I'd already promised to put him up in a hotel for the night, unless his fear of what that night might cost him made the prospect too awful to bear? And what most horrifies me now isn't his misapprehension – after all, what else can you expect from someone with those words splattered all over his chest? – but my own response. I'm a celibate; I've dedicated my life to Christ. So why should I let anyone's assessment of my sexual attraction – let alone that of a boy like that – matter to me at all?

But at least I've learned my lesson. And I vowed never to venture into the West End again: at any rate not on my own, and not at night, and not without a very specific programme. The streets are full of unsuspected dangers... I returned to St Hugh's; I shut myself in my room and fell to my knees in prayer, my mind concentrated by the lack of decoration. I put myself to bed; but I didn't sleep. How could I, once my briefcase had been stolen? I used to need nothing but a simple pattern of childhood prayers to ensure an undisturbed rest; now it takes a litany of pills.

Five

I hope you all enjoyed that brief respite, and are now suitably fortified to continue our walk. I've stopped here outside another pub, but we won't go in; I don't intend to lead you on a pub crawl... Although for anyone who's interested, 'Famous Feet' do organise a tour of some of London's most historic public houses, and I'd be very happy to give you details of that and indeed all our other tours at the end.

No, the pub would have been of particular significance to our next victim, Elizabeth Stride, in view of its name. Like that of many of the sites we visit, this has changed during the past century, and although now known as the City Darts, it was then called the Princess Alice, which was also the name of the large Thames pleasure steamer which had sunk ten years earlier off Woolwich with the loss of some seven hundred lives. May I ask how many of you knew that...? I thought not. Until recently, neither did I. Though it is ironic, isn't it, that we're all here because of five sordid murders, whereas none of us had any knowledge of a tragedy on a far larger scale.

Elizabeth Stride always claimed that she herself had escaped from the wreck, suffering a badly injured jaw as a result. In fact her post-mortem revealed no damage of any kind to her jaw... although there was considerable damage to the rest of her. Her body in the morgue long resisted identification: not, for once, because of the dreadful mutilations carved by the Ripper's knife, but rather the many different pseudonyms she'd at one time or another adopted. I'll spare you the confusion of nicknames, professional names and common-law husbands' surnames which makes it hard enough to follow this story on the printed page, let alone on the streets. And yet our next victim in particular was to pay a very heavy price for her lightly chosen alias.

Elizabeth Stride's is the one murder site that I'm afraid we don't visit. Unfortunately, when he committed his murders, Jack failed to foresee these walking tours a hundred years on; and he killed her rather off the beaten track, about half a mile away in Berner Street. But I do assure you that you're not missing much. If we have to give up any of the murders, then 'Long Liz's' is the one. Quite apart from the constraints of time, it was by far the least spectacular.

For once the Ripper didn't mutilate his victim extensively. Some commentators even claim that her relatively clean cuts debar her from qualifying as a true Ripper victim at all. But that's nonsense. In the view of most Ripperologists, Jack was disturbed before he had time to get down to the real nitty-gritty. But his blood was up; he was desperate for another corpse to savage – and within an hour he'd found one. So follow me to discover just how much he could do, when he finally had the opportunity to hone his craftsmanship to a fine art.

I had no trouble locating the club, which was directly across the road from the restaurant. Although I was surprised to find the door locked and the name in such tiny type. After a moment I pressed a buzzer and after another the catch was released. I went in. I gulped. Even in the passage the air was fetid. And the state of the stairs would have deterred anyone less sure of his mission than me.

I identified the bar by the beat of the music. I went in and was immediately hit by a gust of cold air and a trickle of condensation down my spine. I felt as though I were in a decompression chamber. My eyes took several blinks to accustom themselves to the gloom – although my morals never did. I wrinkled my nose. The room smelt rancid. The bouquet of yesterday's sweat and betrayed expectations hung heavily all around: the animal smell of love for sale and for barter: far ranker than any of the country market smells of my youth. I recognised the risk of intoxication from the stale beer fumes lingering in the air.

A whale of a barman waddled over to me. He was without doubt the fattest man I've ever seen. He seemed to come in two distinct halves: the top half was big, but the bottom was enormous. And as the bar cut him off at the waist, nothing prepared me for the full effect. I wondered how he managed to climb the stairs, and I was later told that they winched him up with the beer crates. Some of the rougher boys sometimes left him dangling in mid-air, but I'm not sure he altogether minded. He had to keep all the drink above waist-height, because there was no way he could bend. Though I heard him ask one of the boys to come behind the bar and bend over for him. And it wasn't until much later that I recognised the ribaldry behind the remark.

After making sure that I hadn't strayed in inadvertently, the barman, whose name was apparently – and appropriately – Slouch, explained the nature of the club and asked whether I wanted to join. To save explanation I said yes; although I didn't use my own name. Actually I used yours... I bought an orange juice and sat down at the side. I didn't know what to do with my hands. So I grabbed hold of the rim of the table, and a sordid stickiness seeped under my nails.

I felt like Daniel cast amongst the lions, but I refused to be deterred. Instead I determined to beard them in their own den. I had to find Jason. Dr Livesey had frightened me. I'd explained that I'd lost my briefcase at Bethnal Green Station – which, whilst only a white lie, still set a dangerous precedent. And he'd expounded all the possible consequences, should the largactil have fallen into the wrong hands... which Jason's undoubtedly were. So I had no choice but to seek him out: not to make a fuss nor even an accusation; but just to make certain he handed them back, or at any rate threw them away.

I took my bearings. The decoration seemed defined by a desperate eclecticism. The walls were hung with foreign posters of American films: the Marx Brothers in Italian, *Gone With the Wind* in French. There were grimy niches filled with empty beer bottles and crudely doctored classical statues: a Michelangelo's David in a dirty jock-strap and the Venus de Milo in a hairnet and black satin bra. The tables were transport-café chipboard, and the parquet floor was acned with cigarette burns. A television flickered over a snooker table. Clip followed clip: current affairs, comedy, adverts – above all adverts, as if it'd been deliberately designed to demonstrate that the commercial break was the apogee of the broadcaster's art. The constantly revolving yellow and orange lights made me feel dizzy and the clientèle appear even more jaundiced; whilst above my head a precarious-looking mirror-ball seemed to be making up its mind whether to revolve or to fall.

I surreptitiously surveyed the other customers. There must have been fifteen to twenty of them and even at first glance they constituted an extraordinary mixture: middle-aged businessmen, most resembling nothing so much as the hen-pecked husbands in saucy seaside postcards, together with much younger companions: some big and brawny, some painfully undersized. One or two even looked as if they should still have been at school, although I put it down to an inadequate diet. I'd always lived in such a healthy world: people who bestrode the earth they owned; here were boys who had to scratch at it for whatever they could glean.

They were distinguished by two marked characteristics: their haircuts and their tattoos. I was later initiated into the deeper mysteries of their specific implications. There were some punks, and some flat-tops, and some skinheads, and some boneheads; and they were as adamant about the distinctions as two theologians disputing the signification of the Mass. And as for their tattoos: one boy had his face enclosed in a spider's web, as if his whole life were equally entangled, whilst another had his back encircled in a dragon breathing fire on its own tail. When he whipped off his shirt, it appeared as though an entire Chinese festival were processing down his spine. I tried to imagine how he ever went swimming. And then I looked at his pasty face and spindly body and I very much doubted he did.

People came and went, although rarely in the same combinations. I watched introductions being effected in the crudest ways. Boys would stand by the fruit machines, nonchalantly pulling the handles, whilst customarily cautious businessmen sidled up behind, throwing their money, or at least their petty cash, to the wind, as they each strove to hit their respective jackpots. How did love ever become so mechanistic? Or were they all simply drunk? There was certainly a constant stream of people towards the lavatories. And I thought of Jason. But my speculations were interrupted by a boy falling flat on his face off a barstool. Nobody picked him up.

After a few moments I went tentatively over to help him, although he didn't seem particularly grateful. I led him to a chair and asked if there were anything I could do. He said I could get him another pint. I was about to protest; but he smiled at me with such a toothlessly vulnerable self-awareness that I decided to save my sermons for another occasion, and moved to the bar. I soon found I was extending my offer quite widely, and I became the centre of a considerable coterie. A boy called Socks put his feet up on the table; his boots sent a shiver down my spine.

None of them could tell me anything about Jason, which, despite my initial frustration, convinced me that the waiter must have been wrong and began to restore my faith, if not in human nature at least in my own judgement of it. They in turn were determined to dispel any misconception I might have that they were rent boys. Although their disappointment, when I made it even clearer that I had absolutely no interest in any of them sexually, suggested that they would have been more than willing to waive their objections for a suitable fee.

I told them I was training to be a priest. I was amazed when they seemed to accept it as par for the course – or rather the customer. Several of them even claimed to have slept with priests and to have enjoyed, though that can hardly be the word, the most sacrilegious perversions. But I'm pretty sure they were simply bluffing for my benefit. Next time I'm determined to put it to the test.

For underneath all the bluff and bravado, the shorn hair and the scars, they genuinely moved me. And once again I felt a deep, a very deep, need to identify with them: like Christ with the publicans and sinners. There were times when I considered his selection of companions unduly narrow. But now I've met those boys I can see what must have impelled his choice. They're young; they exude so much vitality. I can't – I shan't let it go to waste. Though I don't underestimate my difficulties. It was easier for Christ: well, obviously. Quite apart from anything else, he spoke their language... after all his father was a carpenter. Whereas my accent, just as much as my wallet, tends to set me apart.

And yet at heart we're not so very different. My life has hardly been

---

an unchequered path from tranquillity to fulfilment. There was even one occasion when I was forced to resort to violence: at school I hit another boy across the head with a cricket bat. It fractured his skull, splintered his eardrum, and left him permanently deaf in his left ear. Naturally I was appalled; it'd never been my intention to maim him. But I'd been provoked beyond all endurance; for which I was exonerated by my Housemaster, even though I was ostracised by the rest of the House... Of course, I rely on your complete discretion. It's not something I'd care to have widely known. Especially not to the boys. It may help me to identify with them, but it's not at all the way I'd want them to identify with me.

But such an identification only makes my position so much more painful. I see how they're forced to make their living, and I'm racked with guilt. Now I'm well aware that we don't see eye to eye as regards that particular emotion. Forgive me if I'm wrong – no, more than that: correct me – but from what I understand, in your book guilt is itself the original sin: the one that lies at the root of all our troubles; whereas in mine it's the direct result of our original sin that we do, as indeed we should, feel guilt.

So, far from denying it, I welcome guilt; and I often feel we could do with more of it. To my mind it's not neurotic nor malignant nor self-destructive but rather a positive reminder of where we've gone wrong. At its best it can serve a purpose analogous to pain: a moral early-warning system which we ignore at our cost. And so I want my guilt; I need it. And I won't let you take it away.

Besides, guilt isn't only the inevitable consequence of original sin but the natural corollary of free will; as well as the essential seed-bed for Christ. His incarnation is the vital counterpart to the myth of the Fall. It's the point where history and myth meet, where myth is confirmed by history, and history transcends itself to become myth. He freed us from the yoke of sin, in particular original sin, and at the same time justified our free will. Since however little freedom of choice we might have in material terms, in eternal ones our choices have been made crucifixion clear.

Jonathan would have disagreed. He found the whole concept of original sin anathema, referring to it as the Augustinian heresy. It was the one myth which he didn't just want reappraised, but rejected completely. He was as determinist as any Calvinist; although his emphasis could hardly have been more different. To him it wasn't that we were in thrall to our sinful nature, that symbolic snake slimily slithering through our undergrowth, but to the social and economic realities by which we were all to a greater or lesser degree oppressed.

To him Christ's importance was predominantly political. He saw him as an iconoclastic rebel, a social reformer, an alienated outsider: an early Palestinian Che Guevara who roamed the Holy Land with a band of revolutionary freedom-fighters, castigating the rich and handing out loaves and fishes to the poor.

It's easy to make fun of his attitudes; at least it was in the common room of St Dunstan's. It's a rather different story now I'm out in the world. He used to quote me statistics which simply seemed top-heavy; but I've now seen faces which drive the statistics home... And many of them had no choice but to leave home, for reasons so obvious as to have become hackneyed, and not much more about the way that they earned their living, when they had nowhere either to live or work but the streets... And it's not just this new world which I find so hard to assimilate, but the new light it throws on my old way of thinking. What price my free will if theirs is an unaffordable luxury? And what price my religion without free will?

And what price their guilt? If I feel guilty because of my free will, why should I expect them to feel guilty if theirs is a mockery? But that simply extends my dilemma; just as their lack of responsibility compounds the crime. And they drift from crime to crime and punter to punter; and I'm sure it can only be a matter of time before one of them gets sucked into something even more serious. Which in turn only increases my guilt.

But there's guilt and guilt... I've started to feel guilty about feeling guilty, or more specifically about being encouraged to spend so much time talking about it to you when those boys have so little chance to talk to anyone. And yet one of them might do some real harm to someone, whereas the only person I might conceivably hurt is myself – which doesn't count. And don't you feel guilty about only listening to people who can afford your fee? You remind me of a mediaeval indulgence seller who offered the rich the chance to buy salvation whilst the poor were left with the worst of both worlds.

There is, however, one way out: a way for us both to make amends, which is for me to withdraw and still pay for the sessions for you to see some of the boys. Then you could write to Father Leicester to inform him that I'm completely myself again. Not only have I engaged with life, but I'm encouraging others to do so. Then I can go back to St Dunstan's and you can turn your mind to people who really need your help. In fact we'd be killing so many birds with the same stone that it would have to constitute some sort of record. So what do you say? I take it your silence implies acquiescence... Or don't you care? Do you simply switch on a couchside manner? Have you no social conscience as well as no heart?

You're no better than one of their punters. They pick the boys up like old chamberpots in a flea market; and their function is much the same. I told you about the continual exodus to the lavatories. Well, it wasn't just inspired by the volume of beer drinking, as I discovered to my disgust the first time I went myself. As I walked in, I was immediately struck by the acrid fumes of ammonia and three pairs of eyes which stared at me in naked hostility as though I were trespassing: as though my natural bodily function interfered with their very far from natural ones. I was horrified. And under their unabashed glare I proved unable to function at all; which created the very worst impression, for they immediately assumed I must be there for the same nefarious purposes as themselves. While the man in the end stall actually knelt down beside the boy next to him and took his... he took his – I'm sorry – he took his penis in his mouth. In the lavatory. In broad daylight. In front of me.

I turned on my heels. I ran straight back down the corridor. I couldn't breathe. The ammonia hung like asthma about my lungs. Then

I suddenly felt a surge in my trousers. I hardly had time to unzip myself when I was seized by a spasm of incontinence: right there against the wall. I spurted a stagnant stream of shame as though I were a drunk in an underground car park. My one consolation was that nobody came. So I hurried away, desperately praying that in the heat of the day it would soon evaporate; or else that they might think it was one of the boys.

But I made up my mind then and there that I could never abandon them; and if you refuse to help them, it's all the more important I don't. I knew that one day – one Judgement Day – I'd have to answer for my actions and that, however much I might fight against it, nothing happened in vain. My fall: the spilt chalice: the crypt: the Mission: even the spectre of my uncle and my meeting with Jason had all been designed to lead me to the club so that I, in turn, could lead the boys away. And as I walked back into the bar, as if to confirm my resolution, I first caught sight of Rees.

I'm well aware that you're bound to think the worst; after all, it's what you're here for. But I shan't let it discourage me. I'm hardly the first to have had my integrity impugned. Think of Gladstone. After tireless days spent governing the country, he then spent sleepless nights reclaiming fallen women. And all he received for his pains was derision. Some people even went so far as to suggest he might be Jack the Ripper. But he stood his ground. He was no plaster saint terrified that he'd crack at the first temptation. No, he lived his sanctity; he put it to the test. Our Lord made it too easy for us with his 'Lead us not into temptation'. If it were left to me, I'd pray 'Lead us in, Father, please lead us in, and then let us prove our own mettle by leading ourselves out.'

But after one look at Rees, I knew he could be no temptation. On the contrary, in some strange way I felt he was already very close to Christ. It may have been the quality of his suffering or simply that he still seemed such a child. I can see him now leaning over the bar; his hair clipped at the front like an American soldier and in clumps at the back like a circus clown. He wore an old grey jacket buttoned up right to the chin, with a faint check in the material which had all but disappeared in the general grubbiness. And there was a deep air of sadness about him: a stillness that in the hustle and hustle of the club commanded even more respect. He came to move me in a way I'd never known before: as a man identifying with another man's personality rather than a priest identifying with his pain.

I bought him a drink: yet another lager and blackcurrant. He told me his name was Rees... Rees! I'm sorry; I can't help it. I described the club as a place of darkness and it's even reflected in their names: Warren, Darren, Rod, Scott, Floyd and Rees: not one Christian name among them. They've been handicapped from birth. But he alone seemed able to surmount it: by his soft pensive manner and his curiously timeless face. All the other boys could never be anything but 1980s Londoners, whereas he'd seem at home in any period or place. If I were filming a Biblical epic, I'd cast him as an extra – no, why stop at that? – I'd cast him as a saint.

I thought he'd find it easier to talk if we weren't interrupted, so I led him into a quiet corner. As he stood up, I realised he was wearing jeans that were ripped just below the buttocks. From behind I could see his underpants; they were a bright pillar-box red. I blushed; I was glad to sit down. I tried to draw him out, but he was surprisingly reticent as though afraid of giving too much away. And I was struck by the contrast in our positions. There was he, so anxious not to reveal anything too personal; and yet I can only assume he spends half his life revealing his body to strange men. And here am I, forever baring my soul; and yet not since school has anyone seen me without my clothes.

After some gentle coaxing and some not so gentle drinks he did drop his guard a little. Although every so often he'd back away and just repeat under his breath, 'Oh, what a life, what a life' with an awful impersonality, as if it were out of his hands and he could only sit wringing them as helplessly as me. And he had good cause. He was sleeping rough. He'd been living with a friend but they'd been locked out. He muttered something about not even having been allowed to pick up his own stuff. And when I suggested he tried the DHSS, he looked at me as though I came from another planet... Did you know that they're unable to claim any money until they have an address and yet unable to find an address until they can put down the money? I've heard of Catch 22, but they live it: not to mention Catches 23 and 24.

So at night he sleeps in an empty railway carriage in the sidings at Waterloo. He always tries to pick a first-class compartment, not out of some perverse parody of snobbery, but because they retain more of their warmth. Which is more than can be said for most of the people he's encountered during his travels. Does no one in London ever smile? he asked me. And I found myself immediately trying to make up for all ten million of them at once.

He'd worn out his hopes along with his shoe-leather, going after jobs. What made it even worse was that no one ever believed he was nineteen – which I could well understand, since he looked a good three years younger. And yet there was one line of work for which his youth was at a premium: one employer who had no scruples about breaking the law. But then who would ever expect scruples of a pimp? And one afternoon whilst he was begging in the Charing Cross underpass, he'd been picked up and taken to McDonald's by a man who, seeming to befriend him, had proceeded to initiate him on to the game. Game: that's the euphemism of the year – unless you count Russian roulette.

He's under no illusions about the toll his way of life can take both physically and morally. His ambition is to run a second-hand record stall in Berwick Street Market and he swears he'll give up everything else as soon as he's saved the thousand pounds he needs to rent his pitch. He's always loved records: the shape and the shine and the feel of them almost as much as the sound... And as his eyes lit up, I couldn't help remembering Jason. But I decided not to mention him; I'd already drawn a blank with all the other boys and I didn't want Rees to suppose I had a prior commitment to anyone else.

My first thought had been to write him a cheque there and then – well, not exactly there and then, as that might have been open to mis-construction, but the next time we met. Come to that, it would have been easy enough to have helped them all once I'd applied to my trustees. But it would have been far too easy. And I remembered Jonathan's many strictures against private charity: salving consciences rather than solving problems. And, as I looked around at all the middle-aged men leering at the under-age boys, I realised my philanthropy would have been on a par with their philandering. I'd have been purchasing their gratitude as cheaply as their bodies. And I was utterly appalled.

There can be no shortcuts. I'll have to win them by the strength of my example. Love, love and more love: nothing else will do.

Six

September 30, 1888 was a busy night for the Ripper as he rushed from Berner Street, where he killed Elizabeth Stride at about 12.45, to Mitre Square, where he mutilated Catherine Eddowes less than an hour later. But we can proceed down Commercial Street at a somewhat more leisurely pace; and so let's pause for a moment here outside Toynbee Hall, which was one of the many charitable missions set up in mid-Victorian London, whereby the West End could pay its dues to the East End, before, in the opinion of many, one of its number returned as the Ripper to pay dues of a very different kind... So this seems as good a place as any to consider two of the most notable suspects.

Although Jack himself left remarkably few clues as to his identity, the one thing the Ripper inquiry has never lacked is a long list of suspects. Letters poured in to the authorities right from the start, most with the obvious intention of settling old scores. People were perfectly prepared to sacrifice their husbands and fathers, their brothers and uncles. Indeed, the theory I intend to put before you at the end depends on just such an identification. The Queen herself was not above pointing her finger, although understandably not at members of her own family. Her main suggestion was that a check should be made on all foreign seamen coming in on cattle-boats, as she was quite convinced that the Ripper couldn't possibly be an Englishman, and that if by some extraordinary quirk of fate he were, then he could on no account be a gentleman. On both counts she was almost certainly wrong.

Since then, of course, just about every eminent Victorian who was in London that autumn has at some stage or other been subjected to scrutiny. One of the most intriguing was Gladstone, who embodied that Victorian obsession with prostitution I mentioned earlier to such an extent that, as Prime Minister, he would search them out at night and invite them back to Downing Street in order to save their souls. But sadly, at least for sensation-seekers, that seems to be as much as he ever did, and his association with these murders has to be limited to the black 'Gladstone' bag the Ripper was reputed to have carried. Still, even though he was much mocked at the time, it's hard to imagine the present incumbent of Number Ten opening either her door or her heart to any of the modern-day prostitutes who've been so appropriately dubbed Thatcher women.

But although evidently not Gladstone, the idea that we might be dealing with a self-styled angel of mercy, who took his soul-saving mission to devilish extremes, has its attractions – at least for me. For if Christ really did tell the woman taken in adultery to go and sin no more – and that is itself a text of some considerable dispute – then the Ripper might conceivably have taken it as a justification for a kind of moral euthanasia: despatching some of the more notorious sinners out of harm's way. It's the same misapprehension that's led many men who've tried to model themselves on Christ – and I'm no longer thinking solely of Gladstone – to devote a disproportionate amount of their time to the reformation of prostitutes. We – that is they – may well have targeted it as the area of greatest need; but then that need clearly cuts both ways... I digress.

So to return to another of 'the men most likely to': Montague Druitt. Druitt was an unsuccessful barrister who, after working as a teacher, had recently resigned his post. Much was made of the fact that his family considered him to be sexually insane or, as we'd put it, insatiable; although I'm not sure I don't prefer the Victorianism, not as a euphemism but as closer to the truth. For the ultimate consequence of any obsession, and particularly a sexual one, is insanity; believe me, I'm the living proof... that's to say, we're all pursuing the proof right now: a man whose identity had become so subsumed in his sexuality, and his sexuality in itself so warped, that he no longer even desired a human touch, simply the touch of a naked blade.

The combination of Druitt's public-school education and prep-school teaching, together with his sudden unexplained resignation, has led many people to conclude that he must have been homosexual. And, indeed, his suicide at the beginning of December 1888 seemed to offer conclusive proof. For we have it on no less an authority than that of Victoria's grandson, George V, that he thought such men shot themselves. If so, he can have known very little about his own older brother... unless, of course, he knew too much.

Although Druitt himself may have failed to conform to type, he did conveniently drown himself in the Thames, only to be dragged out several weeks later, a hostage to history, or rather to historical speculation. But chronology alone would make him a highly unlikely murderer, particularly as a mere few hours after two of the killings he was to be found on the other side of London playing a game of cricket of such calmness and steadiness as would surely have commended him to the Queen herself: the stiff bat and the stiff upper lip of the stiff-necked English gentleman.

I don't have time to mention all the other suspects, except to say that one of the most apt, even if the most absurd, must be the gorilla who was popularly believed to break out of his cage at London Zoo, make his way across London to Whitechapel, carry out his grisly business and then docilely return to captivity, locking the cage door behind him: all without ever disturbing a soul. You may laugh, madam, and no doubt you're right; but if Queen Victoria found it impossible to imagine that the murderer could be an Englishman, a good many of her subjects couldn't see how he could be any sort of man at all. But not me. Oh no, not me.

Where have you been? I've been trying to reach you all week. You cancel two sessions without a word of explanation. What happened? Did somebody die? Well, don't worry; he wasn't the only one. But I'm not angry: before you jump to your customary conclusion. I may shout, but I'm not angry. I wouldn't give you the satisfaction. But you may like to know that whilst you were playing games with your answering machine, Rees killed a man. He killed him. Do you get the message? So where does that leave your hypocritic... Hippocratic oath?

Didn't I warn you that this would happen? Whilst you've been trying to tease out whatever minor problems I might have, Rees actually committed murder. By any calculation that's two lives ruined instead of one. I asked if there could be any doubt. Not a shadow. It seems he was caught red-handed. I remember as a child asking why it should have been red-handed, and not green or blue or yellow, and being told that it derived from naughty boys who stuck their fingers into jam-pots and left nasty red marks all over the cloth. I want my old dictionary back, with the security of its familiar definitions. And more than anything else I want him. But now I know I shall never have either of them again. And his hands are red with blood.

How could I ever have been so blind: and not just word-blind and colour-blind, but blind-blind? I constantly return to that last evening. I could see he was very depressed, but then he'd just returned from court where his best friend had made a brief appearance. I was surprised, as it was the first I'd ever heard of him. So? he said; he didn't have to tell me everything. No. Of course not. That went without saying. Which was why I was particularly hurt that he had.

I wondered whether I might have met him at the club. But he reassured me with a sneer, just in case I was afraid that I might be called upon to give evidence, that he'd been arrested not long before my first visit. I have to admit I was relieved. My immediate thought was that it must have been for importuning, but it turned out to have been drug-pushing. And that was as much as he'd tell me. When the chips were down, I suppose that I had the manner more of a magistrate than of a mate. And as it'd been three magistrates who'd just decided to commit his best mate to trial, I understood why he shied away. But I couldn't bear to leave him – that is, I didn't think it wise to leave him alone. So I bought him another drink.

I plied him with drinks all evening. I might as well have handed him the murder weapon itself. And do you know what that was? No, I can't – I can't. But his brain didn't seem at all befuddled. In fact, what frightened me most was the clarity of his despair. He kept saying that the world was one great shit heap and he'd be better off dead. And when I gently reminded him of my calling, he turned to me with an expression, which, if I hadn't known him better, I could only have described as hatred, and asked what I knew about his life. And before I'd had a chance to answer, he took it on himself to enlighten me.

At first it recalled the habitual round of children's homes and foster homes, and assessment centres and training schools, which seemed to have marked the rites of passage of nearly all the boys I'd met in the club; with one significant addition: his father had consistently abused him from the age of three. He'd bruised him and abused him body and soul. And his eyes brimmed with tears and filled with pain. He'd destroyed his trust; he'd destroyed his hope; he'd destroyed his innocence. And worst of all he'd even destroyed his faith in his mother, whose loyalty to her marriage had in the last resort proved stronger than her love for him.

I was overwhelmed with sadness. I put my hand on his and tried to tell him I understood. How? He pulled his hand sharply away, as if ashamed, not of his disclosure but of his weakness in choosing to disclose it. How? He said. How? How? The short word hit me like a whiplash. And of course I could find no answer; except that I felt sure that there was some deep, perhaps even primitive, part of me that did.

But there was more. At his parents' request he'd been sent back home when he was fifteen, to see if they could make a fresh start: which was precisely what his father had tried. And for eighteen months he'd abused his adolescence as systematically as he'd previously abused his youth. So he'd finally run away, first to Worthing and then to London, which was how, two years later, he'd ended up sitting in the 'Cockatoo' talking to me.

And so I knew how he felt? He really doubted it. And he spat out his scorn and drank up his beer, with that spurious air of bravado which, as I remembered so well from my schooldays, had been adopted by even the most unwilling initiate who mistook sexual experience for sexual maturity. And just in case it should have proved even more necessary to assert his maturity after those particular revelations, his tone changed yet again as he started to dun me for money.

———

I was about to suggest he came back to the priory; oh, if only I had! But as if he could read my mind, he began to ogle me: to treat me like a punter, making crude overtures and even cruder remarks. I was appalled. It was the first time it had ever happened to me at the club, and that it should have come from him of all people! For he might have been reading my thoughts, but not the reasoning behind them. I wanted to take him home, yes, but so that he could sleep it off, not so that he could sleep with me.

He edged his chair around the table; it made a noise like a stutter. He staggered; the table swayed. He moved closer to me; he leaned over me and tried to put one hand in my jacket pocket and the other on my groin. I couldn't bear it; I shoved him away. He merely laughed. He said he knew what it was I was after, just like all the rest of them; and with that he stood up and bent over as if to make his implication graphically clear. The slit in his jeans then split even wider; his underpants now looked crimson. I blushed and walked away. He barred my way; he clenched his fist so tight that, despite myself, I began to laugh. The concentration had had precisely the opposite effect to the one he'd intended. Rather than making his fist look threatening, it simply looked small.

I worried that I might have provoked him; but instead he began to whimper. He said he needed the money to bail out his friend. He knew that I was loaded; and he swore he'd pay me back. But I was shocked and shaken by the force of his aggression; although it was more than matched by my response... I shouted at him to leave me alone; I wanted no further truck with him. He'd played on my good nature long enough.

I ran down the stairs – if only I could run back up them; I imagine myself running up backwards as though I were re-running the reel of a film. I was terrified that the door wouldn't open and there'd be no escape. He shrieked obscenities which pierced me as sharply as the needles that had tattooed Spider's face. I ran outside. He came after me and I realised that it was the first time I'd ever seen him in the open air. The coloured lights in the club had camouflaged his complexion. His skin looked grey and pimply; and the harsh glare of the street lamps showed up his ineptly dyed hair. I challenged him to say what he wanted – or did he mean to cling to me like a criminal record? Then he shouted one word: one simple word and I still can't believe it: one word with all the judicial disdain of a crack of thunder: Pervert. And as if it had been thunder, it was followed by a downpour of rain.

I ran down the street and I swore to myself that I'd never go anywhere near the club again. But just as God spoke to Elijah through the earthquake, wind and fire, I was convinced I heard the voice of Christ speaking to me through the rain. The words were unmistakable although the accent sounded strangely like Rees: 'For I was an hungered, and ye gave me meat: I was thirsty, and ye gave me drink: I was a stranger, and ye took me in: naked and ye clothed me: I was sick and ye visited me. I was in prison and ye came unto me.' And I knew then and there that I should turn back, but I was too proud: too proud to face Rees' mockery; too proud in case he should think I was going back for more; not too proud to identify with his suffering – oh no, I'll identify with anyone's suffering – but far too proud to identify with the one thing he had to sell.

And in trying not to compromise my reputation, I realise I've compromised my eternal soul. For it's clear that I was far more concerned with what he thought of me than what Christ would... He'd had 'INRI' written over him for my sake; I wasn't prepared to have 'Pervert' hanging over me for his.

Do you see now why I wanted to talk to you? I'm no innocent bystander who unhappily happened to stumble on to the scene of the crime. I drove him to it. If I'd given him the money, he need never have given himself up to a man for whom pain was a passion and sacrilege a stimulant. And so it should be my pride that stands trial for murder: alongside his father's abuse. We're the true criminals, not him. So should I turn myself in or would you rather do it? Will you stand up in court and testify that I wasn't responsible for my actions? Will I bring ignominy on St Dunstan's and embarrassment to you?

One day you'll also have to answer for your actions – or rather your inaction, just like me.

And I do at least have one consolation. No one escapes the final reckoning. And however much Rees may suffer now, on the Day of Judgement my punishment will far exceed his. That's one court where there'll be no special pleading and certainly no benefit of clergy. On the contrary, we who've lived with Christ and then rejected him will be dealt with most severely of all... Or is that the ultimate arrogance? Am I like an arch-criminal who claims that there's no jail on earth strong enough to hold him; and will I only accept my fate at the hands of the most supreme judge of all? Tell me, do many of your clients claim to be the anti-Christ? Is it a common delusion? Well, let me assure you, you're looking at someone who knows it for a definite fact.

I might have guessed that you wouldn't take me seriously. If all religious belief is mere neurosis, then belief in the Devil is sheer hysteria and identification with him conclusive proof that I'm hopelessly deranged. What gives you the right to sit there in judgement on me? And whatever I may think of any other authority, I categorically reject that of your Doctor Freud.

And it seems I'm in good company. Reich himself believed Freud to be considerably sicker than the majority of his patients and his cancer symbolic of the inadequacy of his professional role: the square jaw of his authority crumbling from within. So I should be wary of stroking your chin quite so vigorously. There are evident dangers in such a flagrant attempt to play God.

I might never have found out what had happened if two of the clients at the crypt hadn't made a dart-board out of a Page Three pin-up and a bull's eye out of one of her breasts. We have a strict rule about no sexist behaviour, so I went to rip it down; for which I half-expected them to aim instead at the back of my neck. But what caught my eye at the foot of the page proved a far more effective dart.

It was a report of the remand hearing at Bow Street Magistrates' Court and stated that he was to be held in custody for seven days. I couldn't believe – I refused to believe it. But first I needed to know why, and where, and what sort of custody; and if he were innocent until proven guilty then why had they printed his name? And... But

my mind was racing into the unknown; so I broke all my former resolutions and returned to the club. And as I turned into the street where
I'd last heard Christ's words in the cloudburst, the final phrase came
back to me with a vengeance: 'I was in prison and ye came unto me';
and I was afraid that that might be all that was left.

There were several familiar faces at the bar, but no one approached
me, not even for the price of a drink. And I wondered whether it were
lethargy or if they too blamed me for what had happened to Rees. I
spoke to Slouch; but he only confirmed what I'd read in the paper. So
I asked if there were anything – anything at all I could do to help. He
didn't reply, but nodded towards a figure sitting in the corner, beneath
red and orange flashing spotlights, and surrounded by so many rings of
smoke that at first I was convinced he was on fire. Jack's co-ordinating
everything, he said; Jack's in charge.

I looked over to him and I was unable to turn away. I've had the
privilege in my life of encountering three or four truly saintly men
who've overwhelmed me by their intense aura of spirituality; but this
was quite the reverse. Even from across the room I was immediately
struck by the immense power of his physicality. And I do mean physicality; it had little to do with his actual physique.

I've never paid much attention to bodies. I've consciously tried
to look past them, through them, inside them – you know what I'm
trying to say. And despite Patrick, I've always thought that body language was the very last language I'd ever need to learn: until then. His
body seemed a positive Tower of Babel. And I felt sure he calculated
every nuance as meticulously as a Hell-fire preacher planning his most
harrowing effects.

Hell-fire: we can never get away from it. But if you were tempted to
dismiss what I said before about being caught in the grip of the Devil:
if you think that, if only for the sake of credibility, the concept of Hell
is one contemporary Christians should unequivocally reject, then I
wish you'd been there with me. For there is a Hell beyond all question.
And I was staring it straight in the mouth.

I felt my blood run cold. He blew out a smoke ring and smiled at me. There was no need for any empty formality; we knew one another straight away. I tried to think; but the juke-box pounded incessantly. A boy with hair the colour of seaside rock jostled my arm. Another with a ring through his nose pulled the arm of a fruit machine. Two skinheads with spotty scalps began to arm-wrestle on the dais. And I found myself walking slowly towards him. He held out his hand. His palm was cold and clammy; but his grip felt hot.

Involuntarily, I crossed myself. He smiled and patted an adjoining chair. It was as though he'd been keeping it for me, and yet the seat seemed strangely warm. I examined him closely; I immediately noticed how well groomed he was. His fingernails were meticulously manicured, with perfect cuticles and a nacreous sheen. He had no pulled skin, no calluses, no dirt and no tattoos. He offered to buy me a drink, which felt still more incongruous. And even though I knew I'd need to keep all my wits about me, I said yes.

He walked over to the bar and then turned and flashed me a smile of such incandescent whiteness that it dazzled my eyes. I realised later that it must have caught the reflection of the mirror-ball. His complexion was contrastingly pallid and his eyes ice-blue with cold, sharp pupils. He had a thick mop of jet black hair which all seemed to emanate from the same spot on his crown, like a rag doll's. And his face, although highly animated, was completely devoid of compassion.

He paid for the drinks and as he walked back I thought, for no apparent reason, of Jason; until I realised that, like him, he was wearing a tee-shirt on which his philosophy of life seemed emblazoned. I strained to decipher the wording; in bold letters it read: 'Money can't buy happiness.' And for a moment I wondered whether I might have misjudged him. Until he reached the table and I was able to make out the small print underneath: 'But it can buy everything else.'

He gave me the drink. I raised the glass to my lips out of politeness. I rather wished I'd brought a long spoon... I immediately asked after Rees; I was determined to stick to the matter in hand. I wanted details, but he brushed them aside. I wanted denial, but he'd been caught at the scene of the crime. So I asked about bail, or rather the lack of it. And he told me his solicitor had decided not to apply for it. He was being held in a police cell; so at least he'd have a roof over his head. His gratuitous cynicism disgusted me. But I was relieved that he wasn't in prison; a police cell sounded so much less final. And besides I was sure that there'd be one of the sergeants who'd keep a paternal eye on him. And then I remembered his father and bit my tongue.

So I've failed him in every regard, although I acted from the best of intentions. But then you know what they say about the road to Hell... Maybe I tried too hard. And yet having determined to live my life according to Christ, I had precious little alternative. There again, anyone who aims that high will inevitably fall short. So perhaps I should have lowered my sights. Father Leicester and the bishop must have thought so; which was why they sent me here. They took a calculated risk: kill or cure... I'm condemned out of my own mouth.

I ought to have learned from St Peter. After all I trace my tradition back to him in so many other respects. He even asked to be nailed to the cross upside down in order to avoid any comparison with Our Lord's suffering. Whereas in my heart of hearts, I wanted to surpass it – you may be horrified but I must be honest – to prove myself... what is the phrase?... *plus royaliste que le roi*. So if he'd spent his time with Mary Magdalene and Zacchaeus, then I had to add Barabbas... Barabbas, that Palestinian crowd-pleaser: he hardly sounds much like Rees. I told myself I was just a humble disciple trying his best to follow his master; whereas, as must have been obvious to you all along, I've been an over-officious zealot who's exceeded his brief.

As I sat with downcast eyes, I knew that my only brief now had to be to do what I could for Rees; but first I was anxious to know more about Jack. He'd described himself simply as a friend. So I asked how they'd met; and he smiled and said that in his line of work, he got to meet a great many people. Then I fell into the trap and asked him what line that was; and as his smile flushed scarlet, I realised he could lure me into temptation – into damnation – as easily as a slip of the tongue.

He looked so unremarkable... What did I expect? That he'd have his profession written all over his face: like Spider, whose forehead was indelibly, ironically tattooed with the word love?

Everything else flooded into place, and I realised that he had to be the pimp who'd seduced Rees at Charing Cross. But when I put it to him straight, he just laughed out loud as though Rees were a born romancer; or else he'd picked it straight out of an anthology of tall tales for small boys. Then he tried to turn the tables, asking me to explain my own connection; which I did readily, as I considered it important to establish my credentials. But he looked disappointed, even disbelieving, as though he'd heard it all a dozen times before; which was obviously quite impossible since it was the first time we'd ever met.

I explained how I saw my mission to rescue the boys and he laughed openly in my face, which no one, not even you, has ever done before. He gestured at them quizzically, as if he doubted my seriousness. And then his voice dropped as he forced me to view them in a frighteningly new light.

Their clothes weren't simply a style but quite literally a uniform. Their 'blood and honour' tee-shirts meant precisely that, as did their shorn scalps and metal toe-capped boots. Fascists came in all shapes and sizes; they weren't just flaxen-haired German shepherds. And, he explained pointing to a group of skinheads, some of them had very little hair at all.

I felt sure he must be mistaken. After all, I'd talked to them; I'd drunk with them. Of course, he said; they weren't such fools as to bite the hand that fed them – or at least that supplied them with drinks. But I'd also seen them with their punters: their long, skinny arms hanging loosely around their fleshy necks. Of course, he said, they weren't likely to bite theirs either – unless by special request... But they'd even seemed so affectionate with one another: throwing each other playful punches, rubbing each other's hair – even grabbing each other's genitals. And as if to prove my point, I was able to point to an alcove, where two of the boys were sitting, kissing each other passionately on the lips. But it was then that he made me wave goodbye to my final illusion; it wasn't a kiss they were sharing, but a hashish cigarette. The smoke was apparently the more potent, the less it was adulterated with air.

And at last I understood the significance of their endless joking about circumcision. I'd thought it simply a cruder version of the way at St Dunstan's we might compare the forms of the various liturgies: assessing the tools of the trade. But their interest was far from purely professional, nor even a matter of personal pride, but a political ideology; and one so depraved, that even the most deprived childhood offered no excuse. And I realised too that when I'd laughed at their jokes, however half-heartedly, I'd been implicating myself in those self-same attitudes. I was making myself one with the Nazis when I'd wanted to be one of the boys.

And I could only thank God that I hadn't taken the identification a step further and told them about the boy whose hearing I'd impaired. Since what had finally provoked me beyond all endurance had been his constant anti-semitic sniping... It might no longer have been my faith, but it was still my family, and a number of them had been killed in camps during the war... But now the position had been reversed; and I felt as though I, who should have revered their memories, had instead desecrated their graves.

I needed air, and he followed me down the stairs and into the street. The club seemed more squalid than ever. And as I stood outside looking up at the windows, the silhouettes of heads and arms seemed to form quite different shapes from before. I regained my breath; I regained my composure. There was so much more I wanted to ask him... But time marched on, or so he said which put me in mind of the Fascists – and he was expected elsewhere. If he rushed, he might just make it home for a quick shower; the club always made him feel dirty. And I thought if he felt dirty, then what about me?

I was afraid I might never see him again: which would mean I might never see Rees. He still hadn't told me if there were anything I could do to help or if he'd like me to visit. He promised to put it to him the next time he went. But how would he contact me? I couldn't give him the priory number. It wasn't that I didn't trust him but... No sweat, he said; and I dabbed my forehead. He took out a well-chewed pencil and wrote down his. I noticed he was left-handed and that he held the stump by the lead. He gave me the paper and disappeared.

I stared at the number; the effect proved strangely hypnotic. The figures seemed to dance before my eyes, although the sequence always stayed clear. It looked so bold and hard and self-confident, exactly like him. I felt tempted to rush to the nearest phone booth just to verify the voice on his answering machine; I felt tempted in so many ways. Now I know why Christ taught us to pray 'Lead us not into temptation' and not merely to be bailed out once we'd already fallen in. Besides, Rees hadn't applied for bail; and I was no longer at all sure that I would. I could see that I was standing on the verge of great danger; and yet I remained preternaturally calm.

If I'd had any sense, I'd have thrown the paper straight into the nearest gutter; but the figures had already insinuated their dance into my mind. And I couldn't have turned my back on Rees – on Christ a second time. I'd have been betraying my faith as well as my vocation. And you may think I'm attaching far too much significance to a simple phone call; but when the voices in my head shout 'ring', they sound suspiciously like 'jump'... And this constant self-doubt is like a disease. I sometimes think it would be a good deal easier to try to live my life according to nobody's lights but my own. Easier – maybe; but better? – I doubt it.

And so we're back at square one. Don't you have anything to say? I expected you to advise me. But as usual you just scratch your head and click your biro and hurry the session to a close.

Seven

This is Coulston Street to which we'll be returning later in the tour, as it's also the site of the only definite clue the Ripper left. To your right you see a jellied-eel stall. Are there any local residents amongst you? No? Well I'm told that jellied-eels are the East End's favourite food. I'd be happy to stop for a moment if anyone wants to put it to the test. No? I can't say I blame you; let's keep our investigations to matters historical. And it's now I'm afraid I shall have to disappoint you, as I dismiss everyone's favourite candidate. No, Jack the Ripper wasn't Prince Albert Victor Christian Edward, son and heir to the Prince of Wales.

Much of the renewal of interest in the Ripper over recent years can be traced to the theory put forward in 1970 by a Dr Thomas Stowell, that the figure identified solely as 'S' in the private papers of Sir William Gull, the Queen's physician, was in fact Prince Albert Victor, whom Gull was said to be treating for tertiary syphilis. Although Stowell published his findings in a specialist journal *The Criminologist*, his hypothesis was quickly picked up world-wide and was soon front-page news on an estimated two thousand papers. To the prudish and prurient Victorian fascination with prostitutes was added our own contemporary equivalent: royalty.

Even though Stowell died vigorously denying that he'd ever intended to identify the prince, the attribution rapidly caught hold of the popular imagination. In essence it held that, driven insane by syphilis caught from a prostitute and left with a pathological hatred of women, he'd roamed the streets of Whitechapel, dressed in a deer-stalker, wreaking his revenge on others of her profession by butchering them as brutally as the deer on his grandmother's estates.

Various experts immediately sprang up in the prince's posthumous defence, claiming that since tertiary syphilis takes between fifteen and twenty years to develop, he would have to have contracted it between the ages of eight and twelve, a precocity remarkable even in a prince, and that on the contrary he'd died as had always been asserted in the great flu epidemic of 1892. To this there have subsequently been counter-claims from former royal servants that his death was faked and he lived on hopelessly insane at Osborne House well into his brother George V's reign, dying as recently as 1930.

But whatever the many dark secrets of his life and death, you can be assured that he wasn't Jack the Ripper. The most cursory glance at the contemporary court circulars reveals that on the occasion of one of the murders he was at Sandringham, and on another two at Balmoral: his presence being independently corroborated each time. Nevertheless the heir presumptive to the British throne was still intimately implicated in every one of these murders; and if you come this way, you'll come a step nearer to understanding exactly how...

The first thing to make quite clear is that he's not a rent boy; he's a masseur. He advertises in magazines, not on pavements. He's at the Harley Street end of his profession: your end.

Have you ever considered the similarities between therapists and prostitutes? They're far more marked than those between therapists and priests. You're both masseurs; you massage the ego whilst he massages... I ought to introduce you. You might be able to put a bit of business one another's way. After all we're all clients now: on the couch, in bed, at the crypt. And I think you'd be pleasantly surprised: not for him the swagger and swank of the boys at the club, as they boasted of sleeping with everyone, from major pop stars to minor royalty. He keeps his lips tightly buttoned; even as he unzips everything else.

Of course he could never hope to match your versatility. He's strictly a man's man, whereas your sympathies are far more promiscuous: you flit from men to women to children, hardly pausing even to draw breath... The air in here's so heavy; would you open a window...? And he sweats for his money – believe me, he sweats; whilst you simply sit pretty in that armchair, with your legs crossed and your hands neatly folded on that ever so slightly swelling waistline, but swelling just enough to have the appeal of vulnerability and none of the grossness of excess.

I wonder who has the superior skills. At least he has sensitive fingers; whereas you still haven't noticed, have you? I sometimes think I must be talking to a brick wall: a voice crying out in the wilderness of a little room.

How I hate this room! My stomach sinks every time the taxi turns the corner, and we drive past the grey pebbledashed houses with their slapdash peeling paintwork, and then I sit uncomfortably in the waiting room, flicking through thick magazines whose bland anonymity seems matched only by your own. And if there's one thing I abhor, it's mud-coloured hessian. Though I suppose it provides suitable mulch for your plants. Cacti and cyclamen: how unadventurous! Or have I done you an injustice? Were they chosen on strict Freudian principles: the prickly male and the fragile female, or Jungian: the animus and the anima?

Jack could certainly give you some tips on pictures. I hope you won't think me rude, but honestly, that Canaletto... and those faded wild flowers. At least he sticks his neck out – amongst other things. He has two large paintings: one of three distorted figures screaming and the other of a group of bald women dancing in what appears to be the aftermath of a nuclear attack. I must say I found them rather out of place; but then I have very little basis for comparison, unless with the fragments of erotic frescoes they unearthed in the brothel of Pompeii.

You look pained. Have I missed the point? Are nineteenth-century primroses considered *de rigueur* in the brothel of the mind? Or have I hit a nerve – why don't you hit me? – did your wife choose them? I still don't even know if you have a wife. Tell me something about yourself, for pity's sake! I'm supposed to be making relationships, but the only ones I come anywhere near are the ones I pay for. I pay you; I pay hi... You're not interested in me, only in the colour of my money. I can tell you for nothing; it's scarlet: the colour of sin – crimson: the colour of blood.

———

Do you have any children? Surely you can tell me that? Or are you a homosexual? Don't worry; your secret's safe with me. Can one be a homosexual psychotherapist, or is it a contradiction in terms? Tell me honestly: do you like me? If you'd met me socially, would you have chosen me as a friend? And when I say 'like', I'm not simply angling for an invitation to a vicarage tea-party; I mean 'like': really 'like': sleep 'like': sex 'like'.

No, don't answer. It wasn't a serious question; I don't expect a considered reply. Or do you imagine I'm the sort of man who's so desperate that he has to pay for sex? What would you say if I offered to pay you? How would you feel if I put my hand on your crotch, my lips to your lips – I'm sorry – if I squeezed and squeezed and squeezed? – I'm sorry, sorry – You're a whore: sorry – a whore: help me! Can't you see I'm in despair?

You must be overjoyed. Isn't this what you've wanted all along: to hear me shouting at you: shouting and insulting and lying? Yes, lying. Did you really think that I'd stoop so low as to...? I was simply stringing you along, seeing how far I could go. And I must say I surprised myself; I ought to be on the stage... Although that's another deplorably cheap analogy; the Church is nothing like the stage. The Church is like nothing but itself. And I've cut myself off from it forever.

Do you know the worst thing about prostitution? It's not the act itself, but the attitudes it engenders. I'm getting a prostitute's eye view of the world. And it's no longer a place of good and evil, or innocent and guilty, or even rich and poor, but of buyer and bought. All the world's a market; and innocence is for sale on every street.

I walk down the street and I stare at people from the corner of my eye and I wonder: do they... would they, if the price were right? And I already know the answer: everyone would; and I can pay any price. And it's so pitifully small. For a couple of pounds I can buy a boy a drink, and for thirty I can buy the boy I bought it for. I need never be alone again. And yet nothing in my life has ever made me feel so lonely. And what hurts me most is to know that all the money in the world can never buy what I need. Love: all I ask is a little love. But all that's on offer is sex.

I find no consolation even in Christ. I turn to my Bible and it falls open at the camel and the eye of the needle as naturally as the pages of the school dictionaries all seemed to part at masturbation... Natural: I no longer understand the meaning of words... And in desperation I've resorted to that very chop-logic I've always most despised. I've tried to imagine a needle which is a replica of Cleopatra's, only twenty times wider and higher, with a conveniently camel-sized arch running through. I've even wondered whether they actually had needles and thread in first-century Palestine... What did I suppose they held their clothes together with? Faith?

Faith: I thought mine was rock-solid; but it crumbled to dust at the first touch. I've been deceiving myself, amongst a good many others. Believe me, if a rich man has it hard, then a sophist has it even harder, and as for a rich sophist... I don't have a hope in Hell. But the parable isn't really about money so much as power, or rather the power money brings. Money is absolute power and the power to corrupt absolutely – and not just to corrupt, but to control: to control other people and to lose control over myself; to buy my way out of morality, and to do it with my eyes wide open and my conscience tightly shut. I've finally learned the value of money. And it's measured in Jack.

My one consolation is that I could never corrupt him. There's nothing I can do to him that hasn't been done a hundred times before. On the contrary, it was what he did to me... People destroy each other, which is why you must always keep them at a distance. So take care; I'm a dangerous person. Take Rees... And yet Jack's already damned; and in his damnation lies my salvation, or at least my safeguard. I didn't take advantage of his weakness; he took advantage of mine. I simply phoned him to talk about Rees. But the pretext was as transparent as the pretence. And by the time I realised what was happening, it was too late; my defences lay alongside my underwear, scattered across the floor.

I knew from the first moment I saw him that he'd prove my undoing and yet I embraced it, or at least him, without restraint. He intrigued me; he obsessed me. In a perverse way he seemed the perfect embodiment of the spirit of the age. He's the archetypal small busi-nessman. His sole concern is to maximise his assets – his one asset: his body; which he runs with no-holds-barred, all-holes-bared ruthless-ness, like a well-oiled machine. But my perversity is such that even his productivity fascinated me. I asked him what it took to be a prostitute and whether, under different circumstances, he might have bought me. But he simply smiled and said that he already had.

He smiled and he could have twisted me around his little finger; but it wasn't his finger on to which I clung. He smiled and I would have walked barefoot through the fires of Hell for him. He smiled and I knew I needed him like nothing on earth... like nothing in Heaven. At that moment I needed him even more than God.

I sinned; he smiled and put on a cassette. The music seemed to pound with the insidious beat of sexual coupling. I watched my own seduction with the same fascinated horror as the boys at school watched their seniors attain puberty: the delicious dread of knowing that there was no escape, as the strength which they'd outgrown in childhood suddenly caught up with them. And yet I thought I'd escaped. My body had developed, but not distorted; my growing had been gracious and my skin was still smooth. Christ told us to keep hold of the innocence of childhood; and for twenty-three years I was sure I'd succeeded. I refused to ring the changes; I refused even to acknowl-edge them... And my adolescence curdled in my veins.

He undid my clothes; my body felt so white against the black leath-erette of his sofa. Then he slipped out of his own so smoothly, without any sense of strain or shame. I darted a glance at his chest; it was slight but tightly packed. His abdomen was taut and knotty and seemed to bear the imprints of a sculptor's chisel. If Jonathan had put me in mind of Michelangelo's David, then Jack brought back memories of Don-atello's: a body of great sensuous beauty although built on a less heroic scale; which would insinuate itself not so much by strength as by guile. I thrilled at his proportions. He caught my eye; I looked away.

Feebly I began to fold my clothes. He told me to wait until later; and somehow the breach of etiquette was what brought home the enormity of my fall. And I knew as I watched them drop that my trousers would never slip neatly into their creases again. He lifted me up. I looked at his body and at his excitement; I wondered whether it was just his professionalism, or a tribute to me. And I was thrilled and frightened, and thrilled and appalled.

He led me to the bed. I wanted to slide quickly under the blankets; but there were none: only a thin towel on a bare mattress. I shivered. He touched me; he massaged me from top to toe. There wasn't an inch of me he didn't make his own. My body was a bundle of nerves which he smoothed away to a delicious tingle until I felt as though I were a conjuror's assistant, strapped in a box and floating two foot above the floor. And then he slit the box in two and my upper half was split from my lower – oh my lower – leaving a gap in the middle which was all air: a gap in which he could reveal the full extent of his magical power.

Then my head seemed to break off all contact with my shoulders. It soared to the ceiling from where it looked down on the two naked bodies spread-eagled on the bed. Was this what it was to die? Was my soul floating free of my body? But then why hadn't it sunk straight down to Hell?

I scissored and squealed as my legs began to buckle. And I realised that my head must have reconnected with my shoulders, for all the blood was rushing to it, and then it dipped back to the top of my legs – only it wasn't blood; it was… it was… And it was all over the mattress. And I was sticky – no, slimy: slimy, not wet. And I lay there, not knowing where to look, on a towel caked in the sins of the world and my own sins of emission.

I felt utterly exposed, but I couldn't even cover my shame; I was afraid of staining my hands. And all I could think of was that egg which had exploded in the microwave and how long it'd taken me to clear up the mess.

But Jack knew the form; and he immediately fetched a sponge and a bowl of soapy water and set to work. His practicality only put me to even greater shame. And I wiped myself as best I could and fumbled into my clothes. Then for the first time he showed a little tenderness.

He sat me down on the bed and buttoned my shirt almost as though I were a child. Then he stood behind me and tied my tie and combed my hair, first with his comb and then with his bare fingers. And that moment of intimacy, as I sat in my clothes and he stood in his underpants, almost made up for all the rest. And I felt – I felt... Oh God forgive me for what I felt.

I've supped with the Devil; I've supped of the Devil. I'm no longer fit to be a priest; I'm no longer fit to be a man. I'm fetid; my body is a festering pit. I'm pitiful; my body is pitted with pain. I've committed a fatal crime; I'm an accessory to my own murder. I'm in Hell.

Aren't you scared of me? We're two men alone in a room; neither of us can ever feel safe again. Jack ritualises the violence inside him, but I have all the unpredictability of the neophyte. I may not frighten you, but I terrify myself.

I've sinned; I've claimed my inheritance. I can't escape the burden of heredity. Adam was seduced by the beauty of an apple; but I made straight for the rottenness at its core... not the fruit, but the worm beneath its skin: a worm that slithered and spat between his legs... No! I'm even sinning again in the repetition. And I can only look on hopelessly as the executioners pile the wood for the conflagration of my soul.

I wish Jonathan were here. I'd present him with an image of such evil, and not simply social or economic injustice, but the thing itself. I'd turn him to face Jack and I'd say: there, know your enemy; and then I'd turn him back to me and say: and here, know the madman who knew his enemy and yet who gave himself to him nonetheless. But madness is no mitigation – lack of reason may be, but not lack of morals. What would you have me plead: Father, forgive me, though I knew full well what I did? I'd be laughed out of court.

He asked me for thirty pounds. I was horrified: he'd mistaken me for a client. I was humiliated: he'd never suggested any payment. But I knew better than to show any sign; he held far too much sway over me already. And on reflection I was glad about the money. It gave me power: purchasing power. However much he might despise me, he was hungry for my money. It meant he wouldn't reject me; it meant he couldn't hurt me... Until I realised it meant he couldn't love me either.

No one can love me. I inspire only revulsion. What sentimental hogwash to claim that the more we know people the more we love them, and that if we love them enough we're prepared to forgive them anything. You know me as well as anyone and yet you cringe at the very sound of my voice. Besides, when I claimed that there was no sin too great to be forgiven, I should have qualified it with repentance. How can I be absolved of my sin when I'm constantly reliving it in my heart? And even now as I put on my coat to leave, I'm longing to take it off and begin again.

'Go and sin no more' was what Christ commanded the woman taken in adultery, which I remember Jonathan explaining triumphantly had been discovered to be a later amendment, and not his authentic words at all. But then he could always be relied upon to find some riposte to any injunction that threatened to cramp his style: Leviticus... Deuteronomy... even St Paul had no objections to homosexuality per se, but solely to the sordid practices of temple prostitution. And he may well have been right. And yet to me such arguments are entirely academic. For whereas Jonathan endorsed his sexuality in that it had nothing to do with prostitution, mine has nothing but. And so I'm damned either way.

I've desecrated my faith. I can no longer take the Eucharist. I've substituted Jack for Christ; I've worshipped at his altar and feasted on his body and bile. But that's not all; there's one blasphemy way beyond therapy: a perversion that defies confession. For when I stand at the foot of the Cross, I no longer see the distortion of Christ's agony, but just the thrust of his body. I no longer feel the sanctity of his face or the compassion of his eyes, but merely the rippling muscles of his torso. I no longer share in his Resurrection, but simply the sexuality of his Passion. I've abused the Lord my God; and the Devil has claimed my soul.

Eight

As we walked through the underpass, we left Whitechapel and the borough of Tower Hamlets and entered the City of London. And when Jack the Ripper trod a similar path on the night of 30 September 1888, he significantly took himself out of the jurisdiction of the Metropolitan Police and into that of the City.

It's not always appreciated that when the modem police force was founded in London in 1829, it was divided in two. That officer with the rim on his helmet – no, on your left; do you see him? – belongs to the City force, under the authority of the Lord Mayor; whereas the policemen without rims you find everywhere else belong to the Metropolitan force, under the authority of the Home Secretary.

A century ago there was considerable rivalry between them, and in particular between their Chief Officers. At the Met was Sir Charles Warren, a devoutly evangelical Christian and a frequent lecturer on the Holy Land; together with his deputy, Sir Robert Anderson, head of the CID, who wrote twenty-seven books of popular theology and would have become a minister had he not believed it wrong to take money for preaching – I can only say he was lucky his doubts were so clear-cut. Whilst in the City was Sir Henry Smith, a typical sporting gent, who publicly lamented the passing of the Haymarket brothels and was clearly not a man to concern himself too deeply with the underlying causes of prostitution. Their rivalry bedevilled the entire Ripper investigation and at no time more disastrously than on the night of 30 September.

Earlier that evening Catherine Eddowes, soon to become the Ripper's fourth victim, had been arrested whilst dancing drunkenly down this very street. But perhaps reflecting the more liberal attitudes of its Acting Commissioner, the City Police, unlike the Met, rarely charged drunks unless a specific offence had taken place, aiming simply to give them the chance to sober up in the cells. And at 1 a.m. the Duty Officer decided that Catherine was indeed sober enough to be sent on her way, and she was soon seen returning down this same street. But for once in her life I've no doubt that even Catherine would have preferred to have spent the night under lock and key. And if you want to know the full horrific reason, then please... follow me.

What did you do to that poor woman? She ran past me in floods of tears. Shouldn't you have gone after her? I'd have waited. It wouldn't have been the first time. In Dr Livesey's waiting room there's a notice: 'Thank you for being a patient patient'. You could commission one of your own: 'Thank you for being a considerate client'. I've noticed that doctors usually tend to spell out such things alliteratively. It must be the poetry of prosaic minds.

I see you've opened your window; the weather's clearly growing warmer. Though if you find it close in here, you'd better avoid the police cells where I went to visit Rees... After being interviewed by the Custody Officer and showing him my identification, I was searched – I no longer have the right to call it intimately – and then, to my surprise, allowed in to see him on my own. I took him some cigarettes; he's permitted an unlimited supply. The cynic in me wondered whether it was a ploy to keep down the prison population... There was no cynic in me this time last year.

He's been held there almost three weeks. The prison officers are working to rule and refusing to accept any new remand prisoners. But he seems quite content, almost as though he's discovered his natural habitat. And for the first time since the children's home he knows where he stands, as he sits for hours on the bed or the floor emptying his mind until it's as blank as the white-tiled walls of the cell.

He looked so young; I was expecting the experience to have aged him. But it was the club which had made little boys look like men; this worked the other way round. He seemed so soft and so slight and so slender, I felt I could snap him in two with one flick of my wrist.

The realisation terrified me. I'd found my strength; and I'd found my sexuality. And I was appalled by its proximity. And I was overwhelmed by his.

He'd begun to smell. He'd been the one boy at the club who never had. He told me he'd had no clean clothes in ten days; and as he was talking he began to scratch himself. The sharp, caustic smell filled the small, stuffy room; and I remembered the corpses of saints which were supposed to exude a sweet and pleasant odour. And I was irresistibly drawn towards thoughts of mortality and decay.

I looked at him and I was overcome with sadness. I could only think: there but for the grace of God... but then the thought of that grace mocked me. And there was nothing I could do, since he refused even my offer of a change of clothes. The musty warmth of his own old clothing seemed somehow to reassure him. And besides, he said, he wouldn't be leaving the cell until the committal proceedings. And he began to speculate about the trial and a mandatory life sentence. And whilst I was horrified by his lack of hope, I was at least grateful for his lack of illusion. And all I could reply was that he was very young: so very young; and my comfort felt as cold as his cell.

He told me what had happened. I didn't press him; but he seemed glad of the chance to talk to someone other than his solicitor... And I was amazed at how little he blamed me; he appeared to have forgotten our confrontation. I only wish it were as easy for me.

He met the man at Charing Cross Station, or to be more specific he picked him up in the gentlemen's lavatory, or to be more graphic he fondled his penis in the urinal... I wanted the facts not the details... He turned out to be a wine merchant with offices in Clerkenwell; so the offer of a drink seemed more than just the customary coded chatter. But when he took him down to the cellars, a bottle of wine had been the last thing he wanted to uncork.

He shivered as he spoke; I shuddered as I listened. It wasn't the usual furtive fumble; the man insisted he subjected him to the most obscenely depraved tortures. They exceeded every limit, until finally... you won't believe... I didn't believe... I looked at him as if his solitary confinement had addled his brain. But no: and he continued as calmly as if he'd been describing a game of musical chairs at a children's party. He asked him... he actually asked him... in the name of God, he asked him to crucify him!

No, you didn't mishear, and neither did I, and neither did Rees. He looked around, but instead of nails and a cross, he was directed to ropes and a crossbar: one of the beams that jutted from the cellar's low ceiling as though purpose-built. And the man's wilder and wilder financial inducements removed any residue of doubt.

I'd like you to pray with me. We must beg forgiveness of Christ on behalf of sinful humanity. Was this why he died? Did he suffer the most intense agony on the Cross, simply so that its image should become the springboard for such foul perversion? And for all we know we may have drunk that man's bitter wine.

And he urged him to flagellate him harder and harder in his sniffing, screaming, squirming ecstasy; until he shook from head to toe with a spasm. Only it wasn't simply sexual; for his head dropped forwards and his eyelids flopped closed and his back appeared to buckle under its own dead weight. And Rees panicked; and the only way he could think of to resurrect – no! to revive him – was to slap him sharply across the cheeks. And the angel of mercy had become the angel of death.

He raised the alarm. And it wasn't until he saw the expressions on the policemen's faces that he realised the true extent of his crime. After the initial panic he'd relaxed: almost as if his involvement had begun with the discovery. But when he looked down at the head being covered with a sheet and the slow trail of rich blood seeping from the crown, another alarm went off in his brain.

Why me? he asked. Why Rees? I ask you. And the problem of suffering's one thing, but why is it always the innocent who do? He could never have been one of nature's tough guys, however hard he'd tried. And he'd tried his damnedest. Since we'd first met, he'd had his hair cropped, to meet the demands of a highly specific market. But he simply looked a misfit in a crudely cut crew-cut. So why on earth had the man picked on him to pick on him? Unless he enjoyed the paradox as much as the pain.

And why pain? he asked himself. And why pain? I ask repeatedly. And I've at last come to understand the looks of cynical incomprehension I used to see on the boys' faces and the bafflement behind their tattoos; as they constantly met the degrading demands of men whom they'd been brought up to consider their elders and betters, who asked them not to wash or even clean themselves, but begged to be allowed to do it for them, and in ways at which even a stray dog would have balked. No wonder they felt hurt and humiliated that their only value should be to hurt and humiliate; as they were paid to indulge in private in behaviour for which they'd have been prosecuted elsewhere.

I looked at Rees; and I felt so relieved that I wanted to hug him. How could any jury ever find against him? He was no more guilty than the public hangman. And then I remembered the brief description in the paper I'd torn down at the crypt; and I knew that the verdict could already be taken as read. But I also remembered the English boys whom St Gregory discovered similarly constrained in a Roman slave market. Are they Angles or angels? he asked. And I looked at him again, and my question wasn't even rhetorical: not Angle but angel; not slave but saint.

Which is no hyperbole. Like the greatest of saints he'd followed the precepts and precedent of Christ. Like Christ he took the sins of men upon him and the sins of their flesh inside him. He purged them in the core of his innermost being. And now he's paying the price.

It's so much easier to be a saint in isolation: to stand for thirty years like St Simeon Stylites on a pillar in the middle of the desert, praying for enlightenment and praising God and... Oh no, I can see what you're thinking: the pillar a symbol, and no longer of hope. How I'd hate to have your mind... But now you've made it my mind too. You've done for me, you and Jack. I no longer feel safe even within the privacy of my own thoughts. You've given the very simplest of words double meanings. You may call it self-awareness, but to me it's duplicity. You've toppled St Simeon from his pillar and his bits lie scattered all around.

And as for my own bits... I'm the victim of my burgeoning body. Jack's taught me its underlying geography; its undulating landscape; its contours and crevices and hidden desires. I'm possessed – I'm obsessed and by a common prostitute. I visit him every day. He says I must be a glutton for punishment. It wasn't until he began to whip me that I fully understood what he meant.

He spat in my face. Can you credit it? This face that's now streaked with tears a few hours ago was streaked with spittle. He sucked in his cheeks and gathered a great gobbet of saliva and then spat. And I didn't flinch. I knew it was the closest I would ever get to a kiss. And I yearn for the touch of his flesh: the tough softness and the rough smoothness; but his only response has been to implicate me still further in his savagery. He dramatises the distance between us with scenes of domination and degradation, until even the tautness of his skin comes to feel more like an animal's hide.

He deprives me of everything but his depravity. Yesterday he ordered me to lick his boots. They were hard and heavy and sourly polished black leather. In fact he was completely covered in leather, except for those parts of him which were totally exposed. And he has a special whip like a child's cardboard horn with crepe-paper streamers. Only they're not streamers but matted leather thongs; and when he hits me with them, believe me, they hurt. But I'm prepared to put myself through all that agony in the hope that just once when he puts down the whip, he might run his fingers lovingly over the welts.

Somehow I seem to have stumbled straight out of the schoolroom and into the bedroom of the Marquis de Sade. And the more I squirm, the more he seems to assume I'm enjoying it. He confuses the obvious – the painfully obvious – excitement I feel just to be in his presence with excitement in what he does. And yet I can't bring myself to disabuse him; I'm terrified of losing what little I have.

Like you, he's convinced he can understand me better than I do myself. So the moment I told him where I went to school, he imagined that in some mealy-mouthed way I was simply asking for a harder beating; with which he was more than happy to oblige. It strikes me that your subconscious mind has a great deal to answer for. I want to be loved, not beaten. *Loved*: is it so hard a word to understand?

I'm appalled at quite how little he does understand me. I've stripped myself of all my fears and inhibitions and my faith's prohibitions. I stand naked before him. I'm plucked and puckered like a trussed-up chicken and yet I might as well be hidden inside a cardboard box. I thought I'd at last found my true identity; whereas I've lost whatever I once had. We don't have a marriage of minds or even a coition of bodies, but simply a collusion of labels: sticky brown labels: client and prostitute; and I'm the one who has to lick them on.

And my religion only adds further grist to his mill... and to my treadmill. He assumes that because I believe in God I must be the quintessential masochist. And so he makes me kneel at his feet and call him Master. He says I should be well used to the position; and he wounds me much more deeply than he can know. For I've not attended Mass since Whitsun. I've forsworn Christ as surely as if I'd set up a cross in a cellar. As a child I would often lament that I'd not been one of the twelve or the seventy or even the five thousand: to have known him in the flesh and not just in the sacraments. But now I'm simply grateful that I never had the chance to betray him to his face.

I'm no longer fit to meet Christ in the sacraments. His presence is no longer real to me. Nothing seems real any more except Jack: madness... utter madness. And that's my one last hope: that you'll declare me insane. You could have me committed to an asylum. It'd be for my own protection. Why do you hesitate? You have all the evidence you need. I told him that I was in love with him. Could anything be madder? He simply laughed and said that a good many of his clients thought that at first – so at least there's predictability in my perversion. And I know love is blind, but mine must be in a cataleptic coma... mad: utterly mad.

How can I love someone I don't respect? And yet he's nobody's fool. In a rare moment of self-revelation he told me that not only had he read history at Queen Mary's but he'd abandoned a Ph.D. And he refused point-blank to elaborate. Although I suppose academic achievement would hardly fit his priapic image, which he works on as meticulously as he works out his body in the gym. He explained that for most of his clients he had to pretend to keep the bulk of his brains below his belt. And I admit I find the idea rather exciting: that an intelligent man should so conspicuously try to hide it; whereas the burden of my entire education has lain quite the other way.

In a vain attempt to disarm him, or at least to impress him with my confidence, I mentioned you – oh, not by name, don't worry, but that I came here for therapy. And yet it cut no ice. He considers it a complete waste of time and money; which for him are truly one and the same. He thinks that all I or indeed anyone needs is a good fuck – I'm sorry, but no euphemism could begin to convey his meaning... Do you know that must be the first time I've ever spoken that word aloud? My mouth feels strange... He may think it's what I need; but I've not the slightest intention of complying. Then he really would have complete power over me: over me and inside me.

Besides, although you may think I lead a very rarefied existence, I know enough about the dangers of sexual contact. Jonathan wore a badge last year at college with a pink triangle and the wording 'Silence is death', until Father Leicester insisted he removed it; even though I'd have thought 'Sin is death' would have been more to the point. But what terrifies me most of all is that I can no longer be sure that, were Jack to demand death as the ultimate proof of my passion, I'd have sufficient strength of will to refuse.

You say nothing. Have I stunned you into silence? When the attractions of therapy pall you could always try life as a Trappist monk. Even Jack's more forthcoming. He claimed that all my problems stemmed from self-oppression. For one awful moment I was afraid he was in league with Patrick. Although the term made no more sense to me the second time round. So I asked him to elucidate. And he said that in layman's terms, it meant loving the sin and hating the sinner. But they sounded less like layman's terms to me, than a parody of my most deeply held beliefs.

But then I'd parodied them myself, and in all seriousness. I was a parody of perfection. In a fallen world I thought I could be a man of pure spirit: a man without sexuality. And from that the obvious implication was that I'd be the one man free of original sin. But that was no worthy ambition, but rather the utmost arrogance. The only man without sin was Christ... And if pride comes before a fall, does spiritual pride precede damnation? Is the price of such infernal arrogance my eternal soul?

You don't answer; you can't answer. I need a theologian, not a therapist, just as I need a lover, not a prostitute; and you're neither of you even second best. He has a still more suspicious mind than you. When I offer him friendship, he insists that it's sheer self-interest: if I treat him like a whore, it makes me feel dirty; whereas if I treat him like a human being, it makes me feel more like one myself... Money isn't power; that was merely another illusion. How could I ever have imagined that the man who paid the prostitute called the tune?

I'd like to be a prostitute... He laughed, too. Of course, I know there'll be difficulties; but if he won't meet me halfway, then I must go all the way to him. There's an honourable, or at least a time-honoured tradition. Isn't it said to be the world's oldest profession? That's one thing I can never forget, after having been mercilessly mocked at school for confusing it with the sport of kings... I'll even swap places. Then he can go back to his studies; he can write the definitive history of prostitution. And in the evenings he can visit me.

It's the ideal solution. All my life I've developed my mind at the expense of my body. Now I'll redress the balance. And I'm aware that I still have a lot to learn; but I'm prepared to study all night long just so long as he's prepared to teach me. So what do you say? You're a dispassionate observer. Suppose you found yourself at a loose end and were looking for some congenial company; would I be your man?

I can see you're equally sceptical. But why? Surely anyone can be a prostitute? It's hardly like aiming to be a nuclear physicist when you've a single 'O' level in domestic science. I used to deplore the cult of the outcast; as if the only authentic experience were to be found in the gutter. But now I've seen the light. God isn't to be discovered in stained glass and plainsong and Gothic arches, but in sickness and squalor and sordid, suppurating pain. No! Why doesn't he strike me dumb? Or is even my blasphemy too insignificant? Am I to be discounted even in my despair?

There's one last hope: chemical castration. It may seem drastic; but then my situation demands nothing less. And it's only the words that sound so cutting. If you think of it as just a course of pills, or a few injections... And I'm quite prepared for any side effects. I don't care if I sprout breasts; I'll wear loose-fitting shirts and I'll never go swimming. And it'll be a positive boon not to have to shave. Why do you shake your head? I know they sanction it in prisons; so why not outside? Do I also have to kill someone before anyone takes me seriously...? Or do I have to kill myself?

Nine

We're now in Mitre Square, and in view of what I shall tell you later, please bear in mind that both the mitre and the square are significant elements of masonic ritual. It was to this square, now much redeveloped, that Catherine Eddowes made her way from Aldgate High Street, where we first encountered her and where she was last seen alive at about 1.30 in the morning by three men leaving a local club. Fifteen minutes later P.C. Watkins of the City Police discovered her body lying in front of a row of empty cottages: on the exact spot that you're standing now.

She was horribly disfigured. The Ripper had clearly made up with a vengeance for having been interrupted with Elizabeth Stride. That is, if vengeance were his only aim. As P.C. Watkins said, she'd been cut up like a pig in the market with her entrails flung in a heap about her neck. Her throat had been slashed and her groin had been slit. Jagged gashes in the shape of V's had been hacked through her mouth, her eyelids had been split, and the tip of her nose and her earlobes had been sliced off. This last injury prompted the police to release a letter they'd received, in which the writer claimed he'd clip off his next victim's ear, and which was the first occasion on which either he, or anyone else, ever signed himself Jack the Ripper – the name which has since stuck.

Sir Robert Anderson was certain that both this letter and a subsequent postcard were journalistic inventions, particularly since they were sent to the Central Press Agency and from a postal district which included Fleet Street. All their corroborative detail had in fact already been released, and neither made mention of the one major detail the police had withheld: namely the theft of her womb. The murderer's handwriting was fairly good, although his spelling and grammar seemed deliberately faulty; for example, let's take a spot check: how would you spell 'knife'...? Precisely. And 'while'...? Obviously. Yet he was wrong both times. Whereas 'piece', a word which lends itself to misspelling, he managed perfectly. The police and later commentators remained unconvinced.

In the following weeks the police received thousands of hoax letters, and several people were subsequently jailed. Such deliberate wickedness seemed scarcely credible until I recalled the hunt for the Yorkshire Ripper from my own childhood. The police were misled for months by the tape recordings of the mild-spoken Geordie who claimed to be Jack. It's as if so many small men can see themselves writ large in these sadistic killers, and claiming responsibility is a way of becoming party to the crimes of their dreams. And in one sense they succeed; for if investigations are delayed, either by letters or recordings – if red herrings become wrong tracks, then they may well have blood on their hands. Just as a man who watches pornographic films may not have called the shots but his shadow still falls over the shutter and the frame... I must move on. I must move on.

One 'joker' – I hope you can hear my apostrophes – actually went further and sent a piece of kidney to George Lusk, the chairman of a local vigilante group. The letter, which was calculatedly written in a kind of stage Irish, claimed that the writer had fried and eaten the rest. Sir Henry Smith was in no doubt that it was Catherine Eddowes' kidney, sizzled – or rather sozzled in gin; although it's far more likely to have been some medical students' jape or to have been obtained for a few pence from a hospital porter: the alcohol having served not to drown her sorrows but to preserve the organs after death.

So although Smith was initially delighted that the Ripper had struck in the City, thus giving him the chance to flex his investigative muscles, his conclusions as always proved wildly off the mark. He arrived here shortly after the discovery of the body and immediately set out in hot pursuit; his only problem being that the route the killer had taken took him once again out of his force's jurisdiction – but not out of ours. So let's make our way through the Priory House passage opposite, by the one and only path Jack the Ripper can be said beyond question to have walked.

You've grown a beard. I can never trust men with beards; I always feel they must have something to hide... I'm sorry: it's the same old story. Attack is the best form of defence; and self-defence has become second nature to me.

I met your wife on my way in. At least I assume that's who she was. At last you've slipped up: the mechanics of your consulting-room farce have broken down: the wife and the client meet face to face. But she smiled at me as though she were glad to see me; or was she simply glad to see me alive? It can hardly have done much for your reputation. If doctors bury their mistakes, do therapists commit them? You should have taken my advice and signed me away while you had the chance.

Thank you for coming to visit me. I didn't have many visitors; although the round-the-clock nursing more than made up for it. And to have my very own Filipino nurse smoking and hacking and watching television all night long is clearly the perfect cure for loneliness. Why didn't I think of it before?

Father Leicester came, of course. He condescended to me kindlily like a white settler with a fellow countryman who'd gone native. He presented me with a pot of honey and asked me how I spent my time. I told him I considered the commercial possibilities of canonisation – the marketable merchandise of martyrdom: such as the St Catherine wheel or the St Agnes bra, the St Sebastian dart-board or the St Lawrence non-stick griddle. He shook his head and knelt and prayed, whilst I stared at the honey-pot and racked my brain to remember if there'd ever been a saint stung to death by a swarm of bees.

Did you notice my display of cards during your statutory five minutes? You can hardly have missed the large icon of St Stephen and St John from all my fellow ordinands – I must stop saying that: from the ordinands at the college where I used to train. Unfortunately, it was bent in the post; every time I looked, I saw nothing but the creases. But it's the thought that counts – or so I told myself when I woke up with the tube down my throat... I'm surprised they remembered me; how long is it since I left? My calendar seems like a watch in a painting by Salvador Dalí. And time has become as relative as shame.

Still, I suppose it's a comfort to realise that all those good people are out there praying for me. How long will it be, do you think, until they admit defeat? Or will they carry on for ever until there's no one left alive for whom my name has any meaning and it sounds as obscure as a minor skirmish in the Book of Kings? I'm someone everyone used to know... Although, given that there are many more people dead than alive on the planet, I can at least count myself amongst the silent majority.

I went to see Jack. I put my proposition to him, which was that I should buy him – us – a flat. I was deliberately vague about personal pronouns. After all, the distinctions between us would be blurred in so many far more intimate ways. Man and prostitute... one flesh: haven't you heard; it's the new liturgy? Oh yes, we're all liberals now.

He asked if I wanted to be his sugar daddy. I was appalled – I never want to be anyone's father: not even in jest. Besides, I'm three years younger than him. But I said if he liked he could see me as a kind of sugar brother. He laughed and warned me that clichés had very precise meanings; that was what made them clichés. It didn't do to mess them around. Nor did it do to mess with him.

He sent me away; I'd had more than my allotted hour and he was expecting his next client. Of course, I thought bitterly; he had to give us all a fair crack of the whip – oh, did I crack a joke? Never mind, it was quite unintentional. And there was no one I could turn to: not even Christ.

What could he know of the isolation of my despair or the despair of my isolation? He had a mother, brothers, disciples, friends. Even the prayer he taught us seemed utterly irrelevant: Lead us not into temptation – no; lead us not into loneliness was all I asked. And there could be nobody as lonely as a grown man kneeling at the foot of a cold single bed.

I used to be alone at the foot of the Cross, but I'd meet Christ every day in the Eucharist. Now I see nothing but an empty tomb broken into for nefarious purposes. Grave-robbers have robbed the corpse and necrophiliacs have abused it:

I've been fucked up the arse by Jesus,
He does it to everyone,
He only does it to please us,
He says, 'Here comes God the Son.'

No! Forgive me! Please forgive me! I didn't say that. I'm just the ventriloquist's dummy. The Devil has his hand down my trousers whilst I sit helpless on his knee. I need help... I needed Jack. He was the only one who could save me. I was full of sin and he was the world's leading expert. He alone would authenticate my sin. He alone would assuage my isolation. The Protestant martyrs had at least stood side by side in the fires of Smithfield; was I to burn in the flames of Hell all alone?

No, I needn't have worried; for there was one face I could be sure of seeing: my old friend from Sunday School, Jesus. You look surprised. But why? Surely you must have realised by now: he was the consummate confidence trickster of all time. And through the eternal presumption of the Mass, he found the perfect way to perpetuate the fraud.

And I've finally discovered the answer to the conundrum that has exercised theologians through the centuries. He was neither God, nor man, nor half-man, nor demigod, but demagogue. He may have warned his original hearers that ignoring his message would be like building their houses on sand; but what of all the rest of us who've built up our hopes on hot air? He's led us straight up the garden path: Eden or Gethsemane? They're one and the same.

I've been fucked up the arse by the Saviour,
Which strikes me as rather odd.
I've been fucked up the arse by the Saviour,
At least he said he was God.

Oh God! How can he let me live? Or does even my blasphemy lack all conviction? Is it simply the excrement of my despair?

No wonder Jack rejected me. Whereas I yearned for him more and more. I took to phoning him at all hours of the day and night to check if he were in – to try to catch him out. I weighed up the various tones and tones of voices, the rings and the pauses, the man or the machine. I had to know if he were alone or occupied. Then the overactive imagination in my under-employed body would supply the rest.

Finally, on what was to prove my last night out of captivity, I decided to bring things to a head. I ordered a mini-cab and slipped out of the priory unnoticed to visit him unannounced. We soon reached Westbourne Park. I'd given no thought to either explanations or consequences, but at first neither appeared necessary as there seemed to be no signs of life inside his flat. A cloud momentarily obscured the moon and I suddenly realised how late it was. I jammed my finger on the doorbell and then ran for cover beneath the trees.

I watched with bated breath as he pulled up a window and leaned out, scanning the path. His ivory shoulders gleamed in the moonlight; I was far more aware of the precariousness of his position than of mine. He looked so insouciantly sexual; I could understand how men like Jack the Ripper had been driven to murder prostitutes. I guillotined him in my imagination, picturing the window-sash dropping and his head tumbling clean off his neck and down into my waiting arms. I shuddered. He called out; but I was safe in the camouflage of the conifers. He slammed the window shut.

I breathed again – at least I breathed more deeply. And I suddenly felt as conscious of my breathing as when I was alone with him, and the benign breath of God metamorphosed into the raucous rasps of a pair of rutting animals. But then at heart I was pure animal; and I outlined my two squat horns and my curly hair and cloven hooves...

After waiting for what seemed an eternity, I pressed the bell again. This time I didn't run away; this time he came downstairs. I'd never seen him look so ordinary. He was wearing a tartan woollen dressing-gown with a red tasselled cord, which both demystified and demythologised him. He looked at me with an expression that seemed pitched halfway between relief and fury. And then he smiled; but a smile of such calculated cruelty that it curdled my blood.

I apologised casually for catching him at a bad moment – as though it were three in the afternoon rather than in the morning, adding that I'd tried to ring him but his number had been constantly engaged. That, at least, came as no surprise; he apparently took the phone off the hook last thing at night as his adverts made him a prime target for hoax calls. I was amazed to find I'd been able to lie so convincingly. And I was lulled into a dangerous sense of security as he led me up the stairs.

Thinking back even with a mind ravaged by electricity, the sequence remains clear… We sat in his living room. He poured out a glass of wine as I poured out my heart. He asked me to try to keep my voice down; and when I wondered why, he moved to the bedroom door and pointed to the bed as proudly as a first-time father at the side of a cot. A young man was lying there fast asleep. His beauty dazzled my eyes.

At once I understood everything; but I refused to admit it. I prayed that he might be just another client, although as a rule he took great pains to keep us apart. But he was his lover: Kerry; and I wanted to die. And my honour was compounded with amazement. I couldn't see where he found the time, let alone the inclination. I'd always been led to believe that prostitutes became disgusted by sex, like workers in a sweet factory by chocolate. But the only thing that disgusted Jack was impotence… Why are you looking at me like that?

And I was riven by a sense of intolerable injustice. Why should even a prostitute have found someone to love whilst I was so abysmally alone?

I looked away from Kerry and down at the bed: that hot-bed of both my ecstasy and my despair with its painfully sharp, matt black bed-posts and springy, sweat-stained mattress, which had to be changed every six months due to wear and tear. But now it looked quite different, like a high altar decked out in its Easter colours, with its crisp white sheets and covers in place of the customary, stark brown towel.

But above all there was Kerry. And I gazed at him tucked up in the tousled bedding which still bore the perceptible patina of their love-making, like the delicate pattern of dust on a butterfly's wing. And I was consumed with envy that he'd been allowed inside; whereas I'd had to make do with the surface. And I watched him sleeping enchant-edly – enchantingly, his eyelids fluttering with the sweetness of his dreams. And I searched for evidence of the mechanics of their lust: the belts and boots and clamps and thongs and things. But I only saw Jack's tender touch as he gently teased his shoulder. Was it possible that the love between them was as natural as the love between... between two brothers? And Jack smiled as though he could read my mind.

He asked if I'd mind if he slipped back into bed, as it was begin-ning to feel rather chilly; which seemed to me the grossest understate-ment. And as he took off his dressing-gown, his body looked so much more relaxed than I'd ever remembered. And as he cuddled up close to Kerry, I didn't know where to look... No, that's not true; I knew only too well.

He kissed him awake, before effecting introductions, reminding him that I was the client who'd wanted to take him away from all this – and the extravagance of his gesture reflected damningly on mine. In turn Kerry seemed remarkably unflustered, grinning at me cockily... Oh, ha ha! it's easy for you to smile... I'm sorry; I've even grown suspi-cious of tricks of the light... Then he slipped one arm brazenly around Jack's shoulders: as shiny and smooth as a freshly polished banister, down which I longed to slide.

Each sought out the other's mouth as freely as if they'd been engaged in the art of gentle conversation. They had no shame – and that's not intended as a compliment. I wouldn't have believed it possible to have held a kiss for so long and not drawn breath. But they drew breath as they drew life from one another. Whilst I was left out in the cold, shiv-ering in the hair-shirt of my passion.

They seemed to lose sight of me completely as they lapped each other's warmth and wetness. I coughed; Kerry turned to me sharply. Satisfied? he asked. And I realised he was Irish. Then he pulled Jack up by the chin; I couldn't believe that he'd allow himself to be so crudely manipulated. Did I want a bit of it? he sneered. I was appalled; was he drunk or just disdainful? Well, did I? he rasped. Yes, I said, trying to sound non-committal. Yes, I said, as though I were auditioning for the voice of the speaking clock. Well, I wasn't going to have it, was that clear? And as if to emphasise the full extent of my exclusion, he slipped under the cover and applied himself to Jack's body. And I presumed – no, I knew all too well what he was doing. And the duvet rippled sinuously as though a snake were caught up in an apple-pie bed.

I watched as Jack's lips parted blissfully. He no longer had any need to spit out the sequence of commands and obscenities which had been his professional shortcut to arousal. He no longer had any need to spit at all. With Kerry his face took on an aspect of... beatific sensuality. He was all sense; his senses thrilled; whilst mine shrieked out in torment. I wanted to be in there with them, if not in their arms then at their feet. I wanted to be a bug beneath the sheets or a baby tooth under the pillow or a Christmas stocking tied to the foot of the bed. I wanted to be the sweat on their chests, the hair in their eyes, the saliva on their lips. Surely I had the right to one taste of life before I died?

Anything, I screamed... What? Jack looked at me, whilst Kerry re-emerged from the depths of the duvet. And I offered them anything if they'd only make room for me. I played my final card, and I paid the full price of my degradation, as Kerry let rip with a thesaurus of profanities. He leapt out of bed, his penis blazing like a beacon. He made to grab hold of me; but Jack intercepted him. He asserted his authority; he established his priority. The first stone was going to be his.

What do you want from me? he asked, clutching the roots of my hair so violently that my only thought was release. But he knew full well what I wanted. Love, I said, painfully conscious of the incongruity of my position; I've never felt this for anyone before... What about Rees? he asked, yanking my head back. No, I screamed. And he yanked it back still further until I was practically parallel with the floor. Be honest with yourself, he said, just for once in your life. And at that he let me drop unceremoniously and moved away.

He switched on the television; the screen suffused with colour. At first I couldn't understand why he'd chosen a film of wrestling; until I looked more closely at the two competitors. They were a large middle-aged man and a small pre-pubescent boy. No wrestling promoter would ever have permitted such a miss-matched coupling. But it was a pornographer's dream.

It was my own worst nightmare. I tried frantically to break free. But Jack was holding me fast. My head was fixed as firmly as the camera; whilst my eyes relentlessly recorded the images which seared my soul. I was forced to watch as a monstrous middle-aged man penetrated... no, how could he do it to him? And how could Jack do it to me? I wanted to ask, but my mouth felt clamped and frozen. There was no sound in the room and no soundtrack: simply the suffocating silence of evil. Until I finally found my voice. Why? I shouted. Why?

Haven't you recognised yourself yet? he asked, relaxing his hold for an instant as he pointed towards the screen. He was making no sense... but he continued to point whilst the man's heaving, hulking husk of a body appeared in an all too vivid close-up. And then when the boy came back into view he declared that he was Rees.

I couldn't and I wouldn't understand him. It was the final proof of what I'd long suspected; his sexual excesses had twisted his mind. It was utterly absurd. I'd never laid a finger on Rees. I'd never laid a finger on anyone but him; and even then a finger just about said it all. But at that same moment another image flickered across the screen: a black and white Christ from some Hollywood Biblical epic warning against men who committed adultery in their hearts.

I pressed my hands into my eyes, but Jack pulled them away. At last the image faded, but the horror remained, as the man began to thrust into the boy so hard and so fast that I thought – I prayed – that Jack must have somehow speeded up the film. But there was no respite, not for either of us, as he continued his catalogue of accusations... are you sure you can bear to hear? He claimed that I'd used and abused Rees far more ruthlessly than any of the other men in the club. I'd had every opportunity to help him; but it'd suited me to leave him where he was: confused and vulnerable and reckless – and on remand.

I was astounded. I asked how it could possibly have suited me to leave him in a club which had struck me quite unequivocally as Hell on earth. Of course, he said; that was the whole attraction. What self-respecting Christian could be expected to throw up such a Heaven-sent excuse to visit Hell – to sin vicariously under the cloak of clerical immunity, whilst not even getting his fingers burnt? And I had no answer, and he had no mercy. You're just a spiritual voyeur, he said, a praying Tom.

Then he dragged me to the television and pressed me face to face with both reflections. There I was gross and sweaty and raw and lustful; there I was broken and bowed and buckled under: the reality and the myth. I was afraid he'd push my head through the screen and I'd disappear forever into the pornographic abyss. So I thrust back, while at the same time the boy gave one final heartrending shudder as the man exploded inside him. And my life exploded inside me. And my head went limp.

The picture flickered and died; the moment weighed very heavy. But I knew that if I lost it, I'd be lost forever. So I grabbed hold of his waist and made a final appeal. He'd held a mirror to my soul and a camera to my sexuality. He alone had the power to save me; he couldn't be so heartless as to send me away.

He pretended not to understand; but I told him I knew full well who he was. When Lucifer fell, he hadn't fallen to Hell but to earth; or to be more precise to Bethlehem in four or five BC. But now he'd come again and it had fallen to me to acknowledge him. I'd be the Devil's true disciple, the rock on which he built his coven. And I begged him to take me to him: to sanctify my body and mortify my soul.

He looked at me and his eyes filled with self-assurance as he promised to give me all I'd ever desired: which was no more than I deserved. And I closed my eyes and threw back my head in anticipation of the touch of his lips. But he summoned Kerry and they moved towards me in tandem, and they undid my jacket and unbuttoned my shirt and – I'm... I'm... They took off my shoes and my socks and my trousers and... And I sat as trusting as a newborn baby and gazed up at their naked bodies standing over me, as in a perfectly synchronised sequence they each took aim and pissed.

I sat stunned by the steaming stream of urine. It stung my nostrils; it smarted on my skin. I stared at them in bewilderment through what I thought was a veil of tears. They looked at each other. They looked frightened; they looked guilty; they looked away. And the reality of what had happened finally hit me. And both the manner and the moment of my degradation felt utterly right.

I was a sewer – I am a sewer; I'm the world's sewer. I'm running with the whole world's wastes. They treated me with less respect than a dog would a serviceable tree trunk. Even a dead tree can support fungus – even the Judas tree. But nothing can ever grow from me. I used to find myself in the sacraments; now I must look only to excrement. I've been baptised once in chrism and many times in fire; but at last I was immersed in my true element: a swirling, stagnant swill. And I thanked them warmly for performing the rite.

Jack pulled me to my feet. I gripped his arm; my legs felt as though they'd been filleted. He sponged me and towelled me and helped me to dress; I speculated on the state of the carpet. He ordered a cab from his usual service, although I was sure I detected more than the usual scorn in the driver's eyes. But then that may well have been due to the smell – do I still smell; that is to the world at large...? He said nothing either; he was as inscrutable as the model of the three wise monkeys which bobbed from the mirror as we drove.

I couldn't go back to the priory; the prospect of meeting Brother Martin was more than I could bear. I wasn't worthy to unloose the latchet of his shoes... But the words of the Bible mocked me, especially those of St John the Baptist. For I'd been newly baptised in the Devil's name; and I was worthy of nothing but Hell.

We drove through the pounding rain in which the lights of London dissolved like a wash of water-colour, to a small hotel in the West End that had once been pointed out to me by the boys as somewhere they took their punters – which felt ironically apt. The red light advertising vacancies seemed also to advertise turning a blind eye; and yet there were limits even to its latitude. You could register your arrival under a pseudonym, but not your death.

The porter showed me to my room and brought me a bottle of wine. I reached for my pills, which I'd started to carry about as though I were a spy. I took a last look around the room. The decor proved an antidote to sentimentality. It was quite unembellished except for a laminated Turner seascape and a Gideon Bible. I remembered the Turners at Edensor and my courage faltered; so I turned the print to the wall. But the sight of the Bible simply strengthened my determination. And as I drank the wine and downed the pills which would together drown my sorrows, I slowly ripped out the gospels page by page.

As I started to sink, I began to worry about the smell of my decomposition: God's last laugh and our ultimate degradation. Wasn't the stink of mankind humiliation enough without the added stench of mortality? I moved to the window to try to prise it open when a new idea struck me, and I signed my name in the dust on the glass: a fittingly futile, final gesture. After which I must have passed out.

God moves in mysterious ways; and according to Father Leicester, none more so than the hotel porter, who, confused by complaints about the noise in the neighbouring room, broke in and discovered me. Well, he can believe what he likes but I categorically refuse to accept that God played any part in it. And besides I'd despair twice over of a God so indiscriminate as to have concerned himself with the likes of me. No, it was the Devil who saved me. He'd worked long and hard to gain control of me. He wasn't going to let me slip from his grasp so soon.

Not that I had any intention of trying. While God's injustices drove me finally to apostasy, the Devil's served simply to increase my respect. How utterly true to himself to bring me back from the brink of death and yet not from despair: to refuse even to grant me the absolution of absolute damnation. He knew that for me the true meaning of Hell lay in perpetual isolation: to have communion with neither God nor man, nor even Devil; to be utterly, unutterably alone.

How could anyone have ever made suicide a crime? What punishment could begin to approach the agony of being kept alive? And it's the one life sentence without hope of remission: not in this world, nor even the next. For it's the one sin that can never be forgiven: the one Christ spoke of as the blasphemy against the Holy Ghost. To despair is to negate God's very nature, and to kill oneself to deny any possibility of grace.

So I suppose I've answered my own question. The wonder is that they ever agreed to decriminalise us, although in practice they simply hospitalise us instead. Then they can make us the guinea-pigs for their ineffective medicines and the scapegoats for their unacknowledged pain.

And yet to my mind suicides should be revered, not resuscitated. In these times of ever-dwindling resources we should be lauded as national heroes like Japanese pilots during the war. There should be a Suicides' Corner in Westminster Abbey along with a Tomb of the Unknown Suicide to honour some particularly mangled corpse. Then we can give up our pilgrimages to Lourdes and Walsingham and erect a shrine to the Reverend Jim Jones at Jonestown: the twentieth century's quintessential saint.

But they'd rather revive us with their pumps and pills and potions. How can they be so callous? They'd put a sick dog out of its misery: why not a sick mind? And they treat me as though I've forfeited all right to adult consideration. They roll the medicine trolley through my room like an armoured tank. They keep me away from sharp knives and strong ties and open windows... But I'm learning fast and I've already become a model prisoner – sorry, patient; and the proof is that here I am out on parole – sorry, trust.

Besides, I've discovered a far more poetic form of justice, and one no amount of pills can keep at bay: I intend to contract AIDS. I'll go back to the 'Cockatoo' and pay the boys to take turns to go through me. Until, if only by the law of averages, I'll have no escape. Then when I die, Dante'll have to revise the topography of his Inferno. I'll be so ostracised, I'll be cast in a circle of Hell all by myself.

I can see what you're thinking: it's a double bluff; he's afraid he's already infected and so he's putting the best face on it he can. Well I'm sorry to disappoint you, but Doctor Liebwitz arranged for me to be tested at the clinic and on that score I've nothing to fear.

He was amazed at my chagrin. He'd expected the result to relieve my mind. But on the contrary, it'd been my last chance to regain my faith in God. He might have destroyed my purpose in life; but I couldn't believe that even he'd deny me the chance to let my death serve some purpose: to expiate my sins through my suffering; to be a living sacrifice and the essential embodiment of my prophecy of doom.

But he refused me even the mercy of opprobrium. I'd imagined myself setting up my cross at Charing Cross, ringing a knell and revealing my wounds to the crowd: See my scabs, see my scars; watch me cough and splutter. I'd have accompanied my own death rattle and my message would have been written on a billboard of blood. And I wouldn't have let up until I'd completely lost my voice – no, until I'd begun to lose all my senses and my madness spoke for itself. Then if they'd turned on me and vilified me and spat at me like Christ, the spray of their spittle might at last have wiped me clean.

No! Even in my despair I come back to Christ. It's not he who should inspire me, but Judas. For where would Christ be without him? And where would he be without me? He needs my sin to offset his sanctity, just as he needed Judas' treachery to offset his faith... Of course: that's it! Then I do have a purpose in life after all. I'm a sinner and God requires sinners. Without us he'd be as redundant as a derelict church. So I'll give thanks for my sin, and I'll cherish it: the greater the sin, the greater the service to God.

And you can call off your watchdogs; I intend to live. I intend to outlive both Moses and Methuselah. I'll be sustained by my own sickness; I'll be inoculated by my own despair. And just as Jonathan exposed the distortion of the Old Testament, so I shall do the same for the New. My first step will be to rehabilitate St Judas. He and not Christ is the true son of Man: the only begotten of both God and Satan, and their joint incarnation here on earth. Then I'll found a new sect and profess a new creed and proclaim a new gospel: Despair is Hope, Sin is Salvation, Damnation is Redemption, and Satan is God.

Ten

It was in this doorway, now, as you can see, blocked up, that Jack the Ripper dropped a blood and faeces-stained strip of apron, which he'd torn off Catherine Eddowes' corpse when he fled from Mitre Square. The rag was discovered beneath a scrap of graffiti which claimed that 'the Juwes are the men that will not be blamed for nothing'. And of all the contemporary clues connected with the Ripper, this was to prove the most controversial.

In fact there's no proof whatsoever that the murderer himself had any hand in it. It may already have been up there for some time. There may have been more writing on other walls. No one thought to check. It seems highly unlikely that, with scores of policemen in hot pursuit, even a madman would have paused for a scribble. Unless, that is, he was so tortured by self-disgust, he had to relieve it no matter what. But then why that particular phrase and above all that particular spelling? For Jews was spelt not as one might have expected, but J-U-W-E-S.

As I mentioned back in Hanbury Street, the East End and the City had long been a haven for Jewish immigrants. I also pointed out to some of you, as we walked down Bevis Marks, the gates of the great Sephardi synagogue, the oldest in the English-speaking world, which I'm proud to say numbered several of my own family among its founding fathers. But that was 180 years before these murders. Most of the wealthier families had by then moved out, leaving a very much poorer community of some 60,000 people, along with a strong residue of anti-semitism which had recently been rekindled by the erroneous arrest of Jonny Pizer, a Jew who was originally believed to be Jack.

Pizer had a cast-iron alibi and was quickly released; but not before considerable damage had been done. And it was for this reason, or so he claimed, that Sir Charles Warren insisted that the graffiti be wiped off post-haste, without even waiting for a photographer. For his prompt action, Warren was thanked personally by the Chief Rabbi and publicly in the pages of the *Jewish Chronicle*, but bitterly criticised by Sir Henry Smith and countless Ripperologists ever since.

But before you wipe the wording from your minds, please remember that there is one society for whom J-U-W-E-S is the traditional spelling: the same society that attaches a ritual significance to both the mitre and the square... So was Sir Charles Warren afraid that the message would expose the Ripper as an elaborate Masonic conspiracy? Was the entire Ripper saga yet another, albeit exceptionally savage, instance of the Establishment taking care of its own: and more specifically, of its heir presumptive? Was this the key to Queen Victoria's unprecedented personal interest? But no more speculation. Come with me to the site of the last and most gruesome murder, where I shall reveal all.

I've grown fascinated by the history of psychiatric medicine. After all, everyone should have a hobby. Take ECT: I understand that a farmer was driving his pigs to market when they grew restive; I expect that they must have had some sort of porcine premonition. They squeaked and squealed and kicked against both their fate and the cart, which tipped over into a ditch, sending them flying into an electric fence. He immediately noticed how much more docile they became; and the next thing you know, doctors were applying the same technique to the only other tissue as thick-skinned as pig-skin: the human brain.

And please forgive me if I fail to do justice to the higher mysteries of your profession. But I'm a simple soul; I was brought up on the story of the Gadarene swine. Christ cast out the devils into the herd of pigs. It took twentieth-century psychiatrists to reverse the process.

How could you allow it? You let them send hundreds of volts of electricity through my brain so that I could be led placidly like a pig to slaughter. I'm not an animal! But then I'm no longer a man. I'm an adjunct to a machine. I've been born again: a branch line of the National Grid. Some people give their bodies to science; I gave my mind.

And there was no one to speak up for me – even a prisoner has a Friend, if only my mother… She would never have given her consent; she would have revived me with love, not electricity. Whereas my father blithely signed the papers. And he couldn't even take the trouble to fly over. He claimed that his doctors had forbidden it; he was in agony with his back. So, with excessive protestations of concern, he despatched my stepmother in his place.

Not that I wasn't grateful for her visit, if only because of its effect on the staff at the clinic. Their attitude towards me changed markedly. For a start they called an immediate halt to the ECT. They said I'd come to the end of the course – but the coincidence was too convenient. Nevertheless I allowed them to save face. She insisted that they explain all my treatment. I think it helped that her English was patchy since it meant that they couldn't blind her with science – although that would have been nothing compared to what they'd done to me.

She tried to persuade me to confide in her, but I wouldn't have known where to begin. It's hard enough talking to you and at least you're implicated in the same sexuality. But she could never have hoped to understand; and I don't just mean the language. She'd led such a charmed life, at least to all appearances. She'd only ever confronted darkness like mine within the confines of a picture frame, where it was effectively anaesthetised by art.

But I'm forgetting: how did you take to her? It's no good trying to act the innocent; she told me you'd liaised. I expect you found her attractive. Don't worry; I shan't breathe a word to your wife. And you wouldn't be the first. She has a particular brand of elegance: a typically French combination of sophistication and serenity. She wafts through life with never so much as a hair out of place, not an emotion, let alone a gland. It's no wonder she makes every Englishman fall in love with her. Well, she did my father for a start…

I admit I may not have been completely open with you about my parents. Not that I've been deliberately dishonest… simply selective. I may have given the impression that my father married again after my mother's death; in fact he married shortly before – three or four years to be precise. Though I expect you've already read that in some file; or else I've been dropping clues inadvertently... If you ever decide to give up psychiatry you can always apply for a job picking needles out of haystacks.

And I can also tell you the precise moment when I became aware of something which set me apart from my friends. It was when Father Clement, the village vicar, introduced me to the bishop. I must have been all of six or seven. He asked after my good lady mother; I told him she wasn't well. He was sorry to hear it and turned his attention to my father. I said I'd no idea; I never saw him. My parents were divorced.

He bent down until his flushed, fat face nearly touched mine. I can still recall the smell of him: the sickly, sweet scent of his pampered, pudgy flesh. And he told me never to use that word; it was a bad word. I presumed that it must have been a swear word. And even two or three years later when my uncle took me to see *HMS Pinafore*, and the Captain sang of never using the word that began with a 'd', I was convinced that that word must be divorced: the dirtiest word in my dictionary – the dirtiest word in my mind. My uncle laughed and told me not to be such a chump; the word was damned. And he laughed again and ruffled my hair and... But to me divorced and damned were one and the same.

Jonathan, in his wisdom, thought that was what fuelled my desire for the priesthood. He thrust nails through my vocation as brutally as though I were on a cross. He declared that I was driven by demons in the shape of my parents. I seemed to feel it had fallen to me to redeem them, whilst at the same time taking good care to punish them for all the pain that they'd given me... As you can see, demons make the mind extremely subtle – in his case to the point of stupefaction. I only mention it now to show you how easily I was able to dismiss it: as easily in fact as I dismissed him.

Why should I have wanted to punish them? You can't blame someone for loving someone even if it is the wrong person; any more than you can blame someone else for dying even if you were just a child. So please don't dust down any of your textbook clichés for me.

On the contrary, I'm glad he's found someone to look after him in his old age. And besides they have a family of their own: David and Paul – my half-brothers. He always calls them my brothers to emphasise the relationship, but I always emphasise the hyphen, as I half-heartedly send them my love.

And yet they do seem fond of me; they must either be very deceitful or very naive. I'd have thought I'd have been a constant thorn in their flesh: a reminder of a father they had no part of; a life beyond the Channel and beyond the grave. Apart from which I'm ten years older. We have nothing in common but four pints of blood. And blood isn't thicker than water, simply stickier.

My stepmother brought over their love together with their gifts and their pictures: a series of snaps she'd taken of them playing with my father in the pool. He seemed so relaxed and carefree, as though he'd discovered his second childhood in their first. He was wearing a cork belt to support his back in the water, although it clearly wasn't painful enough to prevent his lifting Paul up on his shoulder. He never lifted...

She said that they'd both pleaded to come over with her, but she'd refused to let them miss school. I felt quite touched until I realised that they must have seen it as a legitimate way to play truant. But she invited me to go and stay with them just as soon as the doctors saw fit. Like all the rest of you she tried to concentrate my mind on the future. But although you may have been able to put nurses inside my room twenty-four hours a day, it's not so easy to put them inside my head.

Not that nurses is the word I'd have chosen; they were just foreign students. I suppose that was why they worked such late hours. Their body clocks were different. They certainly played havoc with mine. And between ourselves, I'm convinced one of them stole my honey. Though I said nothing; I didn't want to cause any fuss. But my stepmother showed no such compunction; she insisted that they be sent packing. And so instead I was kept awake all night by the anorexics upstairs playing Trivial Pursuit.

After that, Robin could only be an improvement; despite the infuriating bonhomie which makes him sound less like a nurse than a Get

Well Soon card. But then you know him of old – was he one of the conditions of my release: like a prisoner's electronic tag? And I'm not being paranoid; it's just that for an agency nurse he seems to have been told an awful lot about me. Although I suppose that's par for the course. Soon I expect I'll be written up in psychiatric journals. Even my most private thoughts will become public knowledge. It's a savage indictment of modern medical ethics; they give me the shock of my life and you make your name... What if they'd given me too much?

My stepmother appeared reluctant to leave, despite the fact that she'd long planned to spend the winter walking across the Andes with a girlfriend. She said she could easily put it off until next year; but I wouldn't hear of it. My motives weren't altogether selfless. I was extremely anxious not to put myself in her debt. What if we quarrelled or I felt like another stab at suicide – not that I do, you understand, but just for the sake of argument? I'd feel duty-bound to defer to her.

So she agreed to go once she was satisfied I was settled – which took rather longer than we'd thought. Not that I had many options. The doors of St Bede's had been firmly slammed in my face... Brother Martin felt unable to take the responsibility, especially when none of the Brothers of the Transfiguration had medical skills. They considered I'd be better suited to a more protective environment. Though their chief concern was clearly to protect themselves.

So we've opened up the house in Little Venice. It was my family's home at the turn of the century, once the Lauderdale Road synagogue was built and they no longer had to walk to Bevis Marks. I shall have it entirely to myself except for Mrs Trewitt, the elderly housekeeper – and resident spy. No one's lived there for years and the interior needs total redecoration. But my stepmother sees that as a point in its favour; it means I'll be able to mould it to my own personality... I suppose I can always leave it completely blank.

Not that my personality will be much in evidence outside my bedroom. I've taken to spending most of the day in bed. Mrs Trewitt tries to tempt me out with titbits. What do I care what I eat? She could bring me pig shit... horse shit... tramp shit from the streets: that's all

I'm fit for. She says I don't make her job any easier. But then no job's easy; having no job's not easy; and having to give up the job you were called for's more difficult still.

And I feel an even stronger bond of sympathy with my mother. She loved her work. I remember her saying that the years she spent nursing were the happiest of her life. But she gave it up to live with my father. While all he could offer in exchange was the presidency of the cottage hospital League of Friends. No wonder she preferred the view from inside her bed.

But then she was in distinguished company. If she wanted a model, she needed to look no further than Florence Nightingale, who'd been her original inspiration as a nurse. What did she do on her return from the Crimea but retire to bed? She didn't give up life – just the wretchedness of everyday living. And yet they don't depict that on the bank-notes. The Lady of the Lamp shines her light on to everyone's pillow but her own.

And if someone who had the world at her feet could find no reason to leave her bed, why should I who carry the cares of the world on my shoulders? I feel like a small child lost on the streets of a foreign city, who doesn't even know the name of his parents' hotel. And before you make a note, no, it's not something that happened to me. Why did you pick up your pen unless to provoke me? I do have an imagination as well as a past. You make me so angry; which is of course precisely your intention. So your therapy becomes self-fulfilling... And you don't simply make me angry; you make me ill.

And if we throw in despair for good measure, then I'm sure you'll agree that I'm better off in bed where at least I don't inflict it on anyone else. Although I no longer reject my despair. It may be an unforgivable sin, but it's also what makes us human. I've read so many different accounts of what marks us out from the animals. Some claim it's that we laugh; some that we make tools; and others that we're self-conscious. But I think it's that we contemplate suicide: in Blake's view, the only philosophical question, and one I've yet to hear that any animal ever asked.

Nothing ever changes. Day and night are just different patterns flickering on the ceiling. I die of insomnia every evening and yearn for death to put an end to the dying. I'm taut with tiredness. It aches in the hollow of my back and chokes at the back of my throat. My skin's stretched so tight, it's begun to flake off. And I flick the remains out of my sheets.

I blink in the morning sunlight as my eyes accustom themselves to another day in the dark. I peer out through the hot hell of heavy lids, too tired to stay open, too irritated to close. The whites of my eyes are veined with red like a spider's web spun out of splintered glass. At last a tear-drop forms. But it isn't water; it's blood.

You urge me to make a move but it takes me all my strength simply to stand still – no, to lie down. As a boy, I recall being overcome with dread that I'd drop dead unless I accounted for every last breath. I sat rigid, terrified to let a single one slip by, until I began to hyperventilate on my own hysteria. Now that childhood fear has come back... History repeats itself, first as ignorance, then as despair.

But you ignore my protests. You've grown tired of playing God and instead you want to try your hand at Christ. And yet you're the very last person to suggest I should take up my bed and walk when it was talking to you that paralysed me in the first place. I can feel nothing but words; I can feel for nothing but words. And the one that sits most uncomfortably on my tongue is sponta... spontaneity.

I've always considered myself a man of the mind; but I was deceived. I didn't think; I merely felt intellectually, which isn't the same. I didn't have a thought in my head – no, that's not true either; I had far too many. What I failed to do was to make sense of them. But all that changed at the clinic, where I was forced to think, and so lucidly that madness seemed the only rational response.

Come and talk to the others, the nurses said; it doesn't do to be so much alone. Oh, but it does. At least when I was alone, I could suppose my pain was somehow exceptional, which made it somewhat more bearable. But to see it reflected: no, not even reflected – reiterated on all those agonised faces: to realise that it wasn't just commonplace but universal... There's so much pain in the world. So much.

Come and talk to the others... Oh, yes. Every patient tells a story. And the hardest thing is that each of theirs made a nonsense of mine. For of all of them mine was probably the simplest. It was the story of a man who believed that God had called him to suffer. And in his innocence he thought he was unique.

You may consider I've been justly punished for my presumption. And I might be tempted to agree if only the sentence weren't so unduly harsh. For my conviction wasn't born of self-importance. I simply believed that if I were ever to stand before a congregation in the person of Christ, then I had to suffer for them too. But my assurance was shattered in the dining-room of the clinic when I realised that people didn't need my suffering... far from it: they already had much too much of their own. What's more, if there were a priesthood of all believers, then there was another of all sufferers. Which left me redundant on both scores.

And now perhaps you'll understand why I'm still so depressed. The doctors may have given me back my life; but they can't give me back my vocation, which was the one way I could find to justify the pain. So can you honestly deny that to retreat to bed is the only possible answer... whilst pulling the electric blanket tightly around my head?

Eleven

This, I'm afraid, is as near as we can now get to Dorset Street which was once the most notorious in London, where even the police would only come – if they came at all – in groups of four. This multi-storey car park occupies the site of the house where both Annie Chapman and Jonny Pizer used to doss. And over there, just where those fruit vans are parked, was Miller's Court, where our fifth and final victim, Marie Kelly, lived... and died.

Clearly a cut above the others, she could afford to rent her own room – indeed, she was the only one of the women to be killed indoors; but when she opened those doors to the Ripper and his knife on that cold winter night, it turned out to be the unkindest cut of all.

Apart from her murderer, George Hutchinson was probably the last man to see Marie alive. But although his suspicions were aroused by her companion's appearance, he was loath to interfere. So he followed them here and watched as she led him inside. But the cold soon took its toll and he returned home. And as I can sense that same November nip in the air again now, I'll be brief. And, in brief, his misgivings were not misplaced.

The sight which greeted Thomas Bowyer, the landlord's agent, when he went to collect Marie's rent the next morning, beggared belief. What little of her remained was laid out on the bed. She hadn't simply been ripped apart, but chopped into tiny pieces. With the exception of her lungs, all her internal organs had been hacked out, leaving her stomach a cavernous void. Her throat had been slit so deeply that her head was almost severed from her neck. Likewise her left arm was only attached to her trunk by a sinewy thread. All the flesh had been sliced off her face, her nose skinned and her forehead flayed. Her breasts and heart, together with strips of flesh from her abdomen, had been neatly placed on a side-table and her liver positioned between her legs. One of her hands had been thrust into her belly, whilst odd bits of offal hung from the picture rail like macabre decorations...

Would you please allow me to finish? I'll be happy to answer any questions later... It took six hours to piece her more or less together. It was the most savage of all the Ripper's murders: the crescendo of his symphony of terror. But it was also the last. Why? Sexual serial murderers don't simply stop... I'm sorry, but I really can't compete with your barrage of barracking. Would you mind saving your comments... very well then, your objections, until the end? Of course my descriptions were grisly; she'd been reduced to scraps of gristle. Now if you please...!

Where was I? Oh yes. Such murderers don't simply stop because they've had a change of heart like you or I... For Heaven's sake, I was speaking hypothetically! No, they're either caught or killed or put out of action some other way... All right, go ahead: the street is yours. Just say what you must, and maybe then we can return to the matter in hand, and the final revelations of the Ripper.

I can no longer make my Tuesday evening appointment. Well, don't you want to know why? I have a job. I've returned to the East End, although not to the crypt nor to anything to do with the Church. I handed in my resignation. They expressed regret, without sincerity. And yet, strangely, they seemed to warm to me once they heard I'd cracked up. And I thought that whatever else, at least I'd never have to see Patrick or Roy or Vange again. Though in the event I'm more worried than ever about meeting Vange.

You'll never guess what it is I'm doing. Come on, you can still try. You give up before you've even started. But then I'm a fine one to talk... I'm guiding two walks a week for a friend who runs historical tours of London, or more specifically I'm visiting the sites and haunts of Jack the Ripper: haunts being the operative word.

I must admit I'd have preferred Literary London or Legal London or Mysteries and Mistresses of Mayfair; but there's not the demand.

Only Jack the Ripper can survive the winter slump. And this year, what with his centenary and all the attendant publicity, there's been a positive boom.

I'm sorry if I'm gabbling but for the first time in months I have something new to tell you. And I feel a new man. You'll have to go away more often. I don't know about you; but it certainly seems to agree with me.

I'll start at the beginning. I'm sure I mentioned my stepmother's proposal that I redecorate the house. Well, she went one further and suggested the name of a suitable designer: Echo Lovett; which is no misnomer, given that almost everything she says sounds second-hand. I expect you'd like her; she speaks your language: the house is my skin, the lighting system my veins... although I hate to think what that makes the plumbing. She claims that redecoration is the best therapy she knows; but I suspect she may be trying to justify her fee.

Forget the redecoration; it's a red herring. Although I'm happy to report that it's already transforming the house. So there may be more to her theory, and her therapy, than I thought. What concerns us is her son, Donald, who's also 'in the arts'. He writes haikus and runs the 'Famous Feet' historical walks agency. And to cut a long story short – which believe me isn't easy with Echo – she told me that he was looking for a new guide: someone he could trust with both the tourists and the takings. And that was where both Jack the Ripper and I came in.

At first I thought she was mad. I'd hardly been on my feet for months; I'd collapse after a hundred yards. But Echo is a woman who never takes no for an answer... most of the time she doesn't listen to your answers at all. It seemed that Donald was in rather a fix. He'd booked himself on two walks at once. She just knew I'd be the perfect substitute. And in the end my resistance gave out. She swooped on me and scooped me up in the vast tangle of chains that dangled about her bosom. Then she kissed me on the cheek three times – she claims to be half Russian – and declared that I had a heart of gold.

I still suspect I was simply the cheapest option... The money isn't much, Donald admitted. And he was right... But then, he'd gathered that that wasn't my primary concern. And I could hardly disagree... After all, what did I have to lose? he asked; and Echo repeated. And when I could come up with no reply, they both took it as read.

In a word, I think that the work, or more particularly the walk, has proved my salvation. It's exorcised many more demons than simply my sloth. Though at first I was acutely conscious of my inadequacy. As I told Donald, I knew next to nothing about Jack the Ripper. But he assured me I'd be able to mug it up in no time. And besides, the delivery was all. He'd provide a simple framework for me to memorise, and I could extemporise the rest.

I followed him round twice. Initially I had a problem simply keeping up; my stiff joints were no idle excuse. But there was something so exhilarating about leading a group of strangers through the settling darkness, that I found the strength to carry on.

And we carry on in all weathers: sometimes, according to Donald, the worse the weather, the better the atmosphere. Although we have nothing to match the dreaded pea-soupers of the Ripper's own day. Someone could disappear without trace from six inches in front of you... I disappeared for far too long. But now I'm back with a vengeance. No, not with a vengeance – with a job.

I observed Donald closely. His delivery was dry and academic, as though that would in itself be enough to refute any suggestion of bad taste. And he stuttered badly over the letter 'r', which gave me added reason to dread the name of the Ripper. But I picked up more than I'd expected, which was all to the good as I only had time for two dummy runs before he sent me out on my own. He came along to support me or, as he put it, for the ride. His unaccustomed levity made his stutter more pronounced.

As luck would have it, for my debut the bulk of the party was Japanese. And as Donald had previously explained, they're every guide's dream audience... The word he actually used was punters, and I thought of Rees... Some groups try desperately to score points, their sole aim being to make the guide look small. But the Japanese are with you all the way. Their enthusiasm's palpable. And they always agree to differ, never dispute... He himself declared himself delighted with my performance; he had complete confidence in me. Which was another first.

And confidence breeds confidence – although not I hope complacency. On my second trip I muddled two of the murders. Not that anyone appeared to notice... I suppose the order's less important than the cumulative effect. And at the end a youngish man tried to tip me. I refused, which obviously embarrassed him. And I felt churlish; he only wanted to express his appreciation. So from now on all contributions will be both gratefully and graciously received.

The money may not be important; but the pay is. It's the first time I've ever had a price put on anything I've done. I've had a value, but that's not the same. And it may not be the career I'd have chosen; it may not be a career at all. But at least it's a start. If I can make my way through the back streets of Whitechapel, I can make my way in the world.

We assemble outside Whitechapel Station. The pervasive poverty effortlessly sets the scene. Although it seems quite different to that of the boys and beggars in the West End. That was the poverty of despair; I saw it in their eyes: a hollow, haggard anger at the depths to which they'd sunk. But this is the poverty of destitution; it's endemic in the cracks in the streets and the marrow of their bones: in the wide-hipped women bloated with batter and their hard-headed husbands big-bellied with beer.

I never thought I'd hear myself talk like this. I've always believed in steering well clear of politics. But somewhere between crypt and club and clinic something changed. And it's certainly coloured the way I guide my walks. I pull no punches; I point the parallels. Jonathan would be proud of me – no, gratified. I'm still not sure about eating bacon being a political act; but walking through the East End undoubtedly is.

How could it be otherwise? There's a wizened old man who perches permanently in a crack in the station wall, his feet encased in layers of heavy plastic like makeshift snow-shoes. He swigs constantly from a bottle of cider, whilst his toothlessness pulls his face in a perpetual grin. Every so often he jumps up without warning and pounds his fists through the empty air, screaming and squalling and whirling like a dervish, with all the frenzy of a disconnected mind. But his stinking squalor seems as far removed from the genteel madness of the clinic as genteel poverty is from the Mile End Road.

And I was reminded of what Fiona told me at the crypt: that it's all very well to put vulnerable people back into the community, but first we have to put the community back into ourselves. And yet any community there once was has been replaced by commuters, to whom the old man is just an incontinent inconvenience: an obstacle to be neatly negotiated, as they hurry through the station forecourt, loudly cursing the passenger under the train at Barking whose despair has reverberated all along the line.

Then I thought of Christ and how he would never have abandoned him; in a mad world he gave his life that we might be sane… Although these days I expect he'd have been certified rather than crucified, and electrodes and not thorns stuck to his head… And if I'd ever intended to pass by, I could do so no longer. So the next time I arrived at the station, instead of the usual wide berth, I gave the old man ten pounds.

And I can hear all Jonathan's objections – he'd have found fault with the Good Samaritan – but from the wild smile on his face and his weird pantomime of pleasure, I felt that although it wouldn't solve any of his problems, it might at least dull some of the pain.

An American who'd booked for the tour accused me of irresponsibility. Didn't I realise, he asked, that he'd spend every cent he was given on drink? So what? I replied, and surprised myself by my vehemence. What right had I to dictate what he did with my – no, with his money? Besides, I'd be deeply disturbed if I thought that our venture into the nineteenth century had helped to revive the distinction between the deserving and the undeserving poor.

You may find it odd for a former ordinand to be tramping the streets of the East End retelling the murders of prostitutes; and yet it could hardly be more apt. I know their stories, I've heard them myself a hundred years on. The sexes may be different but the sexuality's the same.

And I can't understand why so many people, and women in particular, condemn the walks as pornographic. Donald was challenged regularly by abusive pickets; but he explained how to wrong-foot them. In any case, he's quite sure that their dedication will cool in this cold October weather. Nevertheless I have to admit to a degree of trepidation every time I turn a corner. And the threat of confrontation fills the air.

Superficially, I admit, their arguments may sound plausible. But far from glorifying male violence, we're depicting it in its full horror and trying to keep the memory – no, the moral – of those ghastly crimes alive. We murder the women twice over if we commit them to unmarked graves. I still remember my father's anguish when my brothers told him of their school friends who thought the Holocaust was Jewish propaganda; and that was in a country which had suffered the Occupation. And though the analogy may seem glib, the principle remains.

And walks such as ours help to focus on it. We show the true face of evil as well as its mangled torso. And it's a face like yours or mine, not an anthropomorphic old goat. Jack the Ripper was no more the Devil than I was. He was a man long before he became a monster and a myth. And the sexuality of the crimes is all-important. As men we can never relax our guard. We must keep the example of the Ripper always before us: not as an abhorrent aberration, but rather as male sexuality at its most appalling extreme.

At last I fully understand why St Augustine located mankind's original sin so uncompromisingly in the sexual. And as I'm sure Vange would be the first to agree, it was mankind's original sin and not personkind's. This is one instance where the etymology speaks for itself.

So to denounce the walks as pornographic is far too easy. It's just a convenient stick to beat anyone and anything with which they happen to disagree. Their imprecision belies their cause... Besides, if they'd ever care to direct their protests more profitably, I could arrange to take them down some far less savoury streets.

Even so, I'm not sure that I'd protest too loudly. And I suppose it's only right that here I declare an interest – no, not an interest, for Heaven's sake never an interest – but a need. I've started to use pornography. And if I feel more at peace, perhaps it's because I've been able to purge myself. I see it as no different to extracting the venom from a snake... I've always had a horror of snakes.

So if I may play Devil's – or rather man's – advocate for a moment, there may be some merit even in the genuine article. And although it goes against the grain to base a case on the lesser of two evils, if unhappy and unfulfilled people are able to lead happier and more fulfilled lives, then maybe the lesser evil can serve the greater good.

And it was following in the Ripper's footsteps that brought it home to me. I'm so aware of the dangers of my... his... our unbridled sexuality. I've studied him very carefully and my reflection... my reflections revolt me. So what alternative do I have? I know I can never risk coming close to another person; I hardly dare come close to myself. So I keep myself at arm's length. A flick of the wrist and it's all over. I'm neutralised for another day.

Why did you have to do this to me? I thought I was doing so well, but you've made me see that for every step forward I've been taking two back. And as usual you've achieved it without so much as opening your mouth. I feel so ashamed. And it's all quite out of character. I'd never even touched myself before I met Jack. But since then... I'd say the floodgates had opened, if only the image weren't so horribly moist.

He identified a need which, on my own, I'm not strong enough to satisfy. My sexuality has proved too inexperienced for solitude. And so I've begun to buy videos to make up for the lack. I make love to men's shadows instead of their bodies. And even my fantasies are second-hand.

I visit a supplier in Soho; I remembered his name from Jack. He has a shop in an alleyway off a sidestreet. I have to sidestep piles of rubbish and rubble; I have to suppress my own disgust. The display in the window advertises health aids and tummy trimmers, slimming tablets and anti-smoking sprays... I slip inside. Remaindered paperbacks line the shelves: Westerns, hospital fiction and biographies of long-forgotten pop stars. The bottom shelf is devoted entirely to wrestling magazines. Whilst underneath, for those with more esoteric tastes, pregnant women wrestlers re-enact the Battle of the Bulge.

You look sceptical. But there's no taste either too obscene or too obscure, no appetite that can't be met – or rather, whetted; for like the fast food on sale on every corner, the burgers with built-in obsolescence, supplies are carefully packaged to leave the customers drooling for more. So there are men with penises they can tie knots in... in case they should ever forget; women with breasts that stretch to their waists... for men who want more for their money; men-women or women-men who proudly display their superfluities... for the man who has everything, and wants both. Believe me, there's nothing you can't lay your hands on in the fellowship of the sexually perverse.

I flick idly through a magazine whilst I wait to be served. My eye catches a 'polite notice': Anyone caught nicking will be battered. I quickly put my hands in my pockets, and even more quickly remove them again in case the thin grey man in the bright white raincoat should misunderstand. I ask for my films. The manager leers lubriciously, defers ironically and grabs my cash.

I hurry home and shut myself in my bedroom. I draw the curtains and switch off the lights. My heart races. I think of the old ladies I used to visit for whom television was their sole consolation; and I shiver at the company I keep. I'm quite alone. I stare at the screen. And the pictures in my mind make my groin sweat with shame. I watch the men go through their mechanical motions, which I mimic like a wound-up automaton. And I too perform for an unresponsive audience of one.

The films I choose are all perversions. I'm sorry if that sounds tautologous; it doesn't to me. I don't want to watch two golden boys intertwined in a passionate embrace, their privacy undisturbed by the camera, as they revel in each other's bodies quite oblivious of me.

I want my presence acknowledged. I want to be a spectator, not a voyeur. And I want to be stimulated and shocked simultaneously, so I can relieve my desire with my disgust.

So I watch films of men in caves, men in gyms, men in prisons, but not men in beds: men in beds make me feel lonely. I watch fat men, skinny men, squat men, scarred men, buck-toothed men, broken-toothed men, but never perfect men: perfect men make me feel lonely. I watch men in groups, men alone, men abusing each other, men bored with each other, but never loving each other: love makes me lonely. I'm so lonely, so wretchedly lonely. Is there no one out there watching me?

By now I'd have thought I'd be used to it. But however much I may have been prepared for the loneliness of the priesthood, nothing could have prepared me for that of apostasy. To be set apart for no purpose: not ministering to people, marrying them, and baptising their babies, but indulging my vices vicariously on a bedside screen.

And it's not simply guilt that oozes out of me, but fear – and not of impotence or blindness or of excess leading to deformity, but of a dulling of my sensibilities and a deadening of my responses, so that even if I were ever to find someone to love it might well be too late. I'll have stewed for too long in my own greasy juices and be unable to relate to anyone but myself.

So I'm aware that it's a far from perfect solution, but then it's a far from perfect world. In a perfect world all our mothers, and not just Christ's, would have been impregnated through the ear. And these days, when every act of love contains the seeds of its own destruction, pragmatism means nothing less than staying alive. In the war against infection, those men are fighting our battles for us. Whilst we hide behind locked doors and drawn curtains, they're out there in the front line...

I wish I hadn't thought of that. 'Front line' smacks of danger. And it's not as if they take precautions. Their activities are neither sanitary nor safe... Oh no, how could anyone...? I couldn't sit and wa... watch if I thought one of those men might be dying. I remember how my aunt could never bear to see a Rita Hayworth film once she'd read she'd developed Alzheimer's. It'd be far worse if some of those men were already dead. What's more, theirs would be no legacy of elegant Hollywood fantasies, but rather the deepest, darkest fashionings of our guts and our groins.

And who says they took part of their own free will? Or rather how free is free? Oh no, anything but that; that way madness lies... The glazed look in their eyes which to me was evidence of ecstasy might just have been a drug-induced haze. They may have been desperate for the money: any money, my money. And I know very well that I'm only one of many, but I'm still creating a market... a meat-market in my bedroom, an abattoir in my own backyard.

No! I didn't say that. I'm going backwards again and not just through time, but all my good intentions... Is there no escape? I wanted to avoid any kind of power; but the avoidance of it compromises me as much as the abuse. I'm not loving by proxy – I'm murdering. Like Jack the Ripper, I cloak my loneliness in respectability and stalk my prey. But at least he made some contact with his victims, if only at the point of a knife. Whereas I consign mine to oblivion at the flick of a switch.

So the women were right and in more ways than they could ever have suspected. Pornography kills; and you're sitting opposite a mass murderer. No wonder Donald offered me the job, despite my inexperience. He sensed I could find my way through those back streets blindfold. I'm not just the Ripper's centennial guide but his other self... I've never believed in reincarnation until today.

And my next group will find themselves embarked on the walk of a lifetime. I'll finally resolve the mystery that has baffled criminologists for the past hundred years... as I dramatically lower my voice: Ladies and Gentlemen, if you've been searching for the true identity of Jack the Ripper, you need search no further. He's standing here in front of you. Jack the Ripper is me...

Twelve

Jack the Ripper's me. And I'm not trying to sensationalise. I think we've already had sensation enough. Nor am I implying reincarnation; I don't believe in reincarnation – at least not bodily. I used to believe in so many things, but I don't even believe in the Incarnation any more. No matter... You've shown me myself in my true light. Thank you. I've been fooling myself that this is a serious reconstruction when it's little more than a crude vivisection. And I've been cutting up those women all over again night after night.

The irony is that I believed this walk would redeem me. I'd be back in the world, and even if I still couldn't talk to people, at least I could tell them a story: not my own, but Jack's. But now his story has become my autobiography. No, don't be alarmed; I'm not a mass murderer – at least not in the accepted sense of the word. But when does the accepted sense of the word become the acceptable face of murder? For surely that's what we've been witnessing tonight.

And the difference between the Ripper and myself is purely one of direction. He turned his pain and perversion outwards; whereas I've turned mine in. He lived his pornography, whilst I watched and you listened. He was a desperately sick man whose memory is infectious even now. And I've picked up his torch and his knife and, worst of all, his disease.

I'm a murderer of the mind: of it and in it. During the past year I've discovered an abyss inside myself that I never suspected; and unwittingly I've tried to implicate. I've used this walk as a vehicle for my own self-disgust. I've exploited your prurience to express mine. And along with the Ripper's story, I've appropriated his methods. Just as he revelled in his power over his victims, so I've relished mine over you: to tease you with terror – to set you salivating over their wounds...

So now you have it. There's no mystery to Jack the Ripper: merely a mirror. He's me and he's you...

What? I can't believe that you still want more. I'd rather hand you back your money than such an easy escape clause: a smug 'I'm all right, Jack' – oh yes, the puns are as endless as the pain. And whatever I may have said earlier, his identity can never be conclusively established, because he has far too many. He has the perfect alibi: ubiquity, and the perfect camouflage: skin. And the case can never be closed because his crimes still continue. So what does it matter who he was a hundred years ago? What matters is who he is now.

Though perhaps the original is also important, if only to serve as a warning. We mustn't turn our backs on history or even herstory – oh yes, words can change as radically as people – but simply on its exploitation. So if you like, I'll tell you the theory I favour, which I can assure you is no fear-fulfilling fantasy, but the one most in keeping both with my own feelings and the known facts.

First I must tell you who he wasn't. He was not the code-name for an intricate Masonic conspiracy, instigated by the government, to destroy the evidence of a secret marriage between Prince Albert Victor and a young Catholic shop girl, Annie Crook. That was the revelation I'd been leading up to and which was originally put forward by Joseph Sickert, at whose father Walter's studio the pair were purported to have met. According to him, although the lovers were brutally separated, their infant daughter's nursemaid, Marie Kelly, escaped with the child into the East End where, with a group of friends, she hatched a plot to blackmail the royal family: the results of which have been all too apparent tonight.

The hypothesis has undeniable neatness as well as the attraction that all such conspiracy theories have to armchair theorists. It ties up a lot of loose ends, but leaves a lot more entangled. Besides which it has been authoritatively refuted, not least by Sickert himself.

As an employee of the 'Famous Feet' Agency I was still prepared to endorse it; but I herewith resign. And standing at the scene of the crime – my crime – for the very last time, I'd like to suggest another.

It too concerns Prince Albert Victor, although some people seem to find its implications even more disturbing than the thought that he was the actual murderer. But it wasn't the prince, any more than his grandmother's government, but rather John Kenneth Stephen, his Cambridge tutor and intimate friend.

It was Stephen, a sufficiently close contemporary for scandalmongers both then and now to confuse them, who was the patient Sir William Gull identified as 'S' in his private papers. He'd treated him for a blow on the head two years earlier which had accentuated the tendency to insanity to which the whole Stephen family, most notably his cousin Virginia Woolf, was so prone.

Considerable circumstantial evidence supports his candidature. Michael Harrison, the prince's biographer, has convincingly argued from internal evidence the common authorship of the Ripper's letters and Stephen's poems. But even more telling are the frenzied fantasies and murderous misogyny which permeate his writings from beginning to end.

Nevertheless – and happily for the survival of the species – poetic fantasists don't invariably turn into mass murderers. But Stephen, who'd been pushed over the brink by the prince's estrangement, sought revenge on that group of women who were the bedrock of both Victorian society and hypocrisy and with whom, as he could hardly fail to have been aware, the prince had been cynically consorting: indulging the vice that Sir Henry Smith found so diverting in a desperate attempt to purge himself of a love that dared not even breathe its name.

But it was the prince whom Stephen loved, and the damming of his love in turn damned him. And when four years later, by then long incarcerated in a Northampton asylum, he heard of Albert Victor's death, he refused all food and survived him by a mere twenty days.

And as I said a moment ago, I don't offer this up as the definitive solution, but I find it at once the most psychologically true and poetically just: true, in that the killings were perpetrated by a man demented with despair at his own loneliness; and just, in that those very repressive and regressive values, to which the Queen herself has given her name, should have directly inspired the most brutal crimes of her reign.

So in the same way that we each have our own Christ and Hamlet, perhaps we should also have our own Jack the Ripper – no, Whitechapel Murderer. I refuse to use the sobriquet any more. It implies familiarity, which in my experience breeds acquiescence far sooner than contempt. But whereas Christ and Hamlet both exist as words on the page, long before we submit them to either personal faith or critical interpretation, all he left behind were some rather inconclusive messages and a very convenient mirror. Which is why he really can be all things to all people, or at least all men; and so I opt for J.K. Stephen and the grossly unflattering reflection of myself. But I can only pray that the mirror may be tarnished and the reflection distorted, and that one day I'll be able to look both history and myself in the face again and smile.

So there you are, ladies and gentlemen: a candidate of whose existence you could never have dreamed. I've confessed my own complicity after a century. I'm an accessory long after the crime. I see a policeman over on that corner; as there's no rim on his helmet he must be from the Met. I promise I'll go quietly should you choose to press a charge...

I'm afraid I'm dripping on to your carpet, but don't be alarmed: it's *Singing in the Rain* rather than Noah's Flood. I'm Gene Kelly dancing down Warwick Avenue – I'm dancing on air... How often do you go to the cinema? From now on I intend to make it at least once every week and always to something romantic. I want to sit in the dark with a roomful of people and pool our tears. I want to trust to the sanity of a collective fantasy rather than the sick fancies of a solitary mind.

Thank you... I apologise for being so late, but I quite lost track of the time: me on whom every minute has weighed as heavy as the pendulum in a grandfather clock; but not any more. I've resigned – I've thrown up my job – I've forced the issue. Aren't words wonderful? Isn't life wonderful? I can say – I can do just exactly what I mean.

I've always loved words. I suppose it's because I've always loved the Bible. It was where I first found God. But that doesn't blind me to their limitations. This is my body, said Luther... No, this is my body, said Zwingli: a bloody war of words over the simple word 'is', which in the original Aramaic doesn't even exist. And so we for whom the Bible is a dictionary of faith must make the dictionary a bible of definition. Which is why I can never stand by and hear its meanings wilfully traduced.

But the history of words is not the history of humanity, as I realised too late when a group of Women Against Violence Against Women violated my walk. They claimed that I'd appropriated their herstory. I seized on their false etymology to reassert my control. Did they really think that history was derived from his story? Or that the entire English language was a conspiracy to demean them? Did they know no Greek?

Inevitably Vange was in the vanguard, in a grey balaclava which was irreverently reminiscent of a wimple, although I hardly think she'd have learnt her choice of expletives from the Sisters of St James the Great. I was delighted to find myself no longer in awe of her. And her scornful salutation simply steeled my resolve. She seemed to see my presence as a logical progression: as if churchmen not only oppressed women; they also endorsed their murder.

I was goaded into attack by the rest of my party who felt equally affronted, though less by the slur on their integrity than the threat of an aborted walk. In my annoyance I clean forgot that my therapy confirmed their analysis; and that, far from trying to pull intellectual rank, I ought to be making common cause. Patronisingly – which is one word they could have pulled me up on – I offered them the chance to join us: to put their grievances to the test. But it was a challenge only one of their number took up.

His name was Mark. He's a Housing Officer from Southwark... You asked me before about faith. So much of life seems to me an act of faith: does God exist or does he simply fulfil a need; are we truly in love or just in love with the idea of being in love? And you might say your guess is as good as mine; if it weren't for grace. Grace removes the guesswork. And it was given back to me at the time of my greatest disgrace: the grace to know God and the grace to know Mark and, most miraculous of all, the grace to make the connection.

I spoke to him briefly in the pub. I always tried to make myself available for questions; although to judge by some you might have thought I was moonlighting as a pimp. It had come as no surprise to see a man amongst the pickets. There were often one or two, though they were sometimes hard to make out in the androgyny of their anoraks and from their reluctance to muscle in on what was primarily a women's cause... I've subsequently learnt that he's a friend of Vange's, but I refuse to let it worry me. I'm quite sure she won't have mentioned me. I hope – I know I'm beneath her contempt.

It was because he felt less threatened that he'd decided to tag along. And he was interested to hear what else I had to say. He'd always assumed that the word history... Easy mistake, I said. No, it wasn't, he replied; it was bloody stupid. Know your enemy... Words aren't our enemies, I said. And he looked at me steadily. That depends who you are... And I was suddenly conscious of the insults and gibes of effeminacy that the men in the pub were directing at one of their mates, who was trying to climb the central pillar using only his elbows and thighs. And they cut me to the quick.

The rest of the walk passed off without incident, until we arrived at the multi-storey car park which was our penultimate port of call. It stank of urine, which some of the group seemed to suppose we'd laid on specially: a sort of 'smell et lumière'. Although there was precious little light and even less illumination, at least at first. I began my blow-by-blow account of Marie Kelly's mutilations, which drew the usual audible shudders and an even louder response from Mark.

How did I have the gall to call that history? It was sheer hypocrisy. Why bother to invent such an elaborate pretext? Wouldn't it be simpler to organise jack-off parties in a morgue?

His presumably unintentional pun provoked an embarrassed titter; whilst a heavy man with the words 'love' and 'hate' tattooed on his knuckles cracked his fingers and warned him not to talk like that in front of his wife. Mark stared at him, seemingly stunned that anyone could find his words in the least offensive after mine. Then he turned back to me and asked whether I was aware that the Yorkshire Ripper had freely acknowledged the inspiration he'd drawn both from the black museums he'd visited and the pornography he'd found readily available during his youth. And at least that had been confined to the top shelves of newsagents, whereas I was peddling mine openly in the street.

I had no choice but to admit the charge. I was a pornographer. The women had been right. It was I who had the limited vocabulary as well as all the other limitations that entailed. I didn't simply use pornography; I promoted it. No, I presented it. To extend Mark's image, I was like a video of a young man masturbating with nothing more than his disdain of the viewer to keep him hard.

But now that's all in the past. I've thrown out the films and replaced the fantasies. I've owned up to everything, and not just in the confessional or the consulting room, but to the world at large. Although first he had to draw me out still further: What kind of man are you? he asked. I'm Jack the Ripper; I said. And the woman beside me screamed.

I apologised. I was no longer aiming to chill their blood; and I didn't believe in reincarnation, at least not bodily...

Although I believe unreservedly in the Incarnation. At last, my sense of the transcendence of life has returned... But to return to the Ripper: I was by no means his only manifestation. The reason he'd proved so elusive was that he'd assumed so many identities – identities, not alter egos: he was a master of deceit, not disguise. And the case could never be closed because he was still claiming his victims. There was a Jack the Ripper in every man. At which point two of the couples chose to leave.

Is that it, then? our tattooed friend asked. Isn't it enough? I replied. I couldn't believe anyone could still want more. But he clearly believed in getting his money's worth even if it killed him, or rather no matter who else it might have killed along the way. So I decided to take them back to the nineteenth century one final time.

And for the first time I jettisoned Donald's conclusions which until then I'd always followed to the letter: his government-inspired cover-up which had come to seem almost as sensational as the crimes it purported to explain. Instead I told them my own preferred solution, which I would never claim to be definitive; but then nor would I want it to be. That would let us all off the hook... Earlier this afternoon I telephoned Donald to resign my position. And when Echo answered, she scarcely spoke.

I've a further confession: I've done you, or at least your prints, a gross injustice. They may not be great art; but they have an unassuming confidence, a colourful competence, which is in perfect keeping with the room, this strangely comforting room. And as long as you like them... Each to his own: that's what I say... Oh yes, each to his very special own.

I found mine at Aldgate East Station. I was sitting alone on the platform, opposite a stark poster for War on Want, my usual feeling of loneliness at the end of a walk compounded by the events of the evening and the knowledge that it would be my last, when I suddenly felt a hand on my shoulder. Are we going the same way? he asked. I couldn't reply; I was amazed at the wealth of meaning he'd conveyed in such a terse phrase.

He was so relieved to have caught up with me; he'd been afraid he'd have to return another night. I was baffled. Did he realise what he was saying... how he was smiling? Oh, I think I've had my fill of Jack the Ripper, I replied. He was glad to hear it, and wondered who I'd find to take his place? You, I wanted to shout: you, you, you... I don't know, I said; we run a number of other walks: Dickens, Pepys, the banks of the Royal Thames... You, you, you, I wanted to shout, but my propriety betrayed me. Come and have a drink, he said, if you can spare the time. And my courage met me halfway, and the you became yes.

We took the tube to the Red Admiral: a large Victorian pub in Blackfriars with an incongruous collection of butterflies encased on its flock-papered walls. As we squeezed around an already overcrowded table he claimed that the whole of young and trendy 'gay London' went there. And once I'd left my jacket and my briefcase – and my apprehensions and my inhibitions – in the cloakroom, I wondered whether that might ever include me.

But the music drowned all introspection. There was a packed dance-floor; and I was nervous that at any moment Mark might call on me. But he didn't care for the mix. It brought back too many memories of Islington in the late seventies: in particular a band called Human League. So we sat and enjoyed the spectacle. One woman was in a wheelchair with lights that flashed on and off. And she'd made the chair an integral part of her body. She danced; she truly danced. And her fluidity put my two left feet to shame.

Are you sure you haven't painted this room, or repositioned the lighting? Then at least you must have had it unseasonably spring-cleaned? No? I could swear there was something. Well, never mind.

I sipped my lager: another new experience. I spluttered; the foam stuck to my chin. This morning he confessed that that was the moment when he fell in love with me... I realise now why the arm of this chair is frayed... He told me to stay still. Then he moved his hand towards me. Relax, he said; what was I afraid of? And he wiped the foam from my face with the tip of his right index finger; the tip of his left had been sliced off in a woodwork accident at school. Then he smeared the foam on his lips and pressed his finger between them. This time I couldn't hide it. You, I said; I'm afraid of you.

Afraid of me? he said; and yet you roam the streets of Whitechapel after dark? I know what to expect there, I said; I've a story to tell. And it was your story: yours, not the Ripper's, he said, that made me go as a picket and stay to pick up the guide. You didn't pick me up, I protested. Didn't I? he laughed, and carried straight on. I hated you when you were describing the killings; you did it far too well. But then when you broke out and spoke out so bravely I thought it was one of the most wonderfully vulnerable things I'd ever heard... I was amazed; was there a virtue in vulnerability? Had you planned it? he asked. No, I said; it was quite spontaneous. And the word tripped triumphantly off my tongue.

I smiled and sipped and spluttered again. Relax, he repeated; I'm not about to eat you – which is not to say I wouldn't like to try. It's the beer, I said feebly; it's the first time I've drunk it. Really? he asked;

where have you been all your life? That's a long story, I said. So? he said; I'm going nowhere. It's past eleven, I said; won't the pub soon have to close? You're so sweet, he said. That's a phrase he keeps on using. Me sweet? Then he pressed his hand on mine – his knuckles had the strength and glow of ivory – and leaned over and kissed me passionately on the mouth.

His lips had a slightly beery flavour, together with a tang of cigarette smoke, which reassured me. The unadulterated taste of him would have been too much. I felt so happy that I wanted to die – no: I want to live! And I want to live forever. I feel as protective of my future as I once did of my past. And there'll be no more pain. My legs are flesh and blood, not fire and ice and needles... and muscles, such powerful muscles. So you can add another name to the pantheon: Achilles, Hercules, Samson and me.

And Achilles doesn't have his heel, and Hercules doesn't have his labours, and Samson doesn't have his haircut; and I don't have my despair. And I laughed out loud. And he offered me a penny for my thoughts. And I laughed even louder to think that it would only be pennies between us – and proverbial ones at that, not three crisply compromising ten pound notes.

The music was too loud for us to talk and too nostalgic for him to enjoy; and so we finished our drinks and went back to his flat. He wouldn't take no for an answer; he didn't even phrase it as a question. And I was glad. He lives in the Elephant and Castle. I told him I'd never been there; although I'd always been attracted by the name. It's pretty basic, he said; but then I'm a pretty basic kind of person. I was sure that wasn't true, but I felt flattered that he'd thought it needed saying. And I was utterly disarmed by his charm.

Nothing could have prepared me for the flat. My senses reeled. It was in the middle of a row of Victorian villas which were difficult to make out as all the street-lights had been smashed. On his front door he'd pinned a mock-mediaeval sign: *Eintritt Verboten, Ein Haus des Pestes*. I baulked; he assured me it was just a joke. Wasn't it provocative? I asked. He certainly hoped so. And I remembered a phrase about frightened people inoculating themselves with humour. And I followed him in; though I didn't laugh.

We went into the bedroom. He unrolled his futon. I was afraid that I'd end up tossing and turning all night... And so I did, but not in frustration and not alone. He unbuttoned my shirt; I felt like a gift-wrapped parcel. He undressed himself; it was no mere routine, but an almost mystical ritual akin to the vesting before mass. And I felt part of a worldwide communion of lovers: no longer an emotional tourist trying to pass himself off as a guide.

He asked about my boyfriends. I told him I'd only ever had one. He refused to believe it. He said it was such a waste: a beautiful man like me... Don't worry, I shan't embarrass you with his compliments. Though to my amazement, I wasn't embarrassed at all. I told him I'd never spent the night with a man before. He laughed; I was offended. He said I was too sensitive, and then nipped my ear quite sharply as if to prove his point. I yelped. He nuzzled it better; which I said made the pain worthwhile. He laughed again. He was laughing at life, he added quickly. And so was I.

I betted he'd had boyfriends though. And he ran his finger down my nose and replied that that would be telling. And he ran a finger down my spine and down my legs and then up and... I said I was glad. At that moment I wanted him to have made love to every man in the world: although within limits. The more love there'd been in him, the more there'd be for me. And the more men he'd known, the greater the commitment he'd be making when he tossed them all aside. And I nibbled the hair on his chest; it reminded me of Pan: the god of the woodland. All that loves is holy. That night I felt a god myself.

I needn't have feared. Those films hadn't dulled my sensibilities. I found ways of making love to him which were specific to us and didn't conform to some blueprint in my mind. You're so good, he told me; which touched me, as I knew I was just a novice. But he was good enough for both of us and the rest of the world besides. He slid his tongue into my mouth like an oyster. I giggled and gargled and gurgled with delight. The Bible may talk of speaking with tongues, but after years of chapped lips and dry pecks on powdered cheeks, it's kissing with them that means most to me.

He made me feel the uniqueness of my body; and that every lump and clump and crease and crevice and fold of skin and hair was valuable – was invaluable to him. He lingered for what seemed an eternity on what'd seemed an indistinguishable inch of flesh on my side; but he distinguished it by his attention. It was special: it was him; it was me.

And I responded to him. I seemed instinctively to know the ways to please him. They were all very safe and very simple. And he didn't ask for more as if being with me were pleasure enough. And I felt no pressure except the lightness of his skin on mine. And I realised that I'd never before been so close to anyone in either body or spirit and that, despite all my best endeavours, the two couldn't be divorced. The body wasn't just clothes for the spirit; it was the spirit. And I had news for all the ancients who'd endlessly debated the seat of the soul; I knew.

Was this the way to God? Was this the way to God? Was this the way to God? Surely.

I woke up first. Initially I was confused. I'd never slept in another man's bed before. To me a bed had been as private as a coffin. It was only paupers who lay in mass graves. But now I knew what true riches were. And I refused to feel guilty. It was if a great weight had been lifted; or rather the sword of Damocles had dropped and then bounced straight off me like a child's retractable toy.

I looked at his face: his dreamy moon-face dozing on the pillow. I committed every detail to my memory: the heavy-lidded, slightly eastern eyes with their long, thick lashes; the generous, sensuous, Merry Monarch lips; and the short, luxuriant, almost monkish hair. But above all I was transfixed by the freshly sprouted stubble on his chin which was at once the most natural and the most erotic sight I'd ever seen. And I realised to my joy that they too were one and the same.

I slid my tongue tentatively over his jaw, which felt both hard and soft and strong and gentle. And I was convinced that this was the greatest miracle: to wake up and feel life growing beside me. Not to have to go to the window and look down at the garden and commune with the flowers; but to lean over: to see Mark; to see man; to see God.

The light streamed through the curtains. I looked around the room, which was a mess. At first I thought we must have caused it ourselves during the night; and I was glad. I wanted to have disordered his room – to have disorientated his life. But then I realised it was layered almost archaeologically... He stirred. I was impatient to wake him. I pondered the protocol; but my inexperience impeded me. Then he stirred again; and I felt his fingers on my stomach. So I closed my eyes and pretended to be fast asleep.

He proved the most amazing alarm clock. I rubbed the sleep from my eyes as he flicked his tongue in my ear. We made love again... Is that usual? Do you and your wife...? That is on days when you don't have to take the children to school. Or do you have a nanny? I mean for the children... Oh I can't begin to tell you how powerfully his tongue... I'm sorry; I know we can take that as read. When we sat up, he asked if I wanted any breakfast. I lobbed the question back. He laughed and said he thought he'd just had it. So I smiled and said that I felt quite full myself.

I wondered whether he'd want to see me again. I was afraid he might either have been drunk or indiscriminate. But now I know he felt the same this morning as he did last night, and just the same as me. We can't meet tonight because he has some sort of Men's Group. It sounds deadly dull; but I was determined not to show my disappointment, nor be seen to make demands. So he's invited me to dinner tomorrow... And I've arranged to take my toothbrush as well as a bottle of wine.

Thirteen

I'm sorry if you were caught unawares, sir, but then that's the joy of these walks: you can never be sure where they'll lead. Of course if you wish to lodge a complaint that's your privilege; but I can assure you that it will be nothing compared to the one I've lodged against myself. You'll find the address and telephone number on the back of the leaflet. And if anyone else should require one, I've a stack in my briefcase. They also give full details of all our – their other tours. And for a complete change of scene, might I recommend Mysteries and Mistresses of Mayfair or Leafy and Literary Hampstead? Although I'm afraid that unless you can put together a party, you may have to wait until spring.

This is where I leave you. For anyone wanting to use public transport, simply carry straight on down the main road and you'll come to Aldgate East tube station, as well as a regular bus service to both the City and the West End... It only remains for me to thank you for choosing to walk with 'Famous Feet'.

I know you were worried for me, although you'd hate to have to admit it; just as I'd hate to have to admit to any dependence on you. But the analysis isn't all one-way. I can read your mind too; and its drift was painfully predictable. You were convinced he'd prove another Jack – or even a combination of both of them. But your cynicism does you no credit. You must learn to be more trusting. Though it can hardly help to be stuck in this airless room all day long listening to so many sad, sick stories. You ought to go out more: enjoy yourself: meet some new people... Oh Lord! What am I...? That's just what... Oh Lord!

Do you mind if I stroll about? I'm sorry if it distracts you, but I find it impossible to sit still. I have to listen to my body... Yes, it was me who said that. I've finally found my own unique language. Unique but universal: anyone can understand it; you don't need a dictionary, or a degree, or a course in Esperanto. It's the language of the body; it's the language of love... I lie down with my love; I lay down my love. 'A bundle of myrrh is my well-beloved unto me; he shall lie all night betwixt my breasts...'

The Bible is such an amazing book: not only a well of wisdom but an encyclopaedia of emotion; and there's not one it fails to comprehend. I used to be embarrassed by the Song of Solomon. I felt it rather let the side down, as if it had slipped in courtesy of some less than scrupulous editor and was far more suitable for a Hebrew Scheherazade than an Anglican priest. But I was so wrong. If the Bible is a revelation of God's purposes, then the most precious of all is his gift of love. 'And the leopard shall lie down with the kid...' And I lie in bed next to Mark; and he breathes so strongly and resolutely, although without the least suspicion of a snore. And his breath is as hot as his blood: passionate and powerful like a blazing fire – but safe: a fire to warm your hands by, not to burn down a house.

Mark: such a fine name, don't you think? A firm no-nonsense name: the name of the first and my favourite gospel, and the patron saint of the Edensor village church. It suggests accuracy: arrows hitting their mark; achievement: a man of mark; elegance: a mark of distinction; foresight: mark my words. It's a name you can't mimic or shorten: a name that's sufficient unto itself: a truly Christian name.

I wish you had the chance to meet him. You have a lot in common – at any rate he has a degree in psychology. I find that rather alarming. I keep wondering when he'll see through me. But I've no need to worry; it's all past history. He'd have to be a historian, not a psychologist – no, an antiquarian: it's ancient history. It bears not the slightest relation to the man I am now.

He continually asks me about myself. I suppose it must be the training. I was afraid I'd ramble randomly; but I've found it remarkably easy to put my life into some sort of shape. And credit where it's due: whatever else, you have shown me a way into my story. I'm no longer just an unconnected muddle; I've a beginning and a middle and the beginnings of an end.

Not that I've told him everything. I never even mentioned Christ until I realised that Vange had pre-empted me and so I had no choice but to come clean – no, that's not the right phrase at all. And then I emphasised the theological discipline rather than the vocational training, as though my concern were essentially academic. I was afraid that if he knew the truth, he'd lose interest. And at that moment I set more store by his good opinion than my own.

But my fears proved unfounded. He finds my faith a constant amusement. He sees Catholic ritual as the epitome of the homosexual sensibility and me as something from the pages of his favourite novelist: Ronald Firbank. As I'd never heard of him, I couldn't tell whether to feel flattered. So he lent me his collected edition. Although so far any connection seems wilfully opaque. It's strange, but the more people you know, the more books you have to read in order to understand them. I always assumed it would be quite the opposite. I suppose it's what's meant by life imitating art.

His favourite poet was also new to me: Thom Gunn... You must be beginning to think we make love in a library. And yet you couldn't be more wrong. It's just that in bed the other night, whilst he was kissing me but before the kisses became all-embracing, he began to recite one of his favourite poems and then asked me to do the same. I realised that the only two I knew by heart were *The Wreck of the Deutschland* and Gray's *Elegy*; neither of which felt especially apt. So I rolled over and stopped his mouth; he revelled in my taking the initiative. While I resolved to buy an anthology of love-lyrics and study them religiously – no, amorously – from Anon right through to the present day.

I'm head over heels in love; I'm head over heels in life. And most of all I'm in love with his kisses. I never cease to wonder at their richness. How could I have done without them for so long? His mouth is so much deeper and wider than I'd ever have imagined... I sometimes feel like Jonah inside the whale. Is that normal? I've no means of comparison – only of delight. Jack never kissed me. His body was more open than any human being's had a right to be; and yet his lips always remained tightly shut.

I love his nakedness... Jack was his clothes; his nakedness was quite superficial. There was no eroticism; he had to supply that with his whips and leather. The fetish was the message. And his body was as hard as his heart. Try as I did, I could never make him soften. It was like trying to draw blood from a stone. He once told me he'd lose all self-respect if he ever 'came' with a client. What a perverse way to measure self-respect, I thought. And yet it was no more so than mine.

But Mark's brought me more self-respect than I'd have believed possible: and in the most unexpected way. I always thought that if anyone ever did love me, it would be for some quality of my mind or spirit; but he refutes that entirely and claims it's my body that fascinates him. According to him it's an amazing adventure playground: with its swings and slides and climbing frames... not to mention the trampoline. And I find the idea thrilling although the image inaccurate. It makes me sound like a child when I'm a fully grown, no, finally growing man.

So I'm beginning a new life, and how appropriate that it will soon be Christmas. This year I won't have to rack my brains for New Year's resolutions; I'll have to struggle to pare them down. And in my new life I'll be surrounded by new people. Mark's giving a dinner party on Saturday for me to meet a few of his friends. Vange is coming with her girlfriend, Gaia. To be truthful I'm quite terrified; I almost wish I could fall ill... No, anything but that! I'm not superstitious; but I know better than to tempt fate.

There's one guest I'm even more apprehensive of meeting, particularly as he'll also be a host: Adrian, Mark's flat-mate. I haven't told you anything about him; but then initially Mark said nothing to me- Though don't worry; it's all quite above board. They 'lived together' for six years; and when that broke up a couple of years ago they continued to live together without the inverted commas. In one sense I find it reassuring: if my body should ever cease to be an adventure playground, Mark won't cease to be a friend. And yet it's also rather threatening: like stepping into a half-dead man's shoes.

He's flying home on Thursday from Holland, where he's spent the past month studying the latest trends in contemporary dance. He used to be a dancer himself, before he tore the hamstring which hamstrung his career, and re-emerged to found the London International Dance festival, or LID. For all I know you may be a devoted balletomane; I rarely venture beyond the grand tier at Covent Garden. Although after everything he's told me, I long to repair the loss.

And yet, while I can't help but commend his loyalty, I could wish that he'd cite him a little less often. After all, I don't quote Jonathan morning, noon and night – but then the relationship was hardly the same. And I can scarcely expect to have become the most important person in his life after a mere eight days. I'd certainly find it hard to respect anyone so fickle. And yet what does that make me? He's already by far the most important in mine.

Above all, he's given me back my future: which is the most perfect paradox. I've often tried, though without much success, to define my vocation. I even recall a few strained attempts here. But at last I can accept the conventional wisdom which sees it most simply as a gift of love. For that in its widest sense is what he's enabled me to discover. And so now more than ever I'd like to put it to the test. I want to celebrate the Eucharist. I want to baptise babies. I want to bless couples of all persuasions...

But that's just it: because of my own persuasion, I know that I can't. I'm sure I've no need to remind you of the current cravenness of the Church of England. When it comes to love, the Broad Church is still so narrow-minded. Even the bishops are forever falling over themselves to appease the bigots. And yet it's their authority which at my ordination I'd have to bind myself to obey.

Jonathan used to declare that he'd have to cross his fingers when he came to take the vow to uphold the Thirty-nine Articles; which in his view were too many by half. But then he was a born fighter, ever ready to defend his cause; whereas I intend to lead a quiet life. And yet I refuse to live a lie or at any rate one life in the vicarage and another in the vestry: squeezing my identity into a pigeon-hole and hanging my sexuality on a hook.

No, now that I've discovered my gift of love, I'm determined to give it full expression; which I can do far more naturally loving Mark than staying celibate with Christ. And I shall be a priest in my heart, which is no empty form of words, since I no longer see the priesthood as a special case, let alone a special caste. On the contrary, the priesthood of all believers has never felt more real.

So I've written to both Father Leicester and my Director of Ordinands explaining my decision to withdraw from training. Which in turn removes the need for my coming here. I know you'll consider it premature, but I'm convinced it's for the best. I wouldn't like you to think I'm not grateful for all you've done. It's just that the time for reflection has passed; I now have to live. And if you don't mind I'd rather leave straight away. I hate goodbyes; I've already said far too many. But then perhaps that's another word we should restore to its primal meaning: and so 'God be with you', and God bless.

PART TWO

1665 AND 1989–90
PRIESTS AND PLAGUES

One

This traditional village square seems as apt a place as any to introduce ourselves to Eyam, which, although pronounced monosyllabically, is actually rooted in two Saxon words: *ey* meaning water and *ham* meaning home. With its weathered sandstone cottages and slated roofs, its architecture is typical of the Hope Valley – a name which I feel sure you'll consider truly felicitous by the end of our tour – and yet its history is unique.

Last night my invitation to guide this walk was met with almost universal bafflement. I wasn't surprised. Besides, with so little time to spare, those of you who wanted to sightsee might have preferred to make for Chatsworth or Buxton or the Blue John mines, rather than an obscure village with ostensibly nothing to recommend it but its proximity to our Retreat. But I can assure you that that's the least of its attractions. These streets have a story to tell and it's one that merits a mention alongside those of Marathon and Masada. And yet for those of you racing through the battle-weary memories of your schooldays, not a single drop of blood was shed. Their enemy was altogether more elusive: the Great Plague.

There are many recorded instances of pestilence in Western Europe before the epidemics of 1665 and 1666, the most lethal of which, the Black Death, in the five years between 1346 and 1351, wiped out between a third and a half of the entire population or an estimated 25,000,000 people. And in the following three centuries this island saw several further outbreaks, some of which in fact destroyed larger proportions of the population than the one commonly known as Great. And yet I maintain that it's in the exemplary response of this small, sleepy village, that we discover the true justification for such an epithet.

And today I mean to give their tale another airing – and not in some airless lecture hall, but out here in the open. So to learn how the infection spread from the capital 160 miles away to this secluded society of small-holders and lead-miners, and about the path it then took, follow me.

How tedious life must be for you people who know everything. The world can hold no surprises and the imagination no suspense. In the eternal debate between free will and predetermination I wonder where therapists fit in. I don't suppose you'd claim to be all-powerful, but as to all-knowing…?

Of course, you were never in any doubt that I'd end up asking you to take me back. I admit I was over-hasty. Life isn't so simple. You don't just meet your prince and marry him and settle down happily ever after – well, maybe you do if you live in a storybook castle, but it's a rather different story in the Elephant and Castle, at least when you live in your lover's ex-lover's flat with that same ex-lover still very much in residence.

I moved in on Christmas Eve – did you get my card, by the way? – in time for the best Christmas I can ever remember, at any rate since my mother died. And I was determined to let nothing spoil it, not even Vange's Happy Winter Solstice card, nor her gift, '101 Things to do in a Boring Sermon'; I forced myself to smile… Mark bought me these jeans which he said were deliberately a size too small. I still can't make out why. Whilst Adrian's present was indescribably obscene.

But then he takes a positive pride in being perverse. We live in a flat of studied eccentricity. From the outside it looks quite ordinary: the top two floors at the centre of a row of mid-Victorian villas; but once over the threshold every trace of normality has been swept away.

The living-room has been designed, or rather planted, as an African jungle. It was adapted from the decor of a ballet he once presented: after Douanier Rousseau – a very long way after if you ask me. The original decor was considered a failure, but its transformation has been hailed as a triumph. Although what worries me most is what might be lurking in the undergrowth... There are no chairs, simply sawn-off stumps, and clumps of felt ferns and grasses. Luxuriant foam-rubber plants climb the walls and canvas branches drop from the ceiling, studded with exotic insects and birds. An array of coloured lights streams through the foliage, which can be altered to reflect his mood or suit the occasion. And the entire room is a paean to the artificiality which is his philosophy of life.

But the area where he's allowed his imagination freest rein is the lavatory – yes, honestly – which he declares the most important room in any house. You open the door, which the cracked enamel sign helpfully designates 'Gentlemen', on to a working urinal and an equally authentic cubicle complete with graphic graffiti and revolting rhymes. He filched the fittings from the builders who were stripping the one outside his office. Although Mark claims he'd become such a permanent fixture, he must have established squatter's rights.

On my first visit I was quite constipated with self-consciousness, especially as the only paper appeared to be carefully torn strips of tabloid hanging from a rusty ring. And I know it's intended as a joke, but then I've never much cared for lavatorial humour. Mark seems to think that I've no sense of humour at all.

I never know where I stand; I'm treading on tenterhooks... Is that a mixed metaphor? Well, it's hardly surprising when I feel so mixed-up in every way... Almost the first comment Adrian addressed to me was that to know him was to love him. In which case I can only conclude that he's a hard man to know. He makes fun of my religion. Perhaps I do lack a sense of humour; but when I was explaining the subject of my abandoned thesis, Sects and Parties amongst the early Christians, he said that it sounded a hoot and offered to help with the research. It took me some time to work out the reason. And even if I do slur my consonants, would you have made that mistake?

He deliberately sets out to embarrass me. He flirts with me openly and if I ask him to stop, he just winks and says I love it really; when nothing could be further from the truth. I don't find him in the least attractive. I know it's wrong to judge on appearances, but it's as if all his quirky behaviour is reflected in his looks. He's practically bald, which he insists is a sign of virility... though you should know... and yet he wears his scraggy strands of hair in a pathetic pigtail. Then he cultivates a wisp of a beard in the cleft of his chin which, along with his pronounced dimples, makes his head seem almost symmetrical, like one of those drawings that are still faces upside down. And he has two badly chipped teeth, which he claims to have broken in a kiss.

It may well be true; but then I can never be sure... And Mark's not much help. He defers to him at practically every turn. And I'm no longer convinced that their relationship was as equal as he'd like to imply. It's not only that he's six years younger. If it comes to that I'm ten years younger than him; which is not of the least significance. But they're such different people. Adrian's far more flighty and frivolous; and yet in his company Mark changes quite markedly – no, that can't be the word I require.

I'm sure that all our lives would be a lot easier if he could only find himself a boyfriend. He can't help but feel excluded when he sees Mark with me. Though it's not for want of trying; he seems to meet somebody new every other night. Which rarely makes for the most relaxed of breakfasts. I sometimes think he picks them up out of pique: as if to imply that I'm an equally temporary measure. In which case it's my turn to laugh: last, loudest and longest. Ha!

Although it's little wonder he's so unfulfilled when the objects of his desire are so unrealistic. At the moment he's set his sights on an Arts Council messenger whom he insists is as straight as a die. I tried to make light of it and told him he ought to pray to St Jude, the patron saint of lost causes. He said he'd rather stick with St Judy, the patron saint of self-pity. And I was completely flummoxed. I'm having to learn a whole new iconography; and one that's even more self-contained.

Not that there's much scope for my old one. I don't even dare to put up an icon of Our Lady after his lecture on the sexual subtext of religious art. I've always been deeply moved by Bernini's *St Theresa*, but he told me that I wouldn't know a multiple orgasm if it hit me in the face. And as to St Sebastian: did I really have no idea why he was every gay man's favourite saint? I supposed it was because of his muscular definition... Though when he explained the symbolism of the arrows penetrating the flesh I could have wept.

But then he seems determined to reduce everything to its basest level. His friends almost to a ma – to a person, are women and gay men; and when they're together they speak of heterosexual men as if they're practically another species at an earlier stage of evolution who've still to come down from the trees. And yet he's the one who's living in the jungle. While his pursuit of sex is just as obsessive and his innuendo just as crude.

We only have to sit in a restaurant for him to start making eyes at whoever comes to take our order. He sees no harm; it's all part of the service. Besides, he insists that ninety per cent of waiters are gay; which he puts down to an unbeatable combination of ritual subservience and the chance to ruin everyone's meal. And Mark, who claims to deplore every stereotype, loudly laughs.

But when I suggested that he could hardly object to people taking offence at his sexuality when he himself winked and ogled and awarded every personable young man points out of ten as baldly as any nipple-counting *Sun*-reader, Mark flatly denied the comparison... I'd failed to appreciate the subtleties of parody. The distinction was all in the delivery. Considerations of gender were an irrelevance: homosexuals were different from heterosexuals except for what they did in bed.

Though I'm afraid I'm at even more of a loss with paradox... And besides bed is where the bulk of our problems seem to lie – there, I've said it; why don't you smile? In fact it was Mark who insisted I rang. And it can't have been easy for him; he has extremely ambivalent feelings towards all this. He'd originally intended to practise psychiatry himself. But the more he read, the more he saw how it'd been employed as an instrument of oppression. And he quoted with relish the eminent Freudian's slip: 'In my profession psychiatry is no longer regarded as a disease.'

His main objection is to attempt to explain – and hence explain away – homosexuality. No amount of theory can ever hope to encompass human desire. He's as unshakable on that score as the most fervid fundamentalist to whom every comma is a divine command. It's as if he's afraid that too precise a definition could be used as a pretext for a 'cure': a prospect invidious enough at the best of times, but quite iniquitous at a time of a truly incurable disease.

And there's the rub... and the nub of the problem. He's the one who constantly condemns official complacency; he's the one who manages Brockway Lodge – a local hostel for men with HIV. And yet at times he can be almost cavalier. I don't want to go into details... Oh, why should I have to think of body fluids when I want to think of love? I find the whole notion so very distasteful, like the advert for mattresses which illustrates how much sweat they absorb as we sleep. Which in turn makes me think of Jack... No, that's not true! I never think of him at all.

He seems to want to consume me – please stop me if I embarrass you; I no longer suppose my sex life to be your sole concern – he laps up my semen as though it were some life-giving elixir and then buries himself in my bowels, whilst begging me to do the same. But it's not that easy. So in the middle of everything he breaks off to quote me statistics on the protective powers of gastric juices; which, however reassuring, is hardly conducive to romance.

He's determined not to let an opportunistic virus come to serve as an agent of repression. And he's particularly scathing about the equation of sexual activity with death, which has been given new currency; although I thought it was as old as time or at any rate as St Augustine, for whom Adam's sin brought with it both desire and mortality... Christians, he declared; they claim to bring joy to the world and simply fill it full of their neuroses and pain.

And he may well be right. Perhaps I have taken St Augustine and all his works too much to heart. I have quite enough sin of my own without swallowing anyone else's. So my body becomes a barrier, as he rubs himself off on top of me. And his orgasm leaves a slug-like trail across my chest.

He claims that my fears are ridiculously primitive, but they're no more primitive than his desires. His yearning to take me in his mouth and ingest me seems almost cannibalistic. Although what disturbs me most is that they might spring from much the same source. For if Freud were right and the Mass does recall the eating of the primal father, then when I see Mark so hungry for me and I think of myself hungry at the altar I do wonder what exactly it is that I'm eating: his virtue or his virility? His body and blood or...? And I can blot out the image, but not the idea.

But I still love him as much as ever; you must appreciate that. And although it can sometimes be difficult last thing at night, it's always wonderful first thing in the morning. I think that's my favourite time of day: when I wake up and he's still asleep, and I can watch him dreaming or at any rate his eyelids fluttering, which I take to be a sign. If I had dreams they'd all be filled with him... And then I shake him awake and he has to make a move, whilst I can linger languidly. And I relish his irritation which I know to be only skin-deep... and he's so deliciously thin-skinned.

How I love his skin; I'd happily spend all life long exploring it. It has such amazing definition, as though it were already under a microscope: I want to focus on every follicle... And I love his stubble. Sometimes he won't shave for two or three days; but he doesn't look swarthy: simply sultry. And yet stubble fails to do it justice; it's more like a field ripe for harvest. And I'm back in the countryside of my youth: of hops and hedges and haystacks – and hair.

I wish I knew what he sees in me. He's so dark and exciting, whereas I'm so blond and bland. I was nineteen before I needed to shave. Even now at five o'clock my face shows no sign of a shadow. He says my skin reminds him of a peach. And then he bites me. He has more of a problem when he tries to nibble my nipples. He never seems able to find them. And I must admit they're almost imperceptible compared to his, which are so elongated they seem more like earlobes. Would you say that that was a sign of a more passionate nature or just a more passionate life?

I worry about his past life, and despite all my best endeavours it seems to have conveyed itself to him. He accuses me of acting as though his body were in some way unclean – although nothing could be further from the truth: if anyone's body's unclean, it's mine. But at least I had that test at the clinic, so I know I'm exposing him to no danger. Whereas for all sorts of reasons both practical and political he refuses to take one himself.

And it's such a difficult subject to broach, especially since I already have my result... a bit like boasting of passing an exam to someone who's yet to hear. Sometimes I feel that because he's so involved in the issue he must know best; then at others I fear that it might have lulled him into a false sense of security – even invulnerability. And the question's no longer academic because we appear to want quite different things from one another. I'm so happy just to rub up against him; whilst he wants... he desperately wants something more.

But then he seems to see the sexual act as crucial to his whole identity. It's as if it's not simply a bodily impulse but a political imperative, with its public pursuit the symbol of liberation from years of furtive privacy. We didn't fight – we didn't die, he says, simply for the chance to hear *Billy Budd* or see a David Hockney painting. We fought for the right to fuck... And I feel his words pierce me like a personal reproach.

I protest that I'll do anything to please him and I know that that's the one thing above all else that would; so my reluctance belies my claim. Two weeks ago someone doctored the 'No parking' sign outside the house to 'No fucking'; and he swore, not altogether frivolously, that it must have been me. And he blackmails me with my need for him, which is quite the cruellest form of extortion. Last night he declared that it was the only way I could prove that I truly loved him. If not, then we'd gone about as far as we could go. And I'm so afraid that he didn't just mean in bed.

Then he took out a condom like an elastoplast. I still refused. So he took out another and another and asked what if he put on three or even four. I was so nervous that I tried to make light of it. Why was it that important? Hadn't he told me the first night we were together that the best sex was all in the mind? And out of the blue and out of the darkness he hit me hard across the jaw... I know you've been too discreet to mention the bruise. Then he was all solicitude and I was all embarrassment. And we indulged in what Nanny used to describe as making up on the pillow; which always conjured up the most incongruous image of my parents' secret pillow fights... I was such a child.

He continued to press his point. As always he had a ready supply of statistics. He assured me that the condoms were 99.99% safe. And I can't pretend that it's the last .01% which has proved the stumbling block. I don't want to be penetrated! – I'm sorry – I don't want to be possessed! I see his penis like a smouldering poker and I picture Edward II being smothered to death. And I'm afraid.

But to him there's only one valid source of fear; anything else is self-indulgence. And he proffered his prophylactics like a universal panacea. He even offered me a choice of colour, as intently as Echo with her paint-chart. Though when I suggested blood-red he rounded on me even more savagely than before. He swore that the virus had proved a godsend to me. I was the one person outside of the drug companies to have benefited. It had allowed me to rationalise my repressions and legitimise my lack of love.

I couldn't believe that he could be so callous. But do you think that he might have been right? Is there a deficiency in me: a fatal – no please, not fatal – hole in my heart? I need to know. I'm afraid that last year I may have scrutinised myself too closely and now I'm locked into the process. While the danger wasn't so much that pornography would destroy my body's spontaneity as psychotherapy my mind's.

But Mark has set his hopes on you; and I can see no alternative. I'm desperate for help. It must be clear by now that he means more to me than life itself; and if anything were to go wrong... No, that's just another sort of blackmail and I ought to know better. And yet it seems so unfair that after all I went through before I should find myself back here. Once again my future is in your hands. Only now it's no longer my priesthood, but my love.

Two

These are known as the three Plague Cottages and apart from the modern roofs they're very much as they would have been in 1665. It was in this central one, as you may already have gathered from the plaque, that George Viccars, the first – though by no means the last – of the Eyam victims, died... One word of warning: while these three are undoubtedly authentic, several of the plaques we'll come across were put up for the Festival of Britain and are based more on tradition than hard fact. Although since we are traditionalists at least as much as historians, I see no reason for that to deter us.

And tradition has it that George Viccars was an itinerant tailor who lodged here with Mary Cooper, the widow of a lead-miner, and her two young sons. One morning in early September 1665 he received a package of material from London – and later, in the parish church, you'll be able to see what's reputed to be its original chest. As the fabric was damp, he hung it in front of the fire to dry; at which point his fate and that of the entire village was sealed. In case such rashness seems scarcely credible, try to remember that contemporary communications were extremely basic. He may not even have known of the infection that was ravaging the capital. Nor, since it wasn't until the late nineteenth century that the bubonic bacillus was finally identified, could he have had any inkling of the danger of exposing contaminated cloth to heat.

Besides, the heat may not have been critical, as it's been shown that plague germs can survive for a considerable length of time even in dry cloth at a moderate temperature. And there've been many recorded instances of such delayed effect, most notably in Paris where the discovery of ancient infected bandages in a recently demolished building led to a serious epidemic. Whilst in Eyam itself in the mid-eighteenth century five men, digging up what had once been one of the burial grounds, chanced upon some old linen and immediately fell ill: three of them never to recover.

Which makes it all the more remarkable that the villagers don't simply take pride in their past but positively identify themselves by it; these three buildings are named Plague Cottages not simply in the way that a pub might be called the Jack the Ripper, in order to tap a market, but rather to keep the memory alive. For they know that they have the contagion to thank for their rich soil of history. It was George Viccars and Thomas and Mary Thorpe and Edward and Jonathan Cooper, all of whose names you can read in front of you, who fertilised their future and, both practically and poetically, enabled these gardens to grow.

But in September 1665 the plague presented a far more desolate picture; and to chart its course, we must first cross the main road.

Mark thinks that all our problems, both personal and political, stem from religion. And what's more he seems to hold me uniquely responsible for the many centuries of injustice meted out by the Church. I've become his private whipping-boy – oh, don't worry; I don't mean literally; he's not another Jack. And he's adamant that it's quite impossible to be both Christian and gay... Christian and homosexual perhaps. Although I'm still not sure that I fully appreciate the distinction. But he insists that it's as much a contradiction as a Jewish anti-semite: another charge I've had levelled at me before now.

But I no longer have the slightest difficulty in reconciling my faith and my sexuality. I've moved on. Which wasn't simply a question of explaining away a few inconvenient Biblical passages – leaving Leviticus to one side like the lettuce in a salad – but of reassessing the book as a whole. If St Paul can be so self-evidently mistaken in I Corinthians 7, where he couples his call for chastity with the claim that the world will very soon come to an end, why nearly two thousand years later should it surprise us that he can be equally misguided elsewhere? Similarly, why allow ourselves to be side-tracked into academic arguments that the prohibitions in the Old Testament were essentially aimed at ritual uncleanliness, when a similar injunction against allowing people of diseased limbs access to the Temple has clearly never troubled the heads of the nuns at Lourdes?

The Bible isn't an oracle. It wasn't spelt out on tablets of stone, but laboriously transcribed over hundreds of years, leaving considerable scope for individual interpretation and an even wider margin for error. So it's not just the revelation of God to man, but his revelation through him; and the preposition is all. The only certain revelation of God is the Incarnation of Jesus Christ. And not once did Our Lord condemn my sexuality or for that matter anyone else's. In fact he said remarkably little on the subject and what he did was quite specific to the technicalities of divorce.

Not that I could ever go along with Jonathan in his description of the Bible as a sequence of myths, mistranslations, poetic licence and prejudice; or patronise it like a literary critic by praising the poetry as though it were merely a collection of occasional verse. On the contrary, I believe it to be far and away the most profound record both of God's purposes for man and of man's quest for God. Nevertheless, it's dangerously unrealistic to expect divine truths to emerge freely like a moth that's been trapped between the pages of a musty tome.

So at last I've felt able to return to communion. And I choose my word with care. For it's now the fellowship of Christ which I long to share as much as his actual body. But how and where? At St Dunstan's we lived a life of prayer. There was as real a presence in our worship as in our sacraments. But when the community is displaced, the communion becomes just another form of words. And I sit in silent isolation, conscious not of the unity of the spirit but only of the inadequacy of the sermon and the discomfort of the church.

And I take issue with the replacement of the old liturgies, in a misguided attempt at accessibility; as if meaning could somehow be divorced from words. And yet it's not only poetry that's lost in translation, but tradition. We're asked to pray, 'Forgive us our debts, as we forgive our debtors'; which may be true to the original Sermon but always makes me feel like Shylock. Indeed, the whole empty exercise leaves me as unmoved and uninvolved as the Hebrew services of my youth.

I may not have been altogether frank with you *vis-à-vis* my Jewishness. I may not have been altogether frank with myself. My aunt said I simply disliked being different. And it's true that there can be no greater stickler for conformity than an English public schoolboy. But I wouldn't have minded being different as long as it were for a cause in which I believed.

And Shylock's a case in point. At school I learnt to love Shakespeare. One year they put on *The Merchant of Venice*. I auditioned for Lorenzo; I longed to speak the lover's lines at Belmont. But they insisted I played the Jew; even though I couldn't have felt less like an old moneylender: a man with a daughter and ducats and hatred in his heart. I'd never felt hatred at all until then. But the producers could see no further than their noses – or rather, mine.

So, despite my inconveniently Roman profile, they considered me perfectly cast. I continually stuttered over the line 'If you prick us, do we not bleed?' while the other boys laughed at my special pleading. It wasn't that they were particularly anti-semitic, simply ignorant – which I suppose amounts to much the same. They looked themselves up in Debrett and me in the dictionary: I was 'a grasping and extortionate usurer', QED; and I became deeply ashamed of my family's bank. So never let anyone try to persuade you that words can't hurt. I was black and blue.

And how can anyone propose to take the words of the Bible literally when even the dictionary defines them so loosely? And in the hands of my schoolfellows those words became weapons of abuse. So I tried to let them bounce off me. I told myself that I was suffering for Christ. But the bulk of their gibes and the burden of my guilt was rather that it was Christ who had suffered for me – and not on my behalf, but on my account. And beneath the taunts I could hear the strain of the cruellest verse in the entire Bible: 'His blood be on us, and on our children.' Are the millions of pints that have been spilt in the name of that phrase ever since yet another literal revelation of the will of God?

I wanted to redeem myself, and not just from the sin of Adam but from the sin of Israel. And even though I'd yet to be confirmed, I longed to take the sacraments every day so that by filling myself full of Christ's blood my own might be washed clean. I seized whatever opportunity I could; and at Edensor where there was none, I celebrated alone.

I blush – I know I blush – at the memory; but I set up a makeshift altar in my mother's dressing-room where I performed my solitary office every day, until my aunt chanced to discover me. She'd noticed wisps of smoke and was afraid of another fire; I must have been over-enthusiastic in my swinging of the thurible – or rather the kitchen scales which were standing in for it – even then. And she... I'm sorry; I know I shouldn't laugh, but from the look of horror on her face you'd have thought she'd seen a ghost. Although I suppose in a way she had. For in the absence of anything tailor-made I was wearing my mother's wedding-dress as a surplice and her lace shawl as a cope.

She was appalled by my appearance and still more so when she discovered its purpose. I think she'd have found even transvestism preferable to transubstantiation. She fired a broadside at the chaplain to the effect that I must he excused – refused – attendance at chapel, which to my tormentors was further proof that I was endowed with the luck of the Devil – or at any rate the guile of the Jews. Although even they fell silent when they saw what I had to study in its place.

For my aunt was no slouch. She persuaded my father of the urgency of my being barmitzvahed and, moreover, that he should allow me no choice. Even so, what hurt most wasn't his high-handedness but his hypocrisy. I knew he didn't believe in God and certainly not in the God of Abraham, Isaac and Jacob. I'd once heard him say that religion had ruined his life; and he wasn't prone to exaggeration... though still less to elucidation. So I never discovered what he'd meant.

My aunt tried to infuse me with a love of her religion, but I perceived as little joy in it as in the rest of her life. It seemed nothing but an endless struggle for survival; which from where I stand now I know to have been no mean achievement, but which deeply depressed me as a child. Her history, like everything else, was shot through with hysteria; and as she fed me stories of the young German guards who forced Jewish elders to swallow scraps of bacon, I felt that by forcing me to go to synagogue she was exacting their revenge.

Whenever we were in London she made me attend; and Saturday morning soon became the Monday morning of my week. I was given a place of honour in deference to my family. The large plaque acknowledging its munificence was polished and pointed out... to be refashioned in my fantasy as a carving on a cathedral wall. And the weight of tradition hung as heavy on my shoulders as my grandfather's golden-threaded prayer-shawl – which I found myself unwittingly pulling apart.

My chief quarrel lay with the service's relentless masculinity... No wonder churches can be accused of existing solely for old women, when synagogues must have long exhausted the supply of old men... They congregated in their shiny top hats and pallbearers' black as though for a family funeral. And everyone, young and old, wore heavy, thick-rimmed glasses as if they shared some hereditary defect; which in my eyes appeared a blindness to Christ.

And they chattered amongst themselves continuously. The temple may have long ceased to be a market-place; but this seemed nothing but a meeting place. And in the middle of the prayers, total strangers would come up to me and pinch my cheek or rub my chin or breathily, bristlily kiss me, and assure me that I was a credit to my family; which simply increased my discomfort, as I'd already made up my mind to desert.

I could find no release even in the ritual. The cantor chanted the prayers as though he were rolling a globule of spit around in his mouth; but then the whole language seemed so guttural. From time to time, and for no apparent reason, individual members of the congregation would join in; the sounds emerged like the stunned cries of wounded animals. And even during their odd moments of unison the effect was one of dissonance. I felt alien and alone and afraid.

Though what dismayed me most was the sheer incomprehensibility; which wasn't the poetry of tradition, but rather the obscurity of the tongue. I longed to understand, but I could make out neither the sounds nor the symbols. And instead of a priest who spoke with the voice of Christ, there was a rabbi who spoke with the voice of Moses and a good octave lower than the deepest Russian bass.

But my own voice was about to break – at least symbolically – and my barmitzvah could no longer be delayed. My father and step-mother came from France with the boys, whilst distant relatives flew in from equally distant parts. My aunt had arranged a vast reception at the Connaught, which my father considered ostentatious. But as he said himself, he could hardly refuse her her big day... I'd been foolish enough to suppose it was meant to be mine.

She confided in me, as she scrutinised my appearance, that it was her greatest dream that I should become a rabbi. And I'm still convinced that if she hadn't mentioned that, I'd have been able to go through with it. I knew my portion backwards... for obvious reasons. And the legacy of lip-service seemed somehow lighter in a language I could barely understand. But then and there she made me see that I wouldn't just have been betraying my own faith but hers; and my white lie would have been tinged with black.

We reached the synagogue and my father led me to my seat. It was the first – and last – time that I'd ever seen him worship. And his hat seemed to sit even more uncomfortably on his head than mine on mine. I mounted the pulpit and stood alongside the rabbi who pointed a heavy, hairy finger at the text. It was only twelve verses; but it appeared a gyrating mass of squiggles: not swimming but drowning before my eyes.

And I laughed as I realised that it had to be a sign. God had temporarily blinded me, like St Paul on the road to Damascus. And I was convinced that if I listened hard, I'd also hear him speak. But all I heard was the rabbi's gruff impatience: Read. And I shook my head apologetically and walked back down to my seat.

No, I didn't walk – I skipped; I jumped. My father looked appalled, as if I'd fulfilled all his worst expectations, whilst the entire syna-gogue was aghast. I didn't dare cast a glance up at the gallery for fear of catching a glimpse of my aunt. But I knew very well that, like the family portraits at Edensor, her eyes would be fixed on my every move.

All the old men crowded round me; only now they were no longer so free with their kisses. I told them that my mind had gone blank and I'd been unable to distinguish the words. Read it in English, one of them advised. And such a suggestion, in a synagogue where any amount of incomprehension was deemed preferable to the smallest innovation, made me truly appreciate the awe in which my family was held. But the rabbi himself would have none of it and he led me out to his office, whilst the cantor began to read in my place. And I knew that I ought to feel repentant; but on the contrary I felt exultant. I'd stood up – and down – for myself. This was what it was to be a man.

In the office I faced the music: the blustering baritone of my father and the soprano squall of my aunt. I replied that I was unable to deny my convictions, especially when Christ had died for them. Not that I was making any comparisons – that would have been lèse-majesty, worse, lèse-deity – but I also considered I was standing up for the New Testament against the Old.

My father demanded to know how I could have walked out on them... not on him – he seemed to realise that where walking out was concerned he was on dangerous ground – but on my aunt. I found that particularly unjust when, as I was quick to point out, I'd heard him himself describe her as a sour, sanctimonious spinster who'd used all her bad offices with their mother to stand in the way of... something. And –

But then he hit me: the only time that he ever did; and that isn't just a memory, but a fact. I was completely taken aback. It was the precedent that shook me, not the pain. And he shouted that I was a liar: how had he ever managed to produce such a deceitful child? While my aunt sniffed into her handkerchief and sat down heavily on her handbag, which split. And the rabbi looked away as if he had no place in family quarrels, before returning to the service to salvage as much as he could.

We all left shortly afterwards. But what strikes me as odd even now was that no one referred to the meal. Did they salvage that, too? Did three hundred guests make their way to the Connaught and, rather than toast the guest of honour, raise a glass to absent friends? Or was it like the banquet in the parable which, once the original invitations had been refused, was redistributed amongst the poor? I've always longed to know. But at the time I felt that to ask might sound frivolous. And I couldn't bring it up now without opening old wounds.

A few months later my aunt went to live in Israel, where she worked tirelessly on behalf of Soviet Jews. And yet it's all too easy to love humanity in general and neglect those closest to you... Why are you smiling? I suppose you think it's a family trait... She never forgave me. She'd devoted her life to me and I'd devalued it in front of her family and friends and so utterly that she could never face any of them again... I'm sorry. Where have you hidden your tissues? I didn't suspect this would be so hard... But then grief and guilt have always been close relations: at least as close as my aunt and myself.

My father went back to France. And it's not surprising that he should have returned so rarely or that he should have wanted to wash his hands of a son who'd defied him publicly, or even that he should have seen my religion as a deliberate flouting of his authority and my refusal to be barmitzvahed as a reluctance to become a man... or at any rate one like him.

But then he'd have liked to have reduced all my most considered beliefs to a straightforward clash of personalities; whereas nothing could have been further from the truth. And yet I am prepared to admit that when I think of the Old Testament God it is almost exclusively in terms of an authoritarian father: the God of the Patriarchs rather than the Prophets, and that in the past I may have tended to play off one against the other; even to the extent of wondering whether, when he spoke of setting families at odds, Jesus mightn't also have had his own at the back of his mind.

Besides if it weren't for Christ I wouldn't be a Christian – I'll rephrase that: if it weren't for Christ I wouldn't be religious at all... Were I to have to pick one image to stand for the entire Old Testament it'd be Moses on Mount Sinai handing down the Ten Commandments; whilst if I had to do the same for the New it'd be Jesus delivering the Sermon on the Mount: two mountains, two messages, but a whole world in between. And whereas one looks ever forwards, the other is forever looking back; or even more obdurately, looking forwards to the birth of a Saviour who's already been.

But my family is still stuck in the world of the Old Testament, both socially and spiritually, passing on time-worn traditions as though they were time-honoured heirlooms, and insisting on the outward observance of a religion to which they no longer give any credence in their hearts. So that the result is little different from the most primitive ancestor worship with 'Honour thy father and thy mother', or more strictly, 'thy father and thy grandfather', being the first and only commandment that they have to obey.

And they've sacrificed generation after generation on their atavistic altars; as ruthlessly as those mythical Patriarchs whose mute acquiescence in the slaughter of their children found such favour in the eyes of the Old Testament God. Jephthah savagely slew his innocent daughter, whilst Abraham himself was only just stopped in time. And I may be no psychologist, but I've always found that particular expression of obedience dubious in the extreme.

But then Christ came: to offer himself as a living sacrifice and to humanise his father in both senses of the word. He ensured that there'd be no more Abrahams, let alone Jephthahs, and instead he made the taste of blood as sweet as the smoothest wine. How could I ever have supposed that he came to sow dissension when he's the eternal spirit of reconciliation? And maybe one day he'll reconcile me to my earthly father, just as he did long ago to the divine.

Three

Any hope that the plague might be contained at the Coopers and its two neighbouring cottages was soon dashed when, in September 1665, it reached what's now Bagshawe House behind these green railings and claimed the life of young Sarah Sydall. The villagers were forced to acknowledge that it was no longer a private tragedy but a concern for the entire community. And yet with the assumption of responsibility came the inevitable apportioning of blame.

The authorities in London had done what authorities always do and stigmatised the most vulnerable sections of society, chief amongst which in the 1660s were foreigners. And a great wave of xenophobic hatred was unleashed on the Huguenots, two of whom were said to have received various infected woollen goods from Holland. But in Eyam, with its strongly Puritanical streak, the most pressing question was not so much how as why. And given the Old Testament tradition of the jealous God who wreaked vengeance on his enemies by personally sending down pestilence, it's small wonder that they should have racked their brains to discover an explanation for their plight.

The two most popular were that it was either the response to some high jinks during Wakes Week when several youths had drunkenly driven a cow into the church; or else the resolution of a curse laid on the village by two recusant Catholic priests, whom they'd recently insulted... Oh yes, it's easy to scoff; but have the responses to our own epidemic been that much more enlightened? I myself have heard it seriously argued that AIDS was unleashed by germs from King Tutankhamen's tomb when the celebrated exhibition toured America. Well I suppose it's one in the eye for Moses: Pharaoh strikes back at all the New York Jews... Whilst even informed scientific opinion is rife with prejudice. For whether or not the virus can ultimately be traced to monkeys, there's no justification for picturing it as spreading from apes to Africans to Haitians to whites as if it's somehow progressing up the evolutionary ladder, and then from homosexuals to bisexuals to heterosexuals as if it's working its way up the moral one, too. Set in a contemporary context the Eyam reaction seems remarkably restrained.

Nevertheless there can be no doubt that people were beginning to panic: an impression confirmed by the number of rapidly drawn-up wills, at least one of which clearly shows the strain on the rector, William Mompesson, who initially wrote his own name in place of the testator's. And yet such a lapse can be easily excused for, as we can see from this plaque, following on Sarah's death there were five more in October in the Sydall family alone... But unless we wish to add to their number, I suggest we flee the traffic and make our way to the village green; where we'll hear more about the last name on the list. For there can have been no more poignant fate in the entire village than that of Emmot Sydall.

I'll bet you a thousand pounds that you'll never guess where I was last Saturday. No, on second thoughts it'd be just my luck if you'd taken your children to spend the afternoon in Hyde Park... I was on the march: on the march and On the March! From Marble Arch to Kennington Park to celebrate twenty years of Gay Pride. And for the first time I can use both words without qualification. As Mark said, self-definition isn't merely the end of self-oppression but the beginning of self-respect.

I felt truly proud to be walking alongside him. And I even stopped fretting about Adrian, whom I'd never before seen so ebullient, despite the previous night's Indian meal and his ensuing, intimately described 'curry bottom'. He told me that it was his birthday; every queen should have an official birthday, and 24 June was his. Though I also felt humble as he explained that he'd not missed a march in twelve years; and Mark had been on almost as many. While the closest I'd come were two sponsored walks for War on Want and Christian Aid, where I'd led several rousing choruses of 'When the Saints Go Marching In'.

We sang that again on Saturday, or at least I did – until Mark prodded me and I realised that the words had been carefully amended: the saints were gays.

From now on, no matter what the words, those will be my memories. Mark took hold of my hand; and I saw that there were so many others doing just the same: marching hand in hand and arm in arm and shoulder to shoulder. It was every queen's official love day. And I smiled and clasped his hand damply; and we marched on.

I never realised that they knew so many people. They were being greeted and embraced from all directions. Mark swore that one man who'd hailed and hugged him with particular warmth was a total stranger. Then Adrian perplexed me even further by suggesting that they must have met on the Heath. I asked if he used to go jogging. I was soon put wise amidst general mirth and gentle mockery. Adrian apologised for me as though I were a country cousin, but Mark assured me it was an easy mistake. Then he brushed a hair off my face, wiped a bead of sweat from my brow, and kissed me full on the lips as we walked past Buckingham Palace.

We marched on. I was surprised to see so many policemen, and angry that not one of them would deign to smile. They came to protect and stayed to intimidate. Which prompted Adrian to wonder why, since they seemed to have so little else to do, they didn't go and arrest someone for cottaging... which has even less to do with the countryside than jogging has with the Heath; or so I gathered from his subsequent lavatorial tales. Mark told him to save them for his autobiography; at which he flounced and proposed a new genre: 'piss and tell'...

We turned down Victoria Street, which must surely be the most bland and boring in the whole of London. And Mark began to complain that whereas last year they'd been able to be gay and proud in the heart of Piccadilly, this year we'd been relegated to the back of beyond. But any disappointment with the route was more than offset by our delight in the fashions and in particular their diversity: everything from bare chests and tee-shirts, shorts and jeans to full evening dress with crinolines and bustles and three-day beards.

At various times we must have encountered the entire cast of *Gone With The Wind*, and their inventiveness seemed to have surpassed even Scarlett O'Hara's. She'd made a dress out of the drawing-room curtains; but they'd made theirs out of tinfoil and dustbin liners and something very like army camouflage. Which led Adrian to define this year's look as 'military camp'.

Only last year – what am I saying? – even this, I'd have found those Southwark belles a distinct embarrassment. Whatever our differences the imperative was to show that deep down we were all the same. Well, that was obvious – and in the case of the man dressed in nothing but polythene it was extremely obvious indeed. But what now seems far more valuable was their dogged determination to express their individuality with all the courage of their outrage and a good humour which belied bad taste.

Besides which I've come to know and respect another friend of Mark's and Adrian's: Dana, a pre-operative transsexual whose style is anything but flamboyant, but whose self-assertion is no less brave. At first I admit I had a major problem with terminology. They insisted I spoke of him as her, which grated almost as much as when Vange referred to God in the feminine – where at least the castration was strictly symbolic. So I devised elaborate strategies to avoid personal pronouns altogether; which invariably blew up in my face.

But one evening she called round after having spent a night in the cells: by no means an isolated occurrence. She was well known to the police; and apparently in the eyes of the law her manner of dress alone was enough to cause a breach of the peace. So they could haul her in whenever they needed to make up their quota of arrests, or merely felt bored.

And it was then that I realised those distinctions of terminology were far from academic. For whilst to the majority of people she was a freak and even Vange and her friends seemed to find her sisterhood something of an embarrassment, to the police her position, if not her body, was quite clear-cut. And although half of her had become a woman, the other half remained very much a man. And so they'd

---

thrown her into the men's cells where she'd spent the night with two vile and violent young fascists who took full advantage of the anomalies of both. And... I'm sorry... But when later in the march I found I'd inadvertently strayed behind a squat man in a twin-set with a placard 'Glad to be a transvestite', I gladly stayed.

There were placards and banners of all descriptions. Some were elaborately embroidered and tasselled, whilst others were corrugated cardboard sellotaped to a stick. And I relished the combination of the meticulously crafted and the rough and ready. And I realised that if unity were strength then so was diversity; as I marched alongside people of all shapes and sizes, sexes, sexualities and sects.

The age range was equally varied; there were grandfathers and grandmothers as well as brothers and sisters... proof positive, according to Mark, that however young the gay movement might be itself, homosexual intercourse didn't begin with the Beatles in 1963, any more than with Stonewall in 1969. It was found in every country, culture, city and creed. Indeed his own solution to the perennial problem of what distinguished men from animals wasn't that they were *homo sapiens* so much as homosexual. We marched on.

We marched on. And I was appalled to discover that it wasn't just Dana who'd fallen foul of the law; I too had been a criminal all year. Oh, yes, even for consenting adults homosexual acts aren't merely a matter of mutual consent. In fact making love is legal just so long as there are only two of you in the house and one of you owns it, and since neither of you must proposition the other the idea must occur to both of you at exactly the same time... No doubt, as Mark declared, it was purely an oversight that kisses hadn't been similarly restricted to those on closed, dry mouths, and with at least one foot fixed firmly on the ground.

Such injustice makes me see red – politically as well as metaphorically. And I've begun to set my life in a wider context, not just religious and metaphysical but social. To strive for solidarity as well as spirituality. And to the tune of *Frère Jacques*, I found myself joining in the chant:

Homosexual, homosexual,
Lesbian, lesbian,
We are homosexual,
We are homosexual,
We are gay.

And it seemed wonderfully apt that the first song I'd ever learnt in a foreign language should again provide the tune now that I'd truly found my voice.

We surged down Victoria Street towards Westminster. And just as Mark and Adrian had been greeted by faces from their pasts, so, as I caught a glimpse of Church House, faces from mine flooded my memory to greet me. I even wondered if I might bump into Jonathan, who was a veteran – not to say, inveterate – marcher. And I was suddenly convinced he was right behind me; I could feel his breath on the back of my neck. But as I looked round at the row of sweating smiles and sweltering faces, I realised it was simply the warmth of the sun.

We approached Westminster Abbey. I'd have liked to have spent a few moments inside, but I knew that the march would have moved on without me; and my place was up front with my friends... We crossed into Parliament Square, which inspired a new twist to another familiar chant: 2-4-6-8, is your MP really straight? And according to Adrian the answer in a large number of cases was no. But that clearly hadn't entered the head of the Prime Minister who, at least in the person of a female impersonator, stood alongside the statue of Field Marshal Smutts and vigorously conducted a chorus of 'Maggie, Maggie, Maggie... Out, Out, Out'.

But any danger of mistaking the intention for the deed and being lulled into a false sense of euphoria was quelled when I saw that we'd edged forward behind a banner opportunely demanding that we 'Repeal the Section', which was another cause close to my heart. I was as determined to defend the artist's freedom of expression as the priest's freedom of conscience. Freedom was at once indivisible and under threat.

Mark and Adrian had marched against Section Twenty-Eight last year in Manchester; when it was still just a Clause. And Adrian repeated his complaint that it was undoing his whole life's work. After ten years of striving with LID to push back the boundaries of contemporary dance, he was discovering that sexual areas were again out of bounds, at least outside London, as theatre managers who'd previously been clamouring for the companies now held back. Officially they lacked funds; unofficially it was courage as, rather than swirl around 'in a cesspit of their own making', they preferred to twirl through another performance of *Swan Lake*.

The result was inevitably more classical consensus: no deviance nor dissent. Everything had to be bold and brightly coloured, with Victorian values in our lives and production values on our stages. And the irony was that a government which professed to uphold the freedom of the individual was destroying the greatest expression of individuality: that of art... Still, he declared, if they'd driven us out of their theatres, then we'd take our theatre onto their streets.

We marched on. And as we left behind the Mother of Parliaments whose functions were now being flagrantly usurped by Nanny, Mark joked about the irony of such an allegedly meritocratic government diligently promoting the ethos of 'Nanny knows Best'. But the lightness of his tone, more appropriate to Mary Poppins than Margaret Thatcher, suggested that he himself was in danger of being seduced, if not by the propaganda at least by the phrase.

There again, he'd never experienced the awesome authority of edicts issued in the nursery; I had... together with the deep disillusion of finally realising that Nanny no longer knew best, if indeed she ever had, but was blindly laying down the law on matters which she was utterly unqualified to judge.

And Nanny's still getting it wrong and refusing to admit it. She's still laying down the law and taking swipes at anyone who dares to stand in her way. Only we'll no longer take it lying down. We're not in the nursery; we're on the streets. We're out and 'Out', and out and proud. And as we crossed over Westminster Bridge I joined in yet another chant of 'Maggie, Maggie, Maggie... Out, Out, Out' as fervently as I'd once chanted 'Hail Mary, Full of Grace'.

We trooped down Kennington Road, which must be the second most boring in London; but at least we were approaching the park with the prospect of warm grass and cool beer. My legs were beginning to flag, but not my enthusiasm; which was just as well, for the next thing I knew I was carrying a banner myself. Mark had offered to lend a hand to the Southwark AIDS Support Group – or rather he'd offered two, one of which was mine.

Though surprisingly light, the pole was exceedingly sticky. I carried it close to my chest... and my heart. For I knew that to him it wasn't simply one good cause amongst many, but almost the only one worthy of the name. He saw the graves multiplying before his eyes like the acres of crosses in a Flanders cemetery, except with AIDS replacing RIP. And he feared that those four squat letters would prove the epitaph for an entire civilisation. As once again old men sat back while young men were left to die.

He insisted that the solution didn't lie merely in money and medicine but in political will... I suspect that at the back of his mind he still sees the virus as a fiendish plot hatched by a repressive government to curb desire. As he said, they'd tamed every other form of subversion, but sex was the most private and hence the most powerful of all – so what better than to make it deadly: to turn desire into disease?

To which end they'd appropriated the concept of nature, together with an aggressive Darwinism which didn't square at all with their moral fundamentalism. But then theirs was a philosophy that'd always been determined to have everything both ways except – and here he drew himself up with a show of modesty – in matters sexual where there was only one way, which was in itself one too many. Though no doubt in various government laboratories teams of scientists were hard at work seeking to remedy it. After all, why devote resources to finding a cure for a disease which clearly confirmed their idea of natural selection...? Whilst Conservative matrons searched snake-skin handbags for tissues to dab on crocodile tears.

Mine were only too real: salt-smarting tears of frustration and fury; and I strode on at such a pace that I almost wrenched the pole from his hand. But we were immediately faced with a more pressing provocation as we'd reached the entrance to the park, where we were forced to queue for three-quarters of an hour since the police had closed all the others 'to avoid congestion'... I'll say no more. I said enough at the time.

At last we entered the gates. And for one afternoon the park was indeed paradise. I'd known nothing like it since the Pope's open-air mass at Wembley. No, even that can't begin to compare. Have you any idea how I felt after struggling for so long to keep my chin up but my head down – no easy combination – to be amongst thousands of like-minded people whose heads were as high as their spirits? We've been told that there's no such thing as society, but there is a community; and this was the proof.

But then the right, whose self-definition is no longer purely as a political party but rather as the only basis for right-thinking, is as adept at manipulating language as at misappropriating resources; or as Mark put it: at fiddling the dictionary as well as the books. We've reclaimed the streets if only for an afternoon, now we must reclaim the words once and for all. And I don't just mean the insulting ones that are constantly thrown at some of us in jokes and banner headlines, but the longer, quieter ones that affect every one of us: that undermine not only our sense of ourselves but our ability to act.

We condemn ourselves from our own mouths as we're left to use words that have become as discredited as the era they've been made to represent. So society is nothing more than a chimera, socialism anathema, the welfare state the dependency culture and idealism immaturity. While for their own part, political expediency has been elevated to the national interest, historical accident to the natural order, the party in government to the party of government, and their opponents are branded the enemy within.

The expropriation of language has gone hand in hand with that of faith. So though millions live in abject poverty, they still insist that we've been witnessing an economic miracle: as if the moral of the Feeding of the Five Thousand were simply to make the best use of resources rather than to share all that we have. But what else can you expect from an ideology in which the meaning of life has been reduced to eating, competing and excreting, where virtue is self-defeating and chicanery its own reward? Meanwhile the true Christian ideals of Faith, Hope and Charity have all but vanished – well, maybe not Charity so long as the occasion is sufficiently public and the recipient suitably abased.

Napoleon claimed that the English were a nation of shopkeepers; and his gibe is even more pertinent two hundred years on when we've been subjected to the ethics of corner shopkeepers – and one corner shop in particular, where cleanliness is next to godliness, a little hard work never killed anyone, and there's a large notice stuck to the till: Please don't ask for credit as a refusal often offends.

I'm sorry; this must sound less like psychotherapy than soap-box oratory. If you'd rather not hear, if you feel I'm exceeding my brief or your competence, just say so. But I've a lot more on my mind than laying my private ghosts. Besides, Mark doesn't have a monopoly on social concern. We protect endangered species; how about endangered speech? Nevertheless, as we sat on the parched grass drinking sweetly warm beer and drawing inspiration from the music and the friendship, it was possible to believe, at least for a few hours, that we were turning the tide.

The day drew on; and we grew restive. Mark and Adrian strolled amongst the rows of market-stalls with Vange and Gaia; whilst I played frisbee with their son, Brett. All of a sudden he let the disc drop as he noticed what I can only describe as a human gyroscope... at least that's how they described it: you must have seen those wheels within boxes designed to illustrate the principles of rotation; except that here the principle was being applied to people who were being thrown topsy-turvy through the air.

After much cajoling and pleading and the threat of tears, Brett persuaded his mothers to allow him a turn. Mark bought him a ticket and he was duly strapped in and swung round. He shrieked with joy as his fearless, toothless grin disappeared beneath the wheel. I could hardly bear to look, whereas he could hardly bear to come down. And when at last he did, he immediately began badgering for another go.

'Next,' one of the promoters shouted; and Mark thrust me forward. I didn't – I didn't want to understand. Then with a flourish he produced a second ticket. I tried to back away; but I was hemmed in by the tightly packed crowd. I stared at the machine. It looked like nothing so much as a sophisticated thumbscrew to be applied to every extremity of my body: my ankles, wrists, waist and, most terrifying of all, the crown of my head. I stood stock-still; but the bystanders were fast growing impatient. And I knew that if I cried off, I'd be losing not only face, but my whole new personality. So I instinctively crossed myself, provoking a huge roar of laughter, stepped up and was strapped in.

As they set the wheel in motion a great gust of energy surged through me. Never mind the principles of rotation, I seemed more like the man in Leonardo's *Proportions of the Human Figure*, with both pairs of arms and legs encircled in a square. But far from feeling circumscribed, I felt strangely unfettered as I experienced my own renaissance.

Soon I was also seeing double, with arms and legs coming at me from all directions. I orbited the onlookers. But before I could take my bearings I found I was being plunged headlong into the ground. I screwed up my eyes very tightly and tensed my entire body in readiness for the inevitable crash. Then, at the last moment – no, the last moment of a moment, I was whisked away.

I took wing as the machine gained speed and sent me rising and falling and leaping and looping and sliding through thousands of dimensions between body and mind. I viewed the world from so many new and exciting angles: head over heels, heels over stomach, stomach over head. Whilst all around me everyone whistled and clapped and cheered. My shirt broke loose and whipped my eyes; they slowed the wheel and ripped it off me, before flinging me back so quickly that I had no time to object. I was bare-chested, bare-faced, and free.

They spun me round ever faster. My skin caught the deliciously cool cross-currents of the machine, and I began to whoop. I'd found my voice and I was shouting; I'd found my feet and I was soaring; I'd marched and now I was resting. And I whirled onwards and upwards to the ends of the universe. Until, with the gentlest of bumps, they brought me back down to earth.

Four

All in one piece...? Good. The traffic never stops, even this early on a Sunday morning. It would be particularly ironic if the village which survived the devastation of the plague should succumb to destruction by motor car. So let's return to a more tranquil age as we stand at the entrance to the Delph and resume our acquaintance with Emmot Siddal.

In the heroic annals of Eyam, Emmot and her fiancé Rowland Torre supply a subsidiary strand of romance. He was the son of the miller from the neighbouring village of Stoney Middleton – a name which as you'll soon learn proved an apt reflection of its nature. But not Rowland's; and theirs is a classic Romeo and Juliet variant... so much so that I for one could wish that Shakespeare had been born a hundred years later and ninety miles further north. And yet Emmot and Rowland were separated not by the bitterness of feuding families but the impersonal poison of plague.

As her family dwindled around her that fearful October the young girl remained alone with her distracted mother, her sole sustenance being Rowland's visits, until the danger became too great and she forbade him to return; although, in the face of his grief-stricken pleas, she later relented and agreed to meet him behind the village in the safer surroundings of the Delph.

Throughout the spring Rowland maintained his vigil, even though Emmot had long since failed to appear. He refused to give up hope; and legend has it that when the threat of infection was finally lifted he was among the very first to enter the village, rushing from house to house desperate to recover his love. On the way he was stopped by a little lad who, intimate with their story, blurted out that Emmot was dead and had been buried in April in the Delph. And therefore all the time, without knowing, he'd been keeping his tryst by her grave...

So we've glimpsed, in the inhabitants of four cottages, the relentless advance of the infection; clearly someone had to bury the victims. And if you'll continue with me down to the Town Head, we'll discover who that was.

You weigh your wizened words so sparingly. You smile your smug smile, exuding your air of unfathomable wisdom whilst never giving a thing away. Why didn't you warn me? Even little children at a pantomime shout, 'Behind you.' And this was right in front of me; and I walked straight into the trap.

Did you enjoy it? Have you been sharing a huge joke at my expense: you and God? Were the angels weeping with mirth as they watched me take a pratfall? That's the real fall: not Adam and Eve's greed in the garden, but our eternal gullibility as we fall for the myth of an all-loving God.

And you're his perfect representative: therapist... the rapist: that's Mark's philology or at any rate his pun. And if you allege to have seen nothing, then you should change your profession. I was a prisoner of my own story; but you're supposed to put it in perspective. Adrian's curry bottom was a symptom, not a euphemism: he has AIDS.

I'm sorry, I've no right to insult you; you don't claim to be a mind-reader. Your task is to read between the lines, not to supply the missing page. I'm the one who's to blame. You trusted me to tell you whatever I considered important, which I've used as a pretext for the most shameless self-importance. I've diverted you with trivia whilst Adrian... But what about Mark? He's supposed to be an expert. He deals with HIV problems all day long and then mans a helpline every other evening. Shouldn't charity begin at home? And what about self-awareness?

But then there was always an easy explanation. Adrian's been under intense pressure at work. He's permanently fighting for funds. So it's little wonder he's exhausted. And he lives on his nerves and junk food – which is why he looks increasingly drawn. And as for his chronic cough: on his own admission he's been trying to give up smoking for years. Though with the very survival of LID in the balance it seemed inopportune to insist.

And the cough goes on; but life goes on; so he goes on a week's holiday. And he comes back looking worse than before. But then he's been laid low by a severe dose of holiday tummy... to add to the curry bottom. And surely even such a seasoned traveller can react badly to such highly seasoned food? And his skin has become very dry and chapped and crumbly; but that's obviously because he's lazed too long in the sun and not used a powerful enough lotion... And why shouldn't the blind lead the blind when the sighted see only what we want to see?

But no one could have wanted to see him as he looked after his first day back at work: his shoulders hunched and his face haggard and his eyes cracked with crimson; whilst the pupils had dilated into pleas for reassurance which even Mark found himself unable to give. Instead he suggested calling a doctor, at which Adrian grew quite abusive, shouting that they had more than enough bona fide patients without his adding to their load. And Mark put his finger to his lips... and we all put our hands over our eyes, ears and mouths.

The next evening he didn't come home at all, although the real surprise was that he failed to send a message. But even that seemed a good sign to Mark, who was convinced he must have felt so much better he'd stayed over with a friend. So we took ourselves early to bed with a candlelit supper. And whilst we lay giggling with a tray across our stomachs, he lay gasping with a tube down his throat. The crippling fatigue since his return hadn't simply been jet-lag, nor the pains in his chest heartburn. He was diagnosed with AIDS, or more specifically thrush. But although it's possible to have thrush in the mouth and not to have AIDS, there's no ambiguity in the oesophagus. And it'd grabbed him right in the jugular: the new all-purpose four-letter word.

He had to spend the night in hospital. They wanted to perform an immediate endoscopy – that's... but of course, I'm sorry; I don't have to tell you. And he didn't have a chance to tell us; but then I'm not sure he'd have done so anyway. He preferred a little time alone with the verdict, before we all began to lodge our loud appeals. They also gave him an HIV test, even though the thrush was in itself conclusive. Since then he's had tests for syphilis and hepatitis B; they've checked his liver, X-rayed his chest and counted his blood cells. He feels so bruised that he's convinced they must have counted each one individually. And, like a defeated candidate, I clamour for a recount; although the result will never change.

He said that his immediate thought on hearing the news and then that they wanted to admit him straight into hospital was of pyjamas: not of the test nor the tubes nor the prognosis, but that he hadn't worn a pair since he was seventeen. It'd been his first act of defiance: a small but telling gesture against his mother and her straight-faced, straight-laced conventionality. What do you like next to your skin, Adrian? Nylon? Cotton? Satin? Silk? I like sweat, he said. I want to feel the touch of sweat against my skin... And he'll sweat now. Dear God, he'll sweat his life away.

But they provided him with a pair of regulation flannelette pyjama bottoms. Although there was no erotic return to be gained from speculating who might have worn them last: simply the sinking realisation that this was the beginning of the end, if not of his life, then at least of his own control over it. He was in other people's pyjamas and other people's hands.

They discharged him the following afternoon, which was when he told Mark. I wasn't there; I don't know... perhaps I was here? Yes, of course; it was last Wednesday: a week ago – a lifetime ago last Wednesday. What fascinating bit of myself was I regaling you with then whilst they were confronting their own mortality? I can't bear it! I love him... I love him so much.

For five days they kept it to themselves. I could sense an atmosphere, but I thought... you won't believe... to self-importance you must add self-obsession... it was my birthday last Monday, and I was convinced they were planning a surprise party... Have you ever given up a client in sheer disgust? Professional detachment may not be sufficient safeguard. How can you even bear to have me in the room?

In the event the date had slipped their minds; although there was a small pile of cards to greet me in Little Venice: from my solicitor, my trustees and my father. And Mrs Trewitt had baked a cake. I took it back to the flat where, if there's any justice, it'll already be iced with mould. But then I know now that there's none; for later that evening they told me the truth.

I screamed – no, don't worry; my protest was entirely internal. I have the small satisfaction of knowing that I didn't reveal my pain by so much as the flicker of an eyelid or the tremor of a lip. But inside I let rip, and I shall never let up until I've pierced the heart of God himself and a trickle of blood issues from the stone... Whilst my mind has become a livid jumble of lurid letters: Adrian has AIDS and Mark has HIV.

Oh, did I forget to mention that? That's because it's not of the least significance. He's totally asymptomatic; it's a mere technicality. Only thirty percent of people with HIV go on to develop... And I'm aware that the figures are constantly changing, but why must we assume that they'll change the wrong way? We have to think positive... I'd like to cut out my tongue.

He said his piece; I was stunned. It was my birthday; I was bereft. I shall never be young again. But I knew that I had to make my position clear, so I put my arms around his waist and hugged him. I kissed him longer and fuller than ever before. But he brushed me aside and asked if I were trying to give him the kiss of life. Was it part of my training: first aid... last rites? I was about to object when I pictured St Francis Xavier sucking the pus from a beggar.

And I was afraid I might choke. But then he relented and returned my hug, although not my kiss.

I asked him how long he'd known; and he said since Friday. The tests usually took ten days; but through the good offices of the Health Advisers, who'd referred patients to him in the past, they'd pushed the results through in one. And I felt absurdly grateful that, whatever else, he still had his professional standing. I couldn't understand why he'd waited until then to tell me. But apparently they'd advised him to tell no one straight away: the first twenty-four hours were the worst... He only hoped that they were right.

Though it was the preceding twenty-four which had proved the real pain. I desperately cast back my mind but I'd noticed nothing, and I felt deeply ashamed... As I already knew, he'd long decided against taking the test, not from fear so much as scepticism, but Adrian's diagnosis had left him little choice. And yet it'd come as no great shock; in a way he'd been preparing himself for the result since the day that the first of his friends died, while his total immersion in AIDS issues was essentially self-preservation, a vain bid to inoculate himself with information: to plea-bargain with God. And yet, as he watched the nurse squirt his blood into a phial marked 'Infectious', he'd have defied a Mother Superior not to lose heart.

He returned for the result the following lunchtime; but it was only once he was out in the street that the reality began to register. And much to his disgust he found himself hoping against hope that some white-coated technician would follow him out, a sheaf of papers in one hand and in the other a test-tube probably bubbling with blood, shouting at the top of his voice: I'm most terribly sorry, but there are two Mark Gregsons; we've unaccountably muddled the results; yours was the negative one. Please accept our apologies for any distress or inconvenience you may have been caused... Until he realised he was simply paraphrasing the notice on the building site he was walking past.

I wanted to hold him. And yet any gesture felt inadequate or, even worse, inauthentic; and besides, all at once his body seemed to keep me at bay. Too late I understood how lonely he must have felt in the past when he'd complained that I cut him out. While to add to my sense of guilt he appeared so much more alert to my plight than I was to his. He stroked my cheek and told me his one consolation was that I had no cause for concern. Every expert in the world would have to have been wrong for me to have tasted the slightest danger. And I was suddenly mortally afraid.

Please don't misunderstand; I wasn't at all frightened for him.

Any fears on his account would be quite superfluous. I only wish you had a chance to see him, then you'd realise straightaway that he's the picture of health. He ought to be put on a poster to bolster morale. That would – Oh! Oh no, I've suddenly remembered sitting next to him that first evening at Aldgate East Station, opposite a giant poster for War on Want. The thick-ribbed, thin-bodied, skin-tight skeletons of starving children are blotting out his image. I can't even ward them off with words...

And yet I mustn't despair; after all, he hasn't. Not only does he refuse to say die; but he won't even say disease. On the contrary, he seems set to turn being positive into a positive virtue. Which may sound like a play on words; but if so, then it's one from which I draw real hope. Although it should have come as no surprise. He's always been so positive about life in every other respect; this is just one more. Whereas I've simply been confirmed in my negativity: which is an equally double-edged word.

No, my fear is that he'll come to regard my love as a liability; since I know I pose a far more serious threat to him than he to me. Oh, of course I can protect him from my colds and coughs and catarrh, just as he can me from his blood and sweat and tears; but we'd both be betrayed by my doubts. For no matter how hard I try, I can never share his unshakable faith that all he need do is stick a brave smile on his face and a defiant poster on his door and the angel of death will pass him over.

Yesterday I tore the poster down; its ironies had hit too close to home. I was trying to spare them pain; although the effect was the exact opposite. He insisted I replace it right away... And yet what he sees as scorning fatalism, I see as tempting fate.

And is that the greatest irony of all: that his self-acceptance is so assured that he can even accept the virus, whilst it's my lack of infection that stands in the way of mine? I remember how last year I proposed to contract it because I hated who I was and it seemed the most appropriate means to an end. Whereas now it's become almost a means of identification, without which I can never be a fully paid-up gay man.

I'm convinced that when the crunch comes that's where we'll part company, as he denounces those who pass as negative with the same scorn he once reserved for those who passed as straight and dismisses the rest of us as fellow-travellers. I feel so helpless. It's as though he's fighting for his life at the front whilst I've failed my medical. And yet I'm determined to play a part, even if only by carrying a stretcher – no, I'm betrayed by my own metaphor! He is not going to die.

Once again I've no one to talk to but you; I can hardly impose my worries on him. He has to save all his strength for himself and for Adrian, who's neither so well nor so well-informed. But as I watched them together on the night of my abortive birthday, all gripes and grievances swept aside, my grief was shot through with the most shameful jealousy. And perverse as it might seem, at that moment there was nothing I wanted more than to stand in the firing-line alongside them or, better still, in Adrian's place.

Though you needn't be alarmed that I'll take matters into my own hands. At a time when death has become a contagion not a choice, suicide wouldn't only be an unforgivable sin – who gives a damn about sin? – but a truly unpardonable self-indulgence. And yet, if nothing else, let me revel in the irony of having found myself at the time of such universal loss: of once again being both out of step and on a limb. As a child I used to dream and so I was afraid of sleep and of nightmares, and the greatest nightmare of all was death. But now I never dream and so I'm afraid only of insomnia and of remaining forever alive and alone.

And while I may not dream, I do have visions; and as I close my eyes, I can see myself the last man left on earth: the one priest to celebrate in a world full of chantries; the one scribe to record the names in the Book of the Dead.

Five

For many years this house, now much altered, would have been the most feared in the whole village, as it was the home of Marshall Howe, its self-appointed sexton during the period of plague. Just as in London the old women 'searchers of the dead', whose job it was to examine bodies for signs of the pestilence, were regarded by their fellow citizens with a mixture of revulsion and gratitude, so Howe appears to have been viewed as a necessary evil by the inhabitants of Eyam.

And whatever the subsequent reverence shown to the plague dead, precious little was possible at the time. Once again, as in London where the usual funeral procedures were collapsing under sheer weight of numbers, so Eyam, with its average annual death rate of five or six, was suddenly faced with a monthly toll many times higher. Resources were dreadfully overstretched. And although, unlike the metropolis, there were no painful processions to burial pits through deserted streets in the middle of the night, preceded by the awesomely familiar cry of 'Bring out your dead', the village churchyard was soon choked; and it was decided that corpses should be consigned to their own gardens or even neighbouring fields.

To a devoutly superstitious people, that must in itself have been deeply distressing, but the manner of their interment lacked all dignity. The customary offices were suspended. Since the two priests were fully occupied in treating the sick and relieving the dying, the actual laying to rest had to be left to family and friends. But as putre-faction and its attendant pollution were believed to set in very rapidly, obsequies were kept to a minimum and bodies quite literally dragged to their graves with sheets or other cloths tied round their armpits or ankles and then dumped unceremoniously in the ground. And when no family or friends remained to accompany them, there was always Marshall Howe... at a price.

Howe was a lead-miner who, having recovered from a mild dose of plague at an early stage of the epidemic, took advantage of his escape to feather his own nest. For he was one man who acted not so much out of community spirit or Christian charity but with an eye to the main chance; compensating himself extremely liberally for the disagreeability of his task by plundering the possessions of the dead.

But despite his justified confidence in his own immunity, his wife and son proved less hardy; and in August 1666, in quick succession, they died. I'd like to be able to report that Howe subsequently repented and abandoned his cavalier attitude to both the funeral rites and property rights of others, in order to treat them with respect; however, that would be one legend for which there's not the least foundation. And it's said that for a long time afterwards, parents who wished to pacify their children would do so with the threat that Marshall Howe was coming. Which I suppose, like the familiar nursery rhyme 'Ring a ring o' roses', shows how easy it is for the original pain to be assimilated and the memory muffled in a form of words.

And now to resume our death toll: October 1665 had added twenty-three to the six from September; although with the onset of autumn the villagers had reason to believe that the worst was past. Ironically, 1665 had enjoyed one of the finest summers on record – in his diary Samuel Pepys constantly confided his concern with the heat – but the warm thatches, together with the rudimentary sanitation, would have provided ideal conditions for the black rats which carried the plague germs to thrive. And yet, before we continue to plot their putrid progress, let's retrace a few steps to the house of a young girl who contracted the infection with extreme severity but, by means of a highly unorthodox remedy, recovered and survived.

Shall we play my favourite parlour game: if you were a book, what kind would you be? And how about me? Up until last month I'd have confidently said a concordance, but now it would have to be a medical dictionary. I'm a world authority on every symptom known to man – and then some... On Sunday Adrian was taken into hospital.

It was as sudden as a suicide. My day began as usual with the bleep of his pill dispenser... He left his door open on an unexpressed under- standing; which meant I could hear every snort and sneeze and hack of phlegm. He claimed that he swallowed the pills in his sleep. Whilst the bleeps piercingly punctuated my insomnia. And I felt as though I were being paged by death.

It was six o'clock. My eyes smarted resentfully as my mind went through its dawn readjustment, only to be plunged back into night-time confusion by a dense shadow creeping across the floor. It was Adrian crawling into our room with sweat-streaked hair and a torrential fever. We hauled him back to bed. I changed his sheets and towels whilst Mark took his temperature and persuaded him to drink. He complained that his skin felt as though it were being slowly peeled from his chest, like a rabbit flayed by a poacher. Meanwhile his cough had become a croak, and he cawed like a raven... no, anything but a raven: a rook, a frog...

The doctor arranged for his immediate admission to hospital. He was registered and settled, whilst Mark and I tramped the endless cor- ridors past anaesthetised patients on trolleys parked wheel-deep in rubbish, before ending up in the smoke-filled, slop-festering canteen. I dulled every emotion but disgust with endless cups of coffee, until the sharp bleep of his pill dispenser in my pocket prompted a further rude awakening. I fumbled with it furtively. Mark said nothing; his thoughts were eloquent enough.

After lunch we were allowed to visit him. We took our life in our hands and the arthritic lift to the fifth floor. An Irish sister stoutly held it shut as it strained to disgorge its disparate passengers. The implica- tions of our ascent were painfully marked: from the maternity clinic on the first floor to the AIDS patients tucked away at the top. And I felt much as I had when as a boy I'd tried to escape my aunt by climb- ing the turrets at Edensor... out of sight, out of mind.

Adrian was propped up in bed at what appeared an acutely

uncomfortable angle. And whilst his cough had stuttered to a halt, his colour had completely drained. I was shocked to find two tubes stuck to his bruised and bandaged left wrist. But he told me not to worry; it looked far worse than it was... although it felt far worse than it looked. They'd had to take blood from an artery to test the gases... In my ignorance I'd have supposed an artery easier to locate than a vein; and yet it turned out to be quite the opposite – and infinitely more painful. He added that what we could see was nothing; he had bruises all the colours of the rainbow: Richard of York gave battle in vain.

My heart missed a beat, and I was convinced he was raving and that the virus had started to worm its way into his mind. Until I recognised the mnemonic; even though my own childhood seemed just a distant memory and his a cruel mockery. I was about to respond when Mark bluntly interjected that no friend of his would ever be battling in vain. And he squeezed his hand so tightly that I grimaced. But Adrian seemed equally insensible both to reassurance and pain.

He groaned that his body felt like a piece of rotten fruit consumed by maggots. And despite Mark's exhortation, it can't have been easy to retain much self-respect, let alone fraternal solidarity, as he lay in a pile of pink plastic plumbing with a stark Danger Warning stuck to the door. Besides, his nurses' green cotton tunics and trousers were a permanent reminder that he wasn't as other patients, as well as introducing sinister intimations of the martial arts. He lived in constant fear of being asphyxiated by antiseptic. Even his tea tasted of TCP.

And in his enforced idleness his thoughts have turned to prayer. Last week he asked if I believed that in spite of everything, God still loved him: an extraordinary shift for one whose usual practice was to make ribald puns about the Virgin on the Rocks... And I realised how little I knew him and how much more I longed to. Which wasn't sick-bed sentimentality, let alone hindsight – of course not. Why should it be? He isn't dead... And I just stopped short of saying that to my mind the issue was whether, in view of everything, we should still love God. He was carrying enough lumber without the added burden of my despair.

I used to hold that there was nothing as cruel as destroying someone's faith; but I know now it's to destroy his illusions. After all, I've been stripped of every last one of mine... For Our Father has truly excelled himself. It's hard enough that the sins of the fathers are visited on the children and each generation bears the brunt of the one before. But when the sins of the brothers are visited on the brothers, and the lovers' on the lovers, and when those sins are no longer sins at all but loves, then there's nothing and nowhere left to turn.

Although since I'd managed to restrain myself, I failed to see why Mark couldn't do the same. Despite insisting that the worst effect of the virus was secrecy, he flatly opposed telling Adrian's sister... It made no sense. And yet when I questioned him he scornfully called me 'little boy', which had once been a term of endearment, and asked what I could possibly know of such people, with their twee tea-cosiness and garden-gnome gentility, before promptly proceeding to enlighten me.

He comes from a long line of strict Pentecostalists, and as a child in Bolton suffered from a heavy dose of North Country Churchianity. His parents hymned the 'Lord of the Dance' at every opportunity, but they never attended a single performance of his. They viewed his choice of career with open antagonism, and his burgeoning sexuality confirmed all their worst fears. When he first confided in them, they claimed he was sick: sick, sick, sick... And where is he now? Propped up on a pile of hospital pillows. Is it any wonder he refuses to fight?

I'm finally coming round to your way of thinking: that our childhood experiences have scarred us for life. The myth of the Fall was all very well when Adam was the only boy in the world and Eve was the only girl. But the rest of us have fathers and mothers and uncles and aunts. And they bear us and raise us and shape us and shame us. And Adrian's rejected him so emphatically that neither his father nor his sister even informed him of his mother's death. He might never have known if their next-but-one neighbour hadn't felt it her duty to ring him. Although Mark remained convinced that it was more from the hope of a scandal than friendly concern.

If so, she certainly achieved her aim. Having been excluded from the cortège, he pointedly stood at the back of the hall along with the undertakers, one of whom had a thick gravy stain on his suit. The humiliation of that stain remained his abiding memory of his mother's funeral – along with the warmth of his subsequent welcome home. It was then that he chipped his two front teeth. Only it wasn't in a kiss, passionate or otherwise, but rather that, after the tea and the tears and the treacle cake and the still more treacly memories, he felt impelled to fill in the other side of the picture. At which his father, who considered the slightest hint of dissent a slight to his wife's memory, grabbed him without warning and flung him so hard against the dining-room table that he cracked his jaw on the rosewood veneer. Nobody helped him up.

So he picked himself up and he picked up the pieces – of his self-respect as well as his teeth. And he even cracked a joke as he wondered whether, if he put them under his pillow, the tooth fairy might visit him at midnight. Then he left the house, never to return in his father's lifetime, or for that matter even for his death. And his sister had been happy to preserve the gulf... He was Adrian's family, Mark declared; and he painted a picture of him when he still had perfect teeth: a brilliant smile along with a biting wit.

I was afraid I might cry... I'm afraid I still might. I should make the most of my opportunity. I can never cry in the flat. To Mark, tears are no longer a release but a sign of condescension. And he checks me for the slightest hint of that as intently as he does himself for any symptom of disease... I took him in my arms. In principle nothing's changed; we still sleep together, euphemistically as well as practically... though so temperately that even the blankets barely move, let alone the earth. He seems to cling to me more for the reassurance of my presence than anything more intimate. I've almost become his comforter: a role that comes far too close for my own. And I know he needs my love just as I need his acknowledgement that I still love him. But if we made it hard for each other before, we make it almost impossible now.

I was determined not to be deterred by his diagnosis. The night that he told me we went to bed early, and he seemed to be challenging me by the speed with which he threw off his clothes. Whilst I continued to fold mine as methodically as always; to show too much enthusiasm appeared almost as cruel as to recoil. But although I was well aware that our love-making held no risk, the knowledge in my head failed to carry my body's conviction. And we both quite lost heart.

We lay one on each edge of the futon, which had come to seem as cramped as a coffin; and I'd never before felt so conscious of how close we were to the floor. I reached out for his hand and I brushed his leg. The next moment he was all over me. He pulled at me roughly as if he no longer cared to prove his love but simply his virility. He was hurting me; although I was reluctant to protest. He wrenched me up and down; but my fears had become impotence. I focused all my strength of mind and force of will on my penis. I implored it to go through the motions: just once, if never again. How often in the past had it declared its independence; and yet now it slumped cruelly inert.

I recalled my aunt as we stood in the tailor's fitting room and she despaired of my ever measuring up to my own father, let alone hers. Why won't you grow? she asked me, as if I were stunting myself out of spite; whilst the tailor looked away and his acned assistant sniggered. Why won't you grow? I asked myself as I shrank to the size of a pre-pubescent child. But it was no use; he'd taken his hand off me and was concentrating all his efforts on himself.

I fell back in dismay. I was afraid I was about to hyperventilate; but I knew that whatever else, I could never again plead ill health. So I reached towards him as he arched his back against me; and I begged him not to turn away. I longed to make love to him... in the way that he'd always wanted. I needed to feel him inside me, body and soul.

He suspected my motives; I strove to reassure him. He smiled at me and teasingly tousled my hair. And I saw that even if I couldn't give him back his peace of mind, I could at least help to give him back his body. He leaned across to his jeans and pulled out a packet of condoms. I could feel every muscle in my body tense as I watched him pull one on. For some reason I imagined a surgeon slipping on a gown before an operation. And I yearned for a local anaesthetic or, better still, a shot of laughing gas.

I lay back and I could feel him on top of me: his lips... his hips. And I was stung by the impersonality of his sex. I wasn't a lover to be awakened by his passion, but the object of an exercise to be penetrated and possessed. And instead of making myself hard I tried to force myself softer: an invitation, not a rejection; but it was one which he proved unable to accept. And whether from the new image of himself or the unexpectedness of mine, he slid away before he could settle inside me: leaving me high and dry and empty and cold.

We never spoke a word of it the next morning but stared blankly at each other as if we'd simply shared the same bad dream. We cuddled loosely, kissed briefly, and for the first time his breath smelt stale.

We've made love every night since then, but more out of desperation than desire; and from the same fear that impelled my aunt always to dress for dinner: lest the least lapse should herald the beginning of the end... Although when I say we make love, in effect we barely make contact, but simply clutch at each other's loneliness and feed on our mutual grief.

Six

This small house with its attractive black and white doorway is reputed to have been the home of Margaret Blackwell, although the lack of a plaque suggests that no one's prepared to advance too authoritative a claim. Margaret was a young girl who, however inadvertently, took the steps to recovery in her own hands. But before I describe what those were, I'd like to discuss a few of the most common symptoms.

Of course every case would have been different... the cold comfort of doctors through the ages and the one occasion on which an assertion of individuality fails to reassure... So whilst some people perspired so profusely and stank so rankly that no one could bear to stay near, others remained sweet-smelling and bone-dry. Nevertheless many of the symptoms were standard, such as sickness, high fever, violent palpitations, acute headaches, agonising pain in the bowels and the most feared and familiar of all, swellings on the skin: pustules or blisters, buboes, lumps and carbuncles in the armpits, neck and groin. These erupted in various colours: red ringed with blue, or blue or bright purple tinged with black; and they could be as small as a hen's egg or as large as a halfpenny loaf. And no, I'm not sure how big that would have been either, but if you consider that the average daily wage was a penny it must have been a fair size.

The plague was widely considered incurable, although numerous remedies were published – you'll be able to buy facsimiles of some of them from the bookstall in the church. There were cures involving salt and soap, dogs and walnuts, berries and brandy, herbs and tobacco, poultices and pomanders, and even live toads. In London, where prostitutes and people whose bodies were riddled with the pox were popularly presumed to be immune, hundreds of credulous citizens attempted to catch the disease from the Hackney whores in an extremely primitive form of inoculation. Few were disappointed in their first objective; many in the second.

I doubt very much that the Puritans approved of such unorthodox treatment; but perhaps they and indeed clergymen of all denominations would have looked more kindly on the prescription for placing that part of a live chicken known as the parson's nose on the sore to draw out the poison... Yes, I squirmed too; but desperate times, desperate measures. And it might not have been such an old wives' tale, or even as some would have had it, old witches', for later medicine has endorsed the therapeutic properties of many of these potions. Whilst sometimes the most unexpected sources produced the most efficacious results.

As was evidently the case with Margaret Blackwell... Having been left alone *in extremis*, she was seized with such a desperate thirst that in her delirium she grabbed a pan of hot bacon lard and drained it to the dregs. Later, when her brother returned, he was amazed to find her not only still alive but markedly improved. In time she fully recovered and always attributed her good health to the effect of the fat. Which ought to be a lesson to us all – not least to me. I used to be so sceptical of a friend who was practising radical self-help therapies. But from now on I refuse to rule out any: animal, vegetable or mineral – particularly the latter. The benefits are crystal clear.

Sadly however, Margaret Blackwood's recuperation remained exceptional. In the half-year between November 1665 and May 1666 another forty-eight people died; and that was only the prelude to the casualties to come. But as the plague rats continued to carry their germs through the village sewers, it's time to turn to some of their human cousins who, tails squashed between their legs, slunk away.

I bring the most amazing news: Adrian's been cured. Miracles do happen and right on our very doorstep – or at least in West Acton... And it's just too bad if you don't trust the idea nor I the ideology; all that matters is that he's well. Scruples about means and ends are a luxury I can no longer afford. My prayers have been answered and so conclusively that I shall never again complain about double standards. His life and my faith depend on them. 'Things that are impossible with men are possible with God.'

The impetus came from his sister... I didn't meet her so I only have Mark's word to go on; and he's prejudiced against anyone whose name ends in 'een' – although I'm no longer sure if that's cause or effect... She responded promptly to his call, having apparently resolved to be yielding; and they enjoyed a tearful reunion at his bedside: at any rate once she'd ascertained that his tears were safe. She clasped his hand as though through a layer of latex and kissed his cheek as though she were wearing a mask. And while visibly shocked by his gauntly Gothic appearance, her main concern was to regain his soul for Christ.

He'd already been approached by a group of Seventh Day Adventists who took advantage of some inexperienced agency staff to sneak on to the ward and process around singing hymns, pressing their fresh faces into his flushed one and proclaiming the love of God even for 'the leper with his tainted life, and sick with fevered frame'. The callousness of their evangelism revolted me. But whilst they could be shown straight to the lift the moment the staff nurse returned, Maureen's grip proved more tenacious. She clasped his hand until both their palms broke out in beads of sweat... although sweat, she was assured, was safe. And he responded with the same perfect trust which as a child he'd vested in his mother; until this new adult pain was similarly swept away.

His condition began to improve. The doctors were in no doubt as to the cause: the regular supplies of oxygen through his mask and septrin through his drip. But both Adrian and Maureen knew otherwise. He was back in the world of his childhood where he could count on his mother to protect him and, failing that, his sister and, never failing anyone, God.

So Maureen stayed on, although not at the flat – she could never bring herself to sit in the jungle, let alone the Gents – but in Ealing with a friend from the London branch of her church: a shadowy sect of Baptists: the Church of Christ in Triumph Incorporated. And that incorporation looms as large in their thinking as the Incarnation always has in mine.

On his first Sunday home Maureen took Adrian to their morning service. And while I naturally rejoice for both his cure and his conversion, it seems wrong that in order to find Christ he's had to throw out so much of himself; and in particular Mark, to whom he gave the same savage ultimatum that his parents had given him twenty-five years before: his sexuality or his house... I think you can guess his reply. Fortunately Little Venice provided a safe haven and we moved there at once. But Mark has registered nothing but his rejection. He appears to have declined in direct proportion to Adrian's improvement. The fight has been quite knocked out of him and apathy become the only immunity he has left.

I'm so afraid for him. Unlike Adrian, he's set his heart against conventional medicine, insisting it has no more to offer than conventional people – I may be over-sensitive but I'm certain that's a dig at me – and yet it's hard to disagree when with the one drug they have available only the side-effects are sure. Meanwhile he's convinced they expect him simply to sit around and wait for symptoms: a development he flatly refuses to countenance, whilst examining himself for evidence every day.

And so he's turned to holistic therapies. But while the last thing I want is to be a Jeremiah and I'm aware of the link between mind and body – even if in my own case it feels fairly faint – I draw the line at ascribing healing powers to a piece of crystal... And yet his faith holds fast: so much so that I'm beginning to think I must have misunderstood and it wasn't religion he objected to at all but simply its established manifestations, since its shamanistic side exerts such a potent spell. Nonetheless his belief in mind over matter stops some way short of miracles; and he remains deeply suspicious of Adrian's cure.

So for everyone's sake I decided to investigate the church myself. Their London base is in a hall near Wormwood Scrubs. And last Sunday, with considerable trepidation, I crossed the vestibule, which was plastered with primitive paintings, took my place amongst the expectant congregation and sat waiting for the service to begin. Instead of an organ, music was played by a fifties-style dance-band whose slicked-back hair and shiny tuxedos jarred with their late-eighties arrangements. Whilst the worshippers repeated the same few words to themselves as if to induce a state of trance: bless... grace: I am blessed by God's grace.

The lack of variety threw the naivety of their faith into stark relief. I felt uncomfortable and looked around for Adrian, who was nowhere to be seen. But I could sense far more missing than just a familiar face; and then I realised there was no cross on the altar – no altar at all, barely even a communion table. It was as though the Cross were too negative an image for the Church of Christ in Triumph. Instead there were those two great symbols of Redemption draped across the back of the hall: the British and American flags.

I clenched my fist and clung to my sense of mission. A young man mounted the dais; his sure-fire manner and quick-fire delivery seemed more appropriate to a TV warm-up comedian than to a priest. And indeed once he'd raised the temperature to something approaching fever pitch, he hurried off. The ensuing wave of enthusiasm alerted me to the arrival of the pastor's wife. She greeted us with barely concealed condescension as she joked about her fading sun-tan, her family having just returned from a summer spent ministering in Malaya. And I was appalled at the gullibility which had allowed them to mix business with pleasure in such a glaringly disproportionate way.

She then began to mix business with worship as she announced the offertory: the first, as it turned out, of two which were for the missionary work of the church. I bet, I thought cynically, as she entreated us to give as the spirit moved us. And I speculated as to where the spirit would move them to minister next: Fiji? The Virgin Isles? There was no obligation, we were promised, as the plates went round and the money rolled in; we were simply to give as much as God had given us – as much as we rated our salvation. And Tetzel would have recognised his spiritual heir... Then as the plates were taken up to the platform, she weighed them carefully as though she held our souls in the balance, before abruptly shrieking out 'Hallelujah'; and the congregation praised the Lord.

We were then ready for what I'd irreverently come to consider the main attraction: the appearance of the pastor himself. He moved to the front of the dais, oozing greasy self-assurance, with a suntan even more jaundiced than his wife's. His hair curled over the back of his collar and I felt certain that his lip curled, too, as he looked down the hook of his nose at his flock. Once again the television association proved inescapable as he alternately humoured and harangued us, as though he were hosting a game show – albeit one which offered the supreme star prize.

Any vestige of Biblical literalism that may have lingered in me vanished, as he skipped promiscuously from text to text, establishing the most tenuous connections. I was horrified by his lack of sense, not to say scholarship, and still more so when he authoritatively pronounced that every word in the great book was indisputably that of God.

But then he had little time for theological niceties, or indeed niceties of any sort. So there was no private prayer nor contemplative silence. It was as though he feared that it might be dangerous to leave his congregation alone with God. Instead they were invited to sing up and shout out and let him do all their thinking for them. And I recalled another of our St Dunstan beatitudes: Blessed are the simple-minded: for they shall never know doubt.

The pastor clearly knew none, denouncing doubt as the work of the Devil; whilst he condemned other churches and tore into rival traditions, assuring us that communism was dead: which prompted several more 'Praise the Lord's… Although for myself I've never felt Marx's view of religion to have been more apt. Christ came to wash our souls in his redeeming blood, not our brains in such relentless banality. And there's all the difference in the world between my claim to trust in God and theirs to know him – and most of the bigotry, cruelty and oppression in the world, too.

The one note of dissent was struck by his wife, who sat sour-faced like a suburban matron at her husband's business dinner, which, come to think of it, was precisely what it was – it was certainly less the Lord's Supper than the pastor's. The rest of the congregation hung hungrily on his every word: their faces glistening with the glow of devotion; their fervour growing fetid. But when I gazed up, gasping for air, I saw that during the course of his diatribe someone had calculatedly switched on all the overhead radiators. So we could bask in the warmth of his heaters if not his heart.

He evidently believed in co-ordinating his effects... And he concluded with what appeared a favourite theme: the great gulf between sense- and revelation-knowledge. Sense-knowledge was lamentably lacking; it could never tell us which came first, the chicken or the egg. But he, or rather revelation-knowledge, could and did. When God created the world in 4004 BC – I was surprised he didn't specify the exact Monday – he created them at one and the same time: chickens with eggs inside them along with oak-trees bearing acorns and fossils in rocks.

He warned us that the Devil worked in the realm of sense-knowledge by means of illness. I began to blanch; this might have been familiar ground, but it was also growing dangerous. Then he asked if there were anyone there that morning who required the healing touch. The hall was silent; the fear of exposure obviously outweighed the hope of cure. Eventually a woman at the back plucked up courage. He demanded her symptoms; she coughed her reply.

He looked gravely insulted, as though such a minor ailment made a mockery of his powers. But with a long-suffering sigh he told her to place her hand on her heart whilst he repeated the prescribed formula. That done, he immediately inquired if she were cured. As she started to splutter, he boomed that if she were saved then she must be cured. She screeched her assent... her fright had made her whole.

He was now in his stride and impatient to do battle with the forces of darkness. He touted for business so avidly, I almost regretted my good health. Then when no one else appeared, he fell back on the evidence of former glory, calling upon their brother who'd been saved and cured only a fortnight before and who was, of course, Adrian.

From the ripple of anticipation, it was clear that his case had caused a considerable stir. Nevertheless, the pastor reiterated it, adding for good measure that he'd removed the hereditary curse and restored his soul to God. And then, to a frenzied accompaniment of clapping, screaming and stamping, he summoned him on to the dais and urged him to testify... although it was notable that of all the new converts Adrian was the only one whom he failed to embrace.

The hot and humid air grew heady and hypnotic as he primed himself for his final exhortation, warning that anyone who wished to enter the Kingdom of God had first to be born again, and calling on all those who'd been saved that day to 'Come on down' to the front. His wording struck a chord, and I recognised the catchphrase of a quiz show so mindless it'd become a cult amongst my friends at Balliol. Which in turn convinced me that whatever the evidence of Adrian's recovery, my image of the pastor as a game-show host manqué might not have been that wide of the mark... Which came first, the quizmaster or the evangelist? Or perhaps in 4004 BC God created the evangelist with a little quizmaster inside?

But my cynicism was no match for the worshippers' ecstasy as they whistled and whooped and testified. Then, from behind, I heard what for one glorious moment I took to be a hiss; until I realised with horror that people were starting to speak in tongues. And what was more, so was Adrian... And this was a man whose only previous experience of collective hysteria had been to yell, 'Maggie, Maggie, Maggie, Out, Out, Out.'

The pastor then announced a second offertory in terms even more extortionate than the first. And as the band reached a crescendo and the collection plates made a further bumpy ride to the front, I reflected on a church which could so readily dispense with the fundamental symbol of the faith; and I realised that not only was the Cross an embarrassment, it was an irrelevance. They had no need of the sacraments. The offertory was more than just the climax of their service; it was their Mass.

Then, with no more ado, it was over. The band reverted to the rhythms of the dance-floor and the pastor and his wife were whisked away like visiting royalty, whilst the congregation was caught up in an all-embracing hug which at points even stretched to include me. But I refused either to be included or deflected and headed straight for Adrian, who stood conspicuously alone, abandoned by both the shepherd and his flock.

I tapped his shoulder; he jerked around, a blandly beatific smile on his face. He showed no sign of emotion; emotion was clearly a thing of the past which had been removed along with the hereditary curse... I asked him how he was, and he seemed surprised by the question, as though not only was he perfectly well but his health had never been an issue. And it was then that he told me the results of his tests. They'd not been able to detect a single antibody; the virus had completely disappeared.

I searched for words and chose the wrong one: all I could say was that it was 'marvellous'. And he glared at me as though I'd profaned both the pastor's skill and his conversion. The word I was looking for was 'miraculous'... And I was gripped by more than enough emotion for both of us. So I tried to hug him; but his body felt hollow and hard.

We engaged in desultory conversation; and he explained that he was living with one of the men from the church. For a moment I wondered if I'd misheard; until I realised I'd misunderstood, and his speech was now as uncompromised as his faith... Which was more than could be said for theirs; at least to judge from their determination to keep him under constant watch. He told me he'd resigned from LID – to devote himself to the Lord. Every evening he told his story at prayer meetings, in youth clubs and on street corners. And he was grateful for each last indecency, since it served to win souls for Christ.

I think that if I'd suddenly discovered he had a twin, identical in voice, appearance and manner although his antithesis in just about everything else, I could scarcely have been more surprised. This wasn't Adrian, but his shell. And I was sorely afraid that the pastor might have excised his humanity when he'd exorcised his hereditary curse.

We were then joined by two of the ushers who were patently

suspicious of our conversation and anxious to spirit him swiftly away. For my own part I was glad of the chance to escape; but I refused to leave without mentioning Mark. So I asked whether he had any message for him – and as it turned out, he had; but one so smugly sanctimonious I had no intention of passing it on.

They led him away down a subterranean passage and I went home completely confused. Adrian was cured; of that there could be no doubt. I had the evidence of my own eyes as well as his tests. But if God had chosen to work through the pastor then his ways were even more mysterious than I'd thought.

Yet you'd be wrong to dismiss my objections as High Church snobbery or my misgivings as parochial pride, when his methods smacked more of mesmerism than ministry and I'd never attended any service where I felt so close to the Devil and so excluded from God... The problem is that those were precisely the accusations the Pharisees levelled at Christ. And I'm tormented by a vision of the pastor thumbing a text, thumping a Bible and then pointing a finger at me.

And I'm no longer ruminating on theological niceties but wrestling with intense self-doubt. What if their word-for-word approach proves after all to be the true one, whilst I've allowed myself to be seduced by the subjectivity of the age? What if it's I who fail to read rather than they who fail to interpret? What if their literalism gives the lie to my liberalism, just as their full-blooded embrace puts my half-hearted kiss of peace to shame?

Seven

At the top of this rough track you see the ruins of Bradshaw Hall. You're free to walk up to them, but please don't venture on them. In the course of mapping out this tour last week I was clambering on the walls when a villager warned me that they were liable to subside and I was risking my neck. I jumped off pretty smartish, straight into a clump of thistles, which scratched my legs so sharply that I still bear the scars.

But to matters of more moment... Just as in the south Charles II and his court hurriedly left the capital, initially for Hampton Court and subsequently for Salisbury and Oxford, so the wealthy families of Eyam escaped as quickly as they could. First to leave were the Sheldons, shortly followed by the Widow Bradshaw and her daughter Ann, whose home this was. They fled, never to return, and it's reported that recently bought tapestries lay rotting in the corridors without once having been unrolled. From then on the local centre of influence shifted to Eyam Hall, which was completed in 1678, almost certainly with the stone from this house.

It seems fitting that although the rest of the village has been so beautifully preserved both in style and spirit, this should have been left to decay. For it was the ordinary men and women who banded together for the greater good, whilst the rich and powerful cut and ran. And so it's their memories which are still honoured and their cottages inhabited, even as this hall has fallen into disrepair and its owners into disrepute.

That the poor should have borne the brunt of the epidemic was only to be expected; at least here they weren't also forced to bear the blame. In London, on the other hand, the authorities knew it as the 'Poore's Plague', and, just as in Hamburg in the 1890s where the City Fathers laid the responsibility for the outbreak of cholera squarely on the dirt and diet of the lower classes rather than the environmental pollution to which their rampant industrialism had given rise, their ingrained prejudice and institutionalised misconceptions prevented them from taking effective action to contain its spread.

For instance, the Lord Mayor ordered that all dogs and cats should be slaughtered immediately, and official exterminators were richly rewarded. Indeed, it's been calculated that as many as 40,000 dogs and 200,000 cats perished by their knives. And my revulsion isn't simply sentimental; their ill-informed ordinance was counterproductive, since it allowed the plague rats free rein.

In Hamburg, where for commercial reasons the government resisted essential quarantine and disinfection measures, preferring to localise the problem among deprived and defenceless groups, such cynical manipulation had even direr consequences. For it was the ensuing hardening of attitudes amongst the general population that created the climate in which, forty years later, the city would become one of the chief strongholds of Nazi support. And those of us seeking a historical context for our present crisis find the imagery turning full circle: from Plague to Holocaust and back again.

And now we must turn back to Eyam, where the predominant picture could hardly have been more different. I wouldn't have brought you all this way simply to hear an account of a three-hundred-year-old disease, some cowardly desertions, a few lucky escapes and a lot of painful deaths. For first and foremost this is a story of communal co-operation inspired by its priests. And since in June 1665 the Plague Count had risen to nineteen and was once again increasing, it was clear both that drastic steps were required and that, following the departure of the Bradshaws and Sheldons, any lead would be left to the rector. Fortunately he was to prove worthy of the task.

I have nothing to say. But then I no longer feel threatened by the silence. What's the greatest distance between two people? A word.

Although on a practical note, should you ever need to contact me,

I'm back at the flat. I'm living out of a suitcase; but at least it was one I packed for myself. No one has thrown me out. No one has accused me of murdering my brothers and banished me from Eden, even if it was only the temporary haven of the Church of Christ in Triumph. No one has pointed to the lesions on my body, the sperm-shaped scars scrawled in the scruff of my neck and proclaimed them the marks of Cain.

I know you thought... and so did I; but then my medical dictionary is as out of date as your medical training. Do you no longer keep in touch with current trends? Or are therapists and venereologists the Montagues and Capulets of medical practice? Whatever the reason, we were both deceived. For however improbable it may seem, antibodies can be a good sign; they show that the body is still fighting back. Whereas Adrian's resistance is so weak that even that last line of defence has been lost to him and with it his last ray of hope.

My suspicions proved all too well-founded; his cure was a sham. And yet 'I told you so' is no comfort; why didn't I tell him? But I clutched at straws, the way I used to clutch at a crucifix and Mark still does at a piece of crystal; his own faith might have healed him, even though the pastor's had failed... Besides, what was the alternative? The fumbling sympathy of the hospital chaplain? The futile fudge of liberal doubts? I feel so futile! Why didn't I train as a doctor and try to save people here and now? There'll be an eternity to save souls. What earthly use to anyone is a priest?

The pastor himself faced a more immediate dilemma; but true to his designation he turned disaster into triumph. If even he had been unable to save him, it clearly proved he was beyond redemption. Such backsliding was a reminder that they must be ever-vigilant, for Satan was ever-virulent. And he entreated his congregation to redouble their efforts – and no doubt also their contributions – in order to drive him out.

In the meantime he drove out Adrian. He ritually anathematised him, as the dramatic end to a morning service, whilst his flock shrieked and swayed and spat. Even so, when I expressed my contempt for both the man and his methods, Adrian sprang straight to his defence. It was his own sinfulness that was at fault. Some people had faith that would move mountains; and yet his wouldn't even remove a few rogue cells. And his vulnerability moved me even more than his wounds.

It was about a week later that he called me, in the afternoon when he felt sure that Mark would be at work... the memory of their last encounter was too raw to be entrusted to the phone. At first he claimed he was simply ringing for a chat; but then after several false starts and much inconclusive mumbling he began to tell me a little of what had occurred. He even tried to describe his lesions; although nothing could have prepared me for the destruction of his face.

Meanwhile he was alone in the flat. His minders from the church had departed, leaving a trail of devastation and a chain of deforestation in their wake... And forty minutes later I was sitting in his bedroom: the one room I remotely recognised, holding his hand and stifling my shock. I immediately tried to put the place in some sort of order: or at any rate to return it to the ordered disorder of the past. I clung to the illusion of utility; rooms, at least, could be set to rights. And I remembered Aunt Sylvia, in a typical dig at nurses, asking why, if their time were so valuable, they wasted so much on domestic chores. But the answer was evident... Blessed are they who clean and scrub and polish: for they shall achieve results.

I scoured the bath and then filled it full of bubbles, which made my eyes water – or at least afforded me an excuse to cry. I helped him undress, though I may have been more of a hindrance as he was so brittle and bony and flaky I was terrified he might bruise. Stripped of clothes and devoid of flesh his ulcerated body appeared to have been subjected to systematic torture, alternately starved of food and affection, and scorched with the butts of cigarettes.

Even lukewarm water struck him as blisteringly hot. But the extravagance of the bubbles removed the sting as they conjured up memories of his boyhood when he'd regularly sent off to Hollywood for photographs of minor starlets posed unrevealingly in their tubs. And he was transported back to a world before the Fall, where life was as innocently black and white as the pictures and his sexuality as insubstantial as the starlets' suds.

He luxuriated in his bath as I did in his pleasure; then all at once my eyes strayed to the towel rail and I found myself staring at a hospital walking-stick. I felt sick. It seemed less another sign of failing powers than a symbol of desolation: as starkly evocative as Van Gogh's old boots. For Adrian was a dancer. His body had been his medium. And now it was irrevocably impaired. And as if by a process of telekinesis, it rattled abruptly against the rail and clattered to the ground.

I started back guiltily and moved to pick it up, whilst he picked up on some of its implications. A dancer's career had always been short; but now for so many it was even shorter. In America the ballet world wore a permanent black tie and not only for galas... although there were still plenty of those and always for the same cause; as the great and the good and the rich and the famous rubbed shoulders and kissed cheeks, raising money for the dying, paying tribute to the dead. *Ars longa vita brevis* was once the watchword. Now art was expensive, life cheap.

His eyes began to water, and not just from the bubbles, as he bitterly recalled his mother's philosophy and tried to look on the bright side. So many of his dancer friends had used to agonise about what they'd do when they retired; at least far fewer now had that problem... I leaned over and took hold of his slippery, spindly body and tried to infuse him with my strength. But I quite lost my grip when he suddenly sobbed that he'd never dance again, not even for joy. And two tears stepped delicately out of the corners of his eyes and pirouetted down his cheeks... And I'm sorry if I sound fanciful; but it's all that keeps the pain at bay.

Helping him from the bath became a major operation... task. He sat scrawnily on the side, whilst I dabbed him dry and brought him his pyjamas, which he kept opening in order to stare at the lesions on his chest. At first I put it down to disbelief and then morbid curiosity; but it turned out that he was taking his cue from Mark and trying to visualise them away. Except that his imagination, previously so fertile, now failed him; and all he was able to conjure up was the mottled skin of the Devil and the heavy hand of God the Pastor raised against him in wrath. And his tears became an entire corps de ballet... Although he added that he found the swellings strangely comforting to scratch.

It's the loss of his looks which I'd say has hit him hardest. For years he led a life which was just as sheltered as mine – only for wealth read style – as he moved exclusively amongst beautiful people, from the dances he danced and the houses he visited to the holidays he took and the magazines that he bought. Now he's suddenly had to face a new reality... and the reality of his new face.

But it was far from new to me; and I remembered with a jolt where I'd seen it before: on the old man in the Edensor arbour, with the puce, puckered flesh and livid lumps. And yet far from backing away in fear I stood fast in reassurance. Ugliness, I insisted, was not an issue... Although words alone would have done little to relieve his mind, still less his body; so I relied rather on my hands. I ran them slowly over his head and shoulders and teased the lonely-looking hairs on his chest. He crinkled with delight and confessed that it was so long since anyone had touched him. Even the pastor's laying on of hands had been at one remove. And as he kissed each of my palms in turn, I knew that whatever else I had to continue on to and into his groin.

I sensed the conflict of hope and despair that engulfed him. And I seized on the hope as I masturbated him gently... gratefully; for there was still something I could do besides plumping pillows and arranging flowers. And his sexuality, which I'd once found such a threat, appeared the most miraculous manifestation of life. And when he eventually came with a heart-rending shudder that belied his frailty, and I wiped both his thigh and my hand, I felt that not only had I finally laid the ghost of the pastor, but I'd learnt what it was to be a priest.

I settled him in bed and left him to sleep between two thick towels before returning to the kitchen to phone Mark, who he felt sure would refuse to see him... although his stratagem was as plain to himself as to me. And as he'd known and as you'd have expected, he was there within the hour. I made myself scarce as he made his way into the bedroom; their reconciliation struck me as more intimate even than love-making. And within minutes any differences were resolved.

Our immediate task was to take him to hospital. And yet he was nervous. It seemed that after his cure – if it weren't such a sick joke I'd pretend to put 'sic' in parenthesis – he'd abandoned all his treatments, as though to keep so much as an aspirin would display an unforgivable lack of faith. He'd been as impervious to his doctors' advice as to their prognosis, charging them with jealousy; and so he expected they'd show him the door. Whereas to his amazement they've shown him nothing but kindness and respect.

They've given him a bed in a small side-ward which was once a linen closet. And he's gained considerable mileage from the association. But then his wit's about all he has left... While my every visit churns my stomach. I have to ring a bell to enter, and make my way past piles of medical supplies, oxygen cylinders and laundry bags stamped with skulls and cross-bones, into the sour and sweaty atmosphere of the ward. On his first day I filled three vases with freesias for their fragrance; but when I went the next afternoon they'd died. I was seized with superstitious dread and immediately bought three more bunches from the League of Friends, which have so far lasted a week... Do you suppose they breed them specially: a hybrid of hot-house, sick-room blooms?

Not that they afford him any pleasure. He's in permanent, preoccupying pain; for which the doctors can only diagnose more and more complications and prescribe more and more pills. He takes upwards of ten or twelve at a time; and then complains he can feel each one sinking through his stomach like a separate smart. The other day, only moments before spewing them all back up, he proposed a new version of The Princess and the Pea: to be entitled The Queen and the Pill.

He has meningitis, which is what makes it so hard for him to swallow, whilst at the same time necessitating the bulk of the pills. They've put him on five different antibiotics; and even Mark no longer has the heart to protest. That was one disease I'd disregarded amongst all the complicated cancers, pneumonias and paralysis. And

I'm appalled at the reality of his lack of immunity, and I yearn to take him in my arms and cocoon him in my resistance... But then I've also learnt to visualise; and my body appears as a mass of marauding germs.

He's begun to lose control of his bowels, with an infant's incapacity. He's on a course of chemotherapy, but the drugs make him vomit so violently that they have to pump extra fluids through his drip; which in turn increases his incontinence. And it seems unspeakably cruel that having struggled for so long in the face of so many odds to assert his dignity, he should be reduced to such a messy end. Yesterday he spilt a cup of tea all over his sheets. I rushed for a towel. But he smiled wryly and assured me that that was nothing compared to the mess inside. And I was suddenly conscious of a sharp, stagnant smell seeping through the room. My brave face has never been so brave.

At least he doesn't lack for company. So many friends wish to visit him that it's a major job trying to keep to any kind of plan. Killing with kindness seems a very real possibility; and yet, as Vange says, it mightn't be the worst way to go. Sometimes he revels in being the centre of so much attention, whilst at others he just wants to crawl inside his bedding and die. His moods can veer alarmingly and yet he expects all of ours to keep pace. Then he'll turn on us savagely and accuse us of trying to humour him. And we have no redress; no one dares protest for fear of feeding his greatest fear: that of losing his mind.

For the worst horror remains bearable so long as he can give it a name. But if that goes he'd have nothing, not even the chance to escape... to swallow the bitter-sweet pills of suicide and suffer the pain of ingestion one final time. And his fear contains the added pang of disillusion. As a teenager he worshipped twin idols: Rita Hayworth and Vaslav Nijinsky: the goddess of the silver screen and the god of the dance. He modelled himself first on one and then on the other; but his choice seems marked by prophetic irony as he contemplates the insanity of both their ends.

And yet he refuses to give up. It's a calumny to claim that humankind cannot bear very much reality; on the contrary, it strikes me that it can bear an almost infinite amount. When I consider to what it's been reduced, his struggle to keep his hold on reality seems little short of heroic. He deserves the Victoria Cross for his courage – no, we want nothing more Victorian – a pink plaque. And each new day brings a further diminution. Another dawn... another symptom... another treatment. Another false dawn... another forced smile... another despair.

Blessed are they that die young: for they shall have first shot at God.

Meanwhile Mark and I drift further apart than ever. If an optimist considers a man half-alive and a pessimist half-dead, then he's the first and I'm the second. At the hospital we're two sides of the same smile... though I worry which will be the first to crack. Not that I'm allowed to say so; he has the same absolute faith in the power of positive thinking that I used to have in prayer. And I fear for its loss. As he watches him fade, it's as though his whole philosophy has been weighed and found wanting. In the event his self-acceptance has proved as deficient as my self-denial.

We disagree about tactics – no, basics. My sole concern is with what's best for Adrian; and I can no longer accept that this is it. I can't believe that a bed bath and a bedpan, and pissing blood and sweating buckets, and collapsing on the floor at four in the morning in a smear of shit is any sort of life worth living. And I've never held the view that any life is better than none... You look pained; but you know I'm a confirmed cynic. A cynic is someone who knows that everything has a price and nothing a value. You can have that for free.

And along with the other redefinitions – optimist, pessimist and cynic – I've discovered the true meaning of second childhood. It's not only a loss of reason, but a loss of control: the mind's inconsequence and the body's incontinence, as the world churns upside down and inside out... Adrian always set such store by his body, which is now just a series of lumps and bumps and tubes tucked in a sheet – a relief map beyond relief.

Mark is so desperate to save him that he's blind to his own selfishness; his eyes are so bloodshot he can't see the blood. But I look down on his emaciated frame picked clean by the vulturous virus; and murder seems a synonym for mercy. It would take so little: his body's so frail that his spine would snap like a wishbone. His breath's so hesitant; his neck's so thin. Do you think I should take his life into my hands, literally, tenderly: these life-giving, death-releasing hands? Should I lay his panting head back on the pillows and then squeeze?

Each man kills the thing he loves... I think of Rees – there's no comparison. I once tried to take my own life, in the days when it still had a value; or at any rate I still set a value on my despair. But we don't have to be in love with death in order to choose it. It may just be the lesser of two evils. And if evil is simply good gone wrong, as Miss Harper taught us in Sunday school, then despair is no more than frustrated hope.

And yet in a world without hope, let alone a universe, despair is a commonplace, and suicide no longer a philosophical question, merely an empty gesture: a corpse to lay out and bung up. Murder, however, is a very different matter: murder is to love my neighbour as I long to be loved myself; murder isn't simply the ultimate gift of friendship, but the last remaining ethical act.

Eight

This is Mompesson's well. I did warn you it would be quite a trek, but I hope you'll agree that both the scenery and the story repay the trip. And to those of you expecting a fairy-tale wishing-well, I make no apologies either; it's just a simple stone trough. Although I for one wouldn't wish it otherwise.

William Mompesson, the twenty-eight or twenty-nine year old rector – the confusion is history's, not mine – ranks first amongst all Eyam's unsung heroes. When it became apparent that the plague which was ravaging the village had not yet reached the surrounding areas, he persuaded his parishioners of their overriding duty to prevent its spread: in effect to throw a cordon sanitaire around themselves. But the consequences of that decision, both practical and psychological, were immense.

Although they would have been largely self-sufficient, in order to secure such provisions and medical supplies as they might otherwise have lacked, he enlisted the support of the Earl of Devonshire, who arranged for goods to be placed at pre-arranged points around the boundaries, of which this was one. Here the villagers left coins, which were first cleansed in the spring and then disinfected with vinegar, together with records of the plague... which must have made for grim reading, since it claimed another fifty-six victims in July alone. And as you can see, visitors are still throwing in money today; along with sweet wrappers, cigarette butts and – a sure sign of the times, albeit for us an appropriate one – an empty packet of 'Mates'.

Inevitably, over the years there have been those who've sought to discredit Mompesson's motives. It's as though the clarity of his purpose sets their own squalid vacillations in sharp relief. With the bogus benefit of hindsight, they quibble that the elaborate disinfecting process was superfluous, as the microbes could never have lived on the coins. Furthermore, they contend that in urging isolation he was seriously misguided, as the cramped spaces of their insanitary cottages offered the very worst chance for survival; whilst so long as they'd taken certain elementary precautions, there'd have been only minimal danger of passing the disease on to anyone else.

But don't forget that there were no specialised practitioners in the parish; as rector, he himself was expected to be both doctor and divine. And whatever he may have lacked in discipline, he more than made up in dedication. Whereas the professionals frequently failed in both... Take the case of the Chatsworth carter who, having delivered a load of logs to the beleaguered village, caught a chill which his neighbours mistook for plague. They kept him closely confined until the Earl of Devonshire dispatched his personal physician. This worthy gentleman determined to conduct the essential examination not at first hand but shouting from the opposite river-bank, whilst the Derwent, doubtless full of healthy antiseptic properties, flowed freely in-between.

The neighbours' behaviour is understandable; the doctor's unforgivable. And yet before we congratulate ourselves on the ensuing three centuries of progress, it'd be wise to recall the views of many of his successors. 'Don't die of ignorance' may be plastered across the nation's billboards, but it isn't a problem purely for the layman. We're told that the transfusion service is experiencing a severe shortage of blood; nevertheless a recent letter to the *Lancet* demanded that during the present crisis lesbians should be deterred from donating – despite being universally acknowledged as the lowest risk group. And while, as Jonathan said last night, for most men the combination of lesbians and blood smacks alarmingly of vampires, the price of their prejudice could be lives.

On which note I propose we take a ten-minute break. I for one feel a pressing need to devote myself to the spirit of the place and make both an offering and a wish.

It's good of you to fit me in, especially after I've missed so many sessions; but I think that if I hadn't talked to someone, I'd have... May I take off my jacket? It's as hot as hell in here... Please forgive the formality, but the funeral was two days ago and I've not yet had a chance to change. I've slept in my clothes: that is, if I've slept at all. My shirt has turned grey at the cuffs and yellow under the arms. I feel like a man living rough on the Embankment desperately trying to keep sanitary in a public lavatory. I'm desperately trying to keep sane.

I must try to make sense. I must lick my thoughts into shape like a batch of raw recruits. I must order my life with military precision or else I'm sunk. Mark... Adrian... He was buried in an eight-foot-deep grave in a lead, leak-proof coffin. It seemed that after so many years of declaring him to be outside nature they were determined to prevent his returning to it: be it only to fertilise the ground. I intend to form a new pressure group: corpses' rights... I'm sorry. Just give me a moment to calm down.

And yet the peace of the grave is as illusory as the joy of living. There's no respite: we come into this world in our mothers' pain and leave it in our own. And his was much exacerbated by his treatment. They experimented with drugs to the bitter end: with one he couldn't eat, with another he was nauseous, with a third he was constipated and with a fourth he had diarrhoea. So they countered and combined them; and he clammed up and seeped out. And every morning he woke up in a stranger's body and prayed for equilibrium. After one day spent constantly vomiting he asked his nurse why they didn't just cut out the middle man and throw his food straight down the loo. And then he choked on his own joke.

They injected every one of his fifty-seven lesions, which blistered and burst only to return in an even greater profusion than before. One on his leg swelled overnight to the size of a goose egg and then erupted in spurts of blood and pus and squirts of gas. The mess was indescribable. Although at least for three days he was able to look at a body with a chance of resurrection. For three days his cratered skin felt smooth. For three days... No! I can give thanks for small mercies, but not ones that are so short-lived.

In the final week he lost his sight; which wasn't just a darkness, but a disorientation. Whenever he woke, he could no longer be sure if it were the greater darkness of day or the lesser of night. And as he strained for clues and reassurance, he was convinced that after all he had lost his mind. But he wasn't to be afforded even that relief; instead he lost control of his speech. His tongue lolled in his mouth; and he swallowed his words in a slobber of saliva: foaming furiously whenever we tried to fill in the gaps.

I sat for hours examining him with an intensity which would have been intrusive had he been able to see. I performed a post-mortem on his suffering long before he was dead. I registered the hollow, parchment cheeks and the face defaced by lesions; the pitilessly pitted skin and the wide, opaque eyes: eyes that seemed to pierce me with their blankness, eyes that managed to be at once both alive and dead, eyes with retinas detached by despair. I fuelled my fears from the burnt-out fires of his eyes.

And where could I turn for consolation? Not to the priests; Christ's death has been turned into a celebration – a grown-up Guy Fawkes. And not to the poets; even the greatest of them was wrong: his seventh age – his second childhood was quite out of sequence. He should have been the lover or maybe the soldier, not that amalgam of absences: sans anything at all... And where could he turn for consolation? Not to the pastor, who'd thrown his lost sheep to the wolves; and not to his sister: by the time she deigned to appear it was all over bar the mourning. No, his only solace as ever was his friends.

Mark took compassionate leave... although he abhorred the term. He sat very still, desperately tired and absolutely tireless: imperceptibly smoothing the creases in both his bedding and his routines. He did everything that was required, whereas I did everything that was requested; which I knew all too well wasn't the same. I watched him watching Adrian and prayed that in eight years' time I might understand him just as instinctively... But then time was no longer on my side, nor on his.

At least he didn't die in the hospital, but in a hospice: in a room named after Elizabeth Taylor, which seemed to please him even though he wasn't a fan. During his last week he asked me to read to him from *Robinson Crusoe*, the earliest volume on his shelves. Sometimes he'd stop me in mid-sentence, clasping my wrist with the feeble boniness of a ghost-train skeleton, and hold out his hand for the copy. He'd fondly finger its foxed pages, cracked spine and scuffed cover, as though the book were as evocative as the story. I wondered whether he might be searching for something hidden between the pages: a photograph or a note or a pressed flower. But he just croaked at me not to mind him and begged me to read on. Nevertheless I was still too slow, or rather death came too quickly. And he died before Crusoe was saved.

His end was so sudden that even though I was there, I contrived to miss it. I'd like to think that it was so peaceful I wasn't aware; but I'm afraid I may have fallen asleep. And yet, when my experience of death-beds had been confined to *La Traviata*, it was little wonder that I was so unprepared. For it didn't come with a discreet cough and a soaring aria; nor with the sweet scent of roses, let alone camellias; but in a shower of shit and spit and snot and sputum as I hastily grabbed at my handkerchief – and not for my eyes, but my nose.

My initial sensation was of an overwhelming odour: a sewer-sweet stench pervading the room, which my handkerchief simply pressed in further. His death was a verifiable fact; I could smell him inside me. I tried not to sniff. I looked at Mark, who was staring transfixed at his head, so cruelly lifelike on the pillow. I was desperate to know if there'd been any sign of recognition or moment of transcendence; but I couldn't see how to ask. I was – I am appalled by my sloth: no doubt I'd even sleep through the Second Coming.

I stifled a sob; Mark shuffled impatiently. I moved towards him, but he turned away and asked me to fetch a nurse. I hurried out gratefully and then paused for several minutes in the corridor, not simply for breath nor to give them a final few moments together, but because one of my earliest memories had returned: of my mother describing how she'd been trained to wait an hour before laying out a body to allow time for the soul to escape. And I longed to regain such simple faith.

Death was just the first in a long line of indignities... the Lord's Prayer be damned: I shall never forgive Maureen for what she did to Adrian and, through him, to Mark. I'd tried my best. I even called her clandestinely from the hospice to warn that time was running out. But her sole response was a Mabel Lucie Atwell Get Well Soon card which, whether by accident or design, she signed with her surname: with every fond wish from Maureen and Ted Johnson, Roger and Brett. He rasped ruefully that he only had one sister; even *in extremis* he could be trusted to remember her name.

But her reaction to my news of his death was altogether different. All of a sudden her commitments disappeared... I'm sorry; I find what happened next extremely distressing. It's sufficient to say that having washed her hands of him whilst he was dying she was determined to get them on him once he was dead.

Roundly dismissing any charge of morbidity, Adrian had been as preoccupied with the plans for his funeral as wealthier men were with their wills... His will! It would be his final party, and he was determined to be if not its life then at least its soul. He even chose an appropriate anthem: 'It's my party and I'll cry if I want to'; at which point Mark suggested he might also like to choreograph the tears... But he should have saved his breath, for Maureen showed a complete disregard for all our wishes and insisted on her right as next of kin to take charge of the arrangements herself.

And if that weren't enough, and for Mark it most certainly wasn't since they practically came to blows in the chapel of rest, she asserted that she was his executor: which was the first we'd heard. I immediately consulted my solicitor, who confirmed that we had no redress. And so with all the conviction I could muster and considerably more than I felt, I persuaded him to let her take the body. She could never take the memory. And he agreed, for Adrian's sake; for his own, he was spoiling for a fight.

He arranged an effective boycott of the funeral; so I travelled up to Bolton alone. There was a power failure and the train was without heat, light or flushing lavatories; the discomfort felt apt. I was sure that

Mark considered my journey a betrayal, but I needed the consolation of the ceremony. And yet it proved even worse than his dying; it was his denying. Had I known, I wouldn't have gone. Though he managed to have the last laugh, if only by proxy. I shall never be able to read the words 'Family flowers only' without a grin.

The service was held in a mission hall which, from the paintings on the wall and the paint on the parquet, I presumed must also have hosted a pre-school play-group. The hymns were soft-pedalled on a piano that was out of tune; whilst at times Maureen's vibrato threatened to drown it entirely. It would have been charitable to conclude that her grief had shattered her composure: charitable but untrue.

The coffin was wheeled in by an adolescent undertaker who appeared to be on a Youth Opportunities Programme. Death was his one opportunity and he evidently resented it. There was dried blood on the back of his neck whilst the knot in his tie was just a millimetre away from irreverence; and all my thoughts of Adrian vanished in a flurry of untimely conjecture about horseplay in the hearse. He pushed the trolley as gracelessly as a week's groceries; and then pulled to a halt in front of the makeshift altar as though standing in line at a till.

The family took their seats. The congregation numbered around twenty; and I was convinced that I recognised a contingent from the London branch of their church. My worst fears were realised when the pastor himself sauntered in to conduct the service; and I had to clap my hand over my mouth as he brazenly introduced himself as one of Adrian's most trusted friends. Nor could I banish the suspicion that he'd attempt the ultimate test of his powers and try to resurrect him. Although I fast perceived from his abbreviated address and perfunctory prayers that, for him, the sooner Adrian was underground the better... It's not only doctors who have the chance to bury their mistakes.

I resolved not to follow the cortège to the cemetery. The man they were burying was no longer Adrian; and I saw little point in adding to the pastor's audience or my own pain. I walked out through the porch where they'd previously put the flowers. There'd been three wreaths including mine; although pride of place had been given to what I'm sure Maureen must have described as a floral tribute: a large heart of red and white chrysanthemums with his name stuck on in gold.

It was no longer there. Whilst I'd been sitting through the pastor parsimoniously singing his praises and his sister sanctimoniously the hymns, it had been replaced by a giant phallus of white lilies, perfectly arranged around a stake with two symmetrical floral balls. It was anatomically correct to the very last detail: the kind of phallus Adrian would have died for... I didn't mean that... It immediately made up for all the underhand hypocrisies of the funeral. He'd go out as he'd gone on, with a defiant thumb to his nose – no, it's time that I called a prick a prick.

My delight in the gesture was only increased by the mourners' expressions as they approached in disgusted disbelief. They skirted it as though it were the real thing, and then watched numbly as Maureen appeared, supported by Ted and the pastor, only to stop dead in her tracks. She slumped, double-chinned and open-mouthed, as the young undertaker walked up and inquired if she wanted it laid out on the coffin, before sniggering that he wasn't sure it would fit. And I rejoiced in his schoolboy smut.

She quickly regained control, seizing both her sons and propelling them, protesting, back into the hall, as the pastor moved towards the display with all the distaste of a man who publicly appended fig-leaves on to statues whilst privately doodling obscene graffiti in the margins of notes. He bent to lift it; but the weight of the base was deceptive; and he toppled back with a high-pitched yelp, grabbing his groin. Maureen rushed to his aid, aiming, in passing, a hefty kick at the stake, fatally dislodging one of the balls which slithered slowly down the slope.

The lilies proved remarkably resilient as the ball rolled straight along the path and out through the gate. And I wanted to shout a Hallelujah which would have put even that congregation to shame, for the sure sign that Adrian had also eluded them. They'd not been able to keep him from his party after all – he'd been there in spirit: the spirit of outrage which had served him so well all his life. And I hurried home, determined to discover the provenance and divert Mark with the report... If I'd only known.

He'd planned an alternative gathering at the flat to commemorate – or rather blot out – the main event elsewhere. But as I raced up the stairs it became clear that the revelry was distinctly muted – not to say non-existent. I felt apprehensive. It wasn't the occasion for sober reflection. The noise level should have given cause for complaint for years. I fumbled with my key in the lock; it wouldn't fit. I was too exhausted to think straight. I tried again – I looked again; the lock had been changed.

The only logic was the logic of nightmare; and I was terrified that for some reason – some suicidal reason, Mark was trying to keep me out. I hammered on the door. It opened to reveal a stranger: a short, doltish-looking man who smelt of peppermints and perspiration. The door opened; and my world caved in.

The party was over; every party was over. Anyone who holds a party from now on will have me to answer to; anyone who goes to a party will be dancing on my grave. As I've no doubt you've guessed, the intruder was from the Church of Triumph. It seems – it only seems, because I've not yet had it checked and I swear that I'll have every lawyer in London working on it if need be – but it seems that not only had Adrian made Maureen his executor, he'd made over his flat to the church.

I'm convinced that there must have been some sleight of hand; although I admit that his copy of the will looked genuine. I suppose it's possible that in a rush of gratitude after his cure he did sign; but then he'd surely have retracted after his relapse. If only Mark hadn't been so dismissive of the whole business. For my own part I find the flat cramped and claustrophobic; but it's his home. And he must have some rights. After all he's lived there, lover and lodger, for eight years.

I tried to push past; but the trespasser had discovered a bolt and chain which I hadn't known existed. Then with an agility clearly born of years of doorstep evangelism, he sidestepped my objections, adding aggrievedly that Mark had ignored repeated requests to leave from both Mrs Johnson and the church. I was confused. It'd all happened so fast; I'd always presumed proving wills took years. And besides he'd said nothing to me... although he had been behaving strangely. I'd put it down to grief, but then...

So earlier in the afternoon, assuming he'd be attending the funeral, some members of the church had arrived to take possession. This provoked a bitter exchange, in the course of which, according to my informant, Mark lost control and began lashing out so wildly that his friends were barely able to hold him back. And in the melee he collapsed. He has... he has... You know what he has; so why didn't I?

I blame myself; I've neglected him cruelly. And yet as to that he's equally culpable. These last few weeks he's been as careless of his own health as he was protective of Adrian's. And though it amused him to mock my ideal of self-sacrifice as sublimated masochism – I'm sorry, I expect that must be coals to Newcastle – the same might be said of him. He seemed to feel that the more he could push himself to no ill-effect, the more he could point the way for his friend.

And he ignored the flaws in his logic as blatantly as I did his symptoms... So I warn you, don't ever trust my observations, let alone my judgement, again. When I told you he looked jowly; what I should have said was glandular. And his jaundiced skin wasn't just from so much carrot juice... He's in hospital; he has ARC.

Let's be clear about terms; are you clear about terms? I am – I always have been – and now I'll reap the reward. I said ARC, not AIDS. He does not have AIDS: not yet – not ever. As the doctor explained, it's purely a bureaucratic convenience. It means that he's eligible for the full range of treatments; and at least at last he means to accept. So to some extent it could be counted a blessing; it all depends how you look at it. And that's how I intend to look at it... And yet as I sat by his bed and he took my hand, I could feel far more of a change in him than a different three letters after his name.

And I was scared. While the doctors had been quick to attribute Adrian's rapid decline to his lack of drugs, Mark had assigned it no less conclusively to his loss of hope. He insisted that he hadn't died of disease, but of despair. If so, then I was even more afraid for him; suddenly all his resistance – emotional as well as physical – had cracked. And yet despite the discomfort he seemed relieved, as though he'd accepted the inevitable: not of death – please, not of death – but of illness; and he no longer felt the need to fight.

But I've moved in quite the opposite direction. Though he may be inclined to accept his fate, I'm determined to kick against it. And I'm prepared to do battle with God... You may warn that he has superior forces; but I have superior morals. He rejects his children; I stand by my friends. And I refuse to be fobbed off with any more cant about his unfathomable ways. So what if he has some master plan which we're all too stupid to understand? Human happiness is still of value: if not to him, at least to me.

And yet every face that I see is etched with suffering. It's overbalanced the world; and it's threatening to unbalance me. And I no longer gain strength from the heartless homily that it's only by plunging to the depths that we can rise to the heights. If so, why did God create the earth; why not stop at Heaven and Hell without this halfway house?

Suffering isn't ennobling – not for the victim and still less for his friends. So I won't allow anyone else to suffer on my behalf, any more than I'll accept redemption at the price of another person's pain.

But what about Christ? I see you wondering, afraid you must have understood nothing the past two years. Well, you're in good company; I've understood even less the past twenty-four... But I've finally been put wise; and I'm no longer willing to take his pain on trust. The Passion was just an Easter side-show designed to deflect attention from his father's darker purposes, like a royal wedding in a period of political restraint. Indeed, the pastor claimed that God only created the world so that his hot-blooded son would have someone to marry. At the time it appeared an absurd analogy; but now it seems the perfect image for a universal rape.

Although rape was about the last crime of which he'd have been capable. Don't forget that he had no sex. He was a creature of flesh and blood, but not sperm and smegma – not even in his conception:

poor Joseph was completely redundant. Though at least if he were to be born again today there'd be no danger of his inheriting the virus. With a virgin for a mother and a father who took non-participation to unprecedented lengths, he'd definitely be immune.

And it's we who've had to pay the price of his deficiency. Far from redeeming us he effectively condemned us. It'd be true to say that original sin was less the result of the sexuality of Adam than the sexlessness of Christ. For is it any wonder that St Augustine located the Fall of Man between his legs, when to be born without sin and to be born without sperm were one and the same? And while we may no longer have a Holman Hunt view of holiness and at a pinch we're prepared to picture Jesus sweating at a lathe, a set of chisels tucked in his belt and wood shavings caught in his beard, what difference does it make when below the belt he didn't sweat at all?

So in reply to the learned theologian who boldly speculated as to whether he might have been aroused by Mary's unorthodox foot massage: our sinless, spermless Saviour would never even have had to change his sheets.

You may think that I'm simply out to shock, but consider: without sexuality, just what was his humanity actually worth? For how can a man who was incapable of human love, at least in its deepest sense, ever be described as fully human? It's chastity, not charity, that ought to be a byword for cold. To be fully human is to love, and to feel the loss of that love or to see the pain of a lover is to discover the true meaning of despair. Universal sympathies are a very easy option; take it from me: I wrote – or at least I lived by – the book.

Of course you may want to argue that Christ also knew despair. He was betrayed by one friend and denied by another; he was mocked and misrepresented and his message misunderstood... But believe me, the loss of a friend doesn't even begin to compare... Then again you may point to his suffering on the Cross... But what's one day's pain, however intense, set against the dull desperation of a lifetime? Wouldn't you gladly exchange the endless angst for the sharp stab of the nails? And I grant that for a few brief moments he abandoned hope; he who was

God lost faith in himself. But millions of people lose faith all their lives: both in themselves and in him. He had to live with his own death; they have to live with the death of God.

Although to me that could only come as a relief. I long to be able to bury him once and for all and procure such a clear motive for my malaise. I'm aware that it's customary to claim despair as an obstacle to faith; but I find it just the opposite. And if you consider that self-indulgent, all I can say is that, like Christ, you've been let off lightly. I'm as sure of God as I am that this is my finger and this my thumb; but then I'm equally sure he abandoned us long ago.

It may even have begun that very afternoon on the Cross. Yes, that would be the ultimate irony: that the image of faith and redemption throughout the ages should in reality be quite the reverse. Perhaps it was then that he decided we simply weren't worth the sacrifice. Well, all I can say is that I've come to the same conclusion about him. If he's given up on me, then the feeling's mutual. And my impotence will be my power: let him do his worst; it'll afford me further proof of his injustice. The more he plagues me, the more it pleads my cause.

And even in defeat I shall triumph. I used to think that to be worthy of God we had to try to read not only his Bible, but his mind: to do his will, but our own way. Although now I see that I was starting from a false premise, when it's he who isn't worthy of us. But I shan't do the obvious and dedicate myself to evil like a wilful child who cuts off his nose to spite his face. On the contrary, I'll make every effort to do what's right; and yet no longer out of love for him, but out of contempt.

We must show him that if he's abandoned us, we can manage alone. We have to make the best of our lot like prisoners whose serenity shames their guards. It's no solution to go on a dirty protest: to refuse to wash and slowly sink into squalor until all that's apparent is the dirt on our skin, and God can say to himself: What did I tell you? I made these creatures from mud and that's all that they're fit for... No, we shall live in his dung and yet still come up smelling of roses: if only for the sweet satisfaction of proving him wrong.

———

The scales have dropped from my eyes, while the scales of justice have been weighed and found wanting. The Creation was a seven-days' wonder, the Incarnation slumming and the Redemption a sham – what's the use of building a house on a rock when it's undermined by an empty tomb? But if we haven't been redeemed by Christ then we'll simply have to redeem one another: humanity is our only hope.

Nine

I must apologise if my last remarks caused offence. It's not my wish to sow the seeds of contention. I'm aware that this is supposed to be our morning away from such issues. And yet, as must have become obvious, my interest in Eyam derives as much from its metaphorical associations as from its historical acts.

And I couldn't help noticing several of you looking uneasy when I described the sealing off of the village; the idea of a cordon sanitaire seems uncomfortably close to camps. But as yet it's only in Cuba, that most malign of dictatorships, that people with AIDS have been incarcerated. Whereas here the decision wasn't imposed from on high, but agreed communally. And Mompesson remained constantly amongst his charges, not just sharing, but alleviating their woes.

That in turn has led to a further and still more damaging attack on him and one, moreover, that has been made on far too many priests over the years; which was that, whatever its practical value, he rejoiced in the sacrifice demanded of him, and that such self-denial was no more than self-loathing writ large. It's claimed that his heroism reveals the hysteria at the heart of most religious practice... a desire to suffer as long and as painfully as possible in order to share in the Passion of Christ.

I fear that in reporting such calumny I insult your intelligence almost as much as its perpetrators do his memory. And yet I mention it solely in order to dismiss it. Besides, to many of the villagers flight was never a serious option. Plague or no plague, they either had to work their land or starve. Nevertheless, having elected to stay they contrived to make a virtue of necessity; indeed they gave virtue itself a new name. And the horror of their internment, as they found themselves literally numbered amongst the dead, beggars belief. They had no hope; but they show us even now that to have no hope is by no means the same as to despair. For though they may have failed to preserve their physical community, they preserved the idea of that community – the ideal of that community, without which mere survival would have been vain.

They joined in a true communion: a sharing and a sacrifice. And they contained the contagion within the village, but at a terrible cost to themselves... And now, so long as you're all wearing sturdy shoes, we'll take a short-cut across a steep and somewhat stony pathway to the other side of the village and the graves that reveal that cost most clearly.

If one of the critical distinctions between men and animals is that we laugh, then what about God? After all, we were made in his image. So does he have a sense of humour? And if so is it rarefied and refined? Or is the whole of life just a crude joke? On his release from hospital Mark applied for a buddy... no, you'll never guess.

You must have heard of the system: someone to do those things that even his best friend can't do for him. I tried to explain that his best friend would be more than happy, if he were only asked. It seems superfluous, particularly when there must be a great many people in genuine need. What's worse, it feels like an admission of defeat or at least dependence. But I suspect that he sees it as a gesture of independence, at any rate from me.

Although since he crossed his medical Rubicon and his HIV metamorphosed into ARC, he's entitled to far more support – I must take care; I almost said his medical Styx. For instance, he's eligible for a drug made with egg yolks which the hospital wasn't previously permitted to prescribe. What was most galling was that I'd only just persuaded him to set aside his princi – prejudices and allow me to buy it for him on the open market, which he persisted in calling the black. And whilst he grudgingly accepted my offer, by far the bitterest pill was his swallowed pride.

He can't bear to feel indebted. Now that the flat has gone and we're back again in Little Venice, he even wants to pay rent. He mistrusts my concern, accusing me of using him as a shortcut to Heaven: if I can no longer be a priest then I'll go one better and become a saint... And yet I don't feel the slightest sanctity. On the contrary, I'm well aware I've been spared on a technicality – and it's one which I'm ashamed to admit. Love is the supreme virtue; but I've been protected by my own lovelessness. Whereas he declares himself just an incurable romantic. And his flippancy chills my blood.

I increasingly feel that he resents me, and not simply my good health, which would be understandable, but the inexperience which lies at its heart. And when I try to console him over Adrian he shrugs me aside, as though I can have no conception of what he has to endure and he can't be bothered to enlighten me. And I'm afraid he's right. Let the dead and dying bury their dead; the rest of us have no place even at the graveside. Our tears are inevitably adulterated with relief...

Oh, it's so unfair. I yearn for intimacy and have to make do with inadequate imagery. Which is why I still come here. You're the only one who can begin to understand. These last few weeks I've felt so alone that once again I've started to contemplate suicide... Has nothing changed at all in the past two years...? It wouldn't pose any problem. I remember a schoolboy joke about a bastard who ran amok with a pin in a condom factory – although there the intention was quite the reverse. I could lure Mark into love-making and then privately prick the prophylactic: a new blood brotherhood: a bond beyond the grave. In which case, as in no other, the bigots would be right and the wound indeed be self-inflicted, although not from perversity but from love.

And yet no schoolboy joke can begin to compare with God's. Do you, remember Jack? How can you fail? He's filed away somewhere in that capacious memory you call a brain. I ask out of embarrassment, in case you consider the coincidence so great that it must be my own invention. They say that truth is stranger than fiction; although I'm not sure where that leaves therapists. To you most of our truths are fictions anyway... Mark's buddy is Jack.

Yes, even you look startled. So imagine what it was like for me... I missed his first visit. I returned to find Mark cock-a-hoop. He'd warmed to him right from the start and was convinced that we'd all prove the best of friends. I was overjoyed; although I have to admit to a slight twinge of jealousy. But then I invariably feel inadequate after a meal with my trustees. He didn't want to say too much in advance; though when he mentioned he was attached to Queen Mary's College, researching for a Ph.D. in history, I was seized by a strange sensation, which I mistakenly put down to the richness of the lunch.

I met him again on Saturday. Even with his back to me I could feel the familiarity of his presence; and the moment he turned, I was filled with horror – no, the horror was all around me whilst inside I was nothing but air. I went through the motions: that is my body moved slowly towards him, although my legs remained by the door. I was convinced that I must have misheard. Had Mark phoned for a masseur? Had everything sunk as low as that? And his formal introduction compounded my confusion. But I stepped up and steadily shook his hand.

You wouldn't believe – but then you've never met him... I could barely believe it was the same man. He was dressed in a grey thick-knit cardigan, collarless shirt, fawn cords and white canvas sneakers; he no longer even tolerates leather shoes. And this was someone for whom leather had once been second nature, or at any rate a second skin. And he was wearing round, rimless glasses. I'd known he wore contact lenses despite considerable discomfort. He'd insisted that no whore, as he'd styled himself, could admit to being short-sighted; it was enough of a liability being able to read. But then he's no longer a whore and the look in his eyes is quite different. Is it a new-found compassion or simply the absence of strain?

But his change of look had nothing on his change of outlook. I stammered that I'd been expecting an Indian. He laughed sympathetically and I felt strangely at ease. For although my cheeks smarted with the memory of our last encounter – and it was a far more specific smart than simple shame – it was he who'd been genuinely rechristened... no, that's quite the wrong word. He's become a devotee of the Vedic scriptures. He spent six months in India, where he was renamed

Krishnan Krishnaswami – which as you can hear still sits rather heavily on the tongue. Krishna's one of their gods and swami means teacher; it's generally reserved for the name of a guru and was attached to his as a mark of special faith. So if in the past you ever queried my concern with all the Todds, Dwaynes and Garys, and even mumbled to yourself 'What's in a name?', now you know.

One of the drugs Mark takes for his blood exerts a strong effect on his bladder; and while he went off to the loo, we hurriedly agreed to maintain the pretence and meet again at Warwick Avenue Station later that afternoon. He left first; I discovered him sitting on a bollard. And as the weather was mild we decided to stroll along the canal. I felt heartened that whereas two years ago I'd have given my eye-teeth for a moment of such intimacy, the prospect now left me cold.

He was certain I'd expect an explanation, which he at once proceeded to offer. I'd been wrong; he hadn't been surprised to see me. Recognition was an occupational hazard. It'd purely been the context that had unnerved him. And there was one thing he was dyi – burning to ask, although he knew he had no right: Was I also HIV? I was amazed at how much my reply reassured him. He insisted that he wasn't either, and then seemed put out by my composure. But surely, I declared, we've moved on from the world of Moses where infection was spread by divine command? Oh yes, he agreed, there's no justice – a phrase he kept on repeating. When what he meant was that there was no mercy: the pallid palliative of Christ.

He had a boyfriend, Kerry. I met him once; though if you've forgotten then all to the good... He died... I desperately searched for his face, but all I could see was his skin: the dimple in his elbow and the fold of flesh underneath his arm. It was so smooth you'd have supposed him a great lady of the Ancien Régime, with no function in life but to be cosseted and corseted and creamed and powdered, not a boy who worked as a barman and picked up tips and tricks on the side... But this boy with the skin that'd survived the guillotine couldn't survive the virulence of the virus. And as he walked around London trying to make sense of the verdict, he decided to walk under a train. It was at Barking:

a busy station. Several thousand passengers were late home that night; whilst the driver had to be hospitalised for shock.

He threw stones in the canal, not idly trying to skim the surface but passionately trying to plumb the depths... He had to identify the body even though he wasn't able to recognise it. Did I have any idea how it felt to look down at an unrecognisably identifiable body? And I remembered Adrian with his patchwork of polyps. But to spare him I said 'no' even as I thought 'yes'.

There was no one to whom he could turn. He was forced to admit that he had no friends. People were either clients or lovers; and he resented the clients in that they weren't lovers and the lovers in that they didn't pay. He attended a support group for bereaved partners. He told his story. And their sole response was a hug. His voice quavered: there was no human gesture as hollow or humiliating as a hug. It was every bit as hackneyed as a handshake. There was no frustration greater than to long for the fullness of a kiss only to be fobbed off with that endless arms-round hands-off approach. The dynamic was all too clear as they came close but kept their distance, respecting his space but not his needs. How he hated hugs, he repeated, shaking his shoulders. And at first I thought he must be shaking off the memory. But his face was streaked with tears.

I felt at a loss; I wanted to make contact, but I could hardly hug him. So I stroked the strands of hair from his eyes and kissed him first on the forehead and next on the lips. He looked surprised and moved; and we both began to laugh as we recognised the reversal: it was me kissing him. He squeezed my waist and I clasped his hand; which he, ever the realist, diverted discreetly across his shoulder as we circled Regent's Park.

Kerry had been infected not merely by a dangerous virus but by the far more dangerous fatalism of a vindictive world. And for a while he subscribed to it himself as he went for another test – his fourth – and received his fourth negative result; which was no less than he'd have expected given the security of his sex. But Kerry was a near novice – so where did that leave all the theories of divine vengeance? Unless the

Almighty had grown so out of touch that he could be hoodwinked by a common condom... And he vowed that the utter waste of his suicide would never be wasted on him.

At first his resolve was drowned in negativity. Until a one-night stand with a young musician inspired him to a study of the Veda, from which he'd never looked back. He hadn't seen the man since, indeed now he hoped he never would, since his disappearance flattered his sense of destiny and his gratitude went way beyond words.

He'd desired nothing but his body. And yet as he watched him undress, his eyes were drawn to the small silver amulet strapped to his biceps which, he later discovered, contained portions of the scriptures on minuscule scrolls... And he couldn't explain why such a chance encounter should have changed his life. But the next day he bought a dictionary of Eastern religion which he devoured from cover to cover, before making his way first to their temple in Harrogate and then to an ashram in India – from where he'd recently returned.

His first step on his homecoming was to give up his massage. He'd only ever intended it as a temporary measure, to pay off his debts and tide him through college.

And yet he'd developed a taste for the work over and above his new-found income, as he allowed himself to be seduced by his own seductions and abused by his talent for abuse. And he'd transformed his sexuality from a source of uncomplicated pride into a subject of degradation and despair.

He laughed... We all laughed, he claimed, at the tart-with-a-heart cliché, but how about the tart with a brain? He was well aware of the risks he was taking with his own probity; but he argued them away. And yet his self-justification was the sheerest sophistry. He'd long inclined towards Marx; and he depicted himself as the epitome of the alienated worker: the one with nothing to sell but his skin. He postulated it as a position from which to subvert society; whereas on the contrary, since half his clients were married and the other half men of affluence, influence and power to whom he offered a convenient outlet, he found himself propping up the status quo.

And he was drawn further and further into sadomasochism, on one level merely to mitigate the boredom, but on a deeper one to ritualise the disgust. And the blackest irony – didn't I ask whether God had a sense of humour? – was to discover that his clients enjoyed it even more than he did. There was no perversion too extreme for someone to make it his pleasure, and no pleasure too perverse.

But despite his determination to remain a purveyor, he increasingly became a participant. And he lied to himself yet again as he presented it as the ultimate in imaginative sex, when in truth it was the most mechanical. Indeed far from offering a means of liberation it was the philosophy of the prison cell: the tunnel vision of solitary confinement – quite literally, given that De Sade had honed his ideas in the Bastille... Until, with the advent of AIDS, which might well be considered the supreme sadomasochistic fantasy, he was forced to reassess the fantasies which he'd made his life.

And the reassessment of his own life was only the start. His sexuality had brought him a great deal and he was determined to repay the debt. So he trained as a buddy and Mark was his first... what? He couldn't think of the word, though whatever else it might be it wasn't client. In addition, he helped run a project to educate rent boys, where he preached the joys of safer sex with all the missionary zeal of a colonial pastor promoting the missionary position – but with rather more sense.

He drew to a halt just as we found ourselves approaching Camden Lock: the light at the end of the tow-path... or was it the tunnel? We leaned over the bridge; and as we confronted our reflections my eyes took on the lustre of a passing patch of oil. He apologised at length for his prolixity; but I was unboundedly grateful for every word. I gathered my thoughts. My head felt cluttered, though my mind was clear. And my memory had acquired a new meaning. After all this time I thought I'd teased out all there was; but I can see now that there was a limit to how deep I could delve on my own.

I hope you won't take offence. I'm not dismissing what we've done here; but it's not without its constraints. It's hard to gain a perspective from a position of partial truth. And yet there are so many truths even as there are so many stories. And at some point they must all connect. I used to think that that would only be in death; but I'm now convinced that as I reach out to more and more people so I'll come to understand their stories, and the partial truths will make total sense.

Nor am I afraid you'll suspect me of fabrication. For truth isn't only stranger than fiction, but neater. While the arbitrary is clearly the greatest fiction of all.

We took ourselves off for a meal in the nearby brasserie; and Krishnan marvelled at the changes there'd been in me since he was Jack. He insisted that the last thing he wanted was to reopen old wounds but he couldn't forget the occasion when, having come back to find me on my knees, he'd been convinced I was conducting an exorcism. Indeed there were times he'd felt certain that I saw him as the Devil incarnate... I was grateful for the subdued lighting... But I assured him that the wounds were healed and the scars faded. Besides, I no longer believed in the Devil. I still believed in evil, but not as some kind of Manichaean motive force. I lost my belief in the Devil when I lost my faith in God.

He looked perplexed. You no longer believe in God? he asked. Oh yes, I said, I believe in him; I just don't have faith in him. They're two very different things. And he nodded... How can I have any faith in his absolute goodness when I've seen how he abrogates his responsibilities? It's not so much the sins of our individual fathers as those of our universal Father that have been visited on his children, as he leaves us to flounder in a morass of his making which countless apologists have sought to convince us is our own fault.

And so the Devil is simply a cosmic scapegoat: a case less of 'Did he fall?' than 'Was he pushed?' And all I now wish to exorcise are the last vestiges of bell, book and candle that linger like the sickly scent of incense in my veins. Whilst the sole faith to which I adhere is utilitarianism: the greatest happiness for the greatest number. At least its founding father left a relic we can trust: a human skeleton and not an empty tomb.

Ja-Krishnan seemed taken aback, though more by my change of heart than by the whole-heartedness of its expression, particularly as Mark had been equally adamant that I'd one day be ordained. I was saddened to think that after so long he should have known me so little. How could I ever become part of a church where there are priests who deny people with AIDS the sacraments even at Easter, and congregations who find a poisoned chalice in the communion cup?

And God saw everything that he had made and behold it was very good... Well, I'm sorry, but all I can see is suffering. And in case he should have thought, or indeed you do, that I was generalising from too private a pain, I reaffirmed my view that there was one event in everyone's life – one act of God, or more accurately, one inaction – be it fire or famine, earthquake or flood, war or massacre, holocaust or horror, or degrading, disfiguring disease that enabled him to perceive his creator in his true light.

For whatever our responsibility towards one another, it's nothing compared to God's. With him lies the responsibility not just for bringing us into the world, but for bringing the world into being. And, desperate to convince ourselves of his good will, we claim he acknowledged it by sending his only son to suffer on our behalf. Although I'm more inclined to believe that having sacrificed everyone else's children he had no choice but to offer up his own.

It was this sense of shared suffering which once, above all else, bound me to Christ. But I've come to recognise that his was the supreme duplicity... He was indeed his father's son. Do you recall his reply to the disciples' question about the congenitally blind man: that he was blind not through any fault of his own, nor even his parents', but so that the works of God might be made manifest in him? And you still hear that advanced as evidence of his enlightened view. Well, I've no doubt that the blind man considered it a huge consolation... What works? Couldn't God find any other way?

And if that's his response to the problem of suffering, then I reject it along with all the rest of his doctrines. We've been told that by laying down his life he laid the foundations of a new era; and yet absolutely nothing has changed. If he suffered to redeem humanity, why are we still suffering? In an Old Testament world it's conceivable that our pain might have served some purpose. But Christ's death renders it superfluous: an affront to human dignity, if not to God's.

My throat had grown dry. Krishnan poured me the last drops of wine. I was conscious of my flushed face and flustered fervour; but he brushed aside my apologies and assured me that he understood my disillusion all too well. It'd hit him young when, as a good Catholic boy pressed into service at the altar, he'd been seduced by a sidesman on the sacristy floor... And I recognised a further strand to his story which I'd never suspected – but which he quickly dismissed. He'd found a new faith from an unexpected source and an uncompromised tradition; and to his surprise, it'd even enabled him to look tolerantly on the old.

For, unlike his Jesuitical masters, he declared, he wasn't in the business of making converts. On the contrary, he pointed me towards an AIDS project being run by a group of Christians. He'd seen leaflets at the Terrence Higgins Trust announcing one of their retreats. He offered to find out more and I could think of no good reason to stop him, even though I hadn't the least intention of following it up. And then he rang on Monday to tell me it was scheduled for this weekend. That in itself must rule it out as there's no way I can take off at such short notice. How could I leave Mark? Don't answer... Besides, it's being held in some remote village in the wilds of Derbyshire, and it's bound to be fully booked. The idea's a complete nonstarter... In which case why has it stuck in my mind?

Ten

So these are the graves, protected from the winds that cut across the valley by this random rubble circle. Not that I wouldn't be grateful for the breath of a breeze; I find the unrelenting sun a decidedly mixed blessing – who'd ever believe it was October? But at least we can enjoy the serenity of a cloudless sky and the sweeping countryside; apart, that is, from those disfiguring quarries and their deposits of dust. In the seventeenth century the hillside would have been dotted with farms. Whilst on this bank there were two: the Rileys', which we passed on our way up, and the Hancocks', which has long since disappeared.

A plaque in the Riley orchard honours the Talbot family, who originally owned it until the line was wiped out by the plague during 1666. It's thought that the Hancocks, who are commemorated here, contracted the contagion after burying the last of their neighbours: an act of charity for which they paid with their lives. Although the demise of their own farm comes as no surprise considering all seven of these deaths occurred within a single week: the farmer, his four sons and two daughters, with no one but the grieving widow left to lay them to rest, her grim progress witnessed from afar by the flint-hearted villagers of Stoney Middleton.

And we, who've read reports of corpses consigned to bin-bags, of families and friends being denied a final glimpse of their loved ones and undertakers refusing to bury them – or only doing so after negotiating special rates the voracity of which would have shamed even Marshall Howe – can surely feel for this *mater dolorosa* as she dragged her dead husband and children across the deserted landscape, one by one, day after dismal day.

In fact it's only the father's tomb – on which Pauline and Douglas are now sitting – which remains in its authentic position. The six headstones were later removed from their respective sites and reassembled symmetrically and symbolically here... I'm sorry; I didn't mean to drive you off. I consider it no disrespect. On the contrary, as my Na – an old friend used to say, you're keeping the dead warm... And I do realise from the grunts and grumbles that a number of you are beginning to flag. I forget that I'm an old hand. Two years ago I guided walks through the East End of Jack the Ripper – but that's a very different story. Halfway through we'd take a break for rest and refreshment. So although I don't intend to lead you back to the Miner's Arms, I've arranged to call in at the farm on the way down for a jug of their fresh, warm milk. Which is just what we need to replenish our forces before returning to the village proper, where in August 1666 the plague reached new heights, claiming no less than seventy-eight lives.

I've always scorned to seek out the beauty of God in nature. It seemed too easy an option, like everyone being kind to you on your birthday. But why must I make it hard for myself? I need the countryside; I was brought up there. And to see the colours of a May weekend in Derbyshire, with the bluebells in the woods and the cowslips in the fields... Last weekend I rediscovered my life.

Maybe I melodramatise. I have no choice. I'm trying to fix the scene in my memory; and the sheer wealth of images is in danger of wearing it down. So much has happened to me. Shall I plunge you headlong into the torrent of my feelings or guide you gently over, stone by stone? Did you recognise me as I walked into the room or did you think that you must have confused your appointments? Despite myself I feel such hope.

So thank you, Jack... thank you. If it were all part of a deeper plan, how appropriate that its agent should have been you; and that my evil genius should have become my guardian angel. You've been transformed in far more than name... I went on the retreat; I state the obvious. It's safer; then we know where we are. It was billed as for anyone who cared for people with HIV and AIDS. I asked on the phone whether that meant care and concern or care and work, as I'd have hated to participate under false pretences; but I was told that the ambiguity was deliberate and the scope was wide. And I'm grateful too that I left my registration till the last minute; for if I'd received a list of participants I'd have found any excuse not to attend. In which case I'd have lost out on everything, not least the chance to meet Jonathan again.

I missed my connection and arrived too late for dinner. I felt that I'd already been assessed and dismissed. How could anyone hope to deal with the gravity of HIV if he couldn't even manage an elementary change of trains? Nevertheless everyone was most solicitous and I soon had a plateful of food and a head full of names. A young Sister of St James the Great, whom I later discovered to have been a novice with Vange, introduced me to Jonathan... or rather Father Jonathan, who was to lead the weekend; so whatever else, I knew at once that he'd been ordained. We've met before, he said, as he stretched out his hand. I was struck dumb by his composure, and clumsily juggled my paper plate and plastic cup. I managed to clasp his fingers, whilst a sliver of coleslaw slipped on to his shoe.

He was enjoying every moment of my discomfort, and with good reason; whilst I vowed never again to commit myself to anything before discovering the names of all involved. He said I was looking well; I smiled inanely. I didn't dare speak for fear of what might come out. Sister Veronica filled the silence by offering me a cup of coffee. I clutched at the straw... that is, the handle. But when I refused any milk or sugar and he joked that I must be sweet enough already, I lost my grip completely and it spilt right down my leg.

It wasn't hot, I endeavoured to assure them as I held the cloth away from my skin. I smelt the sweetly sodden scent of the wool and sensed that my groin was steaming. I prayed fervently for rescue. At last Jonathan deputed a portly New York priest with a studded belt and spurred boots to show me to my room, since I was quite exhausted by the various mishaps of the day. And as we walked away down the corridor I was conscious of a huge roar of laughter directed at me.

My misery was only increased by the room, which turned out to be a dormitory. And although the atmosphere was less intimidating than school, conditions were even more spartan. Mauro – the priest – pointed out my bunk; it was the top one nearest the door: not simply the last available, but clearly the least attractive. Just looking at it made me feel giddy; but I flung up my bag and thanked him for his help. He went back to the group while I took a shower. I'd wanted a bath, but the enamel on the tubs was hardly encouraging. The shower gushed and spluttered with appropriate ineffectuality; then just when I'd finally worked up an unluxuriant lather, all hell broke loose and I was caught in a gust of scalding steam.

As I returned to the dormitory I looked out at the hall. I glimpsed the hazy silhouettes behind the convivial condensation on the glass. I felt completely confused. I disdained them and I wanted to be set apart... I desired them and I wanted to be in their midst. I climbed up to my bunk and wondered what I'd do in case of fire; I felt like an unsuccessful experiment in the conservation of space. I sat up and bumped my head on the ceiling. I stretched out and wondered if the mattress were orthopaedic or simply hard. I was desperate to fall asleep before anyone else appeared; but a faulty fluorescent light flickered above me. I attempted to regulate it – only to scorch my hand. I stifled a curse and was afraid I might burst into tears; but I refused to let myself, for fear of finding temporary solace. And the situation was far too serious for that.

Some time later they came in and I realised I was wider awake than ever. They made no attempt to keep down the noise; but I was grateful for their selfishness. It made my bitterness easier to bear. Jonathan moved to the bunk beneath mine. That was the last straw; his proximity was almost unendurable. I could hear him laughing and talking as though I'd been just a holiday acquaintance: a Christmas card friend. He began to undress; I slipped over and surreptitiously opened an eye. I caught a glimpse of the top of his head. I'd forgotten his hair was so ginger, whilst his shoulders were a mass of freckles like the heavily foxed pages of a family Bible: I wanted to decipher every phrase... He didn't appear to be wearing any pyjamas... I hurriedly turned away.

I was horrified by the reflex action of the least reflective part of my anatomy. So I slid on to my stomach and played dead.

He jumped into bed. I could feel his body beneath me. I'd have imagined that in a bunk all the pressure would have come from above, but it was quite the reverse: I was aware of his most minuscule movement... his most bated breath. His large limbs looked cruelly confined within the wooden frame, whilst fingers and toes appeared to protrude from every side. After an endless hour I peeled back a corner of my mattress and peered down at him through the struts. For one ghastly moment I was certain that he winked: until I realised it was the overhead light still flickering in my brain.

I hated him for the stillness of his breathing; I hated them all. To be awake alone in company felt even worse than to be standing alone in a crowd. I tossed and turned until I was convinced that the creaking of the boards was bound to rouse someone, and at least we'd be able to talk. I finally felt ready for all the dark dormitory intimacies I'd rejected at school. But I was ten years too late. Besides, no one responded to my tactics, and short of falling out of bed there seemed little I could do. I was considering that when I became aware of a pressure on my shoulder and a light in my eyes. It was Jonathan reminding me that it was 8.45 and everyone else was tucking into breakfast. He smiled; I was going to be late again.

After breakfast we all sat round in a circle – which has never been my favourite formation – for our first group discussion. I was impressed by the diversity of experience linked to the singleness of mind. I don't know who or what I'd been expecting: a few misfit priests and liberal laymen, various churchy women with too much time on their hands... I'm ashamed to recall how I patronised them. Whereas in fact there were men and women of every shape and size. And above all there was Jonathan: Jonathan who dominates my recollections like a head carved in the stone of Mount Rushmore; although he stands entirely alone.

His leadership was inspirational and his enthusiasm unflagging. It was only the second retreat he'd guided, though I remembered how at St Dunstan's he'd been involved in organising several weekends for world peace. He led from the front, the back and the middle. Whether we split into smaller groups or stayed in the one circle, wherever I looked he was there. Indeed I became convinced that at least some of him could only be an optical illusion. But he was blessed with the energy of ten men; and he spread himself thickly around.

He began his own contribution with a text from the gospels. I gulped as I realised that it would be the first time I'd heard him speak formally since... well, you can't have forgotten. He chose the passage from St Mark about the man sick of the palsy whose friends literally raised the roof in order to bring him to Christ.

Our Lord was in Capernaum and already a victim of his own celebrity. He'd become inaccessible, surrounded by a vast crowd of disciples, Pharisees and assorted hangers-on. But when the sick man's friends found that they couldn't push past them, they didn't stand meekly by, twiddling their thumbs in an ante-room until one of the functionaries condescended to let them in; they took action, lowering his bed through the ceiling. And Jesus healed him right away, in the face of the scribes' disapproval. He recognised the man's faith and, more significantly, that of his friends.

Jonathan went on to draw the contemporary parallels which seemed so obvious he felt it necessary to apologise in advance. And yet I don't suppose any one of us found them a jot less welcome. What those men did then, we and so many others were doing today. We were surmounting all the obstacles and fighting to bring our friends to Christ. But if it'd been hard two thousand years ago, it was infinitely harder now when the hangers-on were not simply obscuring our view but obfuscating his message, and the crowds not merely holding us back but putting us down. And yet we must never give up, but rather cut through the dead wood just as they'd done the ceiling. We must break down every barrier even if it meant breaking the law.

He exhorted us to take heart from Christ's subversive gospel. It was no coincidence that those self-styled moralists who demanded a return to the letter of the Bible were far more reticent when it came to his words. They were prepared to uphold the myth of God as a landscape gardener while preferring to ignore all the evidence of his son as a social critic: someone who condemned corruption and inveighed against injustice, who was a thorn in the flesh of authority and could only be silenced when a lance was pierced through his.

I was both exhilarated and moved. Although I felt less responsive to other attempts to reinterpret the gospel, such as whether, if Christ were alive today, he'd have had HIV. It wasn't that I found the idea distasteful – merely unhelpful. It did less than justice to the singularity of people's sufferings to lump them with one who'd been as immune to desire as to disease. No, I pinned my faith on the fellowship of the circle and the unlikely alliances which were emerging on every arc.

There were some who gave us the benefit of their survival and others of their bereavement, some who shared the pain of their incomprehension and others their triumph over despair. There was the cosy middle-aged tax inspector who'd taken early retirement only to find himself working harder than ever as a volunteer. There were the two car-workers from Cowley, to whom AIDS had just been washroom graffiti but who'd been tirelessly raising funds for hospice care. There was the elderly Austrian nun who expressed, in a heavily accented voice and yet words of crystal clarity, the force of her revelation that she had to leave the cloister and work with those at risk, and her extraordinary rapport with a very camp London caterer whom I'd initially resented, but who a few hours later may well have changed my life.

Yes, Krishnan isn't the only one to have discovered his faith where he least expected. It may be that my mistake has been to look for the grand gesture: the blinding light or the wrestling with angels; when all it took was a little pebble which he'd brought back from the Garden of Gethsemane and, in a moment of quiet contemplation, handed round.

I'm not usually moved by relics. However much I try, my scholarly scepticism stands in the way. But for once it wouldn't have mattered if it were disproved by carbon dating or if he'd picked it up from the neighbouring field; it would still have had a beauty all its own. I rolled it in the palm of my hand; its value didn't depend on its attribution. I could feel its natural sculpture, its perfect form. And I perceived the presence of God in its creation as much as that of Christ in its association and a new-found sense of harmony between the two.

I clung on to it as though for dear life. I tried to make it as much a part of me as Mark when he clasped his crystal; and I also sensed its restorative power. To think that I once derided him for pinning his hopes on a piece of rock... And at that moment I felt a great weight slip off my shoulders, even as the stone had rolled away from the empty tomb.

The next morning it was my turn to speak – I should have said that I felt it my turn, for we were none of us under any compulsion. I began by apologising that my connection was so tenuous. Whereas they were all fighting selflessly in the field, I'd been prompted solely by my love for Mark. But then I paused as I realised that there was nothing tenuous about love; it couldn't be diminished by definition. And I found myself looking pointedly at Jonathan – which I could scarcely avoid since he was sitting straight opposite – so I averted my eyes.

I told them my story: much of which I've already told you, except that I only had twenty minutes and not two years. I spoke a little about Mark and rather more about myself: not, I hope, from self-importance, but because to most of them his experience would have been all too familiar, whereas mine was still somewhat remote. Unless they understood the depth of my despair at the time I met him, they'd never appreciate everything he'd done to pull me out.

So I spared them little and myself less as I portrayed my life in all its darkest colours. I desperately sought their acceptance; although a part of me still courted rejection – but then that was what I knew best. And while I spoke to the group, my appeal was directed at Jonathan. I wanted him to forgive me and yet to cast me out; to respect me and to despise me; to promise that we could start again where we'd left off, even as he insisted that nothing could ever be the same.

I only hope that I wasn't as confused in my speech as in my recollection. I forget how I concluded, simply that I gradually became aware of Jonathan's arms around my waist. He was clasping me; I was shaking. He was calming me; I was convulsing. His shirt felt wet; but the tears were mine. He held me so close that I could feel his heart beat. And my own rose up in my breast as, in spite of Krishnan's strictures, I revelled in the warmth of his hug. There could be no mistake: the embrace was entirely pastoral; and yet that was the most I could expect – or desire. Then he took my hand and we returned to the circle, no longer diametrically opposite but side by side. And all around the unity had been re-established. It was a charmed circle; a mystical circle; a circle of grace.

Sunday afternoon was free; and he suggested I might like to walk with him to the village. It was quite some way, he warned. The further the better, I thought to myself – I could do with the exercise, I replied. And he led me off on the most wonderful journey... No, what am I saying? He led me on two.

Slow down, he cried, it wasn't a race – or was I already trying to give him the slip? I laughed hollowly and forced myself to relax into his steadier pace. I inadvertently brushed the shoulder of his battered bomber jacket: the same one that Father Leicester had long ago claimed he'd soon grow out of and which still fitted him like a glove. We chattered about this and that and I was tortured by the triviality. I'd told him so much – too much – about myself; while I knew next to nothing about him. Two years had passed since we met; and for all I knew he might even have married. Though I didn't like to ask.

He described his life since leaving St Dunstan's. Strings had been pulled and he'd spent a final term at Salisbury before being ordained a year ago last summer, as originally planned... He's now attached to a large West London parish, which I'd better not name in case your parents or in-laws or great-aunt Laura happen to worship there; coincidence has made me wary. It's all very 'Faith in the City'; but then that's just what he's always wanted. And he boasts of its deprivation and social problems the way that other priests might point out the reredos or stained glass.

It's also an area which contains a high proportion of people with HIV. Their clergy team works hand in hand with the social services; whilst in his spare time – although he considered the notion risible – he's the local co-ordinator for a support group: Plus IV. When I asked if its members had to be Christians he appeared genuinely affronted, which I found reassuring... he clearly hadn't changed. As he breezily put it, he wears one collar but two hats.

And he isn't married. He lives in a Victorian clergy house with two other missionary priests. That is, they belong to an Anglican society designed to promote additional clergy in areas of special need. Nor does he have attachments of any other sort, which relieves me... Oh, not for my own sake – so you can stop looking at me like that – but for his... It confirms his integrity and shows that his fellowship is a matter of conviction, not convenience since, when he joined, he made a promise of celibacy before a chapter of the mission which, whilst it may not have the force of a vow made before a bishop, remains binding nonetheless.

Even as he spoke, I was thinking back to our estrangement – the intimacy which had evaporated in a cloud of spittle. I told him of my sadness that we'd lost touch – but then I'd also lost touch with myself. I knew that my behaviour had been unforgivable and I wasn't expecting forgiveness... And yet he assured me he'd forgiven me long ago. I may have caused him great pain, but it was past. And the reality was that there we were walking side by side down the road... Although for my own part I'd swear that my feet barely touched the ground.

And though we'd taken a circuitous route, we'd finally reached our destination: Eyam. Have you ever been there or even heard of it? As Jonathan showed me round I seemed to have some dim recollection, but I couldn't be sure. And since my return any mention of the name has been met with blank incomprehension. Which is just typical. Our history books are littered with the names of kings and their ministers and mistresses. We celebrate the most pyrrhic victory in war. But when there's a genuinely inspirational event in the heart of the English countryside, it's barely known.

1665: the Great Plague of London, conveniently close to the Great Fire of 1666: which are two of the dates that every schoolchild learns by heart, inspiring playground rounds and jingles and classroom discussions on primitive sanitation, wooden architecture and the seemingly

Heaven-sent opportunity for the genius of Sir Christopher Wren. But up in Derbyshire, the plague left a very different legacy: a tribute not to the vision of one man but the integrity of an entire community. And as I walked through the village streets I was living proof of its abiding power.

I'd walked through the streets of London telling stories; but the stories had seemed almost incidental to the streets. I'd had to tease them out whilst continually making excuses for the inadequacies of the setting... the buildings that had been knocked down and the others that had been put up in their place. But in Eyam the streets told their own story. The history was not so much in the telling as in the very stones. And to respond required an act less of imagination than of faith.

I was very moved, as Jonathan had evidently expected. And I found an image of the unity for which I'd been searching all my life: of priest and people, families and friends. While in their testament to the spirit of selfless solidarity which had determined to contain the infection, the houses of Eyam spoke powerfully of men like Krishnan and Mark... This was a community truly worthy of celebration. This was history as inspiration, history as metaphor, which had infinitely more to recommend it than history as mere fact.

The parallels exhilarated me and I tossed them back and forth to Jonathan, who once again failed to keep up with me as I raced from house to house. And it was uncanny how they seemed to be speaking to me directly; as I discovered how people could triumph over the most terrible adversity, indeed over death itself, and the present work in tandem with the past. Three hundred years on we were still able to draw strength from them even as they had from one another. So their sacrifice had had further reaching consequences than they could ever have dreamed... It was a story that spoke across the ages in a voice that defied despair.

I also knew that my presence on the retreat could have been no mere chance and that the place was as significant as the personnel. And what had impressed me most were the two priests I'd been walking with: Mompesson in 1665 and Jonathan in 1990. If I believed in rein-carnation... but I don't and I don't need to. This was a tradition of priesthood far more potent than any historical apostolic succession: the priest at the heart of his community, fighting for its survival, what-ever the personal cost.

And in these two figures, so different in every material way and such identical twins in spirit, I recognised both my ideal of the priesthood and my ideal man – although I no longer acknowledged any distinc-tion. For I realised that my original emphasis had been misplaced: it was the man who made the office and not the other way round... And that evening when we came together again in the circle, I took the sac-raments for the first time in I don't know how many months, and I'm sure I've no need to enlarge on all I felt. The retreat itself then drew to a close. But as we went our separate ways the following morning I knew that one day I'd return to Eyam, as surely as the night before I'd returned to God.

Eleven

Thank you all for being such good sports; I'm sure that my credibility with the rector was much enhanced by my milky moustache. Fortunately he has sufficient sympathy with the subject to overlook such an unprepossessing guide. In any case we needn't trespass on his good nature, or indeed his property, any further, as we can see the rectory perfectly well from the bottom of this drive.

Such spots have a special significance for me; and I consider that by now I know you well enough to be able to acknowledge it. On my previous walk, I had only the vaguest idea of my audience. I could hazard a few guesses, but I'm not sure they were all that inspired. And yet the very fact of our coming together for this retreat creates a common bond of sympathy, so I can feel confident that you won't accuse me either of overstating the analogies or of overstepping the mark. And during a contemporary crisis in which many clergymen would rather sit on the fence than stand up and be counted, at most muffling their sympathies and murmuring their regrets, it's imperative to remind ourselves that there is an alternative – and it works.

That alternative may be summed up in two words: William Mompesson... In 1665 he was a relatively recent recruit to Eyam. It was his first parish and hardly his idea of a prestigious preferment since, in addition to its obscurity, it was still suffering the bitter aftermath of two decades of doctrinal strife. Then came the plague, and with it the growing conviction that he'd at last discovered his divinely appointed mission. And yet it was also to bring him much misery; for although he was one of the fortunate few – and they were indeed very few – who survived, Catherine, his devoted wife, was not.

Nevertheless he buried his private sorrow in the wider struggle as he galvanised the village to glory. Remarkably, there are only two recorded instances of attempted flight, both of which quickly came to grief. And, as if to prove that ignorance and ingratitude aren't simply twentieth-century phenomena, when three years after the plague he left Eyam to take up a living in Nottinghamshire, his new parishioners at first forbade him entry to the town, restricting him to a hut in the park until he managed to convince them he was free of the contagion. Nor would they even allow him access to the church. And he who, as we shall shortly see, was no stranger to open-air worship, having once preached so valiantly at 'Pulpit Rock', was forced to preach ignominiously beneath 'Pulpit Ash'.

But that's another village and another story. Let's now try to escape the worst of this heat in the traditional cool of the country churchyard where our first stop will be Catherine Mompesson's tomb.

The sunglasses aren't an affectation, nor am I trying to conceal a black eye... merely red ones. Although I expect to you they'd simply look a little inflamed. Nevertheless I need all the confidence I can muster. I'm reeling under the strain of my recollections; I'm punch-drunk with the past.

I'm not sure... when we last met, had I introduced Mark to Jonathan? No? Well, they took to one another right from the start; so much so, I was taken aback. I've always considered 'Any friend of yours is a friend of mine' the most indiscriminate of compliments. Of course I was relieved; I longed for them to be friends – just not necessarily at first sight. Jonathan encouraged Mark to join his Plus IV support group; and I was again surprised by his enthusiasm. So I welcomed the chance to attend an open evening for lovers, friends and carers... They ought to have added family to the list.

We met in the billiard-room of the clergy house where a giant jigsaw, a Dutch seascape, was laid out on the felt. Mark explained that it was a long-term project: more of a pretext than a puzzle, designed for new members to break the ice... He moved off to greet some friends, leaving me to contemplate the jigsaw; and I felt disappointed by both its sentimentality and its size. They hadn't completed much, but they'd assembled all the edges; and I can remember thinking that if those were ten thousand pieces some of them must be awfully small. I stepped aside; I was suddenly convinced I was going to knock it over... I fulfilled my worst fears.

Would you like a glass of wine? Or was it a cup of coffee? That I don't recall. I was less struck by the offer than the voice. I turned round. I knew him at once: even though I hadn't set eyes on him for fourteen years. No, that's not true. I'd glimpsed him in the hall of the Lambeth Mission, queuing up for a charitable chocolate. My instincts had been quicker than my brain.

His body was much thinner; his hair was much thinner. His skin was weather-worn and he had liver marks on his leathery hands. At least I assumed they were liver marks. But I could never have mistaken the shock of recognition in his eyes nor the slobber of emotion on his lips. I backed away; I was terrified he was about to embrace me. I backed away and knocked over half the jigsaw. Three months work, three months of hard-won confidence and conversation: and I swept it away in one swoop.

There was a dull thud and a muffled clatter followed by a murmur of consternation; and a moment later Mark was at my side. He began to berate me as though he considered himself responsible. I was impossible: no better than a clumsy child who didn't know his own strength... But I was a child who hadn't known his own attraction. And as I gazed at my uncle for the first time in so many years, it all came flooding back.

I knelt down and started to pick up the jigsaw: its thin cardboard pieces had become jagged and sharp. I refused to face him. I tried to blot him out of my sight... to black him out of my memory. Then I felt arms encircling me – his arms; I froze. My heart was in my mouth; I was choking; I couldn't breathe. And his hands were on my wrists restraining me, and around my neck strangling me; and I couldn't understand why no one could see. And I tried to call for help; but his fingers were down my throat trying to tear out my larynx. And... and is the dividing line between madness and sanity as thin as that between present and past? For they were Mark's hands, and Jonathan's, forcing me to vomit up the pieces of the puzzle that I was desperately stuffing into my mouth.

They succeeded. The sentimental seascape was spat out in a splutter of bile. And whilst Mark attended to my uncle, Jonathan led me upstairs. He sat me down on his bed, ignoring my assurance that I'd be perfectly fine if he'd only ring for a taxi, and insisted that I told him everything. Although it wasn't until I started speaking that I realised how much there was to tell. So please don't think I've been holding out on you. As I forced it out, the story became its own discovery. And yet you clearly played a crucial part. For when I spotted him standing in line, all I'd been able to see was my long-lost uncle. It took two years of dredging through my memories to alert me to everything else that I'd lost.

So I withdraw any reservations about the effectiveness of the process. You've proved your credentials beyond any doubt. And yet I'd hate you to assume that that was the key to my entire character: a childhood assault by my uncle: no wonder I'm so confused/repressed/neurotic: strike out where inapplicable, or add on as the case might be. I've warned you before that I'm not an open book; well, still less am I an open-and-shut case history. I don't... I can't deny what happened; what I do deny is that it determined my development; or how would I ever have been able to forgive him as freely as I did?

And you can't expect me to believe that a few local difficulties – my refusal to contemplate certain sexual acts... my reluctance even now to name them – is of any relevance. That isn't inhibition, simply distaste.

I'm sorry; I didn't mean to raise my voice. But this is very hard. I seem to be reliving my revelations, not merely relating them. I don't know which is worse: your silence or Jonathan's questions. He treated me with text-book tact and sympathy; and yet I could tell that it was my uncle who was his chief concern. It was as clear as when Mark recently made love and I sensed him stroking the contours of another man's body: working from memory rather than touch. And I felt indignant; I was sure that if it'd happened to one of the boys in his parish he'd have been up in arms.

And I was in Hell; which I can authoritatively assert is not the simple state of mind so beloved of liberal theologians, but an underground oven worthy of Hieronymus Bosch. And its hub is a spit: a smouldering, scalding spit with a sharp, snagged spike on which I was twisted and turned and tortured, basted in hate and roasted in passion, whilst his hot sweat seeped on to my stomach like burning fat, and my skin cracked and crackled, and my soul...

Why are you putting me through this? Is it not enough to forgive and forget; must I remember and resent? You even prompt me to suspect my own resolution. There may be some things which are buried so deep, we do better to leave them undisturbed. If they're that far down, it must be for a reason, like a consignment of nuclear waste. My uncle is my personal Hiroshima. And the memory leaves me scalded and scarred: a flash of blinding light and then the darkness of unending pain.

I loved him; and he abused my trust as much as he abused my body. He was my strong, safe uncle with the moustache as soft and bushy as his shaving brush – the cavalry moustache which I always found so incongruous in view of his reverence for the RAF. In the holidays I used to run down to the lodge before breakfast to watch him trim it. He'd stand at the sink bare-chested, with his braces hanging round his knees. And I was fascinated by the concentration of his shoulder-blades; his whole back appeared to frown... He was the only man I knew who wore braces; but then he was the only man I ever saw without a shirt. And at Edensor, apart from the servants with their subserviently scornful faces, he was the only man I ever saw at all.

I was ten years old. And my whole education had been designed to keep me in ignorance. Biology was simply nature study: squirrels and badgers rather than birds and bees. Whilst for once even the Bible afforded no help, as its imagery of seed and fruit and loins seemed to have more to do with the larder than with love. And since my abiding image of Sodom was of Lot's wife being turned into a pillar of salt, I presumed that the unspeakable sin must be curiosity – not what was shortly to be thrust on me.

———

It hurt. I was ten years old... I was six years old and I asked Uncle Sinclair why he'd never married. For me marriages were made in Heaven and honeymooned on Noah's Ark. And he laughed and said that the only girl for him had married my father; which was the perfect reply. I wanted every man in the world to be in love with my mother; in those days when love was no hands and all heart. He used to put me between his – stand me between his legs and tell me that I reminded him so much of her... Oh no, you won't lure me down that path. Believe me, it's a blind alley. I've enough on my mind without that.

He claimed he was teaching me to wrestle. He'd previously taught me to arm-wrestle: always leading me to believe I was about to beat him, but then levering my elbow down to the table and holding it there for just a moment too long... So the prospect appeared unexceptionable, although the timing was something of a surprise. And I remember asking whether it wasn't a little late at night. But he said no, late was best. And he told me that we had to take off our shirts, which we duly did. And he made a comment I don't – I can't – remember, to do with my being so skinny, before explaining that he'd start by showing me some holds.

But then he changed right before my eyes, like a piece of trick photography. My safe, solid, slightly stuffy uncle became a monster who was all fingernails and fangs. He turned both me and my world upside down. I choked... I bled. What made it still harder was that the part of me he seemed to be making the most of was that part of which I'd always been taught to be most ashamed: my ugly, fleshy, lavatorial part... And I pulled up my pants like a bloody bandage. And my bowels didn't open for a week.

And at one stroke my vision became murkily incestuous. Instinctively I think I sensed some of the same incongruities in the sustaining myths of my childhood that Jonathan later exposed so publicly: the tree of life not just fertilised by a rotten apple, but fed by forbidden fruit. And yet my hold on life was far too fragile to admit dissension; and so I buried the confusions deep inside me, where there was neither explanation nor resolution – only dull, festering pain.

I suggested to Jonathan that that might even have been the reason I'd found his sermon so disturbing. It'd threatened far more than my sense of propriety. But he thought it wiser that I save such considerations for you. Little does he know... Instead he proposed that I should speak to my uncle; which at first I refused point-blank. It was an intolerable imposition. Hadn't Our Lord himself warned that anyone who offended one of the little ones would be better off cast with a millstone around his neck into the sea?

In fact he ought to count himself damn lucky that I'd decided not to turn him in. Although no doubt he'd have been let off with a derisory suspended sentence... Well, who would suspend mine? I'd been living it for fourteen years without remission. I'd been locked in my solitary shell as though I were the abuser; which, by the law of averages, or at least that of psychiatrists, I might have expected to be. But the only person I'd harmed was myself.

Not the only one, he said softly, and then looked away. But I told him that he should also lay his grievance at the same door. In which case, he asked, just as there were wheels within wheels, mightn't there also be doors behind doors? He knew my uncle's story; he'd heard his confession; I'd added nothing but the names. And yet he couldn't regret them; for he was convinced that God had brought us together for a purpose... At which point, and despite considerable reservations, I agreed to his request.

Even so I stressed that it would have to be later in the week, as I was in no fit state. But then he dropped the second bombshell of the evening which, if not as violent nor as searing as the first, was utterly devastating nonetheless. When I'd picked up all the pieces of my life I'd failed to put two of the most elementary together. Those weren't liver marks on the backs of his hands...

I'll take these off. They're beginning to steam up; and besides you've seen me in tears often enough before... I couldn't take in what he'd said. I'd assumed as he'd offered me the drink that he was there as some sort of volunteer; I'd never admitted any other possibility. Then when I did, I felt infused with a great gust of fellow – or was it family?

– feeling; as I pictured him forced to measure his days by the cracks in pavements, frail and friendless, ravaged at once from within and without. And I vowed there and then to turn my personal Hiroshima into my personal Eyam.

Jonathan hugged me – I thought once more of Krishnan – and then kissed me, a kiss of friendship but still a kiss, before going downstairs to fetch Uncle Sinclair. He was away so long that I wondered if he mightn't already have left. And by the time I heard the knock on the door I'd had ample time to regain my composure; indeed so much that I was afraid I might be about to break down all over again. Then the door opened and he entered, unexpectedly alone.

He looked so much smaller. I don't mean from my childhood memories; but he seemed to have shrunk a good six inches from the man I'd encountered earlier that night... like an ancient textile inadvertently exposed to the atmosphere, which had crumpled to dust. His eyes had become opalescent. I'd heard of people's hair turning white with shock, but never till then their eyes. And they brimmed with tears, for which he stammered an apology. Trembling, I took his hand and we sat down.

I was lost for words and he seemed lost for speech altogether. But the mere fact of our presence was eloquent enough. He kept hold of my hand and gently stroked it as though he were pleating the bed-clothes; and I saw just how ill he was. Gamely he tried to smile; and I couldn't work out why I found it so disturbing. Until I realised that he was wearing a set of standardised false teeth.

My arm soon began to ache and my hand felt clammy; and yet I was desperate not to destroy the mood. I was amazed at how relaxed I felt, as though nothing in my life had ever touched me, let alone him; but I was aware that I had to preserve my composure at all costs. He kept repeating how well I looked; which I found strange, since whatever he may have done, it was fourteen years ago. Then it hit me that his main fear hadn't been of discovery or even of denunciation, but that my presence at the group would reveal an indirect chain of infection that would reflect directly on him.

But I assured him of my good health. He was visibly relieved. Although he still seemed to hold himself responsible for the entire thrust of my sexuality. I denied it vigorously; if anything it would have been the other way round. While if it were the case, I'd consider he'd done me a favour; for otherwise I'd never have met Mark. And though my words were braver than my feelings, my voice must have carried conviction; since for the first time he laughed... And despite the over-statement, I truly believe what I said: I have to take responsibility for my own actions. I can no longer portray my life as some sort of patch-work made up of everyone else's odds and ends.

He gained confidence and told me that there'd not been one day when he hadn't thought of me – and then he checked himself; there'd been some days when he'd thought of nothing but the struggle to survive: the cold and the hunger and the aches and the pains. So he amended it to not one day on which he'd been able to think. And I said that that was over; and he replied quietly that time wasn't as fixed as gravity. If he'd had the courage he'd have killed himself. Instead he'd just wandered the streets, taking refuge with the refuse. In his more maudlin moments he'd been able to convince himself that that was a juster punishment; but the truth was simply that he was too great a coward.

And yet such arguments had been superseded. He had such a short time left to live... I tried to contradict him, but he calmly held up the lesions on his hands... And whilst it was far too late in the day to imagine that he might ever die happy, he'd nevertheless be happy to die having been reunited with me. For apart from my mother, I'd been the one thing of value in his life.

Then why had he left? I asked. At the time what I'd found hardest to understand, and still, to be honest, to forgive, was his disappear-ance... that he should compound the crime with confusion: that he should just take off without a word. Other boys had books they failed to make sense of; I had a body. And I was left to piece it together from my ignorance and guilt.

Guilt, he asked incredulously, whatever for? As though he'd taken on all the guilt of the world the way that Christ had the sin. And I was amazed that he could be so blind; after all it's been evident to you from the moment I sat down. I felt guilty about egging him on – and yet a far more appropriate word might be 'appling' – in the way that I constantly engineered moments of contact: scrapping and scrambling and swimming and even shaving. I remember once unbuttoning his shirt on the pretext of hearing his heart beat; if I wanted to hear someone's heart beat, why didn't I try my aunt's? No, I provoked him beyond all endurance, coiling my trap as subtly and as supplely as a snake.

But he stared at me aghast and then rose up and pulled me to my feet, as though his words contained the authority of a gospel reading. I must never again think such a thing, he exclaimed. I'd given him no sign: none at all. Even if I never trusted another syllable anyone said, I must swear to believe that. He'd needed no persuasion, let alone provocation; he'd been drunk with self-disgust. It was pity he'd felt for me, not passion; for he knew perfectly well why I used to spend so much time at the lodge. It wasn't him I was looking for but my father... And for a moment I took him literally and failed to understand... He was merely the next best thing, he added; although all too quickly he proved the worst.

He couldn't conceive how I could ever have picked up such a wrong-headed notion. Had he had the least suspicion, he'd have damned the consequences and stayed put for however long it took to set me right... But I felt sure that my father thought the same... Had I discussed it with my father? he asked, in a voice pinched with panic. Of course not, I assured him; but clearly somebody must have seen what'd occurred and informed him, which was why he'd ordered him out of Edensor the very next day. And yet he'd been in no doubt as to who was the true offender. And so he'd never let me close to him again, but simply withdrawn into small talk and scorn.

How long had I believed that? he asked. And I had to admit that as far as I knew it was the first time I'd put any of it into words; nevertheless it'd become the central tenet of my private creed... My father knew nothing, he declared. He'd run away from himself and no one else.

He was terrified that what he'd done once he could do again: begging for forgiveness on his knees and then attempting to take advantage of his position; whilst my reproach became a spur to self-loathing which aroused him even more than lust.

I heard his voice, but all I could assimilate was the assurance that my father didn't know; and that therefore my guilt had been entirely of my own making. Then what else could have prompted his estrangement? If not disgust, was it rather disinterest? Had he simply wanted to walk away and forget? Oh no, he exclaimed with alarming vehemence; a man can never forget his son. He can forget anything else but not his son... And I suddenly had a burning insight into my uncle's loneliness. He hadn't been able to love me as a father; and yet the next best thing had proved the worst for him too. For the confusion of identities had in turn led to far more dangerous confusions; when he'd wanted to be touched one way and I another. And it'd been impossible to say where physicality ended, and sexuality began.

And I had no way to account for what he'd done to me: neither to understand him nor to love myself. I had no models, so I had to turn to myths. And I evolved my own myth of my essential corruption which came to parallel that of Adam's Fall... But there was no Fall, either personal or universal. My uncle wasn't the snake and I wasn't Adam; he wasn't Adam and I wasn't the snake. Even Adam wasn't Adam and the snake wasn't the snake. There was no primeval innocence; and there is no original sin.

His assault had coerced my inexperience, not corrupted my innocence... And I finally appreciate the distinction between the words 'innocent' and 'naive'. Which is not one that can be learned theoretically, but only in practice. Since however paradoxical it may sound, true innocence is the product of experience; it's a state of mind, not a state of ignorance. And it won't be found in any childhood garden, whether Edensor or its namesake; but rather in an uncompromising and an uncompromised acceptance of life.

And so at last both my myths can be discarded and with them the whole excess baggage of grief and guilt. Jonathan was right; St

Augustine's heresy has done far more harm than any of those which the Church has exerted all its efforts to extirpate: a heresy, moreover, which was the product of a deeply disturbed mind. For he was a man so revulsed by his youthful sins of the flesh that he deemed flesh itself a sin. And Christians ever since have paid the price of his self-disgust.

But there is no fundamental state of wickedness; and we don't have a propensity to evil, merely the capacity for it. How can it be otherwise when we're made in the image of God, with his two supreme faculties of creativity and moral responsibility? So perfection is neither a lost cause nor a lost paradise. The ideal may lie in Christ, but the potential is in ourselves.

I realise now why he was so keen I should confront my uncle, and you that I should my past. The key isn't to 'forgive and forget', but to remember and forgive. And as I forgave him with all my heart I was richly rewarded. For though it may be more blessed to give than to receive, the greatest blessing of all must be to forgive. And in forgiving him I'm even starting to forgive myself... While Jonathan's analogy held as true as his argument: there were doors behind doors behind doors. And suddenly they all flew open and the room was flooded with light.

Twelve

This parish church is dedicated to St Lawrence, a particularly happy choice since he was the deacon who, when ordered to hand over his treasures to the Prefect of Rome, offered him his congregation; at which the Prefect, whose imagination was lamentably limited, suspected deception and had him roasted to death on a griddle. I've no doubt that had a similar request been made of Mompesson, he'd have felt justified in responding the same way.

Despite the evident antiquity of the churchyard, only two of the tombs date from the period of the plague. The first belongs to an early victim, Abell Rowland; and the second, as you can see, is that of Catherine Mompesson. If you look closely, you can also see how the mason originally misspelt her name and the final 'o' of Mompesson had to be replaced.

But whatever the confusion over her name, there could have been none over her character. Even allowing for seventeenth-century panegyric she was clearly a remarkable woman. Soon after the arrival of the disease and long before any question of quarantine, she begged her husband to quit the village, if only for the sake of his family. But he was in no doubt where his prime duty lay. He nevertheless tried to persuade her to leave without him: a proposal she stoutly refused. So she dispatched their children to relatives, never to see either again; while despite a constitution already wracked by consumption, she remained to work tirelessly by his side.

Then one August day, all their worst fears were realised when, having seized a rare moment of tranquillity to walk together in the fields, she turned to him to comment on the sweetness of the air, a sure sign of rising fever, and subsequently died. He himself recorded her name in the parish register. She was the two hundredth victim of the plague, which in September was to carry off another twenty-four. And as an Eyam poet has written when surveying the scene, with a sentiment far removed from sentimentality, his deepest distress was that he'd been unable to give her so much as a parting kiss... The pain and the parallels are almost too hard to bear.

And her memory is honoured to this day; for every Plague Sunday, which by tradition is the last in August, the present rector's wife lays a rose wreath on her predecessor's tomb... But now let's cross to the church wall to view the memorial to Thomas Stanley, Eyam's other exemplary cleric.

I understand the urge to make virtues out of necessities, but it can be taken too far. There's Uncle Sinclair, confined to bed, breathing through an oxygen mask with measured doses of poison dripping into his veins, and yet he still claims to he grateful. Even in a closed ward he's living a more open life than ever before. He's no longer able to hide behind old air-force slang and a bluff, gruff manner. It's as though at last he's discovered his true identity after years of staring at an identikit picture: one formed from so many false impressions that criminality seemed etched in every line.

He may be about to die, but he has little fear and no resentment. What would have been terrible, he said, was if he'd died of anything else; for then he'd have died in despair. But AIDS was no way as lethal as the lack of love. And he reminded me of my childhood questions on the nature of the after-life... If Heaven were in the clouds, would there be clouds in Heaven? Was Hell really a burning pit? He couldn't speak about Heaven; but Hell had undoubtedly been his life before he fell ill.

He recapped... I'll recap. His life both began and ended in the war. He joined up with such high hopes and soon gained his half-wing. But then his wings were clipped and his fuselage peppered; he was shot down over the Channel where for sixteen hours he was tossed back and forth by the waves. The Westcliff front reappeared as a mocking memory; and there wasn't a single spot of blue to be seen: just jets of jet black, until he supposed the whole sea to be alive with squids squirting their inky juices at him: in his eyes, in his mouth, in his hair, in his freezing flying-suit. Sometimes when he woke up in a bed soaked with sweat he imagined he was back in those icy waters. And they were the only times he felt afraid.

If it weren't for my father, he confided, he'd have gone under – and he didn't just mean the waves. For he continued to drift after the war, using it first as an entrée and then as an excuse, until people lost patience and all he had left was his pension and a head that was still half at sea. But he was offered the job at Edensor, where he could never be sure if my grandmother failed to make the connection or thought it wiser not to ask. He smiled phlegmatically, coughed and put on his mask.

Then when my parents were finally married, no one was happier than he. They were the two people he loved most in the whole world... And a pernicious picture flashed across my mind which I quickly suppressed... What especially surprised me was to learn that my mother had been within a hair's breadth of calling it off. They'd waited so long that she felt the future lacked reality or at least that the reality would prove unsustainable. And he was the one who dissuaded her: she owed it to herself and to my father; although what he meant was she owed it to him. He needed them both so much; and he needed them together. Having a twin sister may have made identity more difficult, but it made identification a great deal easier... and guilt so much harder to bear.

He felt that guilt when he saw her withdraw, first from her husband and then from the world. He felt it again as he looked into my eyes, at once so troubled and so trusting. He was very scared for me and convinced that one day I'd crack under the strain... What he'd never suspected was that that strain would be him. And he fled in horror with nothing but a lifelong overnight-case. He came to London as though he were a fifteen-year-old runaway – I thought of Rees – not a fifty-three-year-old deserter. But if he supposed he was travelling light, he was much mistaken; for he was weighed down with all the guilt of Adam after the first sin, or rather Cain after the second. Did I know what the mark of Cain was? Loneliness. I made no reply.

He found a job in a hotel kitchen. And that soon became the essence of his existence – washing up, pottering, scrubbing floors, pottering; two hot meals a day and no questions asked. They respected one another's privacy; but then that was about the only respect they did have. And for a while he enjoyed his new-found anonymity. He despised who he was and welcomed the chance to reinvent himself. He didn't know if he were believed, but in any event no one challenged him, no one expected anything of him and no one pursued him when he left. Such were the facts of hotel life: the staff was almost as casual as the clientele.

But there was a darker side to that anonymity and he plunged into promiscuity... He rasped and retched; he seemed to be fighting for breath, not to say words... He paid little attention to AIDS, which he considered a disease of the young, although his confidence was to prove cruelly misplaced. And it wouldn't be for the last time; since a waitress he'd thought he could trust revealed his test result straight to the manager, who sacked him on the spot. And he had no redress: no union, no tribunal and no compensation. Those were the facts of hotel life too.

He lost his job and his room and his dignity. He slept rough for over a year and that's no empty form of words: on the Embankment and at Lincoln's Inn Fields and, for a while, in the celebrated Cardboard City, which he claims has become so institutionalised that there's both a word-of-mouth waiting list and a code of conduct as complex as that in any gentlemen's club. And the roughness wasn't so much from the other homeless people as from the young toughs and even children who considered them fair game. He has a scar four or five inches long on his inner arm from a well-spoken boy who skidded up on his skateboard, slashed him, laughed and slid away. I was appalled; but he was resigned. It was an environmental hazard along with the cold and the rats and the rattle of the railway, and the policemen who moved them on at dawn.

I squeezed his hand; he responded with a fruity, throaty fit of coughing. He swilled and swallowed some saliva, then tushed into a

---

tissue; I quickly let go. A neighbour summoned a nurse, who checked his oxygen and drip. And I gazed at the body that shivered and shook and slobbered and slithered. It was no longer one I recognised. Or was it just that our positions were reversed? I remembered his teaching me to skate at Edensor, and lifting me out of the marsh when I fell through the ice. But no one could lift him out of his quagmire; the liquid he was drowning in was in his own lungs. And with a strange synchronicity he asked if I remembered how he'd taught me to skate as a boy... and my revulsion when my boots squelched in the mud.

He was tranquil again, although I was afraid I'd overtaxed him and suggested I left. But he wanted to talk. He couldn't understand why he was constantly told to save his strength. There'd be time enough for silence. So I edged closer and listened... Despite having twice admitted him to hospital, it was purely by chance that his health adviser had discovered how he was living and put him in touch with Plus IV. He'd only agreed to see them for her sake, since it was her unique talent to suggest that whatever anyone's problems hers were ten times worse. And yet he was beginning to suspect it was a deliberate tactic. If so, it'd worked.

He'd always been a Christian, however much he used to offend me by referring to the vicar as a sky pilot – which may of course have been a relic of the RAF... And at their first meeting Jonathan had offered him communion. To many people he played down his priesthood; but he'd judged, and rightly, it was what he needed most. And though his sense of desecration was still greater when faced with Christ's blood, Jonathan banished his fears. He drank before and after him, infusing him with confidence and hope.

He began to take part in a few of the group's activities, and he found that he was no longer alone, either in his symptoms or his sexuality. And it'd taken the one to draw out the other. For the first time in years he discovered he could talk about himself; and what was more, he could laugh. Someone told a joke, at which he chuckled and then felt pierced with guilt. There he was: a person with AIDS, laughing. He should have been tearing out his hair – what little he had left – not enjoying himself as though he didn't have a care in the world. And then he realised: he didn't, not one. And he laughed even louder at the wonder of it all.

He was no longer friendless nor homeless, for Jonathan also offered him a room in the clergy house. And I felt a pang, although whether of remorse or envy I wouldn't like to say. Since then he's moved out into his own flat, where he has help... oh yes... although he continues to assist in the group whenever he can: in meetings, in the office or counselling the newly diagnosed. He's been amazed at how many people find it easier to talk to someone older. And when I revealed that one of them was Mark, he purred with pleasure and contentedly closed his eyes.

I stretched and gathered my belongings. I was preparing to disappear when I caught sight of Jason... Jason – Jason: does that ring any bells? How about if I mention an Indian restaurant, a stolen briefcase? Yes, just as I thought: a whole carillon... I blinked; I hadn't seen him for over two years, but his face had scarcely altered. At first I wondered if it were my memory playing tricks; but no, it was my life. For he made straight towards us, kissed Uncle Sinclair and stared at me.

Fortunately, he failed to recognise me which, quite apart from relieving my mind, removed any vestige of self-importance. My uncle introduced us and explained that Jason was his helper, rather like a buddy only untrained and informal – highly informal. I hadn't known that he had one... But then he hadn't known that he had a nephew either. So he grinned and said that that made us square. Oh, if only we were.

Of all the changes in Uncle Sinclair's life the most important has been Jason. And as I saw his eyes light up, I realised how solemn I must have seemed, treating my chair as though it were a confessional. Whereas Jason flitted from one tall tale to another, to the constant refrain that he must have many better things to do; to which his automatic reply was that of course he had, but he thought he'd better pop in just in case he went and popped off. And their raillery deeply moved me; so that when at last it was time to leave and Jason asked if I'd like a cup of coffee, I readily agreed.

It soon became apparent that he was acutely anxious for my approval; although more, I felt, for Uncle Sinclair's sake than his own. Nevertheless I was taken aback by the speed with which he launched into his story, without ever registering that I'd played a minor part in it myself. Are you gloating? No, I'm sorry. On your psychological ready-reckoner, don't forget to add in paranoia.

He admitted straight out that he'd just been released from prison. He'd been caught trying to push some pills in a night-club: largactil – largactil: don't you see? He asked if I were cold, but that wasn't the reason I was trembling; I felt as though someone were walking on my grave... He was sentenced to eighteen months, which for a first offence was plain vindictive. And he repeated that there was no justice, in a tone so familiar it made me start. He was sent to an open prison in Essex on a detoxification programme, where he worked as an orderly on the hospital wing... and met with the biggest surprise of his life.

He had a boyfriend: Rees... I gulped and tried to pretend it was the coffee. After all, it was a common name – although nothing like common enough. One day he was casually mopping down the ward when he saw him. At first he was convinced he was hallucinating. He was terrified that the treatment he'd been given had begun to affect his brain. But the closer he moved, the clearer his impression became. It was Rees to the life, except for his eyeballs which darted to and fro like an animal torn in a trap. He staggered. He needed to hold on to something, he needed to hold on to him. He wanted to leap straight in beside him, but logic counselled caution. And in any case Rees' face visibly calcified as he pointed to the three black letters on the board at the foot of the bed: VIR... And if you think HIV is hard in the world outside, he said, you've no idea what VIR can mean in the nick.

I didn't know what they meant at all, but his explanation was succinct: Viral Infectivity Regulations. And as for Rees' particular virus... I don't suppose I need to spell it out. Jason couldn't understand; all he could think of was when and from whom. It couldn't have been him; they'd made him take a test straight after his trial. It was standard practice for anyone they considered at risk. While a refusal was rated as a positive result. So how? And later when he'd calmed down, Rees told him everything. And he began to tell me. It's so pigging unfair, he said. I know, I replied, before I could stop myself; he looked surprised... That is, I care.

For I'm the missing link in the chain of liability: the weak link between Jason and Rees. Whereas Jack was no pimp but a true friend who organised his defence from the best of motives, it was my pills which undid them both; since the day after Jason's arrest the police raided their room, sealing it off and leaving Rees out in the cold. He had no money, no clean clothes and nowhere to sleep. But neither the desk sergeant nor the DHSS clerk had a scrap of sympathy. And he was forced to trade in the one currency he had left: his youth.

So I share my guilt with the callous authorities who between them forced him on to the streets... Our ancient judicial code should be amended to 'innocent until found needy'. And there's worse. It's virtually certain that he was infected on remand. The monotony and insecurity of a year in limbo led him to abandon his one remaining restraint; as the drugs his fellow prisoners spewed up from their wives' deep kisses were injected into him, at a price. And all the precautions he'd previously taken went for nothing... He was sentenced even before he was tried.

Jason went on to describe the addicts' blood-brotherhood ritual, which might as well have been a suicide pact. He repeated Rees' account of how he'd complained of feeling feverish and they'd given him a test without the least preparation. He was informed he was positive and then allowed five minutes with the prison psychiatrist before being locked up in isolation for the next sixteen hours. Imagine it: sixteen hours with his head on the block waiting for the axe to fall.

Never mind, the psychiatrist told him as he offered him at most five years to live at the start of his seven-year stretch. With good behaviour, he'd be sure to earn remission from his sentence. Which bleeding one? he screamed; I don't think he used the word 'bleeding'... Which bleeding one?

I needed something stronger than coffee and Jason was hungry, so

I took him for dinner in a nearby trattoria. He confessed he'd been plunged into despair by Rees' diagnosis. It was as if he were no longer a person, but a symptom that had stolen his skin. And his own skin came out in sympathy: a stigmata of solidarity which he scratched raw. But gradually he recovered hope as he registered that Rees wasn't ill. He'd simply been sent there whilst the doctors experimented with a number of new drugs. And though the whole set-up seemed decidedly shady, I recalled Mark's current watchword of 'early intervention' and prayed that for once they'd fit the punishment to the cure.

We toyed with our desserts. The sweetness of the zabaglione proved no match for the tartness of the tale. And yet how extraordinary that they should have come together in prison; when the odds against it were at least fifty thousand to one. But I'd have taken them nonetheless. For when some months later he was released with neither job nor training nor accommodation, nothing in fact but a non-transferrable travel warrant, what he did have was a letter of recommendation from the assistant chaplain, who'd been the only officer to show them any kindness... which he found strange considering he came from the army. And yes, it was the Church Army. And though he didn't tell me his name I felt sure that it must have been Lancelot. But I was afraid it would only arouse his suspicions if I asked.

The letter was to Jonathan, which is why I'd have taken the odds even if they'd been one in fifty million. Such a web of coincidence could never have been the product of mere chance. For Jason to have met his friend in prison and my friend in prison and another friend and my uncle on his release, shows that there's a pattern and a protection and there must someday be a resolution too.

Jonathan galvanised him as profoundly as he did both Mark and Uncle Sinclair. He offered him a room in the clergy house, which immediately put him on his guard – no one did anything for nothing, especially when it came to bed and board. But the only condition he imposed was some occasional help with Plus IV fundraising. And although at first he resented cyclostyling leaflets, licking envelopes and shaking collecting tins, he was no fool, nor, he grinned, was Jonathan; he soon came to see that every penny collected, every signature subscribed and every phone call answered was a way of keeping faith with Rees.

What he didn't bargain on was meeting my uncle. He initially trusted him even less; he'd made it a rule to suspect anyone over forty. And yet Sinclair was different. He didn't make him feel small or interrupt him in mid-sentence as though everything he said were predictable. He didn't act as though old age were in itself some big deal. And he made him laugh more than anyone he'd ever met. So he jumped at the invitation to move in with him... And he suddenly blushed and insisted that he'd told me all that because he didn't want me to think he was taking advantage. He promised to pull his weight... And I could hardly see to pay the bill.

Uncle Sinclair and Jason: who would ever have thought it? I'm reminded of that parlour game where you have to put together some of history's most unlikely pairs. And I've begun to relish the way that, almost in spite of myself, so many aspects of my life are intertwining and a definite symmetry is starting to emerge.

When I first met Jack – or rather Krishnan – again, I felt overwhelmed in the face of a world full of stories. But after Jason I can see that we're all part of the same story and even those strands that don't connect, reflect. And you're in the ideal position to draw them together: a prospect which fills me with hope. So my self-reproach and charges of egotism were redundant. For whether you hear about me from Mark or Mark from Jack or Jack from Rees or Rees from Jason is ultimately immaterial. The perspective may be different, but the pattern is the same.

And even the news about Rees hasn't thrown me. For there was one other thing Jason said, which I hardly like to mention in case you should think I'm blowing my own trumpet or, worse, writing my own score. And yet, as he was describing how much he'd learned from Uncle Sinclair, he added that he only hoped that one day Rees would be able to meet him or, at any rate, somebody like him. But then he corrected himself and said that of course he already had. And it soon became clear that without a hint of calculation he was referring to me.

Thirteen

In passing I pointed out the Saxon cross, the most celebrated in the county which, though rather the worse for wear, still reveals its intricate interlacing of Christian and pagan symbols: the delicately carved angels and the network of knots. The cross was spared the fate of many similar stones under the Commonwealth; but then the incumbent whom the Puritans imposed on the village was at once an exceptional and an exceptionally tolerant man.

His name was Thomas Stanley and his memorial can be found facing you on the sanctuary wall. And yet it wasn't put up until as late as 1891: an earlier tablet in the nave having been reversed by one of his Higher-Church – though sadly not higher-minded – successors; which suggests that even here people's memories were short and their grudges long. Nevertheless, without his backing it's doubtful whether Mompesson, a High Anglican whose arrival met with marked hostility from many on the opposite wing, would ever have been able to maintain such a united front.

Stanley first came to Eyam in 1644 and was replaced and later reappointed during the vicissitudes of the Civil War. He remained as curate to the royalist pluralist, Shoreland Adams, until, unable to stomach recent ecclesiastical legislation such as the Act of Uniformity or to accept the new Prayer Book, he was one of the two thousand clergy who left their pulpits in 1662. He clearly commanded considerable affection amongst his former parishioners; for after his resignation, two-thirds of them continued to contribute to his support. And yet for a time he preferred to leave the village, not to return until Mompesson's induction in 1664.

The following year, despite his religious scruples, he stood squarely behind his rival. And today, when so many evangelical clerics pander to the popular press and public prejudice and writing hate-filled articles can appear a clearer imperative than the Thirty-Nine which they vowed to uphold, it's refreshing to remember one who set aside fundamental differences and fundamentalist doctrines to further the common cause.

Now, if you'd care to wander round inside you'll discover several historic monuments and documents – and a number of more modern souvenirs. Meanwhile I'll collect the key to the Cucklet Church in the Delph, the ad hoc, al fresco altar they used when indoor worship came to present too great a threat. To reach it entails a fair hike to the other side of a ravine so, should any of you decide to opt out, you can always bask in the sun beside the stocks. But take heart, the worst is almost over, for both them and us. October was the last month in which the Plague Count reached double figures, fourteen to be precise. And the Cucklet Church will be our penultimate port of call.

If I'd kept to the faith of my fathers I wouldn't have come here for a month. I wouldn't have gone anywhere for a week. I'd have slit my shirt and grown my beard, covered up any mirrors and sat on a low stool. Whereas for most Christians it's a case of just a couple of days off work and a plate of smoked salmon sandwiches; and for most Jews too now, I suspect. And yet there's much to be said for the rituals of mourning. It's not that they offer consolation so much as a context... the very one death threatens to sweep away. Without which we're left with nothing but condolences and clichés.

I feel so frustrated by his dying: not aggrieved nor particularly grieving, not that it's a great tragedy nor even a bad joke, but bemused by such a miracle of life's having been reduced to a bag of bones and gases and excretions. There was no warning. He was resting after lunch when death attacked him as swiftly as a stray bullet. It was only by chance I was there.

I thought that at least he'd been spared Adrian's obsolescence. He remained conscious and continent until the end. His eyes flickered closed. But then suddenly the vultures of decay launched their attack. His slight body began to swell like the special effects in a horror film, followed by a rasping gurgle like a badly blocked pipe. Blood began to pour out of his mouth, his nose, his ears and even from beneath his fingernails. It seeped savagely across the crisp white sheet. Jason shrieked as his last embrace was lost in a pool of viscous liquid. And the dignity of the moment was quite destroyed.

It was partially recovered at the funeral, where Jason again stood alongside me together with my father in the front pew. It felt very different from the last such service I'd attended. I was amazed at the size of the congregation, which was almost entirely drawn from the friends he'd made since his involvement with Plus IV. Jonathan officiated and his address was both moving and inspiring; whilst I read the first lesson, from Ecclesiasticus, which had been my uncle's own choice: 'Let us now praise famous men'... I glanced at my father: 'and our fathers that begat us.' They used to read it at the burials of Second World War airmen. And at that instant I knew he was one with them once more. 'And some there be, which have no memorial; who are perished as though they had not been.' And as I looked around the church and lingered over Jason, the sentiment seemed quite out of place.

He asked me to be his executor. I was amazed; after so many years in the kitchens and on the streets I'd have thought he'd have nothing to leave. And yet he turned out to have several thousand pounds. When he ran off he left behind all his bank books and papers, for which he never dared reapply in case someone should try to track him down. Until after a time the money seemed to belong to another life and ultimately another person. But shortly before he died he went through all the red tape to recover it. He proposed to leave everything to Jason – so long as I didn't feel slighted. I assured him I'd like nothing more.

Executor: that's a word I well remember from my childhood. One of my cousins died and I understood my father to say that he was his executioner. I was convinced he must have killed him and wondered how long it would be before he did the same to me. But then words have such power; and an unexpected bonus of talking to you is that it's given me the chance to reclaim them and the core of reality within. I was particularly aware of it in the hospice. Death imposes its own rhythm; and I began to weigh every word as carefully as a poet. And the last one I said to him was Adieu. It was as though goodbye were somehow easier in French; I felt distanced by the foreignness of the language. And then I heard myself: Adieu – A-dieu. I started to cry. I was literally entrusting him to God.

I'm sorry. I'm beginning again now. Where do you keep your tissues? Thank you. One way or another I must have kept Boots in business this past couple of years. And right now I find myself apt to dissolve into tears at the least opportunity, even though on the face of it I'm perfectly fine... It's strange, but you always manage to be away whenever I have a crisis. Don't worry, I appreciate that August was the school holidays; and I no longer subscribe to the conspiracy theory of therapy. Nevertheless I have been under considerable strain. I wouldn't have coped at all if it weren't for my father. He'd been due to come to London later in the month; but he dropped everything and flew straight over the day after he heard the news.

Uncle Sinclair's death came as a still greater shock to him. He had no idea that he'd even been ill; and having to fit a face to the acronym was hard. He had to piece together the Sinclair he'd known with the Sinclair he'd lost track of, the Sinclair with whom he'd flown over France with the Sinclair he'd saved from drowning... at any rate at sea. For he insisted that he'd never truly recovered from those sixteen hours in the Channel... And I remember how, as a boy, I was convinced that all his black moods and deep depressions sprang from 'water on the brain'.

And yet, what if there were more to my mistake than I could ever have realised, and the force that surged uncontrollably inside him, and then through me, was simply the backwash of the waves which had left such an indelible image of indefinable horror on his mind that he'd never been able to break free?

My father knows nothing of his assault and I see no reason to disabuse him. It would serve little purpose and only bring him pain. He attributes his flight from Edensor to grief at the loss of his twin.

Although in my view he'd felt that loss many years before. For while I may have been entranced by twins in the theatre – the romantic imbroglios of comedy and mistaken identities of farce – for my uncle the resolution was far less benign. Having experienced such intense intimacy; through the shared bed of infancy and the rough and tumble of childhood, he clearly found the separation from his sister hard to endure. No wonder he tried to blur the distinctions first with her and then with me.

I'm talking too much. After telling you I've learned to ponder every phrase, here I am babbling like a brook. And yet I fancy you prefer it this way. Indeed if you could read me like an open book you'd very soon find yourself redundant: my parentheses give you space. What's more, I suspect that you distrust the calm and collected almost as much as Mark does the straight and narrow. So I'll carry on, leaving you to make sense of what you can.

And as my father struggled to make sense of my uncle, we were forced to acknowledge the one person we always tried to avoid and yet who remained the central figure in both our lives, looming ever larger in our silences; as chillingly as the silence of the grave.

My mother was dead; and I was her only epitaph. We never spoke of her. For me it was simply too raw; and I assumed he didn't care. He used to insist that it did no good dwelling on the past... although he evidently had; which I suppose must have been how he knew. And yet so much remained unclear. No one had ever explained to me why they divorced; it was simply that things weren't right between them. In which case no one had ever explained why they married. Jonathan used to claim that most men lost interest in their wives once they'd had children; it was what lay behind the cult of Our Lady. And yet my mother remained a radiantly beautiful woman right to the end. No, if my father lost interest in anyone it had to be me.

Which is why he abandoned me for so many years: years of burnings and disappearances when I watched the world go up in flames and the smoke of childhood certainties fill the air, years when I felt as unwanted at home as at school in a house where the dead took precedence over the living... And yet he alleged that it was the other way round. Every time he returned to Edensor I withdrew. He saw that I held him to blame for my mother's death; and what was worse I almost convinced him.

He knew that he should have fought for me, but it would first have meant fighting me. And he'd been so weary of all the struggling and desperate for a few years of peace. Then against all the odds they were granted; as he married again and discovered love at an age when the most he might have expected was loyalty. I gulped. I didn't want to delve any deeper. I asked if that meant that he'd never loved my mother. Not at all, he replied, without a moment's hesitation; she was the love of his life.

And all the whys and wherefores of my entire existence came tumbling out. In that case why had he waited twenty years before marrying her? I'd thought of so many explanations from the sensational to the simply silly – and ignored the most straightforward: she wasn't Jewish... But that made no sense: he wasn't a believer. The whole family had merely been nominally orthodox since they built their country houses and spent their weekends out of town. And yet he declared that in the last resort it wasn't his fathers he found it impossible to break faith with, but his mother.

Then he asked if I remembered her, rhetorically... ridiculously since, as he knew all too well, she died before I was born. Indeed she had to die before I could be born. So he painted her picture; and I'd never have believed that such a tiny figure could have cast a shadow so vast.

She came from Vienna and all her life she remained resolutely loyal both to the customs and to the country of her birth. Her family was part of that self-assured, self-absorbed circle from which your founding father drew his original inspiration. For all I know some of them might even have been amongst his first patients – which would be doubly ironic, considering where I sit today. Indeed, they were so self-assured that they refused either to heed advice or to read the warnings. And they stayed in Vienna, first for the annexation and then for the internment and then for the deaths. They stayed as a reproach to the past and a warning to the future. But above all they stayed as a gnawing guilt to those who'd managed to escape.

Which my father no longer could. And he came to believe that it wasn't just the country which over the next twenty years was shown to have won the war and lost the peace so conclusively, but him. For when he attempted to introduce his mother to the one woman with whom he felt he could escape the horror, he found he could never escape the holocaust in her heart. And no matter how much he tried to reason with her, she resisted. She refused to acknowledge the English nurse whose long blonde hair put her in mind only of piano wire. Nor was she appeased by her offer to convert; for to her religion began and ended with blood.

And although he loved my mother and hated his own, he couldn't deny her, even after his father died – especially after his father died; since she seemed to have shrunk into greater dependence than before. So she lived on at Edensor with my aunt, who fired her animosity with her own. She held him to blame for her stifling seclusion, tied to a mother who one day simply renounced English altogether and reverted to her native tongue. And he begged her to leave, to live, to travel. But she'd been brought up on that self-same diet of bitter herbs and bitterer memories. And they grew to vie with one another in filial sacrifice just as they once had for maternal love.

Meanwhile my mother made a home for him in London where a few sympathetic friends addressed them literally as Mr and Mrs, although there was always an official envelope to show up the lie. Until eventually my grandmother died; and three months later they were married in a ceremony muted officially by mourning and in practice by age. And the following year I was born, on a day that was hardly auspicious as it was the one on which a group of neo-fascists attempted to burn down Bevis Marks. And my aunt, who was as superstitious as a soothsayer, never tired of trying to turn a coincidence into a connection: as though it were a portent of my nativity – the flames that appeared in the East.

I discovered that she'd pursued the same line with my father; and for the first time we acknowledged the shared memory as well as the pain. But he couldn't blame his estrangement from my mother solely on other people; the problem had also lain in themselves. In twenty years of struggling to stay together they'd lost sight of their original objective; while their love had grown so tied up with its obstacles that, when they were finally removed, so was its whole *raison d'être*.

They'd come to envisage their return to Edensor as a return to Eden. And yet it soon became clear that my mother felt as out of place as my grandmother on her arrival from Austria half a century before. The one thing that might have pulled them together was children: a house full of children. But my mother was already forty-three when I was born. And if the doctors had had their way, she wouldn't even have had me.

I was painfully aware of the precariousness of my existence. But I had no time to brood, for he gripped my wrist and carried on. They should have had children at the end of the war, he said; and to hell with convention. But with so much already stacked against them, they'd backed away... As though any further illegitimacy would have confirmed the illegitimacy of their love.

Then all at once he seemed horrified that he might have given the impression that he hadn't loved me when on the contrary, the problem had been that he'd loved me too much. He'd become increasingly frightened for me until his fear had verged on lunacy. He'd come to consider it the most arrant selfishness to have fathered a son at all in such a world, quite apart from the greatest folly. To have offered up a permanent hostage to fortune... to have pinned all his hopes on a helpless child.

And he used to dream – that at least hadn't been hereditary – and he described a recurrent nightmare which at the time had played on his deepest dread... He was holding me in his arms and he saw shoes; he was watching me playing in the garden and he saw shoes; he was listening to me recite my two-times table and he saw shoes: mounds and mounds of them piled high in the compound of Auschwitz; shoes of people he'd never heard of but who were as much a part of him as the incision of the *mohel's* knife. Some people were haunted by the corpses; he was taunted by their shoes. And he woke up screaming with terror and streaming with sweat.

His precautions became pathological. I was as cocooned and cosseted as the haemophiliac son of the Tsar. And yet even so it wasn't enough. At times he could scarcely bear to look at me in case some malignity in his glance should do me harm; while at others he was afraid to touch me for fear of a slip of the hand. My mother rounded on him bitterly; but however hard he tried to explain, she refused to understand. She grew convinced that his withdrawal masked a rejection of her. And in the end that became his only way out, as he left us to the protection of his ancestors and moved to France.

But whereas he met my stepmother, whose love gradually recoloured a world drained to the grainy black and white of a nightmare newsreel, my mother was left utterly alone. And she lived on at the castle as though its ramparts were for real and she herself some feudal noblewoman holding the fort until her lord returned from the crusades. And when she eventually realised that her vigil was in vain, she turned all her fury on the house. It was she who struck the match... There. I've said it... And her frenzy fuelled the flames of her own funeral pyre.

He was crying now as we sat together in his hotel suite, whilst a cold cup of coffee congealed by his side and the skin formed a thick scum around the rim. And I recognised the depth of his suffering, as he gazed up in anguish and asked if I had any idea how it felt to have lived through the age of Auschwitz, and survived.

I was silent for a moment and searched my soul to try to answer honestly... not conventionally nor conveniently nor too soon. Yes, I replied; I thought that I had. And for the first time I understood his guilt towards his family and mine towards my friends. And later I took the identification a step further when I looked at pictures of prisoners on their way to the camps; faces I'd never seen before, although I'd seen the eyes: Adrian's eyes; AIDS eyes.

And I established new links, not just the easy analogy of pink triangles and purple blotches nor even the annihilation of entire communities whilst their compatriots looked the other way, but in the guilt of the survivors, the self-loathing, self-lacerating guilt: that same guilt that had tortured him and was threatening to overwhelm me.

But having identified the danger I determined to banish it forever with his help... and with yours. I couldn't have been more wrong when I used to declare so defensively that we needed guilt. It was my last ditch attempt to hold on to the security – no, simplicity, of my child-hood and the fallacy of the Fall. But what's the use of an early warning system that's been programmed to self-destruction? While original sin, with its message of unconditional guilt, is by far the most deadly of all.

And my realisation extended beyond the particular to the sublime. Through his suffering I've finally come to terms with God's... You may find it hard to credit, after all you're one yourself, but for years I considered fathers impervious to pain, which was the exclusive prerogative of sons, both human and divine. And so I engaged in a practice of divide and worship, paying lip service to the Father and true service only to the Son.

But there was as great a sacrifice in the Creation as in the Incarnation; whilst God suffered as much by proxy in the Old Testament as in person in the New. Even the stories of Abraham and Jephthah were emblems of his agonised love. But I refused to see. I made God the Father in my father's image and my father in God's, thereby rejecting them both. But if the rejection worked both ways, then so did the resolution. And through my reconciliation with my father I've found new meaning in the fathership of God.

And I felt so close to my father, so full of love and gratitude, that I also wanted to take him into my confidence and I told him first about myself and then about Mark. He was surprised, but not shocked. He stood straight up and pressed his palm on my forehead as though physically intent on impressing his words on my brain... Whatever else, I must live according to my own lights, not other people's. I only had the one – at least to his way of thinking. And I replied that to mine I only had the one soul. At which he smiled, swallowed some curdled coffee and ordered lunch.

Fourteen

So here we are, almost at the end of our quest. And I'm very glad that none of you took advantage of the escape clause. Although if you think it's been a long haul, imagine what it must have been like for Mompesson and his ever-dwindling congregation; as they crossed over the slippery stepping-stones and scrambled up the bank: the men in their narrow-waisted jerkins and the women in their tight whale-bone bodices, twice every Sunday and several times more during the week. And yet their religion was as vital to them as breathing; and while they may have had to close their church, they never closed their hearts.

I seem to have spent a large part of my life visiting places of worship. Indeed, if I were ever invited on to a desert island with only my eight favourite buildings for company, at least seven of them would be shrines: Chartres, Wells, Ely, St Stephen's in Vienna, the Matisse chapel in Venice... Oh, I don't know; the choice is endless. The eighth, incidentally, would be the house I grew up in, which I intend to refurbish and where I hope some of you – all of you – will one day come to stay. But for the moment that remains a dream, whilst this is before us; and its effect on me at least is immense.

And it's not just the setting, although it remains naturally awe-inspiring with its eroded limestone altar and the niches on either side, but the scale and scope and above all the associations. I'm no geologist and I've no idea how long ago these rock formations evolved. Nevertheless, it's as though God prepared millions of years before for this very contingency; so that when they abandoned St Lawrence's there was an alternative close at hand.

It could hardly have been better suited. Although they wouldn't have congregated as closely as we are now, the existing boundaries of the Delph would have served to unite them; and, since the hillside was less wooded, there'd have been nothing to impede their view of their priest... And have you noticed how far my voice carries even after three hoarse hours? I'm sure there must be a great many ordinands who'd willingly take their preaching practice here. Whilst there'd be no need to arrange any flowers when there are plants in profusion all around.

So is it any wonder that neither priest nor people ever turned away from God when, despite their deprivations, they were constantly confronted with such sure signs of his benign creativity? Just look at the way the sun streams through that crevice, illuminating the stone with all the warmth of the most luminous rose window. What more evidence could they have wanted that their faith was not misplaced? And when in November the final victim of the epidemic, a young boy, died and was buried, the villagers gathered once more in their parish church. As they continue to do to this day, except for the one service held here every August to commemorate the plague.

And their devotion puts my despair to shame. In the past the philosophical problems of suffering caused me almost as much pain as the private heartache. And I had particular difficulty with the passage in St John where, in answer to his disciples' question as to why the man was born blind, Jesus declared it was so that the works of God should be made manifest in him; which, however revolutionary a rejection of personal liability, still seemed a pretty poor reflection on God. And yet if by 'in' you understand 'through' and you see those works not in the blindness itself but in the response it draws from others, then it doesn't merely make sense; it restores faith.

In the same way I once heard the Archbishop of Westminster claim that every time he saw a mentally handicapped person he knew that he was in the presence of a saint, and I rebelled, since it seemed the most cloying, conventional and condescending kind of Catholicism – with the inability to doubt an inevitable adjunct of the inability to reason. But I've come to realise that the essence of sainthood lies in the ability to inspire saintliness in others; just as suffering leads to redemption. Until we all become part of a community of saints; and it's through us, as it was here in Eyam, that God's works are made manifest and his purposes shown.

Well, after that unscheduled homily you'll appreciate my gratitude for the natural acoustic. Now let's return to the village, to that row of Plague Cottages which were the homes of the first victims... and the first fruits of a restored life.

Up to now I've never made much of my birthday. I've always avoided issuing invitations, mainly from fear of assuming responsibility. I think that that must have been one of the reasons I preferred Christmas. It was Christ's birthday – it was everyone's birthday, and so the onus was off me. But henceforth I intend to celebrate whatever I can: feast days, saints' days, anniversaries... every obscure listing in *Whitaker's Almanack*. I mean to leave nothing unmarked.

I never even celebrated my twenty-first; in fact I hardly noticed it. I came of age in my family's eyes at thirteen, in the eyes of the law at eighteen, in the eyes of romance at twenty-one, but in my own eyes only on Thursday. Twenty-five... a quarter of a century: I suddenly feel old – not ancient, but in some way substantial. They say that when you break your leg every other person you pass appears to be on crutches; I'm constantly aware of the ticking of clocks.

And yet after last year I'd have been happy to scratch the date from my diary or at least to be born in a Leap Year and make do with one in four. I remember my intense disappointment that Mark had forgotten; although, as I soon learned, he had every cause. But on Thursday, together with my father – another unlikely pair – he threw a surprise party... They planned it as meticulously as a military manoeuvre. My father commandeered me for a quiet dinner, which proved to be no under-statement. The restaurant could hardly have been plainer and the food was downright dull. And then to cap it all, halfway through the hors d'oeuvre his hiatus hernia played up and we had to leave. On reaching home I could hardly bring myself to say goodnight, and I deeply resented his coming inside.

We found the house in total darkness; while my call to Mark went unanswered. I felt peeved; he'd not been well enough to join us for dinner, but it hadn't prevented his slipping out on his own. Then I panicked: what if he'd had an attack? I raced up to the drawing-room, flicking on the light; and I still find it hard to describe what I saw... Faces first: friendly faces – fainting faces; though the faintness was mine. Clapping. Corks popping. Champagne flowing: fizzing, not flat. Nothing was flat; everything was bubbling. I was bubbling: laughing, crying. Tears mixed with the drink to create an effervescent cocktail... It was my nightmare: everyone I'd ever known come back to haunt me; it was my sweetest dream: everyone I'd ever known come back to wish me well.

I had dreamed; I could dream. Sleep was no longer a reflex rhythm but a nightly adventure... I was kissing; everyone was kissing. A cat's cradle of crêpe paper enveloped the room. Streamers tingled on my neck, tangled in my hair, tickling my eyes. I was handed presents wrapped in paper that was a present in itself. Some I opened; some I still have in store. Several have lost their labels so my thanks can only be general. But if I can't thank them all for their specific gifts, I can thank them with all my heart for their gift of love.

I have so much love; I have so many loving people inside me. The silent scream of solitude has been displaced by a permanent grin. Can one live off memories? Yes, if one can live off love. There was every old acquaintance I'd never forgotten but never expected to meet again. And it was far more moving than New Year's Eve; it was a new life's eve. While it may be my Jewish heritage or, more mundanely, my academic training, but autumn has always struck me as a far more appropriate time for the making of resolutions than the first of January or even Lent.

And I marvelled that they'd been able to contact so many people – had they rifled my address book? I'd never noticed it was so full – while some must have moved and some left the country and some died... I'm sorry... But at the time there seemed to be no gaps. There were relatives and friends from school and college and families from Edensor whom I'd known as a child, some of whom I hadn't seen since they were children. And yet I could remember everyone I was supposed to remember. Even in my emotion I was able to greet them all by name. And I liked myself for that.

I went first to Nanny. I'd forgotten how small she was. Though that wasn't like boyhood summers seeming sunnier; for she was withered with age. She still had the same black fingernail, and the mole on her cheek with the three white whiskers which had alternately attracted and appalled me: all the other women I'd known having been silken and smooth. But then I was a deeply conventional child for whom the distinction between men and women remained the greatest there was; greater even than that between truth and lies... And as I leaned to kiss her, I saw that she was practically bald.

There were boys from school – men now, though to me they were more memories than men and more photographs than either. Indeed there was one boy, Horace Standish, who appeared twice on a school photograph. He raced round the back of the stands and reached the other end faster than the camera. And his transgression remained undetected until the final prints when it was too late to edit him out. The headmaster raged, whilst our physics teacher used him to illustrate the theory of relativity. And now he has a job censoring films.

I spotted Father Clement, my old vicar from Edensor. He used to play cricket for the county; though now he'd scarcely make it to the crease. His sermons were peppered with references to his sporting passion... We may have been batting on a sticky wicket but we must keep a straight bat and our eye on the ball; while if the Devil should bowl a googly... I giggle; but at the time I felt secure. It must have galled him that Christ hadn't stopped at ten disciples; the opportunity for team analogies would have proved irresistible. And yet with St Lebbaeus Thaddaeus as twelfth man, and Judas batting for the opposition, he might have stretched a point.

I shook his hand; his grip felt as fiercely ferrous as ever. And I considered him the very best type of English parson. Then from the corner of my eye I saw Jonathan talking to some of my friends from St Dunstan's. And I concluded that all in all that wasn't enough; there was my very best type of English priest.

I think it was seeing them that moved me most – even Father Leicester had sent his love along with his apologies – although as we clasped hands I felt that our positions had been reversed. I may have been the youngest in college, but I'd overtaken them in all but years. They offered vivid accounts of life in their parishes. And not for the first time since the retreat and my encounters with Jonathan and Mompesson, I felt an overwhelming urge to resume my training... And I can't explain what it is that's holding me back.

I moved from church to crypt as I kissed Vange and welcomed Patrick and Fiona. Sadly, Gaia had to babysit; but whilst I was sorry not to see her, I was glad that it wasn't Vange. For however alienating I may find her manner, I've come to realise that it's not manners that make men, or women – or even wimmin, if she insists... But then I expect you'll tell me, or at least you would if we'd met in different circumstances, that the word manners once meant morals... Which is yet another argument against her verbal hybrids; for in that sense hers are above reproach.

I barely succeeded in steering her clear of Francis Siddall, a Balliol friend who works at Conservative Central Office. He'd hoped to join the Guards and been convinced they'd rejected him on account of his background... I have a strange sense of *déjà vu*, or rather *entendu*, as though I've mentioned that before. I can't think why... I soon found I had nothing whatever to say to him, as I suspected last year when, having run into each other during the tube strike, he took my remark that I was right behind the drivers to mean I must be living behind a sidings. He couldn't conceive that someone he knew socially could be behind them in any other way.

So having exchanged a few pleasantries, I dumped him on my cousin Nathaniel, who'd made small talk a way of life; while I edged towards Lancelot, who was renewing an acquaintance with Jason which had indeed begun behind bars... Although despite our effusive greeting, Jason remained unconvinced by our connection and insisted on introducing us formally, as if Lancelot had simply strayed in off the street. He then shyly offered me his present, an ancient recording of *Turandot*, which was one of the few I opened on the spot. I was thrilled and told him that Puccini had always been my mother's favourite composer; I wondered how he'd known. He smiled mysteriously. But later, when I caught his eye during a toast to absent friends, I saw at once, just as I knew that those friends weren't so absent after all.

He has an encyclopaedic knowledge of all types of records, which he now means to exploit. He's already put part of Uncle Sinclair's legacy towards renting a pitch in Berwick Street Market; or at least I've advanced him the cash on what he quaintly terms his expectations – and I wish you could hear the way he savours the word. For I'm afraid he had very little idea of the intricacies of probate and initially expected the estate to be settled within a week… As he explained to Lancelot, to have their own record stall had long been both his and Rees' dearest ambition. Although he swore him to secrecy until everything was signed and sealed. In return Lancelot told him that Rees had started a correspondence course in business management. And I suddenly had an image of them as the Marks and Spencer of the twenty-first century: Jason and Rees' penny bazaar.

I was worried that I'd been ignoring my family; so I chatted to my cousins and my great Uncle Bernard, the chairman of the bank, and my trustees, who had particular reason to celebrate my coming into my own. I admit to a flutter of unease on seeing Mark introduce Krishnan to my father. But I needn't have worried; he talked exclusively of his research. With which, unexpectedly, my father was able to help.

For the subject of Krishnan's thesis is the Duke of Marlborough's army, about which there are apparently stacks of documents in the archives at Edensor as our ancestors consolidated their fortunes by financing his campaigns… I only wish I'd known more about it at school, where I was constantly taunted by a smug anti-semite whose family had made its money in the slave trade. Since whatever else mine may have had on its hands, it wasn't blood.

My father in turn introduced Krishnan to my stepmother and brothers – note the absence of hyphens; I no longer deal in half-measures. It appeared that David was studying the same period for his *bachot*, although with the emphasis squarely on Louis XIV. So Krishnan offered to take them both on a field-trip to Blenheim, which was sub-sequently fixed for today... in fact they should be there, or thereabouts, even as we speak.

The two boys proved the undoubted hit of the evening, succeeding in charming everyone even when somewhat the worse for champagne. They charmed me right from the start; that is once I'd recovered from the shock of recognition. It wasn't so much that they'd grown up as filled out... They have chests and shoulders and dinner jackets and David even has the beginnings of a beard. They whooped with delight when they saw me, jumped in the air and slapped each other's hands. They didn't slap mine, but immediately embraced me. I was amazed at the genuine warmth of their greeting. And I felt ashamed to recall how wretched a brother I'd been to them. In the ultimate absurdity of my 'sins of the fathers' syndrome, I'd held them to blame for the pure fact of having been born.

I basked in their affection. Then at 10.30 all I wanted was for the floor to rise up and swallow me. For my father gathered everyone together to drink my health. I smiled and squirmed much as I had on those long-ago Founder's Days, when I'd have gladly dropped to the bottom of the class to avoid the interminable trek across the dais to receive my prize. He talked with piercing frankness of how much the evening had meant to him... of how much I meant to him; before adding that if you could judge a man by the company he kept, he could see that he need never have the slightest concern about me. Then he concluded by proposing a toast.

They drank; as I did inadvertently. A bubble lodged in my nose. There were calls for a speech, but all I could do was sneeze; which seemed to relieve both the tension and the need. Jonathan was stand-ing beside me. He held out his handkerchief, which he assured me was quite clean. I swore that I wouldn't have cared if it'd been dirty... I must have been horribly drunk. I fumbled with my glass; I fumbled with my nose. I blushed as he offered to squeeze it for me. I flushed; although whether with embarrassment or pleasure or simply the pres-sure of his fingers, I shouldn't like to say.

The celebrations continued through the early hours. At about two o'clock I began to wish that everyone would go home; by three I wanted them all to stay for ever. And though I didn't sleep a wink I felt fine; until it caught up with me at around six on Friday evening. I expect you can see the bags under my eyes – which is not, by the way, what I meant by feeling older. Adrian used to have a trick with slices of cucumber... Adrian... if only he'd been there. I'd have gladly listened to 'Over the Rainbow' all night long.

Gradually the final guests took their leave. Strangely, it was the priests who proved to have the most staying power. The dawn emphasised the debris which the caterers started to clear. I felt a touch embarrassed, just as I had when Jack came back with the bowl of soapy water... what on earth made me think of that? But it was all part of the service. And they said that by the afternoon I'd never even know that they'd been. And they were right; I wouldn't. But I did.

The very last to go was Jonathan, who kissed me goodnight on the forehead. Although it felt more like a blessing than a kiss. And I tried to count my blessings; but all I could feel was the kiss. I closed the door quickly before I made a fool of myself by attempting to return it. Besides he's taller than me so I couldn't have kissed him on the forehead. It would have had to have been on the lips... Would you mind moving that light? It's shining straight in my eyes.

Thank you... I put my hands in my jacket and pulled out his handkerchief. See, I still have it here. Isn't that absurd? I went upstairs. I began to worry about Mark. He'd been doing so well these past few weeks; I only hoped that the party hadn't proved too great a strain. I peered into his room. He was asleep in bed with Krishnan sitting beside him... Actually I know now that he was lying down; but at the time I saw it as sitting because I assumed that they had a sitting sort of a relationship. Whereas he was slumped and Mark was sprawled.

Later that morning I met my father, who seemed remarkably unruffled after the exertions of the night before. We drove to the bank and lunched with my uncle at the City Club. I suppose one of the reasons that I'm feeling substantial is that I am indeed a man of substance. I'm twenty-five; I've come into my inheritance. Edensor now belongs to me... together with a large portfolio of stocks and shares. All those wars my family financed, all the joint stock banks and insurance companies and domestic credit and foreign credit and national debt and international exchange and bank-notes and bullion have filtered down to me. I'm not just a man with letters after my name; I now have figures: eight to be exact.

It's a vast amount of wealth; but I'm no longer daunted by the dangers, proverbial or otherwise. On the contrary, I see it as a sacred trust. Just as the money was held in trust for me, so I shall do the same for other people. Moreover, even Jonathan congratulated me. And when I questioned his sincerity he replied by producing a fresh gloss on the gospel 'eye of the needle', that passage which seems to have haunted me all my life. He'd read a recent theory claiming it to be the popular name of one of the gateways into Jerusalem. So that, far from requiring a miracle to squeeze through it, all a camel would have had to do was stoop.

Everything was beginning to seem too good to be true – if that's not to deny the entire basis of my theology... Yes, it is; it was simply too good... And there was more; for as I returned home exhausted after the sleepless night, exhilarated by the eventful day, I was confronted by Mark.

He didn't mince words, but told me straight out that in two weeks' time he was flying to India with Krishnan. They'd booked a fortnight ago, but had kept it to themselves so as not to spoil my birthday. He intended to investigate Ayurvedic treatment; after all, it was the oldest healing system in the world. He'd originally turned to holistic therapies in desperation: a rejection of conventional medicine and mores; a plague on both their houses... No, not a plague... But he ran the risk of becoming a medical tourist, snatching bits and pieces from any sympathetic setting, when what he needed was a practice to which he could give his soul.

He believes he's discovered one in meditation... to which he attaches as much weight as I do to the power of prayer. And it isn't some wishy-washy, dippy hippy alternative. Krishnan's explained its scientific basis – and he finds his reasoning highly seductive... as who should know better than I – which is that the key to recovery rests on the level of consciousness, where the difference between curing oneself of a broken arm and a deadly virus is purely one of degree.

For mind and body are as intrinsically linked as body and universe; just as they're made up of the same chemical impulses. So faith that can move mountains is no mere metaphor; since, however infinitesimally, every positive creative thought is changing the constitution of the world.

And this belief in a universal soul of which the visible world is just a material manifestation, along with an intelligence which governs the universe, comes remarkably close to my own conception of God. Whilst his arguments have endorsed another of my most valued affirmations: we are all one body. For he went on to describe how with each breath we inhale we're absorbing millions of atoms that every man, woman and child in the world has breathed during the past week, and one million that everyone in the entire history of the world has ever breathed. Just think: Moses and David and St Thomas Aquinas... and Christ. So even though we may not have lived in his literal lifetime, we're still breathing the air he breathed. What's more, since the atoms in the air were also the atoms in his body, we're in constant communion with him, not just at the altar but at every moment of the day.

Nevertheless it's one thing to affirm the principle, quite another to fly five thousand miles. And yet he insisted that the journey was itself part of the cure. Krishnan had been in contact with his guru, who'd offered to instruct him. And he promised me that it would be far less of a jolt than I might have imagined. For not only had he been studying the Veda, but on his recent trip to Harrogate he'd felt a deep affinity with the other devotees... and one in particular; since it was on their return from the temple that he and Krishnan first made love.

He was sure that I must have suspected... but then it's not only love that's blind. And I admitted that I'd even explained away having seen them in bed together the night before; which was when he confirmed that Krishnan hadn't simply been snatching a few moments' rest.

And all the confusion of the previous weeks – Mark's preoccupation, Krishnan's defensiveness, my own feeling that he'd made love to me as though I were somebody else – began to make sense.

I was amazed at my equanimity. For eighteen months I'd tortured myself with the prospect of losing him first in one way and then another; but now it'd happened I felt neither regret nor relief, simply a sense of rightness as when a well-loved story reaches a well-rounded end. And to my surprise I realised I was happy for them. They appeared ideally suited and considerably more so than either had been to me. And yet I didn't want to lose them either. But he assured me that there was no danger of that, especially when I was suddenly so rich... And I laughed as he cursed his customary bad timing. After which we both grew a little tearful. Then he hugged me hotly, which seemed just like old times; and I clasped him back, squeeze for squeeze.

His grip was taut; his body lean and rangy. Far from ravaging him, his illness had left barely a... mark. He might have lost a little weight, but it suited him; his moon-face had become more of a crescent and his cheek-bones more pronounced. While his whole body felt so vibrant that I hadn't the slightest doubt he'd return in perfect health.

We talked for hours, which also brought back memories. We no longer had to hide, either from one another or ourselves. And we still loved each other as friends if not lovers. Although neither of us suggested that that was better because we knew that it wasn't; I don't think there's anything better than the love of lovers. But then there can be nothing worse than their lies; and at least we'd rid ourselves of those.

He told me how much he'd loved me. And from the wonderful words he used I might have thought he was trying to rekindle the flame. Listen if you don't believe me... I was just about the last man in the world he might have expected to fall for. I was vulnerability when he'd wanted strength, confusion when he'd looked for certainty, Leslie Howard when he'd longed for Clark Gable. And yet I was funny; I was sexy; I was gorgeous... and I'm blushing. Whilst as for my eyes – see, they're nothing special, are they? – but he insisted that I had the most irresistible 'come to bed' eyes.

Even so, he'd realised that he could never make a life with me. He'd truly wanted to – for only the second time. But then Adrian had been part of a very different life, one that had ended long before AIDS; however much people might try to hammer home the connection. With him every day had been like Saturday, or rather Saturday night; which after a while could become wearing. Whereas with me each day felt like Sunday – and he didn't say that merely on account of my faith. He was convinced that in Krishnan he'd struck the perfect balance... Like Saturday night and Sunday morning? I wondered. He smiled.

We held each other close. The embrace established its own equilibrium and I felt that we could maintain it for ever... but then for ever was precisely what we no longer had. He added that he'd have found leaving a great deal tougher if it hadn't been for Jonathan. I trembled. What did he mean? I knew what he meant. He said that I'd made my preference clear from the moment I introduced them, when he'd felt like an apprentice piece presented to a master craftsman. I protested; he smiled and rubbed my nose. But Jonathan's touch had left a permanent tingle which even his failed to dispel.

And it's no use affecting aloofness; I'm supposed to be the one who's tried to avoid human contact... although I'm more than making up for it now. I know you can see through me. I can see through myself as clearly as a plate-glass window; and the goods on display are all shop-soiled merchandise knocked down for an easy sale... So to state the patently – painfully obvious: I love Jonathan. I always have and I always will. There. Now you can forget I ever said it. What's the point? It's a totally useless piece of information, like the breeding habits of the dodo. Some people have doomed love affairs; mine's already extinct.

At prep school I was once asked to recite Rudyard Kipling's 'If' for an end-of-term concert... you know, twenty elementary steps to becoming a man. But the poem of my life begins 'If only', a silly sentimental verse with no rhyme or reason or rhythm, merely regret.

For what Mark refuses to understand, and you to acknowledge, is that whatever my own feelings, there's no way that I can compromise Jonathan's. He's made a pledge; he's chosen the fellowship of other priests before the love of another man. He's resolved his conflicts and I've no right to burden him with mine. What's more, I played a significant part in confirming that resolve; to shake it now would be beneath contempt.

And yet where does that leave me? I look at myself and I see my parents, living in frustration for twenty years, destroying their hopes of a future from a misguided loyalty to the past; and I'm scared of the human cost of my inheritance. Am I my father's son in more ways than I thought? Will his compromise become mine as I also betray my love for the sake of my faith? But the choice isn't as measured as the cadence. We speak of family trees and family circles; and yet what if they're one and the same, and we don't grow out of our roots but simply go round and round, repeating the same old patterns, supposing we're following our hearts when in fact we're chasing our tails?

Fifteen

In a letter he wrote at the conclusion of the crisis, Mompesson described Eyam as a Golgotha; and indeed if you think back to the rock formation of the Cucklet Church, it did rather resemble a skull. And yet our walk doesn't end on a hillside, but back in the centre of the village: a village that must have seemed much like a ghost town with its harvest ungathered, its roads untended, its mines unworked and three-quarters of its population perished. For although there's some dispute over the exact total, it's generally reckoned that 259 of the 267 deaths during these months were caused by the plague. In November 1666 there were only 83 survivors out of a previous figure of 350. But the time had come to rebuild.

Which is why I wanted to finish as we began, outside this row of cottages. But we're not backtracking; for now I'd like to focus on the least renovated of the three: the one on the right. As you can see, the plaque simply records that it was the home of the third man to die of the plague, Peter Halksworth. What it doesn't say is that his widow, Alice, later married a neighbour, Matthew Morten, whose wife and baby had also been struck down. And it's here that they started to re-establish their lives. And it's on that note that consciously – you may consider self-consciously – I intend to end.

But for that, and that alone, I remain unrepentant. Although I came on this village quite unexpectedly – I refuse to say by chance – I returned with full deliberation. I've long needed to discover a congenial community, as I believe everyone does; but particularly someone who finds himself excluded, if only by the prevailing rhetoric, from the wider community in which he's never previously questioned his place. And here in Eyam, by the beautifully kept gardens of the proudly named Plague Cottages in the heart of the Hope Valley – I'm even embarrassing myself –I think that I finally have.

I've also longed to discover a story, one I could both relate to and relate, which would be, if you'll pardon my etymology, at once his story and her story and your story and mine; and in Eyam I feel I've found that too: a story that takes all the gutter-press banner-headlines and turns them on their head. Let bigots twist their prose trying to transform a virulence into a pestilence; this shows them what can be positive even in a plague. And the parallels point far beyond the immediate devastation and suffering. For in the villagers' self-denying ordinance I see the image of many of the people I've come to love and admire best; whilst in their successors' reverence for their memories and respect for their past, I discern the key to all our survivals, moral and metaphorical, as well as in the flesh.

Which is where we must close, as I hear the noonday chimes. I hope you won't suspect me of bribing the rector; but they couldn't have been better timed. For although our current epidemic appears to provide the perfect pretext for the idealisation of the nuclear family in a world where every other nuclear ideal has been blown sky-high, the annals of Eyam offer an opportune reminder that family means far more than the people who share your blood. The village proved itself a truly extended family and a wider word for that is community and a wider one still is society, or at least it was before being authoritatively – no, authoritarianly – declared dead.

And the peal calls to mind the words of yet another priest, the wise and witty dean of St Paul's who phrased his peroration with such poise: 'Any man's death diminishes me, because I am involved in Mankind; And therefore never send to know for whom the bell tolls; It tolls for thee.'

And with that it appears to have stopped.

I'm in your hands again; the moment of truth has arrived. But then every moment is a moment of truth, or at least it should be. And last week I faced up to what it was. I'm sorry I couldn't make our appointment, but I spent most of Monday and Tuesday at Heathrow and then on Wednesday I went up to Derbyshire. I could scarcely tell if I were coming or going. That might almost be the punchline of a joke.

My family flew back to Nice on Monday. I took my brothers on a private tour of the airport; and despite the increased security I was able to take them through several restricted zones. I pretended I had friends in high places, but under concerted pressure I admitted that I'd done my placement there; which clearly sent the priesthood way up in their estimation – although nothing like as far as it's recently soared in mine. And I left them in the departure lounge with kisses and smiles and presents and promises to return very soon.

On Tuesday I was there again with Mark and Krishnan and Jonathan. There was a computer failure at the check-in and we had to stand in line for half an hour. Mark was tired, but he refused to sit down; I think he wanted me to see him fly out fighting fit. But he needn't have worried; I knew he still had everything to fight for. Besides, since he'd come off all his drugs even his cell count had improved. The doctors claimed he was in remission; he replied he was in control.

On Monday I wanted to delay my family's departure; on Tuesday I wanted to accelerate theirs. Perhaps it was because I'd never been to India; I could picture only the distance, not the destination. No, it was far more than that... And we walked together to the gate where I hugged Krishnan, who retreated diplomatically with Jonathan to buy a paper, which left me with Mark. I gazed at him, the usual mass of contradictions with his copy of *The Vegetarian* protruding from his black leather jacket, and I said: Come back soon, come back well, come back just as you are. And he said: Thank you. And he tried to extend it: Thank you for everything. And I tried to dismiss it: It was nothing... No, not for the fare, but for everything. And I said: Thank you for everything too. And he said: That's what friends are for. And I kissed him smack on the lips in the middle of an English airport. And if anyone else pursed his in disapproval, I didn't notice. I felt nothing but the warmth of his mouth: the sweet, light moistness of the memory. And I hurried away.

Jonathan then drove me back to London in his ancient Austin, which had passed through so many hands that he justified it to himself as practically public transport. I did however draw the line at going by road to Derbyshire: not at his driving, let alone his car – whatever you may suppose, I do have some tact – but I persuaded him that not only would the journey be less exhausting by train, but he could also put in several hours of work. He was due to lead another retreat – did I forget to mention that? – and we went up two days early to prepare. Although I spent most of my time exploring Eyam.

This second retreat moved me even more than the first: what with the talks and the tranquillity, the friendship and the fellowship, the prayers and the meals and the dances... yes, I danced. Does that surprise you: you to whom I'm simply a non-stop stream of consciousness? I've discovered my body's flow: not just its language, but its music. And after all the years of self-willed self-division, my mind and my body work as one.

Once again we shared our experiences of Christ and HIV. I remembered how on the previous occasion I'd concentrated solely on the theology: chiefly Jesus' remark that it wasn't the healthy who needed a physician, but the sick. And my reasoned analysis had appeared even more inadequate when set against the general spontaneity. This time I'd determined not to plan but rather to do just as the spirit moved me – a conventional phrase though still a considerable challenge. And if I felt nothing, I'd sit tight. I'd lay myself as open as that.

But when my turn came, I stood. Impulsively I explained that what I wanted to communicate was the sense of grace which had grown in me since that last retreat. I too had felt the agony of despair in the garden... but then the indescribable relief of looking up and seeing that it was Christ on the cross and not me; that at the final moment he'd slipped in to take my place. And the only way I could convey my deliverance was to dance: first the isolation, suffering and despair, and then the resurrection, redemption and joy. And I danced without preparation, without music and without fear. Nor was I afraid to make a fool of myself, since my folly was a part of my dance.

I danced for the group and I danced for Jonathan and, above all, I danced for Christ: Christ who was my Lord, Christ who was my dance. And the Lord of the Dance danced in me; and I knew him in his unique unity. I knew his body and I knew his spirit; and I felt him in my body and my spirit. I was his son and his brother and his lover and his priest. And then the spirit moved me to stillness. And I sat down.

There was no sound in the room apart from the indistinct burr of cars and mowers: the bustle of the outside world serving to emphasise the stillness we shared. And after a moment Jonathan came up and wrapped his arms tightly round me, which provided the cue for a universal embrace: an unscheduled and unthreatening kiss of peace.

On Sunday I took the lead once again. The morning was free; and the evening before I'd suggested to Jonathan that I might guide a walk around Eyam. Since my last visit I'd read everything I could find about its history. And the previous two days, strictly for my own amusement, I'd mapped out a route. To my surprise he'd greeted the idea with considerable enthusiasm; although on reflection his reaction was true to form. But what still astonishes me is that when he mentioned it that night at dinner, apart from two men who were clearly unfit, the whole group chose to come.

The response to the walk was even warmer than to the initial offer. But then it isn't easy for me to differentiate when each experience of the weekend topped the one before. It was a long haul and we must have covered several miles; and yet conditions were ideal: with the streets empty but not deserted and the fields fertile yet firm. And it seemed a perfect way to pass a Sunday morning; since although we'd missed church, we'd discovered our 'sermons in stones'.

I complain that the story of Eyam has been unduly neglected; but then we've long been prone to celebrate victories over others to the exclusion of those over ourselves. So I'm determined that mine will prove the exception. For I've found a walk I can take without resorting to other people's words or to their values. And I mean to take many more groups on it in due course... But I'd exceeded my allotted hour;

and we returned hot-foot to the hostel. Then after lunch Jonathan led another discussion, before we came together for a final time in the most universal story of all.

We drew up our chairs in the customary circle; and Jonathan raised up the Host as we raised our spirits to God. And we shared in Christ's Passion: the greatest of all the double meanings of the language and the divine ambiguities of the Faith. For of the numerous absurdities to which I've subjected you over the past three years, the most grotesque must surely be that Christ never knew the intensity of my love. Since if love means anything, it's identification. And never has one being so totally identified with another as God when he became man.

How could I have ever supposed his universal sympathies were an easy option? Perhaps it was because I was an only child that I found it hard to imagine a love that was all-embracing – or perhaps it was simply that I was a selfish man? But his love knew no bounds. And although it may have involved no direct sexual expression, it was fervently sexual. It was the most complete and creative consummation, through which he fulfilled the desire of every lover and truly became one with his love.

After which he died for us, achieving love's apotheosis and accepting the challenge that's haunted me ever since I first met Jack. And how did we repay him? One of his closest friends betrayed him and another denied him. While two thousand years later we still turn away. Is it any wonder he gave in to despair? As, whatever I may have claimed in the past, he undoubtedly did.

So he had every reason to pray 'Lead us not into temptation' when he knew its torment so well. And his greatest temptation wasn't to throw himself off the pinnacle of the Temple, but to succumb to despair, and throw himself off the Cross. And that would have been more than a sin against the Holy Ghost; it would have been a crime against humanity – against eternity. Since it would have given us all cause to despair until the end of time.

For I see now that true despair isn't to lose faith in oneself, dreadful though that is, or even in the people one loves, which is even worse, but in God and the very prospect of Redemption. As Christ himself did. And his cry on the Cross chills my heart to this day, as he who was God experienced the death of God and became the symbol of suffering humankind.

On the first retreat I grew impatient with questions as to whether, if he were alive today, Christ would have had HIV. And yet the answer is self-evident. His was no dignified death in a palace courtyard; but naked, unkempt, incontinent, torn limb from limb he hung from a tree. His body was lacerated with lesions; the wounds on his side bled like the tumours on Adrian's back... Crucifixion was the most shameful end which the Romans could inflict, just as today AIDS is the most shameful illness which so many people can envisage. And it soon becomes clear why there was no cross anywhere to be seen in the Church of Triumph, since first and foremost the Cross isn't an image of triumph, but of disgrace.

And yet through his disgrace Christ gave us the grace to triumph over ours. As he does to this day. For the real horror of his martyrdom isn't even its manner – after all, St Peter underwent it upside-down – but its duration. His agony wasn't limited to a few hours on the Cross, but extends through two thousand years of our time and the eternity of his. That's what it means to be both God and man: not academic arguments about whether he was conceived through the ear or the vagina, but suffering once in history and forever outside time.

So if, as I believe, Christ is living now, then he's also dying, and of course he has HIV; since AIDS isn't only the scourge of the present day, but the cross. And when in years to come scientists discover a cure and for the rest of us the virus becomes a distant memory, he'll continue to have it; and not merely as a medical metaphor but as a living, bleeding fact. In which case any priest who tries to exclude people with AIDS from communion is also excluding him. For it really doesn't matter who's infected with the virus, whether it's you or I or the person kneeling next to us; in Christ we all are. We are all one body; we all share the same blood. And if the Eucharist is to retain any substance, it has to embody the moment when we assert that unity and share that blood.

So we passed round the chalice in sacramental safety. And as the woman to my right proudly proclaimed it the blood of Christ, I lifted it to my lips and I knew that it was. And I had an intense sense of revelation; it was the most awesome communion since my first. For in that unbroken circle I recaptured all the glow of my original vocation. And I felt at once holy and whole.

And not only has my spirit been refreshed, my brain has been recharged. And although you may well agree with Jonathan that I strive too hard to define the indefinable, with that compulsive need to explain everything which he terms 'ergotism' – no, you didn't mishear – since this will most probably be my last visit I'd like to test my conclusions on you...

I've long felt disenchanted with the myth of the Fall, which isn't only a slander on man but on God, since it invests him with that same spirit of wilfulness which theologians have for centuries imposed on us... how else could the whole of human misery have been pinned on an arbitrary 'Do not touch' notice on a tree? But rather than merely discard it, we need to put something positive in its place: the model of the Flaw.

For just as poetry can produce myths, so science can provide models. And the discoveries of nineteenth-century biologists, which people once found such a threat to their faith, now appear a confirmation. God didn't create the world in six days, maliciously filling it full of fossils and flaws, in order to confront us the following week with both its and our imperfections. But over hundreds of millions of years there occurred an inevitable dissipation of his original creative process... Darwin may have discredited Genesis, but he's absolved God.

So the human race is compromised not by some intrinsic wickedness but by the flaws and faults of our own nature, akin to those in the earth's crust; and for which we're ultimately no more responsible than for the eruption of a volcano. That in no way exempts us from the need to exert individual responsibility; since we all have free will... even those whose freedom of action is most constrained still have freedom of choice. Nevertheless in the last resort that responsibility is limited, just as, at the Last Judgement, it will be God's.

———

And he acknowledged as much by sending his son, whose mission wasn't simply to reconcile his father to us but to reconcile us to his father. Whilst his death afforded a further recognition that the price we pay for being born isn't original sin but existential pain. He can't put an end to that pain – at least not until he puts an end to the world; but by sharing it with us, by suffering both with us and for us, he makes its burden infinitely easier to bear... And yet to say he gave suffering a meaning is far from saying that he made it the meaning of life. So our aim shouldn't be to mortify the flesh, still less to deny it, but to infuse it with the spirit. After all, what else does the Incarnation mean?

Moreover, he offers the reassurance that we need never suffer in vain, since it's the way by which we can come closest to him... Although that's only half true. For, as I drank from the cup and then passed it round in my turn with the same bold affirmation, I realised that of course we had another way – and one that was strictly symbolic. And at that moment I knew that I had to return to St Dunstan's, and make that celebration which had long been the heart of my worship once again the heart of my life.

And yet I've no desire to resume at the point where I broke off – or more accurately, down. For if I've learned anything these past three years, it's that the sacraments in themselves aren't enough. To stand in the person of Christ isn't simply to stand at his altar. A priest has to stand firm and to stand and fight... while he has no need to stand alone. Christ's celibacy is no more incumbent on him than Mary's virginity on a mother... And later that night – and the ambiguity works both ways – Jonathan and I came together in a private passion of our own.

You must have known. Did you say a quiet prayer for me, or did you conclude that if prayers were all I needed, I already had more than enough? Nothing was planned. By six o'clock there were only the two of us left. All the other retreatants had dispersed and the centre staff were still away. We were due to catch the 8.50 train from Sheffield; but after some desultory clearing, Jonathan pronounced himself shattered and proposed staying another night and setting off early the next day... which I agreed was fine by me.

As before, we slept in bunks, only this time he was on top... I'm sorry; I don't mean to giggle... He switched off the light, but the difference was minimal. He's a fresh-air fiend, and the flimsy curtains fluttered against the window whilst the full moon threw shadows on the wall. God bless that moon... God bless that moon! He lay so still that I felt sure he was asleep and I blew him the most brazen kisses, putting my hand to my mouth and then touching the overhead boards. But my gestures must have grown more and more passionate and the shadows more abandoned; for suddenly his voice cut through the silence: if you want to kiss me that much, you can.

I couldn't speak; I thought I must have swallowed my Adam's apple. He lifted his mattress and stared down through the struts. I felt as though we were looking at one another through the bars of a prison cell. And yet I was free... I could just about make out his eyes and the tip of his nose through the gap, and then his prominent eyebrows, which don't simply meet in the middle but seem to quarrel. If you want to kiss me that much, he repeated, you can. Thank you, I said; and I was anxious to lighten the atmosphere. Your bunk or mine? I asked. Oh, yours, he replied. We don't want you falling out.

He scrambled down. His penis peeped through his pyjama bottoms. I laughed, although not from desperation, still less derision, but joy. I made a space for him: first in the bunk and then in myself. I devoured him with my eyes; he devoured me with his lips; we devoured one another body and soul. And I heard again the words: This is the body of Christ; and I knew that there was no blasphemy. On the contrary it was an essential expression of my gift of love. His was the love I'd always longed for: the love I'd always needed. He was the man I'd always wanted: the man I wanted to be.

And yet he was also a priest who'd made a promise of celibacy. And a dense shadow fell across the room and lingered on me. I shivered. He tried to warm me. I questioned him about the promise even though I was afraid he might lose patience. He asked if it'd make any difference if he said it had run out the night before. Yes, I replied, I'd never trust him again. He told me not to worry. Nevertheless it had expired. He was obliged to renew it every six months; and in the last few weeks he simply hadn't had a chance. And in case I considered that too easy, he added that the promise itself had been a pure practicality, to assist him to live the life of a mission priest. At the time he knew of none better; now he was convinced that he did.

Tears trickled down my cheeks but he wiped them – no, he kissed them away. We sought out each other's mouths; we sucked at each other's tongues. Then he quietly asked me if I'd like him to put on a condom; and I said yes. I steeled myself and then yielded myself as he eased into me so gently that the agony was all in the anticipation. His stomach slapped against me; I pulsated with his passion. I felt his arms around me like armour; and I was unafraid. We were lovers; we were brothers; we were twinned in body and spirit. We were Siamese twins joined at the hip. Then he gasped and grunted and I felt him issue into me. I was no longer without issue; I was alive with him.

A sense of peace wafted over me in waves of pleasure. I felt no shame, not in the aftermath nor the recollection; and I knew I would never need to feel the slightest shame again. He cradled me in the crook of his arm, and as his skin felt damp I rubbed it dry with my hair. We lay back, and I wouldn't have thought it possible to create such intimacy. Then he rolled his head and lolled his tongue and kissed me once on each eyelid; and I drifted off into the most rapturous dreams... And I shan't elaborate: except to say that they were rich and rare and red.

In the morning we travelled back to London. Jonathan went straight to the clergy house; and I went home. And for the moment that's how it'll remain. But there are so many places to meet in the middle as well as either end. And we both have much to resolve. I still have to decide what to do about Edensor. I long to reopen it, though no longer as a family house – rather as a retreat house on the lines of the one in Derbyshire, for those extended, 'pretended' families who've redefined my life. And then... Is my watch fast or is it 6.15 already? I've often lost track of the time; but I was sure you had a built-in alarm.

And yet perhaps you've switched it off as a parting gesture... Isn't it odd? After most of our sessions I couldn't escape fast enough; but now that I'm truly taking my leave I don't want to go – or rather let go. Even though I know little more about you now than I did at the beginning, I feel as though we've been on a long, labyrinthine journey, through all of which you've kept me company and much of which you've kept me sane. So thank you. And if I've ever said anything I shouldn't... well, you understand.

I'll slip on my coat before I embarrass you any further. Then I'll take one last look around. I'm trying to fix the scene on my memory. Even the cacti look less prickly... Go ahead, laugh; why not? I intend to at every opportunity. I feel so full of hope. What nonsense to suggest that we weren't put on this earth to be happy! Blessed are the lovers: for they shall be one with God.

I expect that for you it's a case of one file closing as another opens. But before you dispatch me to gather dust on your bottom shelf, there's a favour I wish to ask. As you may be aware I've an appointment to see Father Leicester on Monday. If he hasn't yet done so, he'll be writing for your report. The last thing I want is to pre-empt your findings; but if you'll just give me a hint of what you mean to recommend... He's not alone in valuing your opinion; after all this time you must know me better than anyone. So will you be advising him to take me back?